The
RAYGIN
WAR

LARRY S. GEROVAC

Edited by Molly Sardella
ISBN-13: 978-0-9986995-4-7 (Paperback)
ISBN 978-0-9986995-5-4 (eBook)

Dedication

To my boys: Patrick, Andrew, Michael, Daniel, and
Steven.

TABLE OF CONTENTS

CHAPTER ONE: The Lost Nation

Chief Mahpee burst into the operating room. The veins in his neck pulsed. His steel blue eyes focused on the pale unmoving body of his wife. Her bloody lifeless figure lay on a cold metal table. The big man's lip began to quiver. He heard a wailing and looked to his right. A newborn. As he looked at the baby, he noticed the blanket. It displayed his family totem. Someone had placed a lone white feather on the cart holding the baby. His legs felt weak as the realization hit him. *It's my daughter.* Awarded a warrior's feather for a wound sustained in battle.

Seeing the feather brought to mind a story he heard in his youth. It was an ancient prophecy. So old, his grandfather told him, his people lost track of its origin. *Could the old tales be true?* Mahpee remembered sitting with his grandfather at the full moon ceremonial campfires. Select elders would pass down historical information in the form of stories. *How did it go?* He grappled with the memory. *A princess, warrior born, will lead the People's Nation in a war unlike any of those from the past.*

The baby started screaming and snorting. The noise snapped Mahpee back from his thoughts about ancient legends. *Her voice could drown out a sparrow hawk fighter landing on Nokomis with full thrusters.* He stared at his daughter as she twisted and wiggled inside the open-air bassinet. Tubes in her chest pumped blood into her heart. An IV taped to her head kept her hydrated. Electronic devices had been attached to her little body, in an attempt to keep her alive. She sensed his presence. The wounded little princess began to struggle with wild resolve. She attempted to break free of her life saving restraints. *Only minutes old and already inside her tiny body beats the heart of a warrior.*

Seeing his daughter struggle broke his heart. He had to do something. With the enemy's blood still dripping off his clothes, he shuffled over to his crying daughter. With great care, he placed his large callused hand under her tiny body. The doctor, and nurses, stared in disbelief. The wounded little princess snuggled into her father's palm. With tubes and wires still hanging off her little body, she went to sleep. The chief stared down at the tiny figure of his daughter. Tears began to roll down his cheeks, leaving glistening wet trails on his sunbaked face.

His nose began to drip. He sniffed in the wetness, and in a gentle voice said, "I am sorry this happened to you my little warrior. You must fight. Fight with all your strength."

Mahpee began to rock back and forth to the beat of tribal drums, playing in his mind. He stared at his daughter. If she lived, the coming years would be difficult. Anger began to build like a great storm inside him. Ignoring everyone around him, he sang. "Heya Noha, Heya Noha, We n de ya ho…" They were the words to a war chant his grandfather had taught him. It was a millennium old. His deep, soft voice resonated in a rhythmic pattern off the walls. At the completion of the chant, he spoke to the Great Spirit. He asked for wisdom. The heat of battle still burned deep inside him. His last request was for vengeance.

With his free hand the chief stroked his daughters little face. He bent down and kissed her. With great care, he set her sleeping body back in the bassinet. He walked over to the lifeless body of his wife. He put his right hand on her forehead and whispered a prayer of mourning. *There must be retribution.* He spun around, and without saying a word, walked out of the operating room.

Captain Bodaway caught sight of the chief exiting sickbay. He ran to catch up with him. "Chief Mahpee, we are securing the alien ship and attaching it to Greysail."

"Good job captain. Do any of the aliens still live?"

Bodaway gave the chief a puzzled look, "No, we killed them. Like you instructed."

"In my anger I may have made a bad decision. I will not be such a fool again. Preserve their bodies. Put them in the cryo chambers. If there are too many of them, use coolers. Find out from the med staff at what temperature to store their bodies. Use an aft storage cell if necessary."

Bodaway nodded his head. "We found penned animals, as well as several storage areas on their ship. Some of them contained the carcasses of many different animal species. All the blood has been drained and their internal organs were removed. The meat seems to be going through a decay process. There are flakes of plants smeared all over the skin. It must be seasoning, placed on the meat so it develops flavor as it decays."

"You think the aliens were on a hunting party to replenish supplies?"

"Yes. Based on the crew size they were replenishing consumable supplies for a much larger force. The ship's crew and galley are too small for the amount of food they have on board. The ship is not designed for extended space travel. My guess is they are a scout ship operating at a close distance from a mother ship or base of operations. We found some star charts. At a quick glance, it looks like they stopped to hunt on planets with a gravity near the norm."

"I'm guessing they hunt on planets similar to their home world," said Mahpee. "They are either bold or stupid. Imagine boarding an enemy ship without knowing their strengths and weaknesses."

"What if they thought us to be the People of the Stars? If so, it means they have already appraised the capabilities of our relatives. It also means they do not know of our existence or they would not have boarded us with such lack of care."

"Why did the aliens go after the children? Why didn't they kill us? As they approached they had to know our ship had no weapons," said Mahpee.

"Why the children? It's hard to say," said Bodaway. "I remember reading when some species of bugs go to war with each other they often eat the enemy's children. As for not killing us? I'm guessing, again. They wanted to enslave us."

Mahpee shivered at the thought of aliens eating children. "If they are searching for new food sources, in time, they will discover Nokomis. We must be prepared for a conflict. I always knew someone would stumble upon us sooner or later. I thought our discovery would be by the People of the Stars, not aliens looking for a meal. When we get back to Nokomis, I will meet with the council to discuss our options. We must prepare for the enemy's eventual coming. Also, we must inform the People of the Stars of the threat."

"I'll get Greysail ready if you will oversee the preparations of the alien ship for transport. How is Shanee? I assume she's why you were in sickbay – checking up on her?"

"She died by the hands of our attackers. The med staff managed to save our daughter. Because of injuries sustained while in the womb, my little warrior fights for her life. Pray for her."

At hearing the queen died, Bodaway's eyes went wide and his head moved backward. He looked at his chief's face. He hadn't noticed the wetness of his eyes. Seeing the shock on friend's face the chief feared losing control of his emotions. He turned and headed for the alien ship. For the first time in his life, Bodaway had no words of wisdom to share with him.

The chief entered the alien ship and found his way to the bridge. He watched in silence as his crew poured over the strange controls and equipment. The levers and handles bore no resemblance to those found on human ships. But in the end, he knew a ship is still a ship, so the controls must complete the same tasks. He felt confident the engineers would figure everything out.

The chief stared in satisfaction as crewmembers walked by carrying another alien body.

"This is the last one, Mahpee," said a crewmember carrying the corpse.

Like many aliens, this one also had its head snapped off. The alien armor was strong but the helmet did not connect to the chest or back plate. The design gave the head mobility with little thought to protection. They relied on their exoskeleton too much. He remembered grappling with the first alien. Within seconds he found their neck to be their weak spot. Removing their heads was the easiest way to kill them. It was like snapping a stiff carota plant in half.

Mahpee watched his crew. They prepared the inside alien ship for its piggyback ride back to Nokomis. As they worked, the battle played over and over in his mind. *Nothing made sense. Even though the alien ship was a scout, it still possessed enough weapons to turn his ship into a meteor shower. It was hard to believe such advanced creatures would do something so stupid. Were they following orders? What made the children so important the captain was willing to risk both the ship and crew for? It wasn't the need for food, because they had plenty. It had to be something else.*

One final walk though proved to Mahpee his crew had done their job. The alien ship was ready for the trip back to Nokomis. As he walked back to his cabin he called Bodaway to let him know the alien ship was secure and he was back on Greysail. It didn't take long for memories of his wife to creep into his mind. His heart ached as he stared down the passageway and saw shadows from the past. He watched her specter as he remembered how she walked with him, always smiling, laughing, and teasing him. He wiped the dampness from his eyes.

Work would be impossible with these powerful emotions distracting him. His people and his daughter needed him. He had to push these memories and feelings out of his mind or he wouldn't be able to think. He thought about different ways to regain his focus. The solution hit him – *isolation.*

He decided after he met with the war council he would tell his friends he needed some time alone. He would take two weeks off. They would think he was grieving, but in truth, he would bury himself in his work. By the time he came back, the talk about Shanee's death would have died out. He would grieve later. But for the moment, and his own sanity, he needed to find out how she died.

The queen, being an only child, had no sisters to help her during her pregnancy. Kele, the queen's close friend, volunteered to be Igido. She would act as Shanee's sister during the queen's pregnancy. For nine months, Kele assisted the queen. She became family. Mahpee needed to speak with her in order to find out what happened. He requested she come to his office to talk about Shanee's death.

Within minutes Kele stood in front of Mahpee's open door. She knocked, and entered the room. When their eyes locked, she burst into tears. The chief's eyes glistened once again as he strained to control his emotions. This would not be easy for him.

"Mahpee, I am so sorry. I wish I had been the one to die. I don't know if I can live with this."

He stood up, moved around his desk, and embraced Kele. "What happened is not your fault. I too could blame myself, as could others. I have not asked you here to place blame."

"But, it is my fault. I was with her. I should have protected her."

"Kele, I'm sure you did what you thought right at the moment. I did not foresee the two of you being in the playroom with children when the attack began. We can feel sorry about not making different choices in past events. Or we can try to understand why this happened. I would like you to tell me how the attack happened from your prospective. The aliens did not happen to find the children, but sought them out for an unknown purpose."

Kele gathered her strength and continued with the story. "I remember Captain Bodaway announced we were being pursued by an unidentified ship. We heard the order for all ship's passengers to go to our rooms and secure the doors. We had too many children with us. Shanee decided we should lock ourselves in the playroom. The next announcement stated we had been boarded. We could hear metal on metal grating noises coming from the passageway. Within minutes the aliens were attempting to get into the playroom. They knew we were hiding there. The door held at first. The aliens used some kind of device to melt the metal on the door. Four of them entered the room and began to make clicking noises. At first, it smelled like a field of flowers in bloom." Kele started to sob as she tried to continue with the story.

Mahpee handed her a tissue. "I'm sorry, but I have to ask you to keep going. What happened next?"

"One alien grabbed little Ohanzee and shoved him toward the door. Shanee realized they were going to take the children. When the big bug reached for another child, Shanee ducked under his rifle. She hit him hard in the area between his helmet and body armor. He collapsed. The smell in the room changed from blooming flowers to a rancid acid smell. The alien bodies jerked upright. I could see she surprised them. Before the big bugs could react, Shanee grabbed a second alien placing both her hands on its helmet. There was a horrible crunching noise as she ripped its head off and flung it onto the floor."

"I saw the third alien lift its rifle toward Shanee. I kicked it in its midsection, propelling it hard into the side bulkhead. It seemed disorientated after the collision with the wall so I jumped on it and snapped one of its legs. A loud hissing sound came from the alien's body. I was afraid. I glanced over at Shanee in time to see the fourth alien shove a clawed hand into her stomach. I grabbed my alien by the helmet and pounded its head into the floor until it oozed liquid. When I was able to look at Shanee again, both her and the alien attacker were motionless. I smashed the alien's head to be sure it was dead. Next, I called sickbay for help. She didn't move, I knew she was dead. Oh please, please forgive me," she whimpered. "There was nothing I could do to help her. Nothing. I cried next to her body until a couple crewmen pulled me away so they could pick her up. They took her to sickbay. I'm sorry. I'm so sorry."

"There is no shame in your actions. I must have vengeance against those that have stolen my life. Listen, I have a request I would like you to consider. You knew Shanee better than I in many ways. If my daughter survives…"

Kele interrupted in a high voice, "Your daughter? Her baby lives?"

"Yes, but she fights for her life. If she survives, I would like your help in raising and guiding her on her life's journey." Mahpee saw Kele already nodding her head yes. He knew this to be a big decision, so he held his hand out toward her. "Don't answer now. Give it some thought, and we will talk later." Mahpee hugged Kele one last time. "Shanee couldn't have picked a better friend. Thank you."

Within the next few minutes Greysail started her voyage home. The alien ship rode piggyback on her hull. Word about attack had already spread across Nokomis. By the time the royal ship arrived, a crowd numbering at least in the millions had gathered. Mahpee expected some turn out, but nothing like this. As he looked at the view screen he thought, *half of Nokomis must be out there.* Something was going on here he didn't foresee. As he focused on the crowd, he saw them, the Tellers. *Oh no.* His heart sank. *They found out. Bodaway must have reported the events of the attack. The ceremonial dress meant the Tellers were here on business.*

Mahpee turned to look at Bodaway. He could tell he too had become nervous upon seeing the Tellers. *This would change everything for his daughter. They had the power to become involved in all aspects of her life. All the plans of isolating himself dissolved. To the Tellers, she was the beginning of a prophecy predating the great exodus.*

Mahpee knew all about Tellers because his grandfather had been one. Grandfather often said, "The Council of Tellers are the only ones able to override a chief's order." The council is made up of the most influential members of the Peoples Nation. This council was unusual in it was the first time in history a mystic was allowed to become a member. She seldom interacted with anyone and remained very reclusive. The few times she did appear were followed by great changes within the Peoples Nation.

The crew received word the Tellers wanted to speak with everyone aboard. No one was to leave the ship. Otaktay, the lead Teller, was the first to board Greysail. He went straight to the bridge. Instead of sticking both arms out with palms face down, he reached his right hand out for Mahpee to grasp. This told the chief the meeting would not be a simple questioning it could have life changing consequences.

Everyone on board answered question after question. Following the interviews, the Tellers went with Mahpee to meet the little princess. After they examined the baby, they asked everyone to leave. Mahpee refused to go.

Otaktay put his hand on Mahpee's shoulder. "Do not worry. We are going to perform a healing. We must cleanse the room first." Seeing Mahpee still had doubts Otaktay said, "She is strong, but she needs our help. Her spirit weakens."

It was true. The doctors told him she needed a miracle to survive. The wound over her heart showed signs of infection. He knew something needed to be done to save her. He prayed, but even with the best care, she continued to deteriorate. His grandfather had told him about healings, but it had never crossed his mind to have one performed.

He didn't believe in them. Ideas about cleansings and healings represented a mixture of old tales and half-truths. He looked at his unconscious daughter. He was out of options. *I'll do anything to save her, even this.*

"Okay, perform your healing."

Otaktay smiled, "Mahpee, I know you follow old customs your grandfather taught you. It saddens me to see you do not believe in them. Today, I pray we change your mind. A healing is a spiritual event connecting us with plants, animals, air, earth, water, and fire."

Mahpee started to smile at the thought.

Otaktay gave him a stern look. "Do not forget the omen at your own birth."

The smile disappeared off Mahpee's face.

"You may watch from outside this room. You must not speak a single word. I know how much you chiefs love to talk. Can you do it, not a single word?"

Mahpee nodded his head in silence.

The Tellers began their work. They cranked up the heat, turning the medical room into a sweatbox. Otaktay placed a necklace of small colored cloths tied into little rolls on the princess. Each teller took out a feather tied with leather and began to wave it around the room. Otaktay drew a circle on the floor with some kind of chalk. Mahpee recognized the medicine wheel with the four directions depicted in it. His daughter was at the center.

Each Teller lit a cloth and fanned smoke around the room as they danced and chanted. Soon the smoke became so thick, Mahpee could only see a shadow as something moved near the window. Tears from straining his eyes formed as he struggled to see through the smoke. He began to feel a little lightheaded. He wiped his eyes and saw a dog, no – it was a fox - pacing back and forth. As he strained his eyes, he saw a beaver standing on its hind legs and tail. Mahpee shook his head to clear the cobwebs from his mind. He strained his eyes to see more. He stood up and placed his face next to the window as the wispy shadow of a bird flew by. He watched as animal after animal appeared. An alligator in smoke form became visible on the ground. It looked like it was staring right at him, when everything went black.

Mahpee opened his eyes, and he saw Otaktay grinning at him.

"What happened?" asked Mahpee.

"When we finished the ceremony, we exited the room. We found you lying on the floor, passed out. We discovered a vent was open between the rooms. You must have breathed in too much smoke from the Chuckta bark."

"I saw animals."

Otaktay gave a look to the other Tellers and said, "You mean you saw an animal. Could you identify what it was?"

Mahpee sat upright. "No. I saw animals of all types as if they stepped out of a forest. I saw a fox, beaver, bear, buffalo, there must have been a hundred animals."

The smile disappeared from Otaktay's face.

"What does it mean?" asked Mahpee.

Otaktay patted Mahpee on the back. "It means you were hallucinating from the bark."

"Do not mock me Otaktay. I am still the chief, and this is about my daughter. I demand the truth."

Otaktay took a deep breath. "Each person born of the People's Nation has a spirit animal which watches over them. During the healing ceremony we call their animal spirit into our world to help. Each animal carries a life energy with it. They also represent the individual's different traits. Seeing more than one spirit animal during a healing has never occurred before. To be honest, I don't know what it means. I wish I did."

"If you had to guess, what would you guess it means?"

Otaktay looked at his fellow Tellers. "If any of you has anything to say, speak up."

The look of surprise on Otaktay's face didn't escape Mahpee as an ancient looking female stepped forward. *Why hadn't he noticed her before? She had a patch on one eye and her other eye was a milky white color. She stared right at him as if she could see. Only a handful of people had ever met this Teller because of her reclusive life. She was Nahimana, the living legend. During her vision quest she asked the Great Spirit for foresight. He gave it to her, but took her ability to see. She was the most feared of Tellers. She was the blind mystic.* Mahpee's palms started to sweat.

"I see you know me, grandson of Uzumati. Otaktay speaks true words to you. Your daughter, the warrior born princess, is powerful beyond your understanding. She will become the great leader, as spoken of in the ancient legends. The spirit animals have already shared their energy with her. When she comes of age, she will be a force unlike any other. I tell you now, you will raise your daughter. But we, the Council of Tellers, will choose her education and training. She must develop her full potential at any cost or we are all doomed."

"So I have decreed," said Otaktay. "We will contact you soon, Chief Mahpee. You and everyone else may now leave."

All but the old mystic exited the medical facility. She turned and went back to the princess. Mahpee followed her. The ancient woman made motions in the air with her hands as she spoke in a voice so low he couldn't make out any of the words. She turned so quick to face him his body jerked in a startled reflex.

She was inches from his face and staring at him with her blind eye. When Nahimana spoke, he could smell the spices on her breath. "See. Her wound already heals."

He looked at the scar. *She is right, its no longer red and irritated. It could be a coincidence.*

"Even with what you have seen, grandson of Uzumati, you still doubt?

Can the hag read my mind?

The witch grinned as if she read his thoughts. "I have glimpsed into your future. Do you want to know what waits?" She cackled at him.

His heart raced. He could feel the sweat oozing out of his palms. *I don't believe all this nonsense, but – If I don't believe why am I nervous?*

Not waiting for an answer Nahimana squinted at him. He swore she touched his soul with her stare. "In time, you will betray your daughter, and leave her heart broken. You, Chief Mahpee, will become the rider of the storm. Your fate is sealed." The old mystic turned and walked out before he could ask a single question.

What the hell did she mean? He had never betrayed anyone in his life. He would rather choose death than to betray anyone, let alone his daughter. The hag spoke nonsense. I will become the rider of the storm. Mumbo jumbo. She wouldn't even stay to answer questions. I never want to see her again.

17

Hopes of keeping a lid on his daughter's unusual birth lasted less time than it took to get back to Nokomis. Word spread throughout the Nation his tiny daughter was the warrior born princess from the old prophesies. Later in the evening, the Tellers showed up at the War Council. They warned of impending doom and gave Mahpee everything he requested. For better or worse, it looked like they would be a major part of his life.

The People's Nation broadcast pictures of the aliens and vids of the attack. A few videos from the fight were also shown in all their gruesomeness. The old war drums beat across Nokomis to let the People's Nation know they were at war.

Over the next several years, the scientists learned what they could from alien technology. Labs and universities worked around the clock. They studied the propulsion unit, weapon systems, shields, star charts, and computer systems. The People's Nation incorporated the new technology into their lives. They redesigned their planetary defenses and enhanced their ships of war. Mahpee made sure the People of the Stars received information on the existence of the aliens along with new technologies.

The medical team, along with bug experts, studied the alien bodies. A major evolutionary change in the bug seemed to be in its brain. It still looked like coral, but it contained a membrane, connecting five different locations within the brain. Without a live bug, they had to guess at the membranes purpose.

Evaluations of several stomachs indicated no human remains. They ate decayed vegetables, fruit, and aged meat void of blood. Scientists found four chemical sacs inside the exoskeleton. Each bug was capable of creating thousands of different smells. The entomologists believed the bugs used different aromas as a form of non-verbal communication. Like current day beetles, the enemy could see in the human range and the ultraviolet spectrum.

The People's Nation computers deciphered the alien language by using the star charts and other documents discovered on the alien ship. The Peoples Nation named the aliens Raygin. It was the closest the computer could come to interpreting the alien name. The star charts also caused a profound change in the way astronomers viewed the universe. According to the Raygin, the universe exists in ripples. It's like when you throw a stone in the water. The ripple created by the stone would represent matter, and the area between ripples represented voids. This meant the universe was much larger than expected, and humans lived in the newest ripple. Humans were the youngsters of the universe. Since the Raygin come from the previous ripple, they are older and had longer to evolve.

Each new understanding of alien technology brought changes to the People's Nation. The sole area where no progress occurred was with the Raygin computer system. The design being biological rather than electrical proved a hard concept to grasp. To defeat the impasse, Nashta, an upcoming engineer was assigned to the project.

Mahpee had two main focuses in his life, his daughter and preparations for war. The war effort produced many technological breakthroughs. He was happy with the progress. The real problem was his daughter, who demanded constant attention. He wanted her to have a simple life, but the Tellers always pushed her and tested her abilities. She learned to thrive on challenges. They created a propensity within her for taking risks with high rewards. Because of this, she became difficult to control.

Mahpee knew there was something unusual about his daughter. The day after the attack, she followed him with her eyes when he paced back and forth. Hell, later she even remembered him calling her my little warrior when she was minutes old! A perfect memory from birth, they said. I should never have let them give her the military placement exam. She scored off scale. That started my problems. The Tellers said either I enroll her in the military school or they would take her from me. How could the ancients have predicted the events of her birth in a time before the great exodus? It is all too crazy for me to accept.

Mahpee began to question his beliefs. *The Tellers have filled her head with garbage. If I can get her interested in a man she'll get married, have a baby, and to hell with the prophecies!* He smiled. *I'd love to hear little feet running through the house.*

Mahpee's private communicator beeped. He quit arguing with himself. He looked at the message. It was from his old friend, Chancellor Mongwau, from the university: *Come right away. I have news.*

CHAPTER TWO: Second Contact

The young lieutenant's eyes darted across the screen. Her hands trembled while she manipulated the gains to paint the best picture on the scanner. "Captain, I have an unknown target at the edge of scanner range."

"Are you sure it's not an electronic ghost?" The captain knew each new ship has electrical or mechanical problems to work out on her maiden voyage. The Nomad would be no different.

"We've run several diagnostics, sir. Everything is running at peak performance."

"Okay Lieutenant Muween. Lets see if it's a bug or a real ship. Navigation, come left heading 300alpha15."

"Aye sir. Left heading 300alpha15."

The colonist ship's computer locked out the new singularity drive. The ion propulsion engine activated. The Nomad started a slow turn left and ascended 15 degrees. Unless you were on the bridge, you wouldn't realize the ship had made a turn to the left and changed its inclination. When the ship acquired the new heading, the ion propulsion engine shut down. The singularity drive started with a loud pop. Each pop represented a jump of several light years.

If it was a glitch inside the scanner, the captain figured, it would stay on the screen in the same spot. He waited for the report. At least the singularity drive was living up to its reputation. The new drive would deliver the next great step in human expansion. Picture space as a balloon. Stick your index fingers on opposite sides of the balloon and push your fingers together. The depressed area created by your fingers is a gravity well. A ship travels the small gap from finger to finger. Release the pressure on the balloon. Wham, you travel from point to point faster than light can make the same trip.

"It's gone captain," said Lieutenant Muween.

This is not good news. This trip should have been an easy run. Deliver the colonists to Rayne. Help get them situated, and return home to Adalin for the next assignment. "Thank you Lieutenant Muween. Let me know if you see anything at all on the scanner."

"Aye Captain."

"Commander Tucker, I need a word with you. Miss Ess, you have the bridge. Put us back on course.

"Aye sir, I have the bridge. Back on course."

The door to the conference room sensed the two approaching and opened. Captain Cutter rubbed the back of his neck as he walked in. The captain had flown stalkers during the mining wars and had developed a sixth sense. Right now, it was in alarm mode.

"Mark, I won't lie to you. I'm worried about the ghost ship following us. We are way beyond explored space heading to a planet seeming too good to be true."

The two sat down. Mark said, "I don't understand. We are the first commercial ship fitted with a popper, how can anyone keep up with us?"

"Did you call the singularity drive a popper?"

"Yes sir. It's what all the new engineers call the drives. When the vertilator releases the gravity well it makes a loud pop. The sound is how the drive got the nickname."

"Makes sense, but back to our problem. Do you think the ship following us could be military?"

22

"Anything is possible captain, but I don't see why they would shadow us without letting us know they were there."

"It seems odd," said the captain. "There are always shortages of fruits and vegetables. A probe returns with the location of a perfect planet. The local flora is – you guessed it, fruits and vegetables. Coincidence? I don't know. Something stinks here. Who would follow a colonization ship to nowhere? Anyway, we are close to Rayne. Until we get there I want one of us on the bridge at all times."

"Okay captain. What would…"

"Captain, please report to the bridge." Boomed out of the overhead speaker.

The captain's brow furrowed, "I was afraid of this."

All eyes were on the captain as he went straight to the navigation station. He looked at the screen. *Damn, the ghost ship is back. This time instead of operating at the fringe of scanner range the target is advancing on us.*

"Com, send a message to United Fleet Command," said the captain. He looked at a screen depicting their route, "Location 18736 by 7233. An unknown ship is pursuing Nomad. Intentions unknown. Implementing evasive maneuvers. Expect more to follow. Also, attempt contact with the unknown ship on all frequencies."

"Aye, Captain, message to UFC and attempt contact with unknown ship."

The captain understood it would take months to get the message to United Fleet Command. Still, they had to know, in case something bad happened. The ensign changed the radio to a UFC emergency frequency. Squelch and static was all he received on what should have been an open frequency. He tried the other frequencies with the same results. "Captain, I am getting some kind of suppression on all frequencies. I'll keep trying sir."

"It's critical we get the message out. Keep trying. Civilian ships can't afford the shielded receivers the military ships have. Whoever is moving toward us could be disrupting our com somehow."

"Aye sir, I'll keep trying."

"Miss Ess, I have the bridge."

"Aye captain, you have the bridge."

"Your thoughts commander Tucker?"

"With no weapons our best option is to run. I say we push the Nomad to max speed while still trying to contact them. I don't think this is one of our military ships. What would it be doing out here? Last I knew our military is not capable of disrupting all communication channels. Besides, why would they do that to us?"

The captain moved the ship's throttle from sixty percent to one hundred percent. He flipped a com switch on his seat. "Engineering, this is the captain, we are being pursued by an unknown ship. Were going to attempt to outrun it, so keep your eyes on the popper."

Smitty, the Chief Engineer smiled. First time he heard a winged wonder call the singularity drive a popper! He kind of liked the old captain. "Aye captain, eye's on the popper."

"Commander Tucker, sound battle stations."

"Aye sir, sounding battle stations."

Pop........pop........pop. The Nomad made jumps totaling numerous light years within seconds. Scanners are not capable of operation in a gravitational well. The big colonist transport tracked the unknown ship between jumps.

"Status, Lieutenant Muween?"

"The unknown ship is gaining on us sir. Estimated intercept in three minutes and twenty two seconds."

"Shit. They are way faster than us. Mr. Tucker, warn the ship's crew and the colonists. Com, any luck with response from the unknown ship?"

"No sir. I'm preparing to launch a probe with a looped transmission for United Fleet Command."

"Good job, ensign. Be quick about it."

A security team armed with hand held weapons showed up on the bridge. They positioned themselves at the entrance hatchway. The team leader entered a code into an electronic controller on the wall. A heavy reinforced barrier slammed into position with a thud. Everyone took a second to look at the formidable door. It would take weeks to cut through something so thick.

In the colonists' quarters, activities were chaotic. The lack of information added to the confusion. Seeing the armed security team in the passageways didn't help matters. The captain cut all communications except with security and engineering. If they lived through this, he would make it up to the colonists. The event in progress required his full attention.

"Lieutenant Muween, determine where the unknown ship will exit its gravity well."

"Yes sir. If conditions remain the same the unknown ship will arrive in our space 4,828.032 meters off our starboard side."

"Mr. Tucker, contact security. Have them clear personnel from storage bay four. Unlatch the heavy equipment and lock the inner air hatch."

"Ensign Rolan, how long before you have the probe ready for launch?"

"I need about another minute sir."

"Lieutenant Muween, watch Ensign Rolan. When he launches the probe, use the thrusters to move us starboard. I'll use the stabilizers to stop the ship. On my command, be ready to engage the singularity drive."

Commander Tucker looked at the captain and shrugged his shoulders. "What are you going to do, captain?"

"We may not have any weapons on the Nomad, but we are not defenseless. When we launch the probe I suspect they will track it, and make sure it's not a threat to their ship. If they are military, I'm guessing they will lunch something to chase the probe. For a few seconds, if we're lucky, the probe will distract them. The nomad will shift right. Open the cargo doors, shut down the grav field, stop, release the heavy equipment, and jump."

The captain knew it was a long shot, but this maneuver was all he had. If he lived through this, he would press for a few changes. Future transport ships will need some kind of defensive weapons on them. After hearing the captain's plan the crew was wide-eyed and focused. Their lives depended on the next series of maneuvers.

"Captain, I'm ready to launch the probe," said Ensign Rolan.

"Lieutenant Muween, as soon as the probe clears the ship, activate the thrusters."

"Aye, Captain."

"Launch the probe Mr. Rolan."

"Launching the probe captain."

As Lieutenant Muween moved the ship to the starboard, the captain opened the hatch door. He released the grav field, stopped the ship, and the heavy equipment floated out the bay into the emptiness of space. When he tried to close the bay door, something was wrong. The bay door indicated no seal. The grav field wouldn't work with the door unsealed. *Too late, we have to leave now.*

"Jump, Lieutenant Muween."

"Aye sir, jumping."

The drive popped and the ship jumped light years ahead. Chaos ensued in the colonists' quarters as they lost gravity. The captain's control panel lit up. Alarms started sounding on the helm, the colonists' quarters, and various passageways. Security reported a hold down chain did not fully release. It stopped the bay door from closing. In addition, a large ground dozer got hung up on the chain causing it not to float out. When they jumped, the dozer hit the inside wall of bay four. The damage caused the colonists' quarters to lose their gravity.

The ghost ship released a small fighter to chase down the probe. The next jump put them into the space the Nomad had vacated. The captain pictured the alarms going off on the ghost ship. He hoped their repair teams would be busy assessing the damage. The ploy worked. But the damage to the strange looking ship of war was minimal.

After a few more jumps the ship chasing them was now waiting for them and fired a barrage of plasma weapons. The salvo took out the Nomad's ion propulsion engine and the singularity drive. They were floating in space with no method of propulsion.

"They're going to board us," said the captain, "otherwise we would already be dead. There's still hope."

Not all the crew on the bridge heard the captain. They were focused on the strange military looking ship moving in front of them. The design was not human. It looked like a sleek bug with four appendages. It had a wide body with two shorter arms in front extending forward. Two large legs at the aft end extended rearward. The ship's design made it look like it was leaping through space. The jet-black color blended well with the blackness of space. Weapon mounts bristled across the surface. As the Nomad crew watched, more weapons seemed to appear. They must have been retractable.

The captain flipped a switch on his chair, activating Nomad's com system. "Nomad, this is the captain. It appears an unknown ship of war will be boarding us within minutes. They have taken out our ion propulsion engine and our singularity drive. If they wanted to destroy us, we would already be dead. Do not shoot at them with hand weapons unless they fire first. We still don't know their intentions."

The crew on the helm watched as the black vessel fired its thrusters and maneuvered over the Nomad. The crew heard a loud clang.

"Captain, this is crewman Tiggs from security team six, in the colonists' quarters. They have boarded us - I don't know what the hell these things…"

The sound of weapon fire interrupted their conversation. Tiggs had left his com open. The color drained from the crewmembers faces. The captain looked at Lieutenant Muween and saw she was rocking back and forth in her chair.

"Crewman Tiggs. I said don't fire unless fired on."

"I know captain. As soon as the aliens saw us, they started shooting. We returned fire, but they are wearing some kind of body armor. We lost five crewmembers. We're retreating toward engineering. A few colonists exited their quarters and were cut down. They weren't armed sir. I couldn't tell how many colonists they killed. The aliens look like big bugs that walk upright. They won't talk to us. I don't even know if they can hear us. I'm sorry, but we can't stop them sir."

"Nomad, this is the captain. Do not engage the aliens. They are hostile. Lock yourselves in your rooms and do not exit." The captain hoped by clearing the passageways the killing would stop. He wished they had bigger weapons.

The captain stood up. He walked over to Lieutenant Muween at the navigation station, and said, "Aren't you a linguist?"

Grasping what the captain was about to ask her she said, "I can't captain. The aliens are killing us. I can't think straight, I'm too scared."

"We're all scared lieutenant. If these walking bugs come to the bridge, you may be able to save a few of us if you can communicate with them."

The lieutenant looked around the bridge and realized the captain was right. Everyone looked scared. She took a deep breath, exhaled. "I'll try."

"Walk me through what you're thinking lieutenant."

"Well, since they attacked us, and they shot unarmed colonists, I'd call them an aggressive species. I'm sure they have a strong sense of survival. Most bugs do. Avoid eye contact. If they evolved from insects, we have nothing in common communication wise. Many bugs use chemical scents to communicate. Some can make noises with their bodies, but nothing like what we are used to. The lieutenant's eyes went white as she thought about what she learned in school. "Many bugs are omnivorous, captain. What if they see us as food?"

Sparks started flying from the heavy security barrier on the bridge. The massive door began to melt like ice on a hot day. The crew watched in fear.

"Everyone, stay seated. Keep your eyes on me, or Lieutenant Muween. Whatever you do, do not stare at the aliens. Security, put your weapons on the floor."

The door melted and made a molten mess on the floor. An alien in body armor stepped forward followed by two companions. Their job seemed to be to secure the bridge. One stood on the liquefied metal as if unconcerned. The alien armor design appeared to be stronger than human armor.

I hope the lieutenant can keep her composure. The aliens are butt ugly. They had long antennae hanging forward over their heads. Their arms and legs ended in fingered claws. Instead of a neck they had a thorax followed by a hard-shelled abdomen. Hissing noises were coming from the bodies of a couple aliens on the bridge. Six more entered, followed by an alien with a red decal on its body armor. *Ah, there's the leader.*

The alien with the red decal reached up and removed a partial helmet, exposing two large black eyes. It moved its two maxillary palp appendages, designed to help cram food into its big mouth. The creature walked up to Lieutenant Muween and stood inches from her face. She breathed in, trying to calm her nerves. The smell emitted by the bug leader was like thousands of sweet flowers. It was too much for the lieutenant's olfactory senses. She turned her head and vomited.

The aliens started hissing from tiny holes in their bodies. The leader turned to look at his crew, as if proud of what he did. The captain figured the hissing must be the way they laugh. *Oh great. These repulsive looking bugs are assholes too. So much for advanced civilizations.*

The bug leader stepped forward to confront the captain. The smell changed to resemble the aroma of a sweaty armpit. The monkey's ass smelling leader stunk like hell, but the captain refused to let it get to him. The leader's arm started to twitch, as if the captain had irritated it somehow.

Lieutenant Muween decided to intervene. Without looking into the alien's eyes, she tapped her chest with both hands and said, "Muween". She tapped the captain's chest and said, "Cutter". She opened her arms as if to include the entire crew and said, "Humans".

The alien leader looked at his crew and hissed. The crew hissed back. This went back and forth for about a minute. The Nomad crew experienced a bouquet of smells. Some seemed pleasant, and others, not so pleasant.

The alien leader moved both his clawed arms towards his crew in an encompassing motion. It hissed while clicking twice. The bug spun around and left its crew to gather up the humans.

The crew from the bridge found themselves escorted down their own passageways. They joined with other crewmembers, who were accompanied by their own contingency of armed aliens. Some yelling and screaming could be heard. It was coming from the colonists' quarters.

Every few seconds a plasma rifle fired. The screams were frightening.

The aliens herded the captives forward.

The colonists were screaming, "Where have you taken the children? I want my child back!"

Muween looked at the captain as they walked through the passageways. She started crying.

"What is it lieutenant?" asked the captain.

She sniffled. "Some species of bugs who attack other insects will often destroy the nurseries first and eat any larva they find."

Blood soaked the passageway floors near the colonists' quarters. Plasma-burned human bodies laid everywhere. The bugs shot or mutilated any human attempting to stop them from taking the children. The surviving humans shuffled onto the alien ship. Their heads hung low, not one eye was dry, except for those of Captain Cutter. He put his training to use. He observed how the crew manipulated the various controls hoping they might be able to use the information later.

CHAPTER THREE: The Trip

Mikal Kozlov, the next hand picked governor of Rayne, was observing the loading of Argosy. The Nomad, Argosy's sister ship disappeared over six months ago. There was no sign of either the ship or any of the colonists. A commercial ship discovered a com probe from the Nomad. The military took possession of the damaged equipment. Whispers of slavers operating in fringe space could be overheard in all the outermost space stations. How could anyone lose an entire ship and its contents?

Both the Nomad and Argosy were colonist transport ships. They had no weapons other than some small planetary arms. After finding the probe, United Fleet Command decided to refit the Argosy. They added several laser canons. Against the governor's wishes, 3 light armor platoons also were assigned to duty on Rayne. Rather than using a military transport, the soldiers would travel with the colonists. This had become a standard practice to spare the expense of traveling long distances.

The commanding officer, like the governor, was hand picked for the job. Both individuals were social climbers from connected families. If they did well, their next job would move them further up the ladder. An unbelievable opportunity, considering neither had leadership or command experience.

The next morning at zero eight hundred, the Argosy left load orbit over Trinity Prime. With the new drive developed by the military, the trip would be cut to a few months verse several years. During the voyage the colonists will occupy themselves by getting to know each other and practicing with the new equipment. The military, well, they do what the military always does – prepare for war.

First Lieutenant Phlop attended the initial kickoff muster for the soldiers. He wanted to make sure Sergeant McCormack paid homage to him in front of the troops. They had to learn right off, he was their leader, not the war hardened sergeant. He walked up to the sergeant who spun around and stood at attention. With a voice echoing across the storage-deck, he said, "ATTEN HUT". Representing the troops, the well-seasoned sergeant saluted the young first lieutenant.

The green lieutenant forgot to salute back. He turned to the troops and shrieked in a squeaking voice, "At ease!" The first lieutenant started pacing back and forth as he talked. The troops had a hard time hearing him. "I'm your commanding officer, First Lieutenant Phlop. Please remember the 'O' is spoken as in the word flow. I will not tolerate jokes about my name."

Mac shook his head. *No better way to get young troops to start something than to plant the seed in their heads. A name like Phlop begged to be poked fun at. Many troops died because a military officer's ego was too big to allow them to listen to those with experience.* Mac saw the troops under his care as his children. He would let nobody bring unnecessary harm to them, not even their commanding officer.

The lieutenant squeaked on. "I have an open door policy if you need to talk to me, but make sure you make an appointment. If you follow my orders we won't have any problems. I have a lot to do so I'll leave you in the hands of Sergeant McCormack. Umm good bye." Lieutenant Phlop turned around and walked away.

Mac positioned himself before the troops and said, "Everyone relax! Let me give you a few insights and rules.

First off, call me Mac. You will find colonist duty to be informal by military standards. Unlike many of you, I chose this assignment. You military ground pounders forced to be here, life sucks and you got a shitty billet. Don't whine to me about it. Next, as long as we aren't in a firefight and the lieutenant gives you an order like, get me coffee, bring me a pen, or order this part, do it. If we are in a firefight and he tells you to do something, don't do it. Tell him he has to go through me."

"By a show of hands, how many of you are conscripts." Out of 60 troops, fourteen held up their hands. This didn't surprise him. *Young fleet soldiers all wanted to see action, not watch plants grow while on colonist duty. The military filled in with conscripts when they didn't have enough regulars. I'll make sure most conscripts become part of Third platoon and get special attention.* "How many of you have been in action?" Half the troops raised their hands. Mac shook his head. "I mean real action. Where you had to shoot at an enemy because they were trying to kill you. Show me those hands again." This time, ten people held up their hands.

Mac looked at all ten experienced troopers. "Tinker, is that you."

"Yeah Mac, it's me."

"Well ain't that the shits."

Everyone laughed.

Mac smiled. "How'd you wind up here?"

"I volunteered when I found out you were here."

Mac used a hand signal telling Tinker to not say a word. "Did everyone hear what he said? Now there's someone who knows how to suck up. Come see me after this training session. You troops with experience, I'll be expecting lots of help from you. For now, put on one of the backpacks by the door and follow me."

As he expected, Tinker was the first to move toward the backpacks. Close behind him was a female with a tattoo on her forehead. The rest of the class followed. Mac knew in time, these two were going to be his leaders. He wanted the troops to understand he would never ask them to do anything he wouldn't do himself.

"Ugh," groaned Tinker as he watched Mac pick up a backpack. Mac never did anything half assed. The workout would be grueling.

If nothing else, you could always count on Mac giving his all. The workout pushed the troopers to their limit. As people dropped out, Mac made them return to the classroom, relax, and have some water. Many troopers couldn't believe the salty sergeant didn't yell at them for not pushing on.

By the time Mac stopped the physical training session, Tinker, three experienced troopers, and tattoo girl were the only ones left. He looked over the troopers. The single trooper not sucking air was tattoo girl. He remembered a time when no one could keep up with him during his physical training sessions. Were the anti aging drugs he took in his youth beginning to fail?

"Nice job everyone. Meet me back at the training classroom."

"Fuck," said a trooper, "I'm beat. What's his problem? We're on colonist duty, not the front lines of a war zone!"

Tinker looked at his fellow troopers. "Mac's old school. He believes preparation for the worst scenario will help you to survive in most circumstances. But even with the best training, he says sometimes you draw the short stick, and you're just fucked."

Everyone laughed at the wisdom in the statement. Another trooper said, "At least he sounds honest."

When everyone settled down in his or her assigned seats, Mac started a lecture. Communication was the topic; it was nothing like what the students expected. As Mac talked he used hand gestures to describe different pieces of equipment. For no apparent reason, Tinker pushed his seat back, and ran into the hallway. The class fell silent. Some students looked at the door. Others looked at Mac with a furrowed brow, waiting for him to comment.

"How come no one else left the room?" The class looked at each other. Mac waved for Tinker to come back in.

A brave student said, "No one told us to."

"I didn't tell Tinker to come back in the room, yet he did what I wanted him to."

"Yeah, but you waved him back in."

"Yes," said Mac. "You are correct. I used nonverbal communication to get him back in the classroom. I used nonverbal hand commands to get him to leave. Your problem is you didn't recognize it. I want everyone to learn combat hand commands. Each daily cycle we are aboard the Argosy you will have homework."

The class groaned.

Mac ran his hand across his mouth as if closing a zipper.

Everyone understood the simple instruction and laughed.

"It won't be bad. You will learn at least one command each ship's period. Who knows, one day it may save your life." Mac continued the training session using holographic videos. They covered various communication systems they would be using while on colonist duty.

At the first day's end, the troopers felt exhausted, both in the physical sense and from the constant mental challenges. Mac's training style wasn't a data dump of information, he asked a lot of questions to force his troopers to think. When Mac dismissed the troops he recommended they get to know the ship, and spend some time getting to know each other.

Mac's eyes couldn't help but follow Dreng Matilda, tattoo girl, as she left the classroom. Until now, Mac hadn't thought about another woman since his brother and wife were killed during the mining wars. He tried to figure out what in her stirred his emotions. *Was it her tattoo, big brown eyes, pretty face, long black hair, broad shoulders, or her perfect body? She could become a distraction. He needed to get her out of his head and stay focused on his responsibilities. He knew he shied away from relationships because he didn't ever want to experience losing someone close to him again.*

After everyone had left the classroom Tinker walked up to his old leader.

"So, tell me, what are you doing here?" said Mac.

"I heard rumors the Nomad got attacked in deep space. We lost the entire ship and everyone on it, including my uncle. I started calling around. I discovered UFC planned to refit the Argosy with some laser canons. It sounded pretty serious so I did some more digging. I found out several platoons of light armor infantry would be sent to Rayne. I was told they would ride with the colonists. I called the troop detailer and he told me off the record you took the lead enlisted assignment, so here I am."

"United Fleet Command," said Mac, "doesn't know what happened. They have been saturating unexplored areas of deep space with popper probes. A few of our probes from the same area of uncharted space have gone missing. One returning probe did detect the movement of a ship. It is not one of known design. A few of our battle cruisers have been fitted with the new singularity drive and will shadow us. Once we arrive the ships will search local space for anything unusual."

"So what's up? You think it might be pirates, a rogue government, or one of the big companies?"

"I don't know, but anyone destroying probes is doing something they don't want to get caught doing. I'm glad you're here. Keep all this confidential. I'll let the troops know before we land."

"Will do Mac. By the way, thanks for the nice write up you gave me. I got awarded a battle medal because of it."

He felt good that Vice Admiral Farragut gave Tinker the medal he deserved. After all, heroes don't always live to get them.

"You earned it, Tinker. Now get out of here and have some fun."

After Tinker left the classroom, Mac gathered up his notes. He walked back to his quarters deep in thought. *Colonist duty is a no brainer tour for a combat experienced ground pounder. This tour was different. I don't like deceiving people, but I had to for the mission's sake. The troops needed to get in shape so they could ready no matter what the problem.* He entered his modified quarters, grabbed some workout clothes from the closet and put them on.

His workout hadn't started yet and he realized he was sweating like a fat politician caught stealing. He looked at the environmental controls. *Fuck, it's thirty-five degrees Celsius.* He took off his sweatshirt, called the maintenance department to report the problem. He opened his door to cool the room and started his work out. This little bit of heat wasn't going to deter him.

Mac started with slow moving stretches. He went through muscle resistance exercises and finished with a specific sequence of rolls, kicks, and punches. It took him years to master these exercises. Mac glanced at the door thinking he heard the maintenance crew.

His body jerked and his eyes blinked in reflex. Standing there staring at him, was tattoo girl. She was looking at his war scared body through the open door. "What's up Dreng? Can I help you with something?"

"What were you doing?"

"Exercising."

She put her hands on her hips. "I am not stupid Mac. I know you were exercising. Where did you learn to do those moves?"

Wow, this girl had a big set of brass balls. She always seemed to say what she was thinking. I kind of like it. Mac decided to turn the tables on her. "How long were you standing there watching me?" he asked.

This time Dreng showed surprise as her face turned red, "Oh, I'm sorry. I didn't mean to snoop. I was walking the passageways trying to learn the ship layout when I saw the open door. I looked in and was surprised to see you exercising. The moves, they made sense to me, a pattern with a purpose. I did not watch you. I watched the way your body moved."

"Now I'm disappointed."

She turned red again and looked at the ground.

Mac let her off the hook. "I learned the moves from a Tao monk on Helleron."

"Taoist fighting monks, a philosophical order originating in Old Earth China. Taoists believe there is a force linking the entire universe. The Yin and Yang represents the balance of life."

"Yeah, you're right, very good. I see you are familiar with them."

"I have never met one, but I know to learn their fighting style you must be in their order. Are you a monk?"

Mac burst out in a laugh. Dreng tilted her head in puzzlement as she watched him laugh.

"No, I'm not a monk. I saved a Monk. He wouldn't leave me alone. He followed me like a little puppy for months. He told me until he saved my life, his life would be out of balance. He offered to give me something of value instead of saving my life. When I told him I didn't want anything, he started to follow me, waiting for an opportunity to save me. It was getting to be embarrassing having a little guy in orange robes following me around all day. I relented and told him if he would train me for the three years left on my tour, I would consider the debt paid. He saw the wisdom in the offer and agreed to the deal."

"Will you teach me the Tao style of fighting?"

Mac started to laugh again. "It took me three years and I'm a professional soldier."

"Perfect. I have conscripted for four years."

"Whoa there. I didn't agree to train you."

Mac was trying to read Dreng's face when she batted her beautiful amber eyes at him.

She's a minx, I better be careful. "I'll consider it. But for now, concentrate on learning the basics."

"You will find me quick to learn."

Confident too, I hope she's not too self-assured. It could be fatal. "I'll tell you what. Stay in the top three percent and I'll teach you the Tao fighting style once we're on Rayne."

"You're saying I have to be either the number one or two student?"

"Yep."

She smiled. "I guess I'll be learning your Tao fighting style." Dreng looked down at Mac's crotch. "You must be enjoying my company."

Mac realized he missed the environmental controls kicking in. The body sweat, cold air, adrenalin from the work out, and the company of a pretty girl. It all caused his sweat pants to create a bit of a pup tent at his crotch. He spun around, grabbed his sweat top, and tied it across his waist. By the time he turned around, Dreng was gone. He looked down at his crotch to see the pup tent was also gone. He shrugged his shoulders, *she's right I did enjoy her company.*

Mac took a warm steam shower, kicked back on the couch, grabbed his holographic computer link, and planned the next few weeks of training. He thought about Dreng's dark amber eyes, the cute way she tilted her head. He took a deep breath in and smiled as he recalled her smell. She must have been looking at his crotch and not his eyes when they were talking. Otherwise she wouldn't have seen his body's reaction to her nearness. *Is it wrong to feel good about a female in the springtime of her youth being interested in me?*

Am I a fool? She's so young. How could she want someone like me? She wants special training and knows how to play an old fart to get it. Yet, I know I felt something. Yeah stupid, it was some kind of maternal instinct. Look at you, arguing with yourself, get it together Mac. He brought up her record up on the holograph.

Dreng Matilda, born to colonist parents. Damn, I knew it. Twenty-five true years old. Schooled by parents. Not unusual for colonist children. Holy crap, those results are not normal. She scored a near perfect 1350 on the Fleet Standardized Test. She received an official offer to FOCS. What? She rejected it. No one ever turns down Fleet Officer Candidate School! Let's see, yep, there it is. She requested military conscript duty on Rayne. A four-year contract approved. Something is not right here. Dreng is up to something, but what?

Mac reviewed the records of all 60 of his people. Per fleet regulations each conscript took the Fleet Standardized Test. Scores averaged in the norm falling between 600-700. Some conscripts had no skills, no job, and no hope of getting one soon. It wasn't unusual for young people to refuse to commit to a life in the military. So instead they often signed a short-term contract. Everyone wanted to get away from something or learn skills they could use in the civilian job market.

Hours of reading records made Mac drowsy. He decided to get a good night's rest. Tomorrow's physical training would be even more difficult than today's. Mac pushed each person to his or her limit. He wanted them to undergo the best physical and mental conditioning possible. He had three months to get them into fighting condition.

As the students arrived in the classroom they found Mac standing in front of them. He looked ready to step onto a battlefield. He was dressed in his black, lightweight, body armor, and had a knife strapped to his calf. Everyone else wore the old enlisted field uniform. Mac wanted his troops to use the new battle gear. He watched as some experienced troops laughed at him. It was unheard of… wearing battle armor while training on a colonist ship!

When everyone took a seat, Mac began to talk about the design of battle gear and weapons over the ages. He discussed the development of various uniforms. The students learned how the poor design of shoes had caused an army to lose a war. Soldiers wearing the wrong color uniform allowed the enemy to locate their positions. An all out attack with inferior weapons against a superior force was a death wish.

One of the students raised her hand. Mac nodded at her.

"Mac, were dying in here. It's hotter than hell, can you do something about the heat?"

The students had begun to sweat through their uniforms. "I thought you'd never ask. Tinker, can you open the boxes stacked in the back. Hand out the lightweight body armor to the appropriate trooper."

"You've got it Mac."

"Did anyone notice I'm not sweating in the body armor?" said Mac.

"Asshole," said someone.

Mac laughed. He couldn't tell who said it.

All the troops received their new battle gear. *It's lesson time*, thought Mac. He asked Dwain, one of the experienced troopers who laughed at him, to come forward. Mac reached down and pulled his razor sharp knife out of its sheath. He held the knife by the blade, handed it to Dwain, and said, "Take my knife and stab me in the chest."

Dwain's eyes opened wide. In mock shock, he turned his head, looked at the class, and shrugged his shoulders. He planted his feet, and with lightning quick reflexes, using both hands, stabbed Mac in the heart. The force from the blow knocked Mac over. The troops screamed. Several of them raced out of their seats to help Mac. Dwain stood there with a smirk on his face.

While on his back, Mac shook the cobwebs out of his head, took an extended hand from a student, and stood back up. "Everyone, take your seats. Thank you. Dwain, you can sit down too. Let me make a few things clear about this training demonstration." Mac smiled at the class. "First, don't ask a fourth level trained martial artist to stab you unless you have a good reason." The class laughed. "What I wanted you to learn is the suit may protect you from a weapon like the blade of a knife. But remember, a weapon like a knife has momentum. The suit will never protect you from the impact force of what hits you."

"What about laser or plasma fire?" asked a trooper.

Now they want the body armor. Mac smiled to himself. Self-preservation was a wonderful motivator. "It will protect you from most known chemicals and glancing laser fire. It will repel a weakened plasma stream if delivered from a distance. It will stop projectiles, shrapnel, and knives. What won't it do?"

In unison the class shouted, "Stop the momentum."

"Good. It makes temperature extremes survivable. Its nanotechnology can make the suit blend into the background. Take thirty minutes, get into your suits and meet back here." Mac smiled at the troops. "I have a surprise for you."

Everyone groaned.

Thirty minutes later Mac escorted the students to a holographic deck. This one was special because it included environmental elements. He couldn't wait to use it. *Damn,* he looked at Dreng as he walked behind several students. *Requisitions must have taken the wrong fitting measurements for Her. The battle suit is way too tight.* "Dreng, come here. I'd like a word with you."

When she spun around, it was all Mac could do not to stare at her perfect body. "Your battle suit is too tight. I'll order some more, but it will be months before I can replace the ones you have."

"Don't bother ordering new ones. I like a tight fit."

"It's so tight you look naked."

Dreng looked at Mac, smiled, and said, "I move better when I'm naked."

She turned around and sashayed back to her friends. Mac couldn't help but watch her hips sway back and forth. *I hope no one heard what she told me.* He pictured her naked as she walked away. Mac felt confused as old dormant feelings were beginning to stir.

The troopers saw the heavy backpacks. They were sitting near the entrance to the holographic deck.

"Pick up your backpack. In it you will find a helmet. Put it on, step into the chamber, and wait for me," said Mac. After all the students entered, he walked up to the controls and typed in Mac.mil/storm/5/Ochi. *Today the troops will experience a level five storm on the wet planet of Ochi.* He stepped into the chamber with his helmet and backpack on.

"Everyone who hears me raise their hand." Mac verified the troops could hear him. "When the program starts, we are going to be moving through several storms on the planet Ochi. You will follow me in single file. If you feel you can go no further, call out your name and you will see a green path appear. Follow it to the exit. Go back to the classroom and wait for the rest of us. All I ask is you give me your best."

A storm started and it was a bad one. Lightning flashed, wind blew, and rain pounded. A forest with a path materialized right in front of them. Mac started running and the troops followed. After twenty minutes of hard running Mac heard, "Anderson". Twenty seconds later, "Findley". When their numbers dropped to ten, Mac picked up the pace. Five minutes later, five troopers were left.

"Quit it." Said a voice in Mac's helmet. The voice was female. He was sure it was Dreng.

A few seconds later he heard, "Ughh. Stupid bitch." It sounded like Dwain. Mac knew whatever happened had already played out. If he interfered without being asked to get involved he would be showing favoritism. If Dreng had a problem she couldn't resolve, he hoped she would say something.

Tinker, Dwain, Dreng, and Fishman completed the entire run. Back in the classroom, Mac told the students the uniform of the day would be their battle armor. Everyone's suits were already dry. Mac brought out a new Orion laser rifle. A few troopers familiar with weapons whistled in awe.

"Why are you showing us weapons we'll never be able to use? This high tech equipment is for Tactical Assault Commandos. It's not for standard issue," said Dwain.

"Now it's for TAC and my three light armor platoons," said Mac as he looked at Dwain. "By the way, the body armor is so new, even TAC doesn't have it." Mac thought he could see the beginning of a bruise starting to form on Dwain's face. *Yep, something happened.*

Mac demonstrated weapon safety. He showed the students basic field cleaning and minor repairs for the rifle. He asked Tinker, Dwain, and Fishman to hand out the replica simulator weapons.

Mac said, "These training rifles are the same as a real Orion laser rifle. The single internal difference is the laser is non-lethal ultraviolet with a power supply of 1.6 milliamps."

For two hours the class did nothing but disassemble and reassemble the rifle. Mac showed the troops how the gun broke down into eight sections for ease of field cleaning. The components popped out and back in again for quick repair. He stressed the need to align the pins on the components with great care. Losing the use of your rifle during a firefight could cost you your life. By the session's end, they were ready for field training with the new weapon.

Another long day ended. Mac dismissed the troops and walked back to his quarters. Upon entering his room, he heard a chime on the holographic communications system. He scanned his right hand. An interactive holograph popped up indicating a secure message from the UFC. United Fleet Command, *this couldn't be good. I must have received the message as we passed near Imperial Station.* He hit play. Sitting in front of him was Michael Farragut, the Vice Admiral himself.

"Mac, I wanted to warn you of some troubling information we received. Our probes have found several more war ships in uncharted space. They are not ours. Since we continue to lose probes in nearby areas, we have to assume the unknown ships are not our friends. Nomad is still missing. The planetary President is aware of the situation. He wishes to continue with colonization. Warhammer and the Dagger will follow you to Rayne, they still are not aware you are on the Nomad. Colonists' safety remains the number one concern."

The next morning, Mac greeted the students. "Today's lecture is on recon." As he lectured, there were hundreds of questions. Mac knew the game. *Distract me, and with luck get out of physical training this morning. Not a chance. With enemy ships hiding in uncharted space, we need to be ready for anything.*

One ground pounder put her hand up and said, "Tinker's missing."

"Tinker is on special assignment for me."

There were several comments about Tinker's brown nose, ass kissing, and a few other jeers. Mac continued with the lecture. "Now, listen up. You will receive a recon brief from me. Afterwards, in a single column, two abreast, you will jog to the holographic deck. Tinker will be waiting with your backpacks."

Mac heard a few, 'Aw crap's and a few 'Fuck's. The tone changed when he said, "and your rifles". He looked around and saw a few smiles. To his troops, it meant today would not be another God awful physical endurance test.

"After everyone receives their equipment, I want you to gather together. As a team, I want you to enter the holographic simulator and wait for me. Now, for the briefing: War has broken out with the Zombies. Fleet Command is sending us on a recon mission to Skulderon."

A few experienced troopers groaned.

"For those of you who aren't familiar with Skulderon – it's a desert planet in a binary star system. It is over ninety-nine percent sand. The average daytime temperature is 145 degrees Fahrenheit due to the two suns. During the night it cools down to 120 degrees." A groan came from the troops. "There are only a few life forms left on the planet. Availability of water is limited."

"Long range probes have detected hostile activity to and from the planet's largest oasis. Our mission is reconnaissance. Get in, take vids, and leave without detection. The brass needs to know what the Zombies are up to. Do not, I say again, do not engage the enemy. I will lead you to the oasis and direct the three platoons to their assignments. We will have six standard hours to rendezvous with the one flight out. Whatever happens, don't be late. Are their any questions?"

"If you're leading us to the point of deployment and directing us, who will lead the platoons?" asked Yak, a veteran who hadn't seen real action yet.

"The three top students. Tinker will take First Platoon. Dwain takes second platoon, and Dreng will lead Third platoon."

"What if we're late for the rendezvous?" asked Dwain.

"You and your platoon will be captured or killed."

"What if we're discovered and start taking fire?" asked Dreng.

"If it was me, I'd fire back and be ready to take some heat in the debrief... assuming you make it back."

After several more questions, Mac felt the troops were ready. It was their first mission. The holographic generator would make the undertaking of the task seem real. For those never in combat before, this would be a shock. You can talk about it, watch vids, listen to those who were in a firefight, but until you've been in one, it doesn't sink home.

"Okay, let's go," said Mac.

The troops remembered their instructions: Two abreast, one column. They headed to the holographic simulator. Mac brought up the rear. He kept catching glimpses of Dreng and had to force himself to concentrate on the exercise. He was becoming infatuated with her. *Those dark eyes, the perfect voice, her body... oh shit, focus Mac focus.*

When the troops arrived, Tinker was there with all the weapons and backpacks. He handed out the equipment and assigned the troops to their platoons per Mac's instructions.

Mac walked up to the keypad, entered a security code, and typed Mac.mil/first/5/Skulderon. "All right, put your helmets on, visors down, backpacks on, guns at the ready. Enter the simulator and wait for me."

As they stepped in all they could see was white in every direction. The surface temperature read 250 degrees. Their visors darkened almost to black to allow them to see in the dual sunlight. As the troops moved, their body weight forced them to sink several inches into the sand. This trek would be demanding.

Mac entered last. Without thinking about it his eyes went right to Dreng. "Welcome to Skulderon." He heard the groans in his helmet's speaker. "Follow me." Mac started a slow jog to make sure the weaker troopers could stay with him in the shifting sand.

After three kilometers of jogging Mac stopped his team near the top of a large sand dune. In front of them stood a large oasis with shrubs and some odd shaped trees. The huge leaves created a thick canopy. No one could see the water, but even from here they could feel the moisture in the air. "Tinker, take First platoon to the north for recon. Dwain, take Second platoon to the south. Dreng, you take Third platoon straight ahead. We'll meet back here in five standard hours. I'll be doing some recon on my own, now, go."

In the military this type of training was for advanced special ops. Mac could hear the excitement in their voices. Even Tinker and Dwain had never seen anything so real. The cost of a holographic simulator prohibited its use by ordinary troops. But Mac had connections. The three platoons moved down the large sand hill and began their assignment.

Thanks to the nanotechnology in the armor suits the troops were shimmering ghosts as they moved through their environment. Mac watched them as they began to move into the jungle. He tweaked his helmet visor. He could watch each platoon and see how they performed under their new leadership.

Within ten minutes each platoon discovered a campsite. It contained several environmental pods and small planetary rocket launchers. There were even a couple fighters. Everything was camouflaged to defeat any probes snooping high overhead. Strange looking pieces of equipment lay hidden in the ground foliage. About 250 zombies worked under camo nets putting various components together. All the boxes and crates had strange markings on them. Thousands of containers littered the site.

Mac was proud of all three platoons. They worked hard to get the vids yet remain unseen. Each platoon saw something different. The program tried to get the troops to stay and take more pictures. If they got sloppy the program reacted or if Mac chose to he could force an issue. Tinker was the first to start moving back to the rendezvous point. *Time to go into hiding.* Mac left the area and the simulator kept him invisible to his troops.

Tinker and First platoon arrived twenty minutes ahead of the departure time. When Tinker didn't see Mac he said, "Shit, I knew this was too easy."

Tinker and First platoon climbed the dune. After they struggled to the top, he made the troops fan out, and train their weapons on the jungle. Mac smiled when he saw Tinker display a count down clock on his visor.

Dwain and Second platoon showed up next. They too struggled up the dune and took up defensive positions along with First platoon.

The holographic program tried to get Third platoon to stay longer. The enemy started to move what looked like large rocket tubes out of hidden caves. Mac watched Dreng's reaction. She didn't let the new development distract her. She gave the signal for the troops to leave. Third platoon regrouped and began to move through the oasis back to the rendezvous point. Mac used the computer to force discovery by the enemy.

Two zombies started screaming and pointing at them. Somehow the enemy found them. Laser fire and projectiles began whizzing into the undercover. The troops could smell the trees and bushes burn as lasers hit them. Yak, a trooper who had never seen combat, froze.

Dreng screamed over the roar of weapons firing, "Return fire. Yak, snap out of it!"

Yak ducked down and started to return fire.

"There are too many Zombies to fight and more coming every second. Fishman, you and I will hang back and lay down some suppression fire to slow them down. The rest of you start moving to the rendezvous point. Ham, you take the lead. Now, get going, move it!"

Dreng used hand signals to tell Fishman to cover the right flank while she coved the left. They retreated, popping up and down to fire. Using this tactic the zombies wouldn't be able to identify the strength of their enemy.

First and Second platoon stood their ground. They could hear the battle moving toward them.

"Hold your positions, stay low and be ready to fire," said Tinker.

Third platoon came running up the dune.

Dwain had his thermal sensors activated. He made a quick head count. "We are minus two troopers, and Mac."

Tinker could still hear the weapon fire. "The zombies must be shooting at the two troopers still missing. We've got two minutes before we have to leave."

"Here they come," said Dwain. "I can see about fifty Zombies following them."

"Open fire," said Tinker. The Zombies were forced to stop at the edge of the oasis.

Dreng and Fishman made it to the top in record time. The ground pounders gave the two latecomers plenty of cover fire.

Mac appeared behind the troops. "Follow me," he said, "we've got to get out of here before they bring out the heavy weapons."

Without question, or discussion, everyone followed Mac. After about five minutes of running, the program ended. They were standing at the exit, out of breath.

"Fuck," said Dwain. "It felt like I was in a real battle. My heart's still racing."

"How'd we do?" asked Tinker.

"You did great for your first fire fight. But, we were on Skulderon to gather intelligence, not engage the enemy. Let's go back to the classroom and see how you did."

CHAPTER FOUR: Discovery

In preparation for war, the People's Nation built one hundred sixty-three new Dreadnought class battleships, two hundred seventy-four Swift class cruisers, and three thousand Sparrow Hawk fighters. After twenty-five years, they were still gleaning information from the captured alien ship. Mahpee learned reverse engineering is a slow and difficult process.

Another problem rested with the People of the Stars. It looked like they had not taken any action to prepare for the invasion they were warned about. Still wanting to live in seclusion, the People's Nation came up with a way to help their distant relatives. The People's Nation infiltrated the top engineering schools of their human cousins. They simulated new discoveries their own engineers had already invented. The program to share new information worked. No one realized many people making important discoveries disappeared over time.

By using DNA, the entomologists on Nokomis discovered the big bugs evolved from a predatory species of beetle. The scientists speculated the evolutionary process had taken billions of years. Of all insects, beetles evolving did not surprise anyone considering one third of all insects in the known universe are beetles.

As Chief Mahpee drove his flyer to the university, he thought about the bugs and about his daughter too. *It had been four months since our big argument. Not a single word from her. Blacklisting her from serving in the military was a mistake. What did I expect would happen? There are all kinds of other jobs available. Why can't she see I did it for her? Those damn Tellers filled her head with crap. It's too much responsibility for a young woman. Ancient prophesy my ass. I don't want her involved in the war when it comes. I'll deal with the Raygin myself. I already came too close to losing her once. I can't handle it again. Pushing her to meet men doesn't seem to be working. I'll change tactics and find her a good man myself.*

The chief smiled. He felt better after talking to himself. He grounded his flyer at the university and walked to the chancellor's office still thinking about his daughter.

"Hello chief," said the secretary, "good to see you again. Please go in. Chancellor Mongwau is waiting for you."

He knocked on the big door and walked in. He couldn't wait to get his mind off his daughter. The worrying was going to kill him. He loved his old friend. As a historian, Mongwau always seemed to have a new tale about the lost Nation. He loved to talk about what they went through in the first years of colonization. When Mahpee stepped into the office, a new decoration on the wall caught his eye. The chief walked up to the display, took his finger, and traced the artwork under the transparent cover.

Mongwau could see it tweaked his friend's curiosity. "Do you know what it is Mahpee?"

The chief scratched his head. "No, but I like its look."

"This is a replica of an artifact listed in the cryo ship's records. We retrieved it using Raygin technology. It is a dream catcher. The ancients believed all night air contained both good and bad dreams. If you hang a dream catcher over a bed, the web catches all dreams, good and bad. The good dreams know the path to follow in the web to exit through the feathers onto the sleeping dreamer. The bad dreams get stuck in the web and perish at first light."

"You know, I could use a dream catchers over my bed. My daughter is worrying me to death."

"What? Sweet little Ayashe is worrying you."

"My little warrior is no longer little. The older she gets, the more problems I have with her. I stopped her from joining the military and we had a big fight. She moved in with Kele again. I thought some time away from me would help her. It's been four months since I have talked to her. Last time this happened, Kele worked her magic, and got us talking again. But it's been so long I'm starting to worry. I yelled at Ayashe while I was angry. I said things I regret. I am afraid Kele won't be able to fix it this time."

"I am having nightmares of her fighting thousands of alien bugs all by herself. For some reason, I have to watch and can't help. The attacking bugs overwhelm her. She gets captured. When they begin to eat her alive, I wake up shaking and covered in a sweat."

"Sounds like an anxiety dream to me" said Mongwau. "Do not forget, besides being born and wounded in battle, the Raygin also stole her mother's life. She must right the wrong in her mind or her soul will not sleep. She has been trained by the best our military has to offer. I hear she is a strategist, weapons expert, and natural leader. You know the old stories. So does she." Mongwau squinted his eyes at Mahpee, "Even if you didn't tell her, she learned on her own. You should be proud of her. She has prepared herself for a leadership role her whole life. She has no equal among our people. The student has surpassed the masters. I know you don't want to hear it, but you should let her enter the military. Protect her as best you can, but you must let her become who she wants to be or she will hold it against you forever."

"You're right. I have to do something. Saying no, doesn't work anymore. I'll drop by Kele's place and talk to her tonight. Now, tell me the news."

Mongwau rubbed his hands together. "Imagine two species with different evolutionary paths. The Raygin computer era started with a bio-molecular design. Human computers used an electronic design. The bio-molecular computer they designed uses the chemical building block of proteins. This means if the bio-computer is damaged it can repair itself."

"Their ships are faster than ours because their computers use many multiple loops to do tasks such as jump calculations. The Raygin control their computers using chemical reactions. Remember how Kele described the attack? At first, the air smelled good when they entered the playroom, because they found the children. They were happy. When they got attacked, they gave off an acidy smell, indicating concern. When the queen started to kill them, they gave off a smell like rotten old socks – it's how they show fear."

"So far," said Mahpee, "all I have heard is the aliens can stink real bad. Do you have any good news?"

"The good news," said Mongwau, "is we have our technology and now we have some of theirs. Using Raygin science, we think we can link our nano-circuitry to bioluminescent organisms."

"What do we gain by linking the two technologies?"

"Think of it my good friend. Circuits not slowed by fiber optics connected to junctions and processors. As it stands now, our processors have to communicate with each piece of hardware. A light signal carrying information must get interpreted at each junction. The speed Mahpee, the speed will be unbelievable!"

WAOOM. The sound of an explosion echoed down the hallway walls all the way into Mongwau's office. It was followed by a shock wave of air. Mahpee looked at his friend, their eyes locked, and both of ran toward the labs. As both men rounded a corner, they came upon several scientists and engineers. They were standing outside a lab looking a little shaken. The door was blown off its track, and smoke hung in the air.

Mongwau was bent over with his hands on his knees trying to catch his breath. Airborne debris was still settling.

"Is everyone okay?" asked Mahpee.

Nashta stepped forward, looked at his counterparts and said, "We're okay. Looks like we still have a few more bugs to work out. I'm sure we'll get it soon."

The wide-eyed scientists and engineers shook their heads yes, following Nashta's lead.

"I don't have to tell you to be careful, do I Nashta?" said Mongwau.

"No sir, if I were you, I wouldn't even mention it."

"All right, I won't bother."

As Mahpee and Mongwau turned around to walk away, Mahpee started laughing.

"You were a bit hard on Nashta, weren't you?" asked Mahpee.

Mongwau smiled. "This is serious work here. Besides, he's a good engineer, I don't want him to get hurt."

"You have given me great hope, but tell me, is there anything in the here and now to benefit us?" asked Mahpee.

"It's a good thing I know you are like a child and need instant gratification. Yes, we have boosted the range of our scanners. We also have new equipment able to track ships through space by evaluating the gravity ripples in their wake. It is much like following the trail of a boat as it moves through the water. We have also placed new plasma guns into the battleships and are fitting the cruisers. The fighters can carry plasma warhead torpedoes as part of their offensive weapons. Engineers have added a few surprises to your mini flagship, the Wasp. Consider it a gift from the university."

"I love surprises! Well done."

Mongwau grinned. "I thought you might like it."

The chief's personal communicator beeped an alert. He read the classified message: From Admiral Sewati, Two Probes intercepted by fighters. One probe is Raygin. One probe is from the People of the Stars. Raygin are tracking ship movements within territories of People of the Stars. People of Stars probe tracking People's Nation ship movements near Orenda.

Oh great, Orenda is our shipbuilding planet. The People of the Stars have discovered us. This changes everything. I have to contact them to explain who we are, and what we are doing. In addition, we have to warn them again about the Raygin. They would never forgive us if we knew the Raygin are here again and we said nothing. The chief responded to Sewati: Send data on Raygin probe to our lab without delay. Will arrange to contact the People of the Stars – be safe. Mahpee.

The chief let Mongwau read the admiral's message and his reply.

"I'll get the lab ready for the probe. This is both good and bad news," Mongwau smiled at his friend, "I'm glad I'm not the chief."

"I'm glad you aren't the chief too," Mahpee said. "I better get going. I have to call a council emergency meeting right away."

"Better talk to your daughter, Mahpee."

"I will, I will. I'll do it today. Right after I get word to the council about the meeting tonight."

Mahpee made arrangements for the emergency meeting. The schedule gave him four hours to get to Kele's house, talk to his daughter, and get back. As he drove to see her, he visualized how he would apologize. *I will be sure to tell her how proud I am of her. She had to understand, she means everything to me, always has. I realize now I should have talked to her long ago about my feelings. It hard, because it always brings up memories of Shanee's body on the operating table. After twenty-five years, I still haven't mourned for my wife. It hurt too much.*

I should have reminded my little princess of how I sang to her when she was small enough to put into my hand. How she snuggled on my chest to sleep. How the best part of my day was when I came home from work and got to spend time with her. Instead, I always talked about the Raygin, military weapons, and retribution. I even talked about opening a formal line of communication with the People of the Stars. I did everything except talk about how much I love her.

Mahpee decided he would fix everything between them tonight. He realized he better call to make sure they're home. He grabbed his communicator and called Kele.

"Hello, Mahpee. How are you?"

He let out a big breath. "Fine. It seems there is always something going on. Is Ayashe there? I'm minutes away from your place. I know, I should have called you earlier and spoke to you, but I figured she needed time, and I've been busy. I have come to apologize to her, and you."

"Oh, Mahpee. What have you done this time? You promised me after the last argument with her, you would not be so quick to anger. She should not receive a scolding like a child. She is a woman. I haven't seen Ayashe in about four months. She stayed with me for two days."

"What do you mean? She's not there? Where did she go? I haven't seen or heard from her since she came to stay with you four months ago!"

"What? When she arrived she said the two of you had a big argument. The next day she told me the issues between the two of you were being resolved. I thought you made it right. I should have known better. Mahpee, she left. I assumed she went home to you. She seemed happy. Could she be staying with a friend?"

"I don't know. I'll check. I'm getting worried, Kele.

Mahpee parked his flyer and walked into Kele's home. He gave her a quick hug and asked, "May I look in her room? There could be a clue to her whereabouts."

"Yes, yes, go ahead. I'll call her friends and ask if they have seen her."

Mahpee opened Ayashe's stack shelves. Most of her clothes were gone. More bad news, her prized weapons, two terrillium tomahawks, were gone. He had given them to her two years ago when she earned the rank of master in hand-to-hand combat. Kele gave him more bad news. None of her friends had seen or heard from her in four months.

Mahpee pulled his communicator out. He initiated a search and notify message: To all: Ayashe, my daughter, missing four months. If you have had contact or know whereabouts notify me. Mahpee.

Mahpee was getting sick to his stomach. *What has happened to my little warrior?* The communicator beeped. It was Commander Tokola.

"Hello Commander, you have news for me?"

"Chief, I couldn't believe your search and notify. Per your instructions I took Ayashe to the transport terminal at Finders Station four months ago."

"What?"

"She gave me the diplomatic orders signed by you. She even knew we were picking up Eyota."

"Did she say what she was going to do?"

"She said she was on a quest of sorts for you."

"I don't understand. I didn't ask for anything."

"We helped her convert her rare metals to credits on Finder's Station. Everything seemed legit chief. I'm sorry."

"It's not your fault, it's mine. We had a big argument. She wanted to join the military. I said no, and forbid it. I'm ashamed to say I made it worse by insulting her choices in life. I have to find her and apologize before she does something we both regret."

Discovering his daughter left with a purpose in mind made him feel better about her safety. Not knowing her plans on her first trip away form home, made him worry. He cancelled the search and find. He contacted a few agents. They were familiar with operations within the People of the Stars territory. They were trackers by trade. They would locate Ayashe and get her to come back to me.

During Mahpee's meeting, both the council and the Tellers agreed with him. Treaties must be made with the others. The council would introduce themselves to the People of the Stars. They would carry proof the alien's exist. Both peoples must prepare for the coming war.

He decided to send the delegation on a transport ship rather than a military vessel. *A military ship might seem too threatening. We will carry the body of a Raygin in a cryo chamber as an offering to show the People of Stars we speak the truth. We will show them vids of the attack along with some vids of the Raygin scout ship. With the enemy on the move, it will be wise for both peoples to from an alliance. This is a sound plan.*

It took one week to make the arrangements. The transport ship, Black Fox, left the port city of Tall Pine on Nokomis heading to Finder's Station. From there, the People's Nation would send a formal request to Rhizon. They would ask for a meeting with the Planetary Parliament. If initial communications went well a formal dialog would be opened with the People of the Stars. They would be invited to open an office on Nokomis. The Black Fox also carried five trackers. The trackers would begin their search for Ayashe on Finder's Station. They would go wherever the leads took them.

The war fleet was ahead of schedule. The shipyards upgraded the ships with each new discovery.

The chief stood outside of his dwelling, admiring the night sky. *These are the same stars my ancestors looked at thousands of years ago. It feels good to be ahead of schedule with the war fleet and upgrades to the older ships.* His stomach started to rumble as it reacted to a low level sonic frequency. A high-pitched siren filled the night sky. Mahpee experienced a feeling of dread. It was the planetary alert system. He reached for his communicator. *Damn, I left it inside.* He ran into his dwelling to find it beeping like crazy.

He picked up the communicator. It read: One Battleship and six cruisers detected by planetary defenses. Tracking toward Orenda. Ship design is of People of the Stars. Call me – Sewati. *This is horrible timing.* He grabbed his communicator and called Admiral Sewati.

"Hello chief. I have disabled planetary defenses around Orenda, but not Nokomis. We are attempting communication with the People of the Stars convoy. At present they are ignoring us. They seem willing to risk all to find out what we are doing in our shipyards. They have deployed a system of com probes."

"How long before they arrive?"

"The convoy is traveling using ion drives. We estimate it will take them three standard days to navigate the asteroid maze."

"Nice job Admiral. Let their ships get in position to see our shipyards. Place a couple squadrons of fighters near them so they don't do anything too stupid. Do whatever is necessary, but remember, we want these people to be our friends."

"I understand. When will you be arriving?"

"If we push it, we can get there at about the same time they arrive. I'll keep my com close to me. This is not what I envisioned for the first official meeting between our peoples."

"Do not delay dear friend. To be honest, I've heard my skill at diplomacy is poor at best. I don't understand why. I am honest and to the point. What more is there to statesmanship than this?"

"If they contact you, tell them to stand by for my arrival and I look forward to meeting them, and Sewati – don't add anything in your own words."

"Anything you say my eloquent tongued chief."

"Yeah. Yeah, you are hilarious."

Mahpee disconnected and called Bodaway.

"Hello chief. I thought you might call. You want us to prepare Greysail?"

"No. We better take Wasp this time."

"Where to, and when?"

"We need to get to Orenda as soon as possible."

"You picked the right ship. The crew will be ready in thirty minutes."

"It will take me forty-five minutes to get to the launch pad."

"We'll be waiting."

As Mahpee arrived, he could see the crew completing their prelaunch checks. The Wasp was ready to depart. He couldn't wait to see the new technology the engineers had installed on his ship. Admiral Sewati contacted Mahpee to give him an update. Sewati said the convoy still refused to communicate. As expected, the ships were having problems navigating through the asteroid cloud surrounding Orenda. Once through, the ships would have to contend with the floating workstations. Ships were always under different phases of construction. All the obstacles would force the UFC ships to separate and end the trip in single file. Not a good tactical move, but necessary.

When the Wasp was a couple light years away, it made a final jump and arrived on the opposite side of Orenda. The small ship maneuvered with little effort through a hidden path in the asteroid cloud. Captain Bodaway positioned the Wasp at a point over the shipyard. The battleship and cruisers exited the asteroid cluster. They positioned themselves over the Wasp. Three hundred sparrow hawk fighters armed with plasma torpedoes arrived to surround the convoy.

This got their attention.

The Wasp com center lit up like the night sky over Old Dry Lake on Nokomis.

"Unknown fighters. Stand down, or we will fire."

"Hello, People of the Stars. Welcome to Orenda. I am Chief Mahpee, leader of the People's Nation. Welcome."

"Chief Mahpee. This is Admiral Harding of United Fleet Command. If you are the one in charge have your fighters stand down or we will fire."

"Now, now, Admiral Harding. We have allowed you into our shipyards so you can see for yourselves, what we are doing. The fighters are here for our safety. After all, you invaded our territory and would not communicate with us."

"First off Chief Mahpee, you did not let us anywhere. Second, you are building ships of war. Third, you attacked an innocent colonization ship, the United Federation ship, Nomad. Now, have your fighters stand down or we will destroy them."

Mahpee's private com beeped. He looked at the message: *Ten Dreadnaughts standing by. Should calm him down.*

"Admiral Harding, as I said, we let you see for yourselves, what we are building. We tracked you here, shut down the planetary defenses, and I came here to talk to you in person. We did not attack any of your ships. We will not stand down in our own territory until we come to some type of an agreement. Look around you."

Ten large ships from the People's Nation's appeared around the convoy. The com station went silent. Admiral Harding and his team were evaluating their new circumstances.

"Okay, Chief Mahpee. I'll concede. You let us come here. If you didn't attack the Nomad, why are you are building ships of war?"

"My ship came under attack by an alien race called the Raygin twenty-five years ago. My wife died in the attack. We have been preparing for a war we know is coming. It is the reason we are building ships of war."

"I'm sorry about your wife. I have to ask, do you have proof of what you say?"

"Yes, Admiral Harding. We have already sent a diplomatic contingency to Finder's Station. Their job is to open communications with your people."

"Who are you? Why are you in unprotected and uncharted space?"

"We are the descendants of the Indian Nation of old earth. Tens of thousands of years ago when the sun consumed the Earth, my people took part in the great exodus. The cryo ship carrying my ancestors to a safe new world malfunctioned. We lived isolated, lost and alone for thousands and thousands of years. We made our home on a planet we call Nokomis. Several years ago, after we designed the singularity drive, we located your people."

"Chief Mahpee, I think you just told a wonderful story, but it's a lie. We developed the singularity drive about a year ago in one of our military sponsored schools."

"Admiral Harding, we placed one of our engineers into your engineering school. He acted like he designed the new drive while attending your top school. We wanted to share the new technology with you. The name he used while in your school was Michael Etton."

"Every engineering person in the universe knows Michael Etton designed the singularity drive. He disappeared after the first trial run of his creation. Your proof is all common knowledge."

"Nashta, or as you call him, Michael Etton is an engineer on my ship. Nashta, come to the viewer. Here he is captain. Do you have any young engineers that were in class with Michael Etton? If so could you get them and let the two talk?

"Give me a couple minutes."

While they waited, Bodaway gave council to Mahpee. He told him to bring the whole convoy back to Nokomis. Seeing their home world would end many doubts. It would be good for both peoples. Mahpee agreed. As usual, it was good council.

A young, blond haired, engineering ensign, appeared on the viewer screen. "Mike, I can't believe it's you."

"Tim. It's so good to see you. How is your mom?"

"She's okay. It turned out to be a neurological reaction. It came from a chemical she started spraying on the fruit plants to get them to grow."

"Great. Tell her I said hi."

"You know you're famous? Why did you leave without saying good bye?"

"I left you a note. It's as much as I could say at the time."

The young ensign looked at the captain and said, "It's Michael, sir." He looked at the view screen again. "Great talking to you Mike, Maybe we can talk more later, but for now I have to go."

"Tim, when all these issues are resolved let's get together and visit. Take care buddy."

"Chief Mahpee, can we meet face to face?" said the admiral. "We have a lot of talking to do."

"I have a better idea, if you are willing. We will send you the location of our home world, Nokomis. I'll ride with you, we will get acquainted, and you will become the first People of the Stars to visit us."

"Great idea. Tell me, why do you call us People of the Stars?"

"There are so many of you on so many planets, we did not know what else to call you."

"Funny. I guess we have populated a lot of solar systems. How do you want to do this? Would you like me to send a shuttle for you?"

"Would it be possible to park my small ship, the Wasp, on one of your landing decks?"

"Chief Mahpee, you'd be doing us a huge favor. Our engineers would love to look at your technology."

"We have a deal, Admiral Harding. My ships will stand down."

Captain Bodaway maneuvered the Wasp onto the Constellation. The first order of business was to allow their human cousins to tour the Wasp. Captain Bodaway showed off the little ship to the Constellations' lead engineer, Commander Gynn Roads. Meanwhile, Mahpee was escorted onto the bridge to meet Admiral Harding.

As the chief walked by engineering on the Constellation he heard the familiar pop caused by the singularity drive. The convoy had started its historical trip back to Nokomis. As he walked with his escort he counted off seven seconds before he heard another faint pop. The speed at which the People of the Stars fitted the new drive into their ships amazed Mahpee. Both peoples had much to learn from each other. He had to admit, when it came to the military, they were efficient.

The escort led Chief Mahpee to the bridge elevator. As he stepped out from the elevator Admiral Harding was waiting and honored him with a salute.

"Chief Mahpee, I'm Admiral Harding."

Mahpee held his hands at chest height with his palms outward saying, "Admiral Harding, my people are informal. I would prefer you address me as Mahpee, if you don't mind. It will make the trip much easier."

"Okay, Mahpee it is. I can see the strong link to your ancestors. You know we still teach our history students about the Indian Nation's disappearance? It was pandemonium during the exodus. I checked our computer.

We don't have a complete data bank of your language but we did have your name. It's from the Nation called Sioux. It means sky."

Mahpee laughed as he recalled the story of his naming. "My family had been working on our farm near Lone Tree, on Nokomis. When the time arrived for me to come into the world, it caught my mother by surprise. As she gave birth to me in a field of wheat, my mother looked up and saw the sky, or mahpee, as spoken in our native language. My father told a different story. He said at the same time my mother looked up, a Sky Hawk, the fastest predator bird on Nokomis, flew overhead. My father believed it an omen from the Great Spirit. My mother refused to see the Sky Hawk, for seeing the bird at the moment of a birth, was an omen of war. My mother's name for me stuck, but my father always called me Mahpee Chatan, Sky Hawk."

"What a great story. I can't wait to sit down and hear…"

A young ensign walked up and said, "Admiral, forgive me for interrupting. We received an emergency communication via the experimental tachyon transmitter."

"Well don't stand there, what did they say?"

The young com officer fidgeted, and looked at Mahpee.

"You can speak in front of our new friend. His name is Mahpee. Let's hear it ensign."

"Aye, sir. The new com transmitter still has some issues to work out. We deciphered the following partial communication from Imperial Station. The junior officer read the paper: Under attack. Six unknown ships…"

"Is there more to the message?"

"Yes sir. There was more, but the data got corrupted during transmission. We can't raise them on the tachyon or by using the com probe link."

"If Imperial Station is under attack, it may be the new threat Mahpee informed us about, an alien race called the Raygin. No one else is out this far except for colonists and the military. Navigation, set course for Imperial Station."

"Aye Admiral. Setting course for Imperial Station," said the senior lieutenant at navigation controls.

"Com, relay the message to the convoy and inform them of our change in plans. Continue attempting to contact Imperial Station. Let me know if you are successful."

"Aye sir."

"Helm, how long will it take us to get to Imperial?"

"Twenty-seven point four standard days sir."

"Damn, I hate operating at these distances. When you broadcast to Imperial Station give them our estimated day of arrival too."

"Aye sir, making blind broadcasts to Imperial Station."

"I apologize Mahpee. We have to change our plans. Looks like you were right, these damn Raygin are after a fight. We can let you and your ship off before we change course."

"If you don't mind a little help, the Wasp may be small but she has tremendous fire power. We also have some new tracking technology. We may be able to help once we get to Imperial Station."

"You honor us with your commitment. Over the years, I have learned to accept help whenever it's offered. Thank you, Mahpee."

Before the convoy began its sequence of jumps, Mahpee fired off a probe. It contained information about the attack on Imperial Station. He also let his people know he was going to assist the People of the Stars. Updates would follow.

CHAPTER FIVE: Survival

The Nomad survivors, except for the children, were herded into a large holding area. It was deep inside the alien ship. The passageways were dark, but the aliens seemed to navigate with little effort. The Nomad's captain, Jahra Cutter estimated they were about mid ship. The aliens entered and exited the holding pen constantly. There were two platforms raised about two to three feet of the ground. An armed guard stood on each dais allowing them to oversee the human captives, and if necessary to interact quickly.

Every time the door opened the captain could see the bugs carrying dead human bodies. He feared Lieutenant Muween could be right. Humans were a food source. Yet, the aliens took extra effort to capture the humans alive. Because of this, he believed they would also become slaves. Since the aliens took the children separately they must have a purpose for them, he just didn't understand their motive.

The alien ship contained a labyrinth of dark hallways. Ribbed surfaces lined all the passageways. It looked the walkways were hewn out of a block of lava. Aboard the ship, the captain noted most aliens did not wear armor. They seemed unafraid of their weaker human captives. As a precaution, the bugs brought armed guards when workers entered the pen.

Without body armor everyone could see the bugs' black exoskeleton. It seemed stiff and not flexible at all. Captain Cutter speculated *even without body armor, it would still be hard for an unarmed human to kill a bug. There must be a weakness we can exploit. I hope we have a bug expert among the survivors.*

The enemy's plan all along must have been to capture humans. Look at the pens. They were designed for human prisoners. Not good news for us. It means the aliens have been planning this for years. An invasion of human space must be imminent. Hell, this might even be the beginning. Intelligence about the enemy is critical. We have to gather every piece of info we can about our captors. I have to get us the hell out of here.

Once things settled down the aliens placed two bugs armed with plasma rifles on elevated platforms in the pen. They hadn't gone out of their way to bother anyone, yet. The humans were free to move anywhere within the pen except near the guard platforms. The captain watched as the crew and the colonists each formed clusters of their own people. He knew if they were going to survive, he had to change this behavior.

During the trip the captain made sure the colonists knew they could count on him for help. He established a good rapport while walking through their spaces to check on their needs. He also removed barriers to their preparations for colonization. *It is time to capitalize on the bond I created.* He walked over to the colonists.

"Hi, I remember some of you. I'm Captain Cutter. I'm looking for the governor."

A muscular looking young man stomped to the group's forefront. "The fucking bugs killed him when he tried to reason with the butchers as they took the children. They killed everyone trying to stop them. Are the rumors true? These bastards see us as a food source."

Still looking them in the eye the captain said, "It's too soon to tell, but I'll be honest with you, it doesn't look good for us."

A woman with tear tracks in her eyes and wet cheeks said, "What are we going to do captain? Can we even do anything at all?"

"I'm here now to talk about our options. I need to talk with your biologists and engineers."

The muscular looking man said, "I'll get them, but first tell me what you're thinking?"

"I was a pilot in the mining wars. My fighter got shot down behind enemy lines and I got captured. I learned to never give up hope, and always have a plan. Every living creature has a weakness. We need the biologists to speculate on what the bug vulnerability is and figure out how to exploit it. The engineers may be able to identify something within the ship's design we can use to our advantage. For instance, our bodies are more flexible. The bug ship designers may not have considered the human anatomy when they built their ships."

Another woman stepped up. She had several open wounds on her arm. "They took my daughter, captain. I want to help too."

"Okay, I want you to find the colonist doctors and nurses. I suspect the bugs won't be helping us so we need to start helping ourselves."

Everyone in the group started to ask the captain how they could help. In time, he came up with a task for each person. This wasn't going to be easy, but he needed to give them hope. Everyone scrambled to complete his or her assignments. The captain walked back to his crew and told them what he had done. They were glad to hear the resistance against the bugs had begun.

The next several days would be crucial if they were to survive. As the crew discussed their options, the bugs turned down the lighting to simulate nighttime. The captain didn't want to draw attention to groups of humans roaming around at night. He put the word out to sleep and not be active at night. The captives would work during the simulated daylight hours so as not to draw attention.

As soon as the lights came on, a group of five people walked up to the captain. An older woman stepped forward and held out her hand. "Hello captain, I'm Nihna. I have a doctorate in biology. I am the lead biologist and back-up entomologist for the Rayne colonists. We heard you wanted to talk to us."

The captain took Nihna's hand and shook it. She didn't realize it yet, but her people would play a major roll in saving all their lives. "Hello Nihna. I'll get right to the point, I want to create a plan to break us free. Tell me, what are the strengths and weaknesses of these human abducting cockroaches?"

Nihna gave a small smile and said, "Well captain, these bugs not being cockroaches is a plus for us. If they were, we would be in big trouble. You can cut the head off a cockroach and they will still put up a fight. It is difficult for us to understand how this evolution could have occurred. Our best guess is we think our captors evolved from Carrion beetles."

"Okay, tell me about Carrion beetles."

"There are five hundred thousand types of beetles found in the universe. These bugs and Carrion beetles have many similar characteristics. To begin with, Carrion beetles evolved with black bodies and different colored heads, as did our captors. Many other species of beetles have colored shells. We have seen nothing but black exoskeletons. The Carrion emits chemicals to irritate other bugs and animals. Some entomologists believe the chemical smells are also a form of nonverbal communication. The mandibles, antennae, and atrophied wings are also indicators of characteristics shared with the Carrion beetle. We can't be positive without DNA testing, but it's our best guess."

"Do they have weaknesses we can exploit?"

"If they stayed true to their ancestors, they may have a few weaknesses. They love to eat decaying flesh, ripe fruits, and rotten vegetables. If given a choice, they prefer the decayed meat. These types of beetles have an aversion to feathers, organs, sun baked skin, or fresh blood."

The captain recalled catching glimpses of beetles carrying human corpses in the passageways. Each bug wore protective covers and weird looking hand gloves.

"In a lab environment we use porcelain or resin coating to contain them. Colonies like damp underground dwellings and large water sources. They cannot survive when exposed to extreme heat. Compounds containing formaldehyde, pyrethroids, or carbamates, are poison to them. They will not eat anything covered in mold. The temperature most ideal for them is 15 degrees Celsius." Doctor Nihna looked at her team and said, "Anyone have something else to add?"

"I do," said a thin, young adult, wearing thick-lensed glasses. He stepped forward. "They have a hive mentality. They like to lay their eggs in decaying organisms. The Carrion beetle has four stages: egg, larva, pupa, and adult. The nest is always tended around the clock. The young would be easy to kill, as it takes time for the exoskeleton to form and harden."

"That's more information than I hoped to learn about our captors, nice job," said the captain. "Do you have any chemists among the colonists?"

"We had two, a husband and wife team. We lost the husband during the attack. Ruth Bernardo is the surviving chemist."

"Great. I know I'll need more input from your team, but for now that's enough information to start planning a way to get us out of here. Do me a favor. Without drawing attention to yourselves, watch the bug guards. Make note of anything you think might help us. I'll spread the word we are making a plan to get us out of this mess. One final request before you go, could someone find Ruth for me?"

Doctor Nihna nodded her head in the affirmative, and the team started to walk away. The thin young man that spoke up earlier turned around to face the captain. "They took my younger brother, captain. My older brother died trying to stop the aliens. If you need a volunteer with knowledge about insects, I'm your man. My name is Tews. I'm the colonist's primary entomologist."

"Thank you Tews. I know we're going to need your help in the future. I'll keep it in mind as we make our plans."

As the captain watched Tews shuffle away he wondered if the young man could handle what was coming. He remembered his own captivity during the war and recalled he promised himself to never judge a person by their looks. Many average looking people went on to become heroes.

The captain spotted several colonists picking their way through the mass of people. They strolled in a meandering path, so as not to draw attention to themselves. He wondered if they were more volunteers. One by one, the colonists showed up next to the captain.

"I figured you could use some of their help," said Smitty, the Nomad's chief engineer. "There's several more engineers, but we didn't want too large of a group moving through the colonists and crew." Smitty looked at the newcomers. "This is Captain Cutter, he needs our help to get us out of here."

"Hello everyone. We need to gather as much information about these bugs, the ship, and their weapons as we can. I met Nihna, the colonist's lead biologist, and Tews, the primary entomologist; they gave us some good info about the aliens. I have a plan in mind, but we are going to need as much information as our engineers can give us about the ship."

75

The engineers came looking for hope, and the captain had given it to them. It was going to take some time, but let them know they had a chance. Their eyes glinted with new optimism and their slouched shoulders straightened. They agreed to start analyzing the ship from an engineer's perspective.

For his plan to work, he still needed a chemist. A woman from Nihna's team found Ruth and brought the captain to her. She warned him ahead of time Ruth had a mental collapse and was not doing well. When the two of them came upon Ruth, she was sitting on the floor. She was oblivious to everything going on around her. Captain Cutter had seen this same behavior many times during the war. Ruth's mind couldn't make sense of anything that happened to her, so it shut down. She was in shock.

The captain walked up to Ruth and sat on the ground next to her. She stared through him, as if he weren't there. People looked at Ruth and shook their heads at the captain. They had already tried to get through to her, but were unsuccessful. They put her where they could keep an eye on her. Setting her near, but not talking to her was the wrong action to take even though the colonists meant well. She needed to talk, to be part of a conversation. If not, in time she would snap.

"Ruth, I'm Captain Cutter. I need to talk to you about some important plans. First off, I want to tell you I'm sorry your Raphael died. I heard he tried to stop the aliens from taking the children. He was very brave."

Ruth started to shake. This was a good sign. She was remembering what happened. Cruel, but she needed to let her emotions out, not bottle them up. In the military, the captain learned a surviving friend needed support from others. Sometimes a few kind words were enough. He also had to show Ruth she was needed by the other survivors.

"We need to stop these bugs from killing more of us. You have knowledge that can help us. Ruth, we need you. Can you do that Ruth? Can you help us?"

The captain watched as tears began to roll down Ruth's cheeks. It was more than he could take with everything else going on. He started to cry too. The captain who was still sitting on the floor had to look away from Ruth so he didn't send her into a deeper depression. *Oh great, I'm here making her feel worse.* The captain felt an arm cradle his head. Ruth had reached out to comfort him. They both cried for a while. It helped them both.

In a shaky voice the captain said, "Ruth, we have to stop these bastards. I have a plan but I need your help."

"What do you need?" Ruth managed to sniffle out.

She had snapped out of it. He knew what she wanted. He had to capitalize on her desire for revenge.

"Ruth, I met with biologists and entomologists. They identified several weaknesses we may be able to exploit if we can create the chemicals."

"What chemicals?" asked Ruth.

"They said we needed formaldehyde, pyrethroids, or carba, uh, let me think, it was carba something or other."

"Was it carbamates? They are a general class of synthetic organic insecticides."

"Yes, that's what they called it. Carbamate. Can you make any them?"

"Oh sure, I could make them all with the right chemicals and a lab."

"How about here, in this holding pen, with what is available?"

"To create formaldehyde requires recovering gases made by burning certain materials. In this pen it would be impossible. To make pyrethroids requires access to large volumes of flowers, Chrysanthemums or Tanacetums. I don't think it's possible given our environment."

The captain got a sinking feeling. He had hoped they could create a chemical to kill the bugs.

"Now, let me think. For carbamates I need ammonia, and carbon dioxide…"

The captain interrupted Ruth, "It was worth a try. I'll come up with a plan B."

"Not so fast captain. Carbon dioxide and nitrogen are both in the air we exhale. The nitrogen will be irrelevant to the chemical reaction. I can come up with a way to capture our exhaled breath. The next problem is ammonia. Humans have small amounts of ammonia in their blood; it's toxic and it gets filtered into the body's waste. If we force people to dehydrate, their bodies will produce more urea than normal. It will come out in their urine."

"Won't people forced to dehydrate to that level die?" asked the captain.

"No, we can rotate volunteers. We will let the urine sit for a while to reclaim the ammonia – yes. I can do it. The problem is I won't be able to identify the concentration levels. We could have a twenty percent or a ninety percent concentration. The best thing to do would be to test spray some on a guard and observe its reaction."

"Ruth, you're a genius."

"No, it's simple. I want to kill these bastards."

"How long will it take you to mix up a batch?"

"It will take several months or so to get everything done. Even if we start today."

"Lets start now," smiled the captain. "I haven't had anything to drink since last night. I'll be the first to pee for you."

"I have to make some preparations first. In the mean time, don't you dare pee."

At hearing this, the captain smiled and hugged her.

"I won't."

In the next months the engineers located air ducts and electrical lines. They also found door control mechanisms, communication systems, and junction boxes. They speculated about the ship's design, and what held the ship together. A team of engineers worked on fashioning weapons. They used the metal and super plastics found in belts, clothing and shoes. It turned out the alien scanners had missed many items. They also planned to take whatever they could from the ship or guards when the time was right.

The plan seemed to be going well as the colonists and crew worked together. The captain felt a strong vibration. The rumbling shook deep inside his body. *I'll never get used to the low frequency sonic wave*. It was the bugs calling them to eat. Two separate troughs slid out from the wall near where the guard stood watch. One trough contained some kind of creamy substance for solid food. The other one contained what appeared to be water. The captain couldn't help but picture pigs at a trough. *Could humans be no more than cattle to our captors?*

The captain walked over to the bathroom area and began to formulate the rest of his plan. The room had ventilation and was auto cleaning. The facility had one way in, and one way out. Upon exiting, users received a spray of fast drying disinfectant. It kept their bodies disease free. The engineers found two hidden ventilation shafts in the bathroom facility. One supplied fresh air and the other sucked it out. *This is the jackpot.*

The crew set up a work area for Ruth. She worked squatting near the ground so the guards couldn't see her. There were several colonists assigned to assist Ruth. Their job was to prevent her from being seen by the bugs.

When the captain walked up to Ruth, she was so intent on her work she didn't notice him. After a few minutes, he used a soft voice and said, "Ruth." She still didn't notice him. This time he added a little more volume, "Oh Ruth, we need to talk."

She looked up, saw the captain, and tried to stand up, but couldn't. The captain had to help her up. She had been squatting so long, her legs wouldn't extend.

"Ruth, you need to take better care of yourself. I can smell your success in making the ammonia, but if we don't do something the bugs will know it too. Is there any way to mask the ammonia smell?"

She wiped the hair from her face as she looked at the captain. "Yes. I should have thought of the smell."

"I'm glad we caught it before the guards noticed. What can I get you?" asked the captain.

"Bring me a few of our fattest people."

The captain laughed. "You're kidding me right? You don't need fat people? Do you?"

"Yes, I need fat people. I noticed the gruel provided by our captors is salty. We can solve our problem if our heavy weights will volunteer to exercise and sweat. Their sweat contains salt I can recover from their clothing. The salt is all it will take to mask the ammonia smell." Ruth smiled at the captain. "After twenty years as a top level chemist, here I am using pee, bad breath, and sweat to make chemicals."

"The captain reached over and hugged Ruth. I thank God you are here. You may be our salvation."

Ruth smiled and buried herself in her work once again. Creating a strong pesticide in this environment was no simple task. Nothing about their plan was simple. The captain had everyone involved in preparing for the escape. Not one person said trying to take control of the ship was a crazy idea. Everyone knew it was this, or nothing.

The engineers developed a simple mouth sprayer. They used the Venturi effect to create a low-pressure delivery system for the poison. The user needed to blow into a hollow tube connected to the container of insecticide. Care had to be taken not to suck in while their mouth was on the hollow tube or they would get a mouth full of chemicals. The captain marveled at what the human mind was capable of in a pinch.

The captives wanted explore the ship by to using the air ducts while Ruth completed her work. The captain said no. Not until the poison was ready. If they were discovered, the captives had to do as much damage as possible. After some heated discussion, the crew and colonists agreed with the captain. Being prepared for the worst while hoping for the best was the most prudent approach.

Since it would be helpful for the person spaying the bug to understand bug physiology, the captain decided to talk to Tews. The idea was to dilute the original spray in the hopes of getting a reaction from the bug. They did not want to kill it and ruin any future chances they may have had of taking over the ship.

As the captain walked up to Tews he asked him, "Do you still want to volunteer to help take out the bugs?"

"More than ever, captain."

He looked at Tews, "I'm a little worried you won't be able to jump on the guard's platform. Or to spray the insecticide into the bug's face."

Tews started to laugh. "You have proven why you need me to do this. Carrion beetles do not have lungs or breathe through their mouths, captain. They have tiny holes in their bodies called spiracles. The air moves into them, it travels into tiny tubes called trachea, which act like lungs. While spying on our bug hosts I noticed they are capable of expanding and contracting their exoskeletons. This pumping action causes more air to flow into their spiracles. Once the air gets to the tracheal system a simple diffusion occurs…"

"Okay, okay, you can stop, you win. You've proved you're the right person for the job."

"Thank you captain."

"Don't thank me for putting you into danger. If you are caught, the bugs will kill you. I had other plans for your expertise, so do me a favor and stay alive."

"I'll do my best. Do you think you could create a distraction for me?"

"I'll do one better. At feeding time, I'll have a fight break out. The two opponents will bump into you, knocking you onto the guard platform by the food trough. One antagonist will climb onto the stand to jump on his opponent. We will have people yelling and screaming at the two fighters to get the guard's attention. You should be able to approach undetected and spray it with the insecticide."

"Sounds like a plan, captain."

Everyone felt the ship lurch, as if they had hit a speed bump. The captain knew right away what caused the bump. There was another, followed by a third. *The ship is in a fight. Hits to the ship's shields caused the lurches. The shields must have held. He wished he could see what was happening.* The lights dimmed and the humans could feel the ventilation stop. A rumble moved throughout the ship. It happened four more times, each no further than a minute apart.

Smitty ran over to the captain. "Did you feel that, sir? I'd bet all my credits the drain of power was some kind of weapon system."

"You're right Smitty. It can't be a laser, it's got to be something else."

"This ship took three direct hits. No busted lines, loss of power, or breached bulkheads. We gotta stop these butchers. Whatever they did after their weapon fired, we weren't hit again. I'm guessing they took out whatever was firing at them. I hope it's not more humans."

The colonists and crew began to speculate on what had happened. Everyone seemed to agree, their ship had been in some kind of firefight. A little while later everyone heard the sound of metallic clanking. You could feel the vibration through the deck. After about fifteen minutes the pen doors opened up. Eight armed bugs wearing body armor entered the compound. Two worked a portable scanning device as the other six stood at the ready. A body hydro of human captives was forced to walk though a portable electronic scanning device.

A stream of hundreds of humans started shuffling into the pen. The firing of plasma rifles reverberated through the passageway. In shock, anger, and with tears running down their faces, the new captives moved like livestock into the large pen area. A scuffle broke out when a captive wearing a military uniform walked by an armed bug. In an act of defiance, he spun around, grabbed its gun, and moved backward through the detector.

Alarms sounded as the courageous sergeant tried in vane to fire the rifle at the guards. When he pulled the trigger, nothing happened. The bugs started clicking and hissing. One used its exoskeleton forearm like a club and bashed the human on the head, knocking him out. It took back the stolen gun. A few colonists from the Nomad dragged the unconscious man away. They moved into the mass of human bodies and disappeared from view.

The people from the Nomad descended on the new prisoners in an effort to glean information. The captain understood the new prisoners would have a thousand questions. As he made his way to the new arrivals, the old captives parted giving him a clear path. It meant a lot to him because it conveyed an acceptance of his leadership. Everyone stopped talking when he walked up to the group.

"Hello, I'm Captain Cutter from the Nomad." The captain held his arms open, "Everyone here is from our ship. We were carrying colonists in an unarmed ship to the planet Rayne. These bugs attacked us and took us prisoner. We have been here for months, and still don't know what the aliens want with us."

The young black haired man stuck his hand out toward the captain. The two shook hands. "Captain Cutter, I'm Gus. I am from the maintenance staff on Imperial. I know most everyone on the station. You know how it goes. A new space hub means lots of problems to fix. Everyone needs a maintenance worker sooner or later."

"Gus, we need to gather all the intel we can about our bug captors. Can you tell me what happened from the beginning?"

"Sure. Anything you need. It started when I got a call from engineering. Some military personnel on leave were having problems with our view screens. They were in the central gravitational ring. When I got there, sure enough, the screens were down. I got my equipment out and tried to scope the signal, but it was gone. We have a back up transmitter, so I switched to it. I saw the signal appear on my scope."

"I heard a military guy say, 'What the hell are those'. By the time I looked up, the screen was blank again. I performed a scan for the signal but it was gone. Like the first one, it disappeared."

"Did you find out what caused the signal loss?" asked the captain.

"No, but that's when I remembered we had hardwired the cameras when we built the station. The manufacturer forgot to send the transmitters to us. Later, we installed the remote transmitters and left the wires in place. I switched to the old low voltage analog signal created using a galvanic gel. This time the screens came on, and the signal didn't disappear."

A man walked up to the captain. "When the aliens attacked us, we lost all communication too. They must have a harmonic frequency generator. It dampens the wave function of any wireless transmission. It's high tech electronics. Our engineers are working on it, but we don't have any yet. I can't believe these dumb ass bugs are capable of designing something so complex."

Gus tilted his head and blinked at the newcomer.

"Gus, this is Smitty, the Nomads Chief Engineer," said the captain. He turned to Smitty. "You're right. The bugs seem to use high tech gadgets, but I have not seen proof of a greater intelligence." Turning back to Gus the captain said, "Sorry Gus. What happened next?"

"We couldn't believe our eyes. We saw six alien ships. They looked like big bugs and they were firing at the military war ships docked at the station. Our ships were sitting ducks."

"Was anyone able to fire on the alien ships?" asked the captain.

"Yeah. The aliens were so busy taking out the docked ships they didn't realize they gave us time to activate our big defensive guns. The alien ships took hit after hit, but their shields held. They wasted no time in neutralizing the station's weapon system. When they boarded us it was total chaos. It became a game of hide and seek inside the station," Gus shook his head and said, "I lost."

"Anything else you remember, Gus?" asked the captain.

"Hey, come on. Someone give me a hand down here." It was the young sergeant who snatched the bug's gun. He managed to get himself upright into a sitting position. A few colonists helped him up. He looked at the people around him, smiled, and said, "Thanks for getting me out of there. I was counting on you helping me. I'm Sergeant Frank Spazinok. My friends call me Spaz."

"What do you mean?" asked the Captain. "You were counting on people helping you?"

"Well, it's like this: I already knew their gun wouldn't fire. A few ground pounders and me ambushed some of their search teams and tried using the alien weapons. We never got their rifles to work. My guess is they have some kind of DNA coded safety mechanism. I moved backwards through the scanner while holding the rifle at my right side on purpose." Spaz pulled out an old-fashioned synthetic needle gun from a sleek holster in his waist. It was an outlawed weapon used to circumvent carbon-based scanners. "I wanted to make sure I got this past them. I thought it might come in handy."

"Spaz, that was pure genus," said Smitty. "Captain, we could use Spaz to help us plan. He's a nontraditional thinker. We could use his talent."

Spaz grinned. "I'm willing if it will get us off this death trap."

"Okay, Spaz. You've earned a spot, if you're interested," said the captain.

"Hell yeah. Sign me up."

"The bugs you took the rifles from, did you kill them?" asked the captain.

"Yep, we killed a few of them. Our hand held weapons were useless against their armor. We found a woodcraft shop that sold wood framing tools to colonists. The tools we took had points, sharp edges, and were about eighteen inches long. After a few attempts we learned if we jammed the blades in through top opening of their armor, the bugs died."

"That would be the thorax," said a thin, anorexic looking man. "Located near the top and below the thorax is where the all the bug's main organs are situated. You couldn't find a better place to stick a long sharp object."

"Spaz, meet Tews." At hearing himself give the introduction, the captain said, "That's got a certain ring to it, doesn't it? Tews is our resident bug expert. His knowledge is what's going to help us all get out of here."

"Tews, huh? Yeah, I could see it. Spaz and Tews the gutsy duo. You could be the brains..." Spaz reached over and acted like he felt Tews bicep, "and I guess I could be everything else."

Everyone laughed, even the captain. The sergeant's personality had a positive affect on everyone near him.

With all the new information coming in, the captain said, "We need to regroup and discuss our plan of action. As far as we know, the humans from Imperial Station are the only ones to engage the bugs. We need to share our information with each other in the hopes we can use it to escape. Whatever happens we have to get word back to our government about these aliens."

The next few days there were many meetings. A sharing of every scrap of information about the bugs and their weapons occurred. The engineers learned the enemy ships used plasma canons on the station. The bug ship lowering its shields as the plasma cannons fired is what the captives felt during the battle. This was useful information.

It was almost time to send a two-member team into the ventilation system. They would map out the ship and learn what they could. Spaz volunteered because of his military experience. Tews was the second team member because of his knowledge about bugs.

The next day the plan to test Ruth's poison was put into motion. Two rather large colonists started fighting at the food trough. One fighter slammed into Tews, knocking him onto the guard platform. Before the guard could react, the other fighter leapt onto the elevated platform and dove at the other human. The guard brought his rifle to the ready. Tews blew into the insecticide delivery system and slid off the platform in one smooth motion.

The captain watched but nothing happened. The guard stood there with his weapon pointing at the two fighting humans. Tews decided he had to do something before the guard fired at them. He launched himself into the guard's feet. The guard fell over, paralyzed stiff as a board. The commotion got the other guard's attention. Everyone started screaming and running away.

The guard on the floor began to move, as his partner approached with its rifle at the ready. It stunk like all hell. The fallen guard stood up, while the other guard clicked and hissed at it. Soon both of them were clicking and hissing at each other. It sounded like they were arguing. Tews watched the guard he had doused with insecticide. It forced its chest to heave, causing a larger flow of oxygen to enter the respiratory system. Tews could see the drug had already worn off. The bug was back to normal. The second guard pushed several humans over on its way back to the platform. You could tell the second bug was mad. It looked like it thought the other bug had fallen asleep and fell over.

Tews went straight to Ruth. "Ruth, would it be possible to mix some kind of substance into your concoction to make it sticky. I need the insecticide to stick inside the bug's body. If a bug heaves its chest the insecticide will resist being pushed out of the spiracles."

"Yeah, I can think of a few simple creations that will work. I'll add it to the mix. How'd the insecticide and mouth aerator work?"

"At current potency, it paralyzed the bug for about one minute. I can't wait to see what full strength will do on these baby-eating bastards. The mouth aerator worked better than I could have imagined. Just be careful not to make the bug juice too thick."

"We'll test it after I change the mix. I'll have it ready by the end of day."

Next, Tews met with the captain and Spaz to discuss tomorrow's foray into the air duct systems. The engineers developed a few simple tools for the two to use as they traversed the air vents inside the ship. They would have light tubes to hang around their necks so they could see and have both hands free to crawl. Ruth found a way to create dry, odorless, chalk, to mark on the vent system. She was sure it would get confusing as the turns and twists started adding up.

The team agreed with the captain. It would be best to leave in the morning. The team would mix with the mad rush to use the bathroom facilities.

"For once, my lack of height makes me a valued commodity," said Spaz.

Tews started laughing. "Spaz, I'm shorter than you and less muscular. Look at you! You have too many muscles and they will do nothing but bind you up. I think I'm a more valued commodity on this team!"

"You're wrong Tews. Oh sure, you have bad posture, making you appear shorter. But when you straighten I am the shorter person."

"I see the problem, it's my hair. Mine is curly and yours is straight and sits flat, making you seem shorter when you are not," said Tews.

The captain smiled at the banter. "This is the first time I ever saw two people argue about who is shorter. Most of us can't fit into the vents. That means both of you are valued commodities to the rest of us, and we appreciate the risk you are both taking."

"Did you see Tews, when the captain looked both of us in the eye, he had to look even lower at me? It proves I am shorter than you, my dear friend."

"Uggh. Let me settle this now before you two start arguing in the vents and get us all killed. By the power vested in me by United Fleet Command, on this day, I declare Tews and Spaz to be the exact same height," said the captain.

"Spaz, can he do that?"

"I'm not sure. Let's assume he's right until we can check Fleet Command regulations."

The captain smacked his forehead with an open hand, making a loud pop. Everyone laughed.

The next morning, Spaz, Tews, and the captain made their separate ways to the bathroom facility. Smitty was waiting for them and had already removed the vent cover.

He showed the two volunteers how the alarm system linked to the magnetic cover and how to bypass it. The two new friends prepared to enter the vent.

CHAPTER SIX: Second Platoon

For close to three months, Mac honed the skills of his troops, preparing them for a possible battle. He needed to talk to his ground pounders about the possible danger they might be facing on Rayne. Rumors were already flying. Missing probes. There were sightings of strange ships in deep uncharted space. Space pirate attacks and proof of secret military missions. Some rumors were far fetched and others were closer to the truth.

The singularity drive development created problems for the government and military. As soon as large organizations could get their hands on the new drive, the race would be on. Who would be the first to claim the new worlds, rich in raw materials or new food sources? The government was hell bent on getting the colonists to lay claim to the new fringe planets.

There was one other giant problem for colonists. They would be too far out for proper government protection. Like the last great expansion of humankind, there would be opportunists. Slavers would steal people. Pirates would steal goods and claim jumpers would steal land. Unscrupulous corporations would take whatever they could. In past times the military had to place outposts on each new planet.

I need to have a talk with my troops, but first I need to choose my platoon leaders. Previous rank doesn't matter. I need people that can lead and at the same time not put lives at risk. Hand-to-hand combat competition starts today day. I'll make the top three soldiers for the three-month period platoon leaders. Along with the new position, I'll give them a field rank advancement. Tinker was a lock for leader of First platoon. Neither Dreng, nor Dwain can displace Corporal Tinker. The real fight is for Second platoon.

Right now, Mac knew Dreng to be in second place, but she could lose her standing to Dwain if she didn't have a big win in hand-to hand combat. Mac thought he knew what would happen. Dwain, with his specialized training would take first place in the hand-to-hand competition. Though in itself, winning wasn't enough to guarantee him Second platoon. Dreng had to lose in her fight with Tinker for Dwain to become Second platoon leader. On the other hand, if Dreng defeated Tinker she would become Second platoon leader. The three top ground pounders were each getting a platoon, but status went with the lower numbers. What Dreng lacked in experience, she made up for with her natural leadership abilities.

Mac paid close attention to Dreng. Sure, he watched her because of her hot looks, but he also felt like she was holding back in her performance. He noticed during physical training exercises she didn't give her all. Oh she was good, always in the top, but he could see she never gave her best. Mac didn't like anyone slacking off. In combat, to survive, he needed to know the skills of each person under his immediate command. A weak link was okay, as long as he knew he had one.

Today, I'll force Dreng to do her best, he thought. *If she doesn't she will drop below Dwain in the standings. For me to teach her the Tao fighting style she needs to show me her best. Hell, I want to teach it to her, but she has to earn it! A bet is a bet. It's all in her hands. No more hiding talent.*

In the old days there were no levels of fighting skills in hand-to-hand combat. You learned every trick and move you could, because you wanted to live. I was an angry young soldier wanting revenge for my family's death.

Someone was going to pay for it, so I worked day and night on my skills. I became a proficient killer at a time when the military needed killers. They loved me for it. In a way, Dreng is like me. There seems to be a passion driving her. I need to know if it is self-serving or something else. Can I count on her?

Guys like Dwain are dangerous. Being a showoff, hothead, and overconfident can get you killed. But even Dwain has potential I know I can develop. Tinker I know. I can put my life in his hands and not worry. Dreng is someone I'm not sure of yet. She's going to have to work hard to beat Tinker in order to keep Dwain from wining Second platoon. Time to head to the classroom and see what develops.

When the students showed up, the chairs in the classroom were gone. A large tumble mat covered the entire floor. There was a large white circle in the mat's center. Several ranking diagrams hung on the wall and would be filled with names as troopers won or lost their bouts.

Upon entering the classroom, Tinker looked at Mac. "You bastard."

"Sweet talk will get you nowhere with me." Mac directed everyone to move against the wall and take a seat. He began to explain the competition. "Students will fight for place, one through sixty. Each student will participate in several fights.

A chorus of "Oh, fuck" sounded.

Mac smiled and went on. "I will score based on a point system. Each match will last no more than ninety seconds." Mac looked at Dwain and said, "How long does a fight to the death last?"

"Could be seconds," Dwain pointed his finger at the entire class. "None of you are going to last more than seconds against me."

About half the class went wide-eyed, at Dwain's statement. He could be intimidating.

"Does anyone here think they can beat Dwain?" asked Mac.

No one commented, not even Tinker or Dreng. Mac looked at Dreng and for the first time he saw a worried look on her face.

"Well Dwain, it looks like you may have an easy time during this competition. Now, let me give you the rules. A tie after ninety seconds will gain you no points. A decision in your favor after ninety seconds will get you one point. A death strike or crippling blow will earn you the match and two points. If you harm a fellow trooper on purpose, I will put you in the brig. I'm the referee, and you will always follow my instructions. Understand?"

As Mac looked over his warriors, everyone nodded their heads. He started the tournament with the least experienced soldiers, to break the ice. The competition went as Mac expected. Dwain annihilated everyone he faced. Tinker did the same. Dreng won her battles, but again, Mac could see she was not fighting to her full potential. She missed opportunities to strike. During the entire competition she had yet to use a grapple hold.

By the third day, there were three troopers tied for first place. All three had not lost a match. Mac decided it was time to force the issue. *First Tinker will fight Dwain and lose. Next Dreng would fight Dwain and she would lose. In the end, Tinker and Dreng would fight. No sloughing off would happen here. All three would have to give it their best. After three months of evaluations, at this point Tinker was first in class and couldn't lose.* As Mac had planned, the match between Tinker and Dreng would decide who got which platoon. *I love it when a plan comes together.*

"Next match, Dwain and Tinker," said Mac.

The students started to cheer, "Go Tinker. Get him Tinker."

Tinker was an excellent leader. Dwain was good too, but he knew it, and let everyone else know it too. His ego often got in the way of being a great leader.

They stepped into the circle, shook hands, and bowed to Mac.

Mac stepped between them, raised his right hand, and when it dropped, the fight started. Tinker ran forward with speed no one realized he had, dropped to his knees and swung his right fist at Dwain's leg. Dwain's eyes opened wide as he shifted his weight backwards causing Tinker to miss. Dwain began to move forward. Tinker continued to spin on his knees in a complete circle, landing a left fist against Dwain's left knee.

When Mac said, "Point, Tinker," his voice reverberated off the classroom walls.

Dwain's eyes narrowed as he glared at Tinker. ""You lucky fuck. That was weak."

Mac knew it was a weak strike, but it was still a point. Smart fighting by Tinker.

Tinker moved in again, thinking Dwain's hands were too high to stop a blow to his groin. Tinker was right but Dwain blocked the blow with his left knee. He spun to the right on his right leg and gave Tinker a solid blow to his left arm.

"Point, Dwain," said Mac, as the troops voiced their displeasure with a low rumbling "boo".

"How'd ya like that, asshole?" said Dwain.

Mac knew it was an excellent move. Dwain set Tinker up.

As the two maneuvered for position Dwain jumped high in what looked like a double leg kick to the chest. Tinker took a half step back and set his arms to block Dwain's feet. The leap took Dwain higher in the air than Tinker anticipated. Both of Dwain's feet came downward and knocked Tinker's arms down, causing his body to bend forward. Dwain gave Tinker an incapacitating blow to his exposed head.

Mac stepped between the two fighters, "Match, and two points to Dwain."

Dwain started jumping high into the air while pointing his finger at Tinker. "I got you. You weak little son of a bitch."

Mac gave Dwain his moment, he stepped into the ring's center and both fighters shook hands.

"Take a break everyone, be back in thirty. Dwain, do you think you can handle another fight?"

Dwain looked Dreng in the eyes, threw a few punches at an invisible foe, and said, "Fuck yeah, I'll be ready. I owe that little bitch."

Mac had seen trash talkers fight before. They always tried to intimidate their opponent. He hoped Dreng could see through the boisterous comments. "Everyone take a thirty minute break, and when you come back it will be Dwain and Dreng in the circle."

The class cheered and clustered around Dreng. Dwain walked out all alone. No one stood with him. After these last couple of days, his fellow troopers hated him even more. Dwain didn't even try to make friends. At the breaks end, Dwain entered the classroom the same way he left it, alone.

Dreng walked into the classroom with her head held high. She saw Dwain already standing at the mat's center stretching and loosening up. Mac hoped she understood he was attempting to intimidate her by not giving her room on the mat. As Mac looked Dreng over for signs of nervousness or stress he detected the flush spots on her skin. *I'll be damned. The little minx had already loosened up.*

Dreng walked up to Mac and in a soft whisper said, "Why? Why make me do this?"

Mac cocked his head as he looked at her. The bluntness surprised him, but it was a quality he loved in her. He whispered back. "You forced me to do this Dreng. I told everyone I needed their best effort, so in a pinch, I know what I can count on. I'll be honest, I like you, a lot."

Dreng's eyes turned downward and her face flushed even redder.

Mac saw the reaction and realized what he said. "No, no, not that way. I don't know you like that. I mean, as a leader you have good qualities, but to be honest, I don't trust you. You are playing some kind of game, and lives may be at risk."

Dreng couldn't look Mac in the eyes. She continued to look down at the mat. "I am not playing a game with you or the troopers, Mac. I'm sorry you feel I'm not trustworthy but my actions are out of necessity. Can we talk after class today."

"Sure, but no games. I want total honesty." Dreng stood so close to him, he could smell the orange she ate for lunch mixed with the sweat from her workout. *She's intoxicating. Look at her, she's too young for you, you old fart. I don't know why I'm even worried. After Dwain beats her, and she has to fight Tinker, any chances I had will be gone. For the troops' sake, I have to see her at her best when she fights Tinker. I hope her psyche can handle it.*

"Okay, total honesty." Dreng flipped her hair in a sensual way and said, "Afterwards we can get to know each other." She smiled and turned around before a stunned Mac could respond.

What the hell was that? Mac watched her take up a position next to Dwain and began to stretch a little.

Dwain smiled at her and said, "I'm going to get you for swinging me into the tree."

"You should have kept your hands to yourself. You must be stupid and need another lesson," said Dreng.

Dwain's head came close to exploding. His face turned red with anger. "In a few minutes, my hands are going to be all over you and I'm going to hurt you, bad. It will be worth time in the brig. It won't be my first trip there. No one can help you, not even Mac." Dwain sneered at her. He turned to Mac and in a loud voice said, "Come on Mac, let's get on with this, I'm getting tired of stretching."

"Dreng, are you ready?"

Dreng glanced at Dwain, smiled, and said, "Give me another minute."

Mac could see the situation had flipped. It was Dreng who was messing with Dwain now. His red face proved her delaying tactics had gotten to him. "Okay. One more minute."

Dwain rolled his eyes as everyone watched the two of them. Dreng bent over and placed both hands on the mat. *She was every bit as flexible as Dwain, and by far, better looking. Did she just bend over with her hind end facing me on purpose?* He jiggled his head no, not believing the thoughts he was having. *Oh, come on Mac, snap out of it. Focus. This is too important to be daydreaming about a girl who could be my daughter.*

"Time," said Mac.

Both fighters entered the ring and stepped toward each other. They shook hands and stepped back to the circle's edge. Mac stepped between the contestants. He raised his open hand and slammed it down like a hatchet as he moved back. Before a second ticked off the clock Dwain moved in on his opponent.

He stepped forward, moving his right foot followed by his left foot. It left him in a well-guarded stance. As his left foot planted, he swung his right arm in a powerful roundhouse punch toward Dreng's head. Dreng saw the punch developing. With lightning quick reflexes, she turned her right shoulder to the left and down. At the same time she balanced on her left foot. Her right foot came into the air and hit Dwain's exposed head. Not enough for a deathblow, but everyone saw the surprise on his face.

"Point, Dreng," The troops went nuts cheering.

Pissed off, Dwain looked at the troops, pointed his finger at them and said, "Shut up, or you're next."

Dreng took the opportunity to launch herself at Dwain. When Dwain turned back to face Dreng, she had already launched herself with her legs bent, her feet hit his chest. In the same instant she grabbed him by the shoulders, pulling with her arms. To everyone but Mac, it looked like she used leverage, but the move was all brute strength. She pulled Dwain over her as she kicked her legs out, sending him sprawling through the air. *Who is this girl*, Mac wondered?

"Point, Dreng," said Mac, bringing an even louder cheer than the first one.

This time Dwain didn't take his eyes off her. He decided to rush her and use his greater strength in a grapple move. He made a bull rush trying to grab her by her narrow waist. In a surprise move she fell backwards, grabbed his arm and pulled him onto his back. Before he cleared her body, she grabbed his ankle, and spun so she was positioned between both his legs and perpendicular to his knee. She wrapped his right leg just below his knee with her right arm.

She made a mistake. Dwain's legs were even stronger than his arms. In a matter of seconds, Dwain would maneuver himself on top of Dreng. He had to admit, she put up a good fight. She grabbed Dwain's right foot with her left hand and put reverse pressure on Dwain's right knee. For the second time, Mac couldn't believe the fighting ability of this girl.

"Point, Dreng," said Mac.

This time there was more murmuring than cheering. Dwain got up rubbing his leg to restore circulation. Had this been a real fight, the injury would have gotten Dwain killed. The timer sounded, ninety seconds had flown by in a flash.

He stepped between the combatants. "Dreng wins by decision, one point for the match." *I didn't see this coming. Our talk is going to be even more interesting.*

The two combatants shook hands in the middle of the circle. About fifteen troopers ran up to Dreng to congratulate her. Dwain stood all alone watching. His head hung low, his shoulders slumped, but his eyes focused with hate on Dreng.

Mac continued with the fights. He saved Tinker and Dreng for last, but the fight didn't matter in ranking. Tinker already had earned First platoon. In a surprise, Dreng had secured Second platoon by defeating Dwain. No one knew the standing so there was still tension in the air before the fight.

"Tinker and Dreng, take up positions. This will be the last fight."

Everyone cheered.

Mac could see confusion in Dreng's face. *He still didn't understand what was going on here. After defeating Dwain with such flair, she should be able to defeat Tinker too.* Mac dropped his hand for the last time.

Tinker was first to attack. Everyone saw the surprise on Dreng's face. Tinker fought safe in the past, always looking for a weakness in the challenger, but not this time. He gave Dreng three quick punches to the face, which she deflected with little effort. It was a ruse designed to block Dreng's vision. Tinker delivered a knee to her stomach. When she bent down from the impact, he used an overhand chop to her neck landing the blow with the force of a feather.

Mac stepped into the circle. Tinker delivered a perfect deathblow. "Match Tinker, two points."

Dwain slammed the floor with his palm. The other troopers flocked around Tinker and Dreng to congratulate them.

Mac had everyone except Tinker and Dreng take their seats. He looked at the two combatants and said, "Now finish."

Tinker and Dreng stepped onto the circle facing each other. They walked to the mat's center, shook hands, and bowed to Mac. It became instant chaos. The troopers hooted, hollered, and clapped their hands. Mac was glad to see they even congratulated Dwain.

It took two minutes for the cheering and congratulations to run their course

"I want Tinker, Dreng, and Dwain to step forward into the circle," said Mac. "The rest of you take a seat." When everyone settled down Mac said, "It's been three months of traveling which means you have also had three months of training. Soon we will be landing on Rayne. I want to thank everyone for the hard work they have put in." Mac pointed his arm towards the three troopers in the circle, "These three deserve special recognition because they are at the top of the class standings."

The door to the classroom opened, and in walked the long lost, Junior Grade, First Lieutenant Phlop.

Mac looked at the lieutenant and said, "Perfect timing Mr. Phlop, I was about to promote these three troopers to platoon leads."

"Sergeant McCormack, you should know better. I am the senior ranking officer. It's my call to make promotions and at this point I am not sure I agree with you."

Mac's right eye twitched. He was at his tipping point.

"It's too cold in here, turn up the heat in this classroom. Tomorrow, I want everyone back in standard uniform. Not dressed in those silly leather outfits. I should have gotten involved in your training earlier. I'll be taking over from here on out." The Lieutenant pointed at Tinker,

Dreng, and Dwain. "You three take a seat. I can see I have to set all of you straight right now. Sergeant McCormack, please leave the room and wait in my office."

It took all of Mac's strength resist grabbing the young lieutenant by the neck and shaking some sense into him. "Mr. Phlop, we need to talk first. Mac gave a hand signal."

The students, all stood up, and left the classroom.

"What's going on? Who told them to leave? What are they doing? I'll have them court martialed for insubordination. This is a treason," said the lieutenant.

Dwain was the last one out and left the door ajar behind him as he said, "Fucking Mac is in hot water now. I want to hear how this goes down."

"You don't know Mac. I'll bet you a hundred credits, the lieutenant backs off," said Tinker.

"You're on. I may not know a lot, but I do know is a first lieutenant always outranks a sergeant. Now shut up for a few minutes and listen."

"Sergeant McCormack, I am well aware of your background as a war hero. But, you still violated military protocol. I will be putting a letter in your file along with your cohorts."

"Mr. Phlop, how many commands have you had?"

"This is my first."

"I suggest you listen to what I have to say. First, a rank of commander or above is required to authorize promotions in the field. We were in the field as soon as the Argosy left the orbit of Trinity Prime. If a commander or above is not available, the senior non-commissioned officer may award promotions. By the way, that's me. Submission of UFC Field Promotion Form 1500 must follow."

"Second, the body operates best at a temperature of 21 degrees Celsius. The hypothalamus regulates ideal body temperature to control infection. Deviation from ideal temperature causes the body to reallocate resources. This hinders the learning process. Third, United Fleet Command has authorized the use of our high tech uniforms. I want the troops to be familiar with them."

"The students left the classroom because I gave them a non-verbal battle command. If you put a letter in anyone's file other than mine, without telling me first, this will be your last command. If you ever interrupt my training again, I'll have you busted to an ensign. You cared so much about the troops you spent all your time sticking your nose up the governor's ass. You're a green leader and if you ask me, dangerous. You could have come on the holographic training sessions with us. You would have learned something, but you chose not to."

"You can't talk to me like this, and those holograph sessions are make believe."

"Lieutenant, I already gave you more respect than you deserve. If you didn't like what I said, take it up with Fleet Command or change."

"Oh, I will sergeant. I'll take this up with Fleet Command. I've got news. It's you who is going to lose your command. At the first opportunity, war hero or not," said the lieutenant. He spun around and stomped away.

As soon as the lieutenant was out of hearing range Dwain said, "War hero, what fucking war hero? All I see is a baby sitter."

"You know Dwain, you're dumber than you look. Mac has served in multiple wars. He's received about every commendation the Fleet has to award."

"If he's so good, why's he still a ground pounder?"

"The word is he turned down an offer for meritorious advancement to Commander. They say he told the Vice Admiral, once a ground pounder always a ground pounder."

"Sounds like a fairy tale to me."

"Watch your mouth Dwain. I served with Mac. I've seen him in firefights, and if you want to live, I'd stay by his side and listen to him."

"Humph," said Dwain.

"Mac's signaling for us to come back in," said a trooper. "Let's go."

Everyone sat back down, not saying a word. Mac didn't realize the troops had heard every word exchanged between him and the lieutenant.

"I apologize for the interruption. As I was saying, Tinker will be lead for First platoon. Dreng will be lead for Second platoon, and Dwain will be lead for Third platoon. All three of you please step back into the circle."

Mac took something out of his pocket, walked up to Tinker, and placed a pin on each side of his collar. "Congratulations Staff Sergeant Tinker." Tinker grinned ear to ear. The troopers hooted and hollered their approval. Mac pinned both Dreng and Dwain with corporal arrows. They got the same cheers from the troops. He swore Dreng winked at him as he pinned her. *Is she messing with me?*

Tinker looked at Dwain and said, "You owe me a hundred credits."

"I'll pay you when I see the credits in my account from this promotion."

Everyone laughed because the military was known to be slow in paying for field promotions.

"That's enough for today. Once again, congratulations to our sergeant and new corporals. Now get out of here before I come up with something else we should be doing."

Everyone leapt out of their seats and took off except for one trooper and Mac.

"Mac, can we do this talk in your quarters. I would like to keep what we discuss between you and me."

"Yeah, we can go to my quarters. I have to tell you, if something you have to say affects the other troopers, I may have to tell them."

"Fair enough. I'll let you be the judge. How about in thirty minutes?"

Did she bat her eyes at me? Come on Mac. Get your head out of your ass. "Yeah, thirty minutes from now is fine."

Dreng turned around and sashayed toward the exit. Mac's eyes couldn't resist watching her hind end sway in rhythm from side to side. *Damn, she's hot.*

Dreng spun around and caught him watching her behind.

Mac could feel his face redden.

Dreng smiled, turned around again, and continued walking toward the door. Over her shoulder she said, "See you in thirty, Mac."

I am an idiot. She caught me watching her butt. Now I'll be thinking about her catching me when we talk. I feel like a school-aged kid. What the hell is going on with me? Is she playing me? Does she like me, is it my imagination, or is it nothing at all? I don't know what to think with this one.

As he walked to his quarters, confusion about Dreng continued to occupy his thoughts. He was glad the old rules of not dating subordinates ended over a thousand years ago. Sometimes, on remote duty, military personnel were the only ones around.

I could ask her for a date, but what if I read her wrong? I have always felt good about reading people, why is Dreng so difficult? Awe shit, all these signals I think I am seeing is nothing more than a wishful imagination. I need to focus on taking care of my troops. She could have become anything she wanted. Why would she choose to become a ground pounder, why not take a commission? Look at yourself, Mac. You can't keep her out of your mind for even a minute. Is a meeting in my quarters a bad idea? Hell, I can't even remember if it was my idea or hers!

Mac entered his quarters. He gave himself a chemical shave and took a bio-shower to kill any odor causing bacteria. He thought about what he was doing, getting all gussied up for a visit by a pretty girl. Instead of nice clothes, he put on an old set of sweats pants and a retro UFC tee shirt.

Mac hoped the lieutenant would get over being mad and think about what he had done. This wasn't school anymore. Lives could depend his actions. Life could be difficult for a young junior grade lieutenant. You have to realize most of your troopers have more experience than you. You must accept it, use their experience to everyone's benefit, and set your ego aside.

Mac had an odd feeling. He walked to the door and swung it open. Dreng jumped, she was about to push the com button.

"How did you know I was here?" Dreng looked on the wall for a camera. "Do you have a camera hidden somewhere?"

"No, I guess I had a hunch."

Dreng smiled and cocked her head a little. "On my home world they would say you and I are linked because we share a sensory connection."

Is she coming on to me or is it my imagination again… I can't read her worth a shit. "Where's your home world?"

"Are you going to invite me in or will we be talking here at the door?"

"I'm sorry, come in. You'll have to sit on the floor. I don't use chairs."

Both Mac and Dreng squatted down and sat cross-legged facing each other.

"My father and I did not use chairs, so I am use to the floor. He made me follow some old customs. That is what I need to talk to you about. But first, could we talk a little about you, Mac? Tell me about yourself."

"Not much to talk about. I've been in the military most of my life."

"So, let me get this straight, your life story is: you were born and joined the military? Wow, it's an amazing story and it's so interesting. It's a story they could write volumes of books about."

Mac frowned. "Look, I haven't done much with my life and we're here to talk about you."

"Will you answer me one question first?"

"All right, one question."

"Do you have a preference for men?" asked Dreng.

"What?" came out of his mouth. Mac couldn't believe what he heard. Plus, his ego felt a little wounded. *She must have saw me looking at her at least once every minute of the day. How could she not know I am interested in her? I thought I was too obvious.* "Why would you ask such a question?"

"Do you think I'm attractive?"

Oh, God, this discussion is going nothing like I envisioned. He could feel his face blushing from the blood running to his cheeks. "Well, I can tell you, you look better than the guys in the class." Mac smiled, thinking he gave her the perfect comeback. *I let her know I think women look better than men, and she herself is attractive. Perfect.*

"See, that's what I mean," she said as if talking to herself and not Mac. "I give you the perfect opportunity to say yes, and instead, you tell me I look better than a guy. Your words are not encouraging to a woman."

"I don't understand," said Mac.

"How I proceed from here depends on how you respond to a couple simple questions. Do you find me attractive and do you like me? Mac, you are so clear and precise about everything you talk about, can't you do that for me now?"

All right, I won't give her any more clever answers. "Yes."

"Stop doing this to me," she begged. "I need you to be clear. Are you saying yes, you find me attractive, yes you like me, or yes you can be precise in your responses?"

Mac swallowed hard, *this is more difficult than it should be. I have never felt this way about a woman before.* He looked Dreng straight in the eyes. "From the moment I first saw you, I felt a tug on my heart, the likes of which I have never felt before. You are the most beautiful women I have ever met. You have a pretty face, gorgeous eyes, a perfect body, and I even love your tattoo. The more I have gotten to know you, the more I like everything about you." Mac looked down at the ground and in a nervous reaction shuffled his feet. He had never laid himself so far out in the open for anyone. He had a feeling he seldom experienced. He was... scared. *What is she going to think?*

Dreng smiled at Mac's shyness, leaned over, and gave him a long hug. She pulled back from him, looked him in the eyes and said, "Thank God. I have done everything but beat you over the head in trying to get you to notice me. You ignored all my advances. I thought you might prefer men over women."

The pressure broke. Mac started laughing. Dreng couldn't help but to laugh along with him. He explained the insecurities he felt. He told her each time she flirted with him, he told himself he was reading too much into it. He put into words how it was driving him crazy.

"Mac, you think too much. Sometimes you have to stop and listen to your heart."

Mac reached across and grabbed Dreng. They rolled on the floor. He took hold of her sweat top and lifted it over her head. *Wow.* She was wearing a beautiful white, silk like camisole. *Looks like someone came to seduce me. I must be the luckiest guy in the universe.*

"Whoa, there. What are you doing?" said Dreng.

Mac grinned. "I'm listening to my heart."

"I don't think it's your heart talking."

They both laughed like children. He moved to grab her, but she pulled back. She walked to her backpack, swaying her hips as she walked. His eyes were spellbound by her perfect body. He was a dog in heat. She took out two old fashioned pine-scented candles. She placed them together, and lit them both as she spoke some words in an odd language.

She turned giving him a mischievous smile. He couldn't wait any longer. He sprang up, embraced her, and gave her an affectionate kiss. She allowed him to remove her camisole. His eyes went to the scar between her breasts. With great care he took his finger and ran it over the old injury. He whistled.

"Now, there's a story I'd like to hear."

"Dreng lifted his hand off her scar, and placed it on her breast. First, finish what your heart started and I'll feed your brain's curiosity afterward." Dreng reached over and covered both of them with a soft, light blue, blanket.

Later, after their joining, as Dreng called it, she began to explain where she came from.

"Mac, do you know the great exodus story about the lost Indian Nation?"

"Of course, it's still taught as part of Ancient Earth History classes."

"Let me tell you what you don't know about the story. During the trip to Deca, what was to be the Indian Nation's new home, something went wrong with the cryo ship. The computer didn't wake-up my ancestors, it let everyone sleep and they sailed right by Deca. The solar sails powered the ship for one thousand fifty-seven earth years."

"You're shittin me! Right? You mean your ancestors are the lost tribes of old earth? I've got a thousand questions. First, what prompted the ship to wake everyone, after such a long time?" asked Mac.

Dreng touched his arm. "Patience my love. There is much more to reveal. Let me tell the story before you ask your questions."

He could feel his face flush. *No one ever called me 'my love'.*

"Our ancient records indicated the ship was falling apart. The electronics' aged beyond repair and too many metal components wore out. Add the failing life support, micro meteor damage, and the result is a ship beyond repair. To answer your question, the ship initiated emergency protocol on its own. The computer found the nearest habitable planet, entered orbit, and woke up the crew. Once the crew figured out what happened, they woke everyone."

"The ship's drive stopped working. They were in a geosynchronous orbit around an unknown planet. The planet was large with an equatorial radius of 85,000 kilometers. The crew measured its gravity at two and a half times Earth norm. With the ship's life support failing, they had no option but to make the new planet their home."

Mac had studied up on colonization before this assignment. "They can't have survived that kind of gravity," he said.

"The bio scientists warned life would be possible, but difficult. It was. The scientists laid all hope on the body's ability to adapt. They believed we would adjust within several generations. Records say fluid imbalances and stress on weaker hearts caused lots of deaths. We lost many elders in the first year. By the third generation of births, nature started to change my ancestors."

"Change? You look the same to me. Except a lot more attractive than normal."

Dreng tilted her head and smiled. "Our cells developed micro sacs to increase oxygen storage. Muscles became denser. Connective tissue became flexible and stronger. Greater oxygen levels in the blood caused an

110

increase in cerebral convolutions. The size of our heads didn't change, but there was an increase in cognitive abilities." She continued to talk for some time before she gave Mac a chance to ask questions.

His first question was about her. "Can you show me how strong you are?"

"Stand up." Dreng moved behind him, put her hands onto his hips, and lifted him above her head in one easy motion. Mac was staring at the ceiling. She set him back down on his feet. "Could any of your other girlfriends do that?"

Mac smiled, liking it that she considered herself his girlfriend. He got butterflies in his stomach thinking about what the words implied. *Yes, it would suit me fine.* "To be honest, I have never had a girlfriend."

Dreng made a face, as she looked him in the eye.

"I told you, I like women. I have been with women. It's I have never had the time to invest in a relationship."

"Mac, you have joined with me. Are you telling me it carried no deeper meaning to you than a physical feeling?"

"No, I'm not saying that at all. With you, it's the opposite. I love everything about you." *Oh no, I've done it now. I said love. Why did that come out of my mouth? Stupid, stupid, stupid! I find a girl who likes me, and I rush into a relationship. Everything I ever read said never ever tell a woman you love her after first sex.*

Mac was so busy fretting over saying he loved everything about her that he didn't see her approach. Her lips locked onto his as her arms embraced him, sending him to heaven once again. His heart was pounding so hard, he was afraid she could hear it. *So much for all the crap I had read about girls.*

Dreng released his lips, and stepped back. "Do you have any questions?"

111

"Yeah, I have a few. What you said explains a lot. But tell me why did you take a four-year consignment on Rayne?"

"It would seem the answer to your question is fate. I searched the databanks at Finder's Station. I came across a United Fleet Command recruiting video with you in it. Your story was interesting. Your looks appealed to me, so I hacked into a docked military battle cruiser. I read your military biography, which seemed sketchy at best. The deeper I dug, the better the story got. They were hiding something about you. When I found you would be going to Rayne as the senior NCO, I decided we needed to meet. Besides, you and I share a common problem."

"Your mean you signed up to meet me?"

"Yes, but in a way it was my father's doing."

"Your father wanted you to meet me? Come on now. That's hard to believe."

"It's true, but as I said, in a way."

"Sounds like what we in the military call weasel words. They're used when someone doesn't want to lie, but has to answer a question."

"Okay, I said I wouldn't lie, and I didn't." She smiled. "I used weasel words instead. Don't be a jerk. Quit digging. Yes, I did all this to meet you, and – a little more."

The last time I heard so many weasel words was during a court-martial.

"You should be more worried about our common problem than why I took a military consignment."

"Okay, I'll let you off the hook. I guess a girl can have a few secrets."

Dreng hugged him.

"Tell me about our common problem."

Dreng told Mac everything her people knew about the Raygin. It blew him away. The universe existing in rings shocked and intrigued him. She covered ship design and weapon systems. She described their bio computers, plasma rifles, body armor, and propulsion system. He learned about Raygin physiology all the way down to their soft web like brain tissue. It was one bombshell after another. It was too much to make up. It had to be the truth.

She described the Raygin in detail. She discussed how the People's Nation shared technology with the People of the Stars. How they infiltrated schools, businesses, and the military itself. Why? They did it to share their important discoveries with us and still stay isolated. They let their human cousins think they discovered the singularity drive, longevity drugs, weapons, and so much more. Mac did a quick verification of everything she said using joint databases on the ship.

Dreng was either a spy or was telling the truth. If she were a spy, she didn't have to come clean. She could have stayed under cover. She also passed on the opportunity to go to Fleet Officer Candidate School. It would be the best place for a spy. Where she was now, she wouldn't have access to secret information. He concluded again, she had to be telling the truth.

The conversation with Dreng filled in all the blanks. It even made sense, with the culprit being aliens. Mac decided he had to get a message to Fleet Command as soon as possible.

"Dreng, my people are walking into what could be an enemy forward operating base. I have to meet with the ship's captain and get him to drop a com probe. I have to warn Fleet Command."

"Sorry to be the bearer of bad news. The problem is too big. Our peoples are going to have to work together. Mac, can you do me a favor and don't tell the troops about me? I'd rather they not think of me at as an outsider. I'd like them to learn who I am before they judge me."

"Sounds like we are in the same boat. I have some confessions I have to make tomorrow."

"Should I be worried?" asked Dreng.

"No, it's nothing like that. I'll tell the troops tomorrow."

"Okay. You go make your notifications and I'll go back to my room. I'm looking forward to tomorrow."

Mac tried to get in contact with Lieutenant Phlop, but the lieutenant wouldn't answer his calls. He left him a message. Next, he contacted the ships administrative officer. He asked for an emergency meeting with the Argosy's captain and the governor. The admin officer explained the captain and governor were both busy with preparations for their arrival at Rayne.

Mac didn't want to flex his muscles. Not yet. Not until he spoke with his troops. He told the admin officer, "Did you hear me say I have an emergency? Can you at let him know it's why Master Sergeant McCormack is asking for the meeting right now?"

"I'll call the bridge, but don't hold your breath waiting for a meeting."

"Thank you. I'll wait on line," said Mac.

Three minutes later the admin officer came back on line. "Master Sergeant McCormack. The captain said to escort you to the private planning room on bridge level. He and the governor will be waiting for you. I have to tell you, you must have connections to pull this off. Please meet me at the ship's admin office."

The admin officer escorted Mac to the planning room. She stepped into the room to introduce him. The captain stood up, moved in front of Mac and shook his hand like they were old buddies.

"I've been hopping to shake your hand one day. I'm Captain Jake Tanner. We've met before. Do you remember me?"

The young admin officer turned around and left the conference room.

Mac smiled as he studied the captain's face. "I know who you are captain. We met on Titas, the large moon of Traykon."

"I wouldn't call it met. I'd call it you saved my life."

The governor looked at Mac with new interest.

"I was a young pilot on my first mission during the mining wars. I was brash and cocky. I got myself shot down by a better fighter pilot behind enemy lines. I survived the crash but was hurt bad. I couldn't remove myself from the cockpit. I was stuck until help arrived. I freaked out when a team of five mercs started to move in on me. It was well known mercs didn't take prisoners unless there was money in it for them. I wasn't worth anything. They were crossing an open field in front of me when I heard a buzz inches above my head. It was so close I felt the air as it dragged behind the projectile."

"The gun's nickname is a buzzard rifle because its projectile makes a buzz sound," said Mac. "I still use one when given the opportunity."

Captain Tanner laughed and patted Mac on the shoulder. "I thought the mercs had the worst shooters. Five shots at me, and I was still alive. I was so scared I was shaking. I looked up to see how close the foot soldiers were. All I saw was five dead mercs in the open field. An armored med vehicle picked me up only minutes later. The crew said a ghost called in my crash coordinates. I'd never heard of a ghost. They said a ghost is a crazy ass military sniper who operates behind enemy lines. I told them about the buzz sound I heard inches over my head. They laughed and told me the only one using a Buzzard was crazy ass Corporal McCormack. Thank you for saving me. Now, tell me how can we help you?"

After about fifteen minutes of talking, Captain Tanner agreed to launch a com probe for him. The governor sat with his arms folded. He had not said a word, up until this point.

"Are you proposing we not colonize Rayne? We have a presidential order. Do you want all the work to get us here wasted? I won't have it! If I understand what you are saying, you don't even have proof the Raygin exist. We are going down, with or without your protection."

Mac thought, *another politician willing to risk everyone's life to protect his empire*. "How about this? You put my three platoons on the ground. Monitor us while hiding behind a planet. Give us three days to snoop around, and if there are no signs of aliens bring all your people down. If aliens are here, or show up while we are on the planet, leave us, and get word back to the UFC."

The governor agreed to a three-day delay. He refused to tell the colonists the alien story without proof. To Mac, it sounded like Lieutenant Phlop may have already spoken to the governor. At least he didn't have his hand forced too early, thanks to the captain. He would have time to explain everything to his troops.

Mac created the message for United Fleet Command. True to his word, the captain launched the probe. Mac went back to his room and got a good night's rest.

The next day, he started the morning by briefing his troops. "We are already receiving data from Rayne. Today the temperature is 25 degrees Celsius, and the humidity is 45 percent."

The troops cheered. It was perfect weather for reconnaissance operations.

"Planetary orbit commences in nine standard hours. We will be the first humans on Rayne. Our job will be to take three days to scout the planet. We need to ensure it's safe for the colonists. We load the skiff today. Thirty minutes after planetary sunrise we leave for the planet's surface. Departure is at 0732 ship time."

The troops cheered again. They didn't understand the danger yet or they wouldn't be cheering. The Argosy was a big ship but after three months everyone couldn't wait to feel the pull of real gravity. There is nothing like the feeling of sunlight on your skin. The air on the ship is well filtered, but it would be nice to smell the aroma of a healthy planet.

"What I'm about to tell you is restricted information. Keep it to yourself."

The words got everyone's attention. Not the best start to the day, but he wanted his troops ready for what they might have to face. No surprises. The room became silent as everyone focused on his words.

"I know everyone has heard stories about the Nomad. The truth is, what we know of it has been kept a secret. It's a need to know basis. Now, you need to know. So, here's what happened. A commercial ship found one of Nomad's probes near a shipping route. The body was so plasma burned all we recovered was a partial message. 'Implementing evasive maneuvers' is all it said."

"Since Rayne is deep in uncharted space, the military thought it was a conspiracy carried out by the Priest Synod or a corporate consortium. There were some who thought it could be a secret group operating within our own government. They might be able to steal the plans for the new singularity drives. It might also be possible to have a secret group operating within the military to steal plasma cannons without anyone noticing."

A trooper voiced her concern to Mac. "Why are you telling us now? What information has changed? Did the UFC send us here knowing the risk?"

"I'm telling you now because I have learned more information. I have confirmation the threat is from hostile aliens who call themselves Raygin. I'm willing to bet they are operating somewhere out here in uncharted space. Before we left Trinity Prime, the UFC didn't understand the risk, as we know it now. They sent us here to protect the colonists, from other humans. Besides us, they sent two battle cruisers to protect everyone. The UFC war ships have been shadowing us all the way here."

"I didn't sign up to fight aliens," said a conscript.

"No, you didn't. But, remember what I told you earlier about luck? Right now yours is shitty. Let's see if we can change it."

"It's not fair," said the same conscript. "You've been in wars, battles, skirmishes, firefights, and who knows what else. You're comfortable with fighting. More than half of us have never had someone point a gun at us!"

"Everyone has to start somewhere," said Mac. "You had three months of holodeck training. I have made sure you're as ready as practicable within the time parameters we had. All of you are more ready than I was for my first skirmish. Each scenario you went through was something I experienced in my career. Dwain, remember what you told me after the Skulderon holodeck program ran? After the shooting broke out, you said your heart was racing. The program was based on what occurred on Darkmore."

"The same Darkmore the mining wars started on?" asked Dwain.

"Yep. It was my first firefight. I can still remember how my heart raced. The difference between your experience and mine is, I shit my pants. I didn't even know it until we climbed aboard the armored transport."

The classroom went up for grabs as everyone laughed at him. Troopers slapped each other as they pictured him running with his pants loaded with crap. He glanced at Dreng. She smiled at him, and wrinkled her nose. He assured them, other than experiencing a real firefight, they were as ready as they could be. To be a little afraid and apprehensive was okay.

"Now, let's get back to business. The aliens evolved from a form beetle with an appetite for meat. You can bet they think nothing like us. They evolved from a hive mentality, whereas humans evolved with independent thought. Without getting too into it, they come from an older location in the universe we didn't know existed. They have had more time to evolve and make scientific discoveries. The weapon systems on their ships are more advanced than ours. Their ships are faster, but their body armor is weaker than our new armor. Let's face it, we need to steal some of their technology. Until our technology catches up we are better off fighting on the ground than aboard a ship."

"The Nomad never made it to Rayne, so why do you think the aliens may be here?" asked another trooper.

"Put yourselves in a bug's exoskeleton," said Mac, drawing a laugh from everyone. "What do you have to have if you are going to start a war?"

The troops started yelling out answers. Mac heard, "ships", "weapons", "trained personnel", and "supplies".

"You are all right. I am afraid Rayne may be a supply planet. Don't forget, their technology is a little more advanced than ours. If I were in command of a war fleet, and could have an ideal situation, I would get my food supplies from local areas. Supply lines are dangerous. The enemy can break them or trace them backwards and destroy a war effort."

"Humph, this is unbelievable. Now we have a sergeant who thinks he is commanding a war fleet," said Dwain. "I thought you said the Raygin are carnivorous? Isn't Rayne full of fruits and vegetables?"

"Raygin evolved from beetles. The bugs we know are omnivorous and like vegetables and meat. Like humans, I am willing to bet their palate didn't change as they developed."

"So, Mac, the question becomes what are we going to do?" asked Tinker.

"Our primary job is to protect the colonists. The first order of…"

The door to the classroom smashed open with a loud bang and interrupted Mac's discussion with the troops. Lieutenant Junior Grade Phlop stood all red faced. His body shook with anger as he pointed his finger at Mac. He squinted his eyes at him, "What have you done, you crazy son of a bitch? You went over my head, and made a fool of me with your crazy speculations about aliens. You're removed from the position of senior NCO. I don't care what you say. I'm still the ranking officer. Do you understand me? Now get out of my sight."

Mac looked at the lieutenant, took a calming breath and turned around. He reached into his ready bag, and took out an official looking envelope. "I didn't want it to happen like this, but you forced my hand." Mac walked over to Lieutenant Phlop, and held out a document with Vice Admiral Michael Farragut's seal on it. The lieutenant snatched the envelope out of Mac's hands. To: First Lieutenant Junior Grade Theodore Phlop. It indicated it was from: The Office of Vice Admiral Farragut, United Fleet Command.

The lieutenant broke the seal, opened the courier envelope, and pulled out a letter. He began to read as everyone watched in silence.

CHAPTER SEVEN: Imperial Station

On the trip's sixth day the convoy experienced a problem. A battle cruiser developed a drive synchronization glitch. The convoy stopped to let the engineers fix the problem. During the down time, Mahpee demonstrated the weapon systems on the Wasp. He used a few nearby asteroids for target practice. The admiral couldn't believe the tiny ship's firepower.

Mahpee asked if he would like the Wasp's engineer to work with the Constellation's engineering staff to modify her weapons systems. Although against fleet regulations the admiral accepted the offer. Gynn Roads, the Constellation's chief engineer, worked with Nashta. It was the first official agreement to share technologies between the two peoples.

The engineers repaired the drive, and the convoy was back on its way. For weeks there was no news from Imperial Station. Everyone understood the threat, so upgrades occurred at a feverish pace.

The speed with which the ships could make major modifications amazed Nashta. They were so well equipped they didn't need a shipyard for the minor refits. But even with all their capabilities, they couldn't incorporate the more complex structural enhancements. Those and the miniature circuitry for the tracking systems would have to wait. Nashta sent upgrade designs to the engineering staff of each ship in the convoy. He helped the Constellation first.

The engineers were working with the Wasp's crew on the battleship's new plasma canon.

"Nashta," said Gynn. "I noticed your whole crew is wearing the same leather outfit. Is it a uniform, or some kind of popular clothing on your home world?"

Nashta almost choked on the sweet cube he was sucking on. Ignoring the question, he said, "Do you have a sharp knife? I need to cut this joiner line."

Gynn grabbed her knife and held it out to Nashta.

"Can you hold the knife while I run the wire across the blade?"

"Yeah, but I have a joiner cutter. Let me get it," said Gynn.

"Nah, it's okay, this will only take a second."

While Gynn held the knife, Nashta ran the joiner line across the blade with a lot of downward pressure. Gynn had to plant her feet to hold the blade steady. Nashta slipped the joiner off the blade, causing Gynn to stab him with a solid upward thrust to his chest. With a groan, Nashta fell to the ground face first.

"No", echoed off the metal walls. Gynn raced to flip Nashta over onto his back so she could see the wound. Smiling at her was the happy face of Nashta, still sucking on his sweet cube.

"The leather looking suit is not made to make me look handsome. It's a pliable armor suit using nano technology we developed."

Gynn released a deep breath and said, "You asshole! Why couldn't you just tell me? I can't believe you're in the military."

"Please, don't be mad at me. We are not so formal as you are. My people value a sense of humor."

"You mean all your people are like you?"

"Oh no. Of course not."

"Thank God."

"I am considered much too serious on Nokomis. It is a reason why my people chose me to go to your schools."

Nashta finished the joiner splice. With his peripheral vision, he could see Gynn smack her head with her hand. He chuckled to himself, knowing she couldn't tell if he was serious or kidding.

"We have already supplied the method of creating nano bots to your military. We also gave them a schematic for armor suits. I suppose it may be years until you see them created for field use. I can send you the schematics and design layout if you'd like. You might be able to create them on the ship."

"Yes, it would be helpful. I feel bad because so far all we have done is take. I don't know how we can ever repay you."

"We share an ancestry, at least, at one point in our past. Besides, we have found a method of compensation…"

A wavering alarm sounded on the Constellation's Internal Com system. It was a call to staff battle stations. All personnel had to report to their pre-assigned positions for battle readiness. Weapon systems would be charged and the new shields would be at full strength. General quarters meant the ship was entering a dangerous situation.

"Nashta, I have to report to engineering. You better go to the Wasp," said Gynn.

*****

Mahpee stood on the Constellation's bridge. He watched as the magnified remains of Imperial Station came into view. Large segments of unrecognizable structures floated in space. He could see tens of thousands of bodies drifting within the debris field. The ship's crew locked the viewer onto the lone surviving gravity wheel. The admiral deployed transport skiffs to search for survivors. This was senseless butchery. He ordered the cruisers to look for any trail left by the enemy. Parts of Imperial Station were still under construction. It had a human population of about sixty thousand.

Within minutes a skiff arrived at the lone gravity wheel. After flying around the wheel, they chose the best spot to anchor the transport shuttle. They began to burn through the ring's hull to allow the search team access to the passageway. The convoy watched the search and rescue on vid transmissions. Once inside, the team found hundreds of stiff, bloated, floating bodies. The search party split up into two groups. They began a systematic search in opposite directions.

It was odd. The cameras showed a few bodies floating in the passageways were wearing spacesuits. It meant a few people survived the initial assault. The chief wondered, *Why would they be in the hallway?* He watched a crewmember check the electronics on a dead person's spacesuit. The display indicated the users depleted their oxygen weeks ago.

Commander Tark, the search party's lead officer said, "Alright, everyone look hard. These people in spacesuits died long after the attack, not during it. I'm sure they gave their lives for a reason. Let's find out what they were up to."

The Constellation's bridge crew monitored the search parties. Everyone watched as they made their way through the ship. They could see the view from each team member's vid cam.

"Commander Tark, this is team two. We found something. A weld is on the outside the pool door."

"Commander Tark, this is Admiral Harding. A skiff pilot reported she is getting a strong electrical reading near your location. The engineers tell me there is no power supply they can find in the station's schematics. Nothing justifies the electrical signal we are receiving."

"Thanks admiral. We will proceed with caution. Mari, bring the sound transducer and place it on this welded door."

Mari plugged the instrument into her helmet. She placed the tiny transducer against the door. She shifted the component around, and she heard: "Mark, I know heard something." It was the high pitch of a child's voice.

"Alright, alright. Everyone, stay still and shut up for once," said a different voice.

It sounded like someone in control. BANG, BANG, BANG. Everyone on the bridge jumped. Mahpee was sure the noise must have broken Mari's eardrum. The screen showed her hands scrambling to turn down the signal strength.

"Someone, get me a pipe or piece of metal, hurry."

A crewmember handed her a metal bar. Mari banged the bar against the door. BANG, BANG, BANG, BANG. She listened again, but this time with the self-adjusting volume turned on.

She heard, "See, I told you."

"Good boy, you were right Teddy. I hit three times and someone responded with four. If it were the bugs, they would have gotten us by now. Everyone, this is important, be quiet." Mark hit the metal pipes. He banged three times in a quick string followed by three bangs with a two second interval between strikes. He ended with final three bangs in rapid succession.

Mari clapped her hands, "SOS, he banged out SOS. They are using the old Morse code. Computer, what is Morse code for 'help comes'?" A series of dots and dashes appeared on Mari's faceplate. She pounded out the sequence, and listened.

"It's help, everyone. Help is here."

Mari heard what sounded like a whole bunch of kids cheering.

"Admiral, this is Commander Tark. We are going to set up an air interlock, so we can burn the weld holding the door. It will keep the oxygen in the room when the door opens. It may take a while, but we can do it."

"Admiral," said Mahpee, "we have a chemical plasma welder on the Wasp. We designed it from Raygin technology. It can burn through all of our metals in seconds. You're welcome to use it."

"Did you hear that commander?"

"Yes sir, send it over. By the time you get it here, we'll have a make shift air interlock built."

While team two built an interlock onto the pool door, team one proceeded with its search around the wheel. Most compartments had plasma holes in the exterior walls as big as a Catari fishing trawler. It was a miracle the wheel had stayed intact. A skiff arrived and piggybacked onto the search party's transport ship. A crewman arrived carrying the new cutting tool.

"I hope you know how to use it," said Commander Tark, "because I don't."

Nashta read the name on the commander's chest label. "Hello commander Tark. I am Nashta, from the People's Nation. I am a Wasp crewmember. I helped design this cutter, but I never used it in zero gravity. This chemical reaction generates a lot of heat and sparks. I have a shield for the cutter, but I'd like someone watching me over my shoulder. All I ask is you make sure I don't burn a hole in my suit. My chief would kill me."

Everyone laughed, except Nashta. It got quiet when the Constellation's search and rescue team didn't hear Nashta laugh. They thought it was a joke. The chief smiled. *Nashta played them like people sitting in the front row of a comedy club. Clever, he let them stew for a few seconds, thinking he may have been serious.*

Nashta started laughing. "I'm kidding, lighten up. The chief doesn't care, but it is my favorite suit."

The commander smiled, and shook his head. He pointed to the door. The team members closed themselves inside the interlock. They left their helmets on in case something went wrong with the cutter. Nashta started the plasma cutter, placed the tip onto the new weld, and started the chemical flow. Sparks flew, like he said they would.

In thirty seconds the cutter broke through the weld. The team sniffed the gas levels from inside the room with their high tech equipment. It was 78 percent nitrogen, 21 percent oxygen, and one percent other gasses. Perfect. The search party put the temporary interlock door into place. The helmets came off, and everyone walked into the pool area.

The bridge watched twenty-one children cheer when they saw the human adults. The children ran to get hugs from their human rescuers.

Mari walked up to the boy holding a pipe. "Are you Mark?"

"Yeah, how'd you know?"

"We used a sound transducer to hear inside the welded door. We could hear you directing activities. Using Morse code was smart of you."

"Since I'm the oldest child, the parents put me in charge when the bugs attacked. My dad is a fighter pilot in the Fleet Command. He taught me survival techniques as I grew up, so I knew Morse code."

Nashta walked up to Mari and Mark and said, "Why didn't the bugs come in and get you?"

"We don't understand what stopped them from coming into the pool area. Every time they opened the door, they'd act goofy, like they were drunk. They always turned around, made loud clicking noises, and left."

"How did you survive without air?" Asked Nashta.

"After the bugs blew up the station, a few adults in spacesuits found us in the pool area. The pool has its own batteries to maintain a graviton field. They used spare batteries to set up a powered oxygen generator using pool water. They created what they called an air scrubbing system." Mark started crying. "The air kept leaking out the door. They couldn't weld from inside without creating poisonous gases. They had to weld the door from the outside. They sealed us in and them out."

Mari grabbed Mark and hugged him. "What they did was brave. They saved all of your lives."

"I'm going to get even with those bugs. I'll kill them, I'll kill everyone of them."

Mari didn't know how to respond to Mark's anger. She let him vent until he started to slow down. "Mark, what the bugs did is horrible. We aren't going to let them get away with this, but for now we need to focus on helping the children. Okay?"

"Yeah, right. I need to make sure the kids are safe. It's my job."

The UFC ships sent their smallest space suits to the search team. The children needed them to move from the poolroom to a transport skiff. The children were comfortable with Mark, so Mari let him help suit them up. In the meantime the engineers sampled everything. They wanted to know what kept the bugs from entering the swimming pool area. The crew took lots of poolroom vids. Mahpee hoped the answer could be a game changer in a war with the bugs.

Federation ships of war have limited accommodations for children. The admiral decided to send a cruiser to drop the children off at Finder's Station. They would also initiate notification of next of kin. The children would be transported to a safe location. The admiral had two children himself and told Mahpee he wanted to ensure these kids were well taken care of.

With Mahpee's approval the cruiser would carry some vids back to the United Federation of Planets. They would see the shipyards at Orenda and the Peoples Nation ships of war. The Admiral also included schematics and specs of new technologies. Once everyone saw the devastation at Imperial Station and the thousands of dead bodies floating in space, the wheels of war would begin to turn. He hoped the humans were up for it.

The children's rescue took six standard hours. During the evolution the computer analyzed the number of bodies in space and determined thousands were still unaccounted for. The cruiser found traces of six alien ships, but could not tell where they went. Mahpee volunteered the use of his new technology onboard the Wasp. His engineers found clear disturbance paths in the gravitational fields of space left by all six alien ships.

The Wasp had to search for the alien trail each time they completed a jump. Most ships travel in a geodesic line. In curved space it is the shortest distance between two points. This made hunting the Raygin ships a little easier. Computers always picked a route with the least changes in direction unless evasive maneuvers are implemented.

The Wasp led the convoy because of her advanced tracking capabilities. Bodaway dictated the jump timing, direction, and inclination. Mahpee rode on the Wasp in the hopes he would be the first to engage the Raygin. He still owed them for what they had taken from him. After days of jumping, the computer was taking an abnormal amount of time in locating the alien trail.

"Mahpee, the computer says the alien ships split up here. Five stuck together on the same direction. One split off going a new direction," said Bodaway. "What do you want to do?"

"Let me check with the admiral. My gut says follow the single ship."

"Com, open a line to the Constellation."

"Go ahead Mahpee, the line's open."

"Constellation, this is Mahpee. The Raygin have split up. Five ships are continuing in the original direction. The sixth is heading somewhere else. I'd like to follow the single ship. We sent you the tracking data, ask the Admiral what he'd like to do."

"Mahpee, Admiral Harding here. I have some limited star charts for the area we are in. Based on your computer projection the lone ship is heading towards Rayne. Let's follow the single ship."

"Okay admiral, let's catch some bugs."

"If we can't catch them, we need to exterminate them."

"I'm with you. I have an old score to settle. Admiral, can you send the star charts you have of this area?"

"I'll have them to you in a moment."

Mahpee thought about the new computer system installed on the Constellation. The admiral told him Fleet Command put their newest combat computer in his ship. They isolated it from the ship's main computer. Every femtosecond of calculation goes toward engagement strategies, maneuvers, and firing sequences. It seemed like a clever idea. Mahpee decided he would talk to the university about the idea.

The People's Nation enhanced their systems too. According to Mongwau they were on the verge of another huge break through. The problem was the convoy needed computing speed now. *I hope the Constellation's computer is a match for the alien bio based computer system the university seemed to love so much.*

After the star charts arrived, they got underway again. Mahpee excused himself from the bridge. He wanted to take a closer look at what the admiral sent. He was sure there was going to be a battle, and he wanted to be ready. He walked down the main passageway toward midship. He could hear the singularity drive in the engineering compartment. Mahpee counted off seven seconds between pops. Instead of turning into the small conference room he decided to make sure Nashta was ready.

Engineering was the last compartment in the ship. When Mahpee arrived he caught the tail end of a conversation. "... I don't understand. What do you mean not efficient?"

Mahpee stuck his head through the door to see whom Nashta was conversing with. He looked left, and right, no one was in engineering other than Nashta. Worried about his young chief engineer Mahpee said, "Nashta. Is everything okay?"

"I don't know."

"What do you mean, you don't know? What's wrong?"

"I was running some tests to ensure everything is operating at peak performance. When I ran my computer system diagnostic, the artificial intelligence said the computer is not efficient. Enhancement underway."

"Good job, Nashta," said Mahpee.

"You don't understand. I was using direct input, not voice mode. It talked to me. It should not have been able to use voice mode. It is improving the computer without my direction. Something's wrong, and right now I have no idea what. I don't even know what it's changing or doing to improve the computer! I need time to figure this out."

"Whether the computer is working or not, we will be in the battle. Make sure we're ready."

Nashta shrugged his shoulders. "I can't. I don't know what the computer is doing. If we go into battle without the computer we all need to prepare our death songs."

CHAPTER EIGHT: The Vents

Spaz entered the opening first. He jumped up grabbed the vent's edge and hoisted himself into the ventilation shaft. The fit was tight, but there was enough room for them to crawl on their hands and knees, one behind the other. He figured by leading the way, he would have the advantage of seeing possible danger first.

Spaz could see Tews frown as he looked at the distance from the floor to the opening.

"Come on Tews, I have a date later."

Tews jumped up, grabbed the vent, and tried to pull himself up. Smitty watched the entomologist's feet kick for a few seconds and decided to give him a boost. Tews's thin arms didn't have enough strength to jerk his frame into the vent. Smitty positioned himself between Tews's legs and pushed upward.

"Phrrrrrt"

"What the fuck," said Smitty, "You farted on my head! I should have let you dangle there."

Spaz started laughing so hard tears came out of his eyes. In return Smitty squinted at him.

"Sorry Smitty, I didn't do it on purpose. The bugs are giving us some kind of milk mix in our food. I'm lactose intolerant, and I don't have my meds."

"I'm glad I'm in front," said Spaz, "or it would be a long day."

Now it was Smitty's turn to laugh. "Spaz, you poor bastard. The vent you're in is an exhaust line. When Tews shits his pants, the smell will follow you, the whole way.

I'll have the captain put you in for a medal. Now get going."

Awe great. "Hey Tews, will your farts attract the bugs?"

"You're confusing Carrion beetles with Dung beetles. Carrions will stay away from feces. I suppose it could be good news for us."

"Enough fart and shit talk. Get going before I climb up there and get you moving myself," said Smitty.

Spaz turned on the light stick hanging around his neck. The duo started inching their way through the vent. They kept turning around to see their vent getting smaller and smaller. When they could no longer see it, they heard Smitty put the vent cover back in place.

After several minutes, Tews stopped. "Spaz, my legs are beginning to cramp. I need to stop for a few minutes."

"Don't worry, it's normal. I cramp up too if I exercise too much. When you feel a leg cramp coming on, stop, sit down, grab your feet and stretch your leg. It should go away in a minute or two. The more we move through the vent system, the sooner your unused muscles will adjust."

"Yeah, you're right. I haven't exercised for a decade. I sit all day researching, so I'm sure my muscles have atrophied." Tews worked on his muscles, stretching his legs and pulling on his feet as the two talked. "You know, Carrion beetles like to tunnel underground. It makes sense they use tunnel designs in their everyday lives. It's an efficient use of space. A ship constructed of tunnels and chambers provides greater structural strength."

"So, you're saying these bugs are smarter than us?" asked Spaz.

"No, I'm saying it depends. If they have been around longer than us, that's good news."

"Why? What difference would it make?"

"If humans and the bugs evolved during the same time period, it would tell me the bugs are smarter than us. If

133

they evolved millions of years before us, it would mean we are smarter than they are. At this moment in time, their technology is a little more advanced than ours, so it would give them an edge in a war. We have to discover a weakness, have a breakthrough in our own technology, or steal their science."

"What about the large number of warships we have throughout the universe?"

"I hate to ruin your hope, but Carrion beetles are like roaches. If you see a few of them, there are always thousands more. The bug populations have always outnumbered human populations throughout our evolution."

"Crap, Tews, you're full of good news aren't you? Now I'm depressed."

"Don't be, the way I see it, we are much like the bugs in this ship. They are taking advantage of our weaknesses and we are looking for weaknesses in the bugs to exploit. Along the way we can try to steal anything we can. Bugs and humans evolved along different paths. I'm sure we will each have technology the other species did not think about developing."

"Now you're talking buddy. Let's steal their technology. Hell, let's think big. We can steal their whole fucking ship! Come on, let's get going."

If not for the light sticks, traveling through the dark vents would have been impossible. Spaz saw the first fork coming up. One path continued on the same level and the other took a gradual slope downward. Spaz took his homemade marker out and drew a horizontal line with a descending arrow on the joining wall.

"Look Tews, here's how I'll label the passageways. I'll identify the direction we travel with a line and on the joining wall I'll put an arrow, like this." Spaz drew a horizontal line connected to a descending line with an arrow. Behind the horizontal line, he wrote the letters HP.

"To get back to our holding pen, reverse the arrow. In case we get separated, we can each follow the directions as we diagram the ship."

Tews shook his head at the notion of being alone in the vent system. "If it weren't for you I'd be fighting my fear every second. Do me a favor, never get separated from me."

"Let me tell you something a soldier once told me. He said fear is not real."

"The person who told you that is a liar," said Tews.

"Let me finish jackass. He said fear is something you create with your thoughts. It's a choice you make. The danger is real, but not the fear."

"Spaz, your full of crap, but thanks for trying. Do me a favor. Don't get separated from me. That's what will help me the most."

Spaz gave up on trying to help Tews's accept his fears. The two explorers continued to crawl in silence until they came upon a passageway. It led to what appeared to be a storage room. They were both silent while they checked for any sign of occupancy. After several minutes of surveillance, they agreed, the room was empty. Spaz bypassed the alarm wire, pushed the magnetic vent cover out, and pulled it back into the vent setting it aside.

Spaz slid into the room first and helped Tews down from the vent. The room contained twenty cargo boxes. Each box had color markings and unfamiliar writing on the top and side.

Spaz whistled. "Look at the wall behind the boxes. We're in a mini armory. We have these on our ships. Look there," Spaz pointed, "the racks are missing four rifles, it could mean– "

Spaz stopped talking as the door opened and a bug walked in carrying two rifles. Tews froze in fear. The bug's body jerked in surprise when it saw him standing in front of it. It let off an acid smell. Spaz figured it was a warning for other bugs, so he kicked the door shut. The bug dropped one rifle as it tried to raise the other one. Spaz jumped on its back and tried to strangle it before it could shoot Tews.

The bug dropped the second rifle, and used its forearm to club Spaz on the head. The bug looked at Spaz. He was groggy and couldn't move. For the moment he no longer posed a threat. The bug turned and started moving toward Tews. Spaz watched as he tried in vain to get his own legs to move.

Tews started to move backwards. He reached for the aspirator located in his carry bag. In his haste, he tripped over his own feet and fell on his back. The big bug wasted no time. It moved over him, and raised its arm to deliver a fatal blow. Spaz heard a familiar sound.

Phrrrrrt.

Tews farted. Smelling the vaporous odor, the big bug froze. Its arm was high in the air ready to strike. The confusion gave Spaz the time he needed to jump on its back while pulling out his needle gun. He fired two shots into the big hump part of its neck. The bug dropped with a thud. It died staring at the face of Tews.

Spaz started laughing.

A stunned Tews, still shaken said, "What happened?"

Spaz was laughing so hard he had trouble breathing. He managed to spit out, "Your fart killed it!"

"Get out of here, you're lying."

"Oh yeah, wait till Smitty hears about this. He knows first hand how bad your farts can be. Why, I'll bet you get a medal for being the first person to kill a bug with their ass!"

"You're a funny man. Now get serious. I need to know, what happened to the bug?"

Spaz showed Tews his needle gun. "I put two darts in its – what did you call that big hump? Its thorax."

"Yeah, the thorax. I can't believe two tiny darts killed a big bug."

Those two tiny darts release six prongs in sequence after impact. It causes a corkscrew effect as it opens. The dart leaves behind a four-inch hole. With two darts, I figured I'd hit at least one vital organ. It's good I wasn't too far away. These guns are designed for short range use."

"Nice work. You saved my life."

"The way I figure it, your fart saved your own life."

"You aren't going to let this go are you Spaz?"

"Nope."

"Come on, let's grab some guns and get out of here."

"It's no use to take them, remember? They won't work."

"I have an idea, give me a minute." Tews grabbed his homemade knife, fabricated by the engineers. He stuck the bug with it, and obtained a smudge of blood. "Hand me a gun." Tews took the gun and placed his now bloodied finger in the claw hole but nothing happened. "Crap, I was sure this would work. Wait, I have one more idea. Do you have the yellow marker Ruth made for us? It has phosphor in it."

Spaz handed the marker to Tews. He watched as Tews smeared the marker all over various places on the rifle. This time when Tews slide his bloodied finger into the claw hole, they both saw a weak light.

"I'll be damned," said Spaz, "how did you know to do that?"

"I remembered learning a lot bugs can see light in the ultraviolet (uv) range. By using the phosphor marker, the uv light gets absorbed by phosphor material. In turn, it gives off light in the 400 nanometer range making it visible to most human eyes."

"It's like I said, you're the brains, and I'm everything else."

"Yeah, but let me ask you this Spaz, who killed a fricking bug? Bad ass you, or chicken shit me."

"Touché Tews. Well played."

The two looked at each other and began to laugh. Tews squeezed bug blood into a container, so they could operate the stolen bug rifles later.

Spaz walked over to a crate and opened it. "Holy crap, look what I found! We hit the jackpot, it's loaded with plasma rifles." They both started to look inside the other containers. Each box contained twenty-two new plasma rifles.

"Looks like they're ready for some kind of ground fight," said Tews.

"This is great," said Spaz. He looked up at Tews to see a shocked look on his face. "No. I mean it's not great their ready for ground fighting. It's great we found all these guns here. If we took guns from the rack, I was afraid they would notice right away. Now, we put these two guns back in the rack and steal the rifles from the containers instead. I say we put the big ass bug into an empty box. With any luck, we will be long gone by the time they find it."

They set a bunch of guns near the vent and crammed the dead bug into a box.

"This place is making me nervous. Let's get moving," said Tews.

"You're right. We still have a lot of exploring to do. Climb into the vent, and I'll hand some rifles up."

"Spaz, I can drag no more than two rifles at a time."

"I know. It's all right. I'm limited to carrying about four while crawling in the vents. We do like the military does it. We stage a bunch of rifles somewhere we can pick up later. We can get them all up in the vent for now. Afterwards we will move the guns out of sight, and finish exploring the ship. When we go back to the pen, we can send people to pick up the rifles."

"Okay, good idea. Hey Spaz."

"What."

"I want you to know, you're more than muscle to me. You are an intricate part of our team."

Spaz grinned. "You're sucking up to me so I don't tell Smitty you killed a bug with your fart, aren't you?"

"Yes."

The ventilation duo moved forty-four rifles into the vent ducts. They placed them in a location where they were out of site, but retrievable. Spaz took the lead again, and started crawling down the same passageway.

After about five minutes of crawling, Spaz could see the light coming from another vent ahead. He turned to Tews and pointed his finger in the direction from which the light was reflecting. As the two made their way to the vent in silence, they could hear a commotion coming through the vent cover. The two peered though the slats in the cover to see what they had found. It was the galley, the ship's kitchen.

Bugs moved in and out of what appeared to be a series of storage units. They placed what looked like decaying vegetables and meat into clear containers. The scene below looked like a restaurant preparing food for customers. But, the bugs weren't scurrying inside the walls; they were doing the food preparations. The bug in charge reached its scaled fingers into the tray and pulled out a large piece of decaying meat. It held the flesh up near its mouth, and snatched it with its mandibles. The bug gripped the large piece of meat and ripped it in two and forced both pieces into its mouth. It chewed a little bit and swallowed.

The bug eating the meat started clicking and hissing. In a flurry of activity dozens of bugs grabbed the prepared trays and left the kitchen. The few bugs left kept preparing the food. Spaz had seen enough and moved back into the vent shaft. Tews watched the bugs for several more minutes.

He too crawled back into the main passageway. "Gross."

"Yeah, I agree, it sucked. I can still remember being a junior trooper and having galley duty. Once you've worked in a galley, you never want to eat another ship's meal. Come on, we have to keep going and look for things we can use."

After seeing the galley, Tews changed, he got quiet. Spaz gave him time to collect his thoughts. He wondered if he was struggling with his younger brother being eaten by the black bugs.

"Look at this Tews. It's some kind of fire suppression system. Must be something important ahead."

The two kept crawling and within minutes they began to hear bug hissing, clicking, and a range of smells. They removed their glow lights and scooted up to the vent cover. There were bugs moving every which way in the large room. Next to each walkway there were walls with what appeared to be dark holes carved into them.

As the two humans watched the activities, they could see the bugs crawling out of holes in the wall. They clicked and hissed at each other, and let off various odors. Some smells pleasing, and some not. Spaz knew from his own experience on various ships they were looking at a berthing area.

He decided they saw all they could see here. It was time to move on. He hand signaled to Tews, and the two started making their way through the passageway once again. Spaz reached the final vent cover situated at the shaft's end. He peeked into the room. It contained one hole in the wall, a display case, a table, and a body armor suit hanging from the wall. It had a red insignia on it. This room must belong to the captain. In the display he could see: a fleet rifle, a plasma burned helmet, and the cleaned skull of a human. There were also several pieces of scrap metal and over it all a screen playing a looped video of Imperial Station firing her defensive guns. The son of a bitch had a victory case!

Spaz was pissed. Tews touched his shoulder and motioned to move on. Spaz shook his head in the affirmative and led the way back to where the passageway split. They made several trips placing the plasma rifles in the main vent for retrieval later. Spaz finished up by writing on the wall: Armory, Galley, Berthing Area, Bug Captain's Berth.

"Okay Tews. Let's go this way now."

"Spaz, something is bothering me about the bugs."

"Me too. The more I learn about them the more I hate them."

"No, I mean there's something strange. The bugs we are familiar with have tiny little brains. Yet, they are able to recognize and remember different humans. They can even count, remember shapes, recognize danger, and much more."

"So what's your problem?"

"These beetles have evolved larger bodies with proportionate heads. I don't know if the brain size has anything to do with their intelligence. I'm sure their thought processes are different than ours. My problem is since bug ships are more advanced than human ships I expected to see more advanced technology throughout the ship. The only place I have seen or heard about their advanced technology is the ship's propulsion, shields, and weapon systems. It doesn't fit."

"You know Tews, you're right. Something was bothering me too. I couldn't put my finger on it until you said it. The way they pen us, the lack of security, the lack of personnel screening, the bug's crummy berthing quarters, the cheesy vent shafts, even their actions don't show great intelligence. We need to talk about this when we get back, but for now, let's finish exploring."

Tews stretched his legs a little more before they continued creeping along on their hands and knees inside the vent shaft. It wasn't long before they came upon another split.

"Want to go straight, or to the right?" asked Spaz.

"Let's go right. Give me a minute, my legs are killing me."

Spaz watched Tews rub his legs. He evaluated the entomologist's fragile physical condition. His friend was pouring sweat, stretching his legs, rubbing his knees, and arching his back. The hunched over crawl was taking its toll. Even his breathing seemed a little more labored. He's on his last legs, its time to give him a mental bone.

"Hey Tews. How about we do two or three more stops, and call it a day."

"Thank God. I didn't want to say anything, but I don't think I have much more energy left in me. I'm not use to all this physical activity."

He grinned and gave Tews some encouragement. "You did good."

Spaz grabbed the marker and drew a line attached to an arrow on the joining wall. They started their trek again. After several minutes of crawling they both began to hear the repeated pop from the alien singularity drive. The alien engineering department had to be ahead. From the next vent, the two humans peered into the engine room. It looked strange compared to human standards.

Spaz whispered in Tews's ear, "Fuck. Look. No wonder their ships are faster. They have two drives in tandem."

"Look at those bugs injecting green goo into that piece of equipment. I have no idea what they are doing. If I had to guess, I'd say it keeps all the equipment running. See, those small lines are attached to everything, including the two drives," said Tews.

"Look over by the wall. I'll bet that's their shield generator. See how big those lines are going into them? They need a lot of power, and the conduits to them come out of each drive. It could be why their shields are stronger than ours. They have more power going to them. We have to get Smitty in here to look at this set-up. Come on Tews, let's get out of here."

The engineering passageway was a dead end. The two started crawling back to the main vent when Tews stopped. Spaz didn't have to ask why. The symptoms spoke for themselves: frequent stops, he talked less, had a headache, and a feeling of weakness. Tews was on the verge of exhaustion. He watched his friend go through his ritual. He rubbed his calves, stretched his legs, arched his back, and massaged his neck. He sat without saying a word while he tried to find more strength. He felt bad for Tews, but if they wanted their freedom, he had to keep moving. A lot of people were counting on them.

Tews broke the silence. "You know, this ship is huge, but we haven't seen as many spaces as we should have by now. There must be other vents isolated from ours".

Spaz felt surprised. His friend never seemed to stop thinking. "You may be right. There have been a couple long lengths of vent shaft between rooms. Makes you wonder what else this ship is carrying. If that's true, how do you suggest we explore the entire ship?"

"You don't want to know, but I'll tell you anyway. We would have to go out a vent, and into a room. Next, we would have to leave the room and travel perpendicular to the passageway, find another vent and remove the cover. Hop in and begin exploring again. We'd have to do it all over again to get back to the pen."

"I have to tell you, I'm not a fan of your idea."

"I'd calculate our success at less than ten percent."

"We have to find another way to explore the ship because that's not going to happen," said Spaz.

"If we could take over and hold engineering, our chances of success increase to about thirty percent."

"What if we poison the crew before we take control of engineering?" asked Spaz.

"That is a great idea. I would guess our chances of success increase to about forty percent."

"One more question. If you round forty to the nearest increment of fifty what would that be?"

"Fifty, I know you're not that stupid. What are you getting at?"

"I'll tell you what I'm getting at. Stupid me just increased our odds of success to fifty percent, and I can live with fifty-fifty odds."

Tews shook his head. "Come on. Let's get going."

"Do you want to go back to the holding pen?" asked Spaz, hoping Tews would continue on instead. He didn't mind the rest stops, but their lives were at stake. They needed the intelligence. He crossed his fingers, hoping Tews would push on.

"Man, I'd like nothing more than to go back. My head's pounding, my body aches, and I have sweat so much I'm starting to smell like you."

"Be careful, my musky smell is what attracts the females."

Tews burst out laughing. "Yeah, maybe female dung beetles."

Spaz started crawling towards Tews. When he was close enough, he grabbed his head, and started pulling it towards his armpit.

"Stop. Stop it. You win. I'll keep going, you little rat bastard."

Spaz released Tews, smiled, and said, "What made you change your mind?"

"If I'm going to pass out, it may as well be on my terms, not yours."

"Come on buddy. Let's go find a way to kill more bugs."

Spaz held out his fist. Tews smiled and gave him an exploding fist bump. They started to crawl again. When they got to the main vent, Spaz labeled the arrow on the wall with the word engineering. The glow sticks still put out a decent amount of light, but not enough to see down the long main corridor.

In time, they came upon another T.

"Which way Tews?"

"Let's go left."

"Okay, but I have a bad feeling about your choice."

"So we go right instead."

Spaz grinned at Tews. "Okay, but I have a bad feeling about that way too."

Tews couldn't help but laugh. "Did I ever tell you my parents wanted me to study psychology? This caused a great conflict within me, because I wanted to focus on bugs. My solution was to study both fields at the same time. In the end my parents accepted my love of entomology. Why is this important you might ask? I recognize crazy when I see it. I also know you're trying to distract me from my physical pain with what you perceive to be witty wordplay. You must have learned a few simple medical tricks in military field training."

"You know Tews, a simple thank you, would have been fine. Did it work?"

Tews stretched his back and rubbed his neck. "I'll be darn. My headache is gone." He smiled at Spaz as he patted him on the shoulder. "Thank you."

The two friends kept crawling. The length of vent seemed to go on forever. Spaz passed an isolation point in the air moving system. Something important was ahead again. He stopped to let his partner catch up. "Do you want to rest?"

Tews stopped and sat in silence for a moment. "Can you hear the clicking? It's bugs. They're talking to each other."

"I can't hear shit."

"Let's keep going. I want to see what they're up to," said Tews.

Spaz stopped crawling when he came upon a small cavity offset from the main vent. He stuck his head into the dark tiny room. It seemed loaded with high tech electronic equipment. "Look at this. It's some kind of transmitter and receiver. It's hard wired and has a back up power supply. What's it doing in a vent?"

"Its placement had to occur during the ship's construction. Someone wanted to hide the equipment. There has to be hundreds of locations better suited to place this antenna system," said Tews.

"Do you think they have bug spies on their ships? Man, look at the little antenna. I've worked with hundreds of transmitters and receivers in my military career. I have never seen anything so small. What are they transmitting and receiving? Communication systems placed inside a ship with all this structure around it has to have all kinds of interference. I know they don't think like us, but no human engineer would put a transmitter and receiver deep inside a ship."

"We aren't going to solve the issue here," said Tews. "Let's keep going."

Spaz led the way once again. When he got to the point where he could hear the bugs clicking at each other, he stopped. Both he and Tews removed their light sticks to avoid drawing attention to themselves. In darkness, they crawled to the vent cover. Jackpot. As the two peered through the vent slats they could see the ship's bridge. A 360-degree view screen showed a planet and two other bug ships sitting stationary.

Spaz counted fifteen bugs on the bridge. At the center of the open area sat an elevated spoon shaped chair with a big bug in it. The chair swiveled left and right as the bug clicked out orders. The one in the chair had to be the captain. It hissed and clicked some more. Two bugs appeared on the screen. These had to be the other bug ship captains. Each captain clicked and hissed. It looked like they were arguing about something.

The ship they were on rocked as if it collided with another ship. The air entering the vent smelled as bad as one of Tews's farts. Alarms started sounding. The captain hissed and clicked. Spaz looked at the 360-degree view screen. One alien ship was being blown to pieces! Spaz resisted a cheer as he saw six human ships and scores of fighters with weapons blazing. They caught the bugs with their shields down. They must have jumped knowing the bugs were here. Spaz couldn't move as he watched with awe. The fighters were firing at their ship. The battle's action absorbed all of his senses.

The bug captain pulled a lever. The ship jumped to life, and maneuvered as it fired at the humans. Spaz wanted to help but Tews was tugging on his arm. Spaz forced himself to leave his view from above. When they crawled a little ways into the main tunnel Spaz said, "What are you doing? I want to see the battle. We have to help them somehow!"

"If we can get back to the captain and attack the ship from within, I calculate success at fifty percent without rounding. Are you listening? That's only true if we attack the bugs during this battle!"

"Why you sitting here yacking? Let's tell the captain," said Spaz.

With adrenalin pumping through their veins, the two friends scurried to the holding pen like hungry rats to food. By the time Tews and Spaz got back to the pen, everyone knew something major was happening with the ship. The captives could feel power surges as the ship maneuvered. They also felt strong jolts knocking them off balance.

The captain assembled representatives from each group of captives. Everyone listened as Tews and Spaz described their findings. When they talked about what they saw on the bridge moments ago, it got instant attention.

Smitty agreed with the vent crawling duo, it was the time to strike, while the crew was distracted. For once, everyone agreed. Urgency forced them to develop a hasty plan of attack. They would take over the pen, engineering, and the bridge. They would also send a team to the armory to acquire more weapons and cause general havoc.

They split the weapons. Ten weapons would stay with those in the pen and fourteen would go with the engineering group. Of those remaining, fourteen would go with the group attacking the bridge, and six would go with the armory group. The pen would get two additional rifles when they killed the guards. Each vent team would have thirty humans. Each team preselected riflemen who dipped their fingers into the blood Tews brought back. Each team also took a small container of blood, in case they needed more riflemen.

Smitty and his group were already heading towards the vent. Their mission was to take control of engineering, neutralize the ship's weapons, and isolate the drives. The second team started to crawl toward the bridge. The pen captives began to count to three hundred. At three hundred, two flashes from plasma rifles lit the pen walls. Both guards slumped into the arms of their captives. Spaz grabbed one rifle and another captive with blood on his finger took the other weapon. They moved toward the pen door.

CHAPTER NINE: The Landing

Lieutenant Phlop started to shake as he read the order. "Commodore? There's no such rank as a commodore. This is some kind of a joke gone wrong McCormack. You're going to pay for this! Hah, you in command? You're nothing more than a non-com." The lieutenant pulled a gold tube out of his pocket, and placed it in his mouth, and sucked in. Mac knew Lieutenant Phlop was puffing Ep Flavors on the trip. It was a disgusting habit practiced by the rich. It gave the user an epinephrine rush and was suppose to boost the firing of neurons giving the user a mental burst.

The lieutenant held the orders up for the class to see. He looked at the troops and pulled a fancy chem-tube from his pocket. It was a type of lighter the colonists used on remote planets to start a fire. He ignited the lighter and held the hot flame to the orders. Nothing happened. He grasped the orders and tried to rip them in half. He pulled and pulled to no avail. With each attempt to destroy the orders, Mr. Phlop's face got redder and redder.

Mac grinned. *The neuron boost must not have worked.* "Let me give you a little history lesson Mr. Phlop. During the mining wars, messengers often had to deliver orders by hand due to radio silence, jamming, or plain old com problems. It's why Fleet Command started making the orders out of spun Inconel. Its impervious to fire, and the strongest man in the universe can't tear it," said Mac.

Lieutenant Phlop looked around the room. He pointed to Dwain and said, "Take Sergeant McCormack into custody."

"Does the paper you're holding say Sergeant McCormack is a commodore?"

"Yes, but it's a lie."

"Sir, I hate to tell you this, but it looks like an official document. Commodore always outranks a first lieutenant. No disrespect Mr. Phlop, but as I see it, Mr. McCormack is your superior. In fact, if I remember my military history right, he has a lot of power. Not even fleet command, or for that matter, not even the president can override a commodore's order during times of war."

The lieutenant looked at Dwain in disbelief. "This phony war hero has fooled everyone. He's not even college educated. This is mutiny!"

Mac had taken all he could. Most of his ground pounders were not college educated. It didn't mean they weren't intelligent.

"Mr. Phlop, I'm ordering you to leave this room. I want you to think about your future, because you are on the verge of not having one in the military. We will talk after you have time to think. Now go." Mac pointed at the door.

The lieutenant spun around, and stomped off like a frustrated, angry child.

Dwain was the first one to break the silence. "So, Commodore McCormack, what are you in charge of?"

"I work through Vice Admiral Farragut. I am in charge of special operations."

"Fuck, no wonder we got all this fancy equipment," said Dwain.

Mac shrugged his shoulders. "Rank does have certain privileges."

"How come no one knows you're a commodore?" asked Dreng.

"We kept it a secret. As a sergeant I can move without notice within both the military and civilian organizations. A commodore draws way too much attention."

"What do we call you now? Sergeant or commodore," asked Tinker.

"Neither. Call me Mac." Everyone laughed. "Look, nothing changes. We still have our primary job to do: to protect. Only now we protect the colonists, our ships, the crews, the folks back home, and everyone in-between."

"What's the game plan? What do we do now?" asked a trooper.

"Tinker will take charge and be responsible for loading our equipment onto the skiff. I have several containers on the hanger deck labeled UFC.Specop.Rayne. Make sure they get loaded and be gentle, the contents are fragile."

"What's in the containers?" asked Dreng.

"I brought a little surprise that might be useful if we have a problem. Whatever Tinker needs, Dreng and Dwain, I want you to make it happen."

"Who's in charge of which troops?" asked Dwain.

"You're both corporals now, work together and supervise all three platoons."

They both nodded their heads.

"Tomorrow, when we deploy on planet, each of you will wear your body armor with a scout pack. This includes a helmet with face shield, and you must each carry a rifle. Beyond that, I am flexible. You can carry a back-up weapon. Hell, you can even carry additional supplies, pictures from home, or anything you want. I don't even care if you bring five pounds of sweets to share with everyone."

The team jostled each other and laughed.

"Keep in mind anything extra is your responsibility to carry. With that said, I have to go to the bridge and use their com system to talk to the Warhammer and Dagger. Now get loading. When I'm done, I'll meet you by the skiff."

Mac called the com group and explained he needed to use the ship's communications system. When his request was denied, he explained he was Commodore McCormack and this was not a request. The com officer laughed.

"Look Sergeant McCormack, I already know who you are, and I admire your creativity. I am aware of the link between you and the captain, but he's asleep right now. We don't let anyone on a whim come to the bridge to use the ship's com system. You can fill out a transmission slip, we will prioritize it, and in time, your message will go out. It's the best I can do right now."

"Never mind," said Mac. I'll take care of it myself. He broke the link and headed for the bridge. *Time to see if his staff was right. They said I could get into secure areas I didn't even know existed. Right now, I'll be happy if I can get access to the bridge.* He walked through the passageway to the direct elevator and put his hand over the scanner. The light turned green, the elevator door opened, and he stepped in. The elevator door closed and when it opened again he was standing at the entrance to the bridge.

A big metal door blocked his entrance. He stepped onto a trigger mechanism causing his whole body to be scanned. A computer-generated voice greeted him with a, "Good morning Commodore McCormack." *I have to remember to thank my team.* Mac stepped through an opening and was standing on the bridge.

A com officer stood talking to the person in the captain's chair. Mac could hear her say, "It's not a mistake, the computer said commodore on deck."

Mac didn't have time for games. He walked right up to the watch captain. "I'm Commodore McCormack, who are you?" Mac had the attention of everyone on the bridge.

"Forgive me, Commodore McCormack, but we were not told we had a commodore on this flight. I am Commander Staltz. I have to ask, how you got onto the bridge?"

"I was traveling under the alias of Sergeant McCormack. No one on this ship knows who I am. I no longer have the need to travel under a false title. As for your second point, a commodore has unlimited access to everything. Right now I need to use your com system. If you refuse, I will seize your ship and do it anyway. I don't mean to pressure you, but this is time sensitive. What's your decision Mr. Staltz?"

The commander looked worried, but he made the right decision. "Lieutenant Tybur, show the commodore the com system and give him anything he needs."

"Thank you commander, you made a good decision."

Mac walked over to the fancy com station, and studied the controls for about thirty seconds. "I don't need your help Lieutenant Tybur, I'm familiar with the com system's operation." He put an earpiece on, switched the system to privacy mode, and activated a sound dampener. Next, he broadcast a coded message on a military use frequency. "Tango Tango Three Charlie Foxtrot, I say again, Tango Tango Three Charlie Foxtrot." He sat in silence as he waited.

The broadcast activated a series of events on the Warhammer and Dagger. Both ships' captains would open and read sealed orders from United Fleet Command. Neither captain realized the orders existed. *I hate all secrecy, but when the Argosy left Trinity Prime, they didn't know who had attacked Nomad or the probes.* He waited as the minutes ticked off. The two ship's captains didn't realize it, but they were hand picked by Mac. During the battles they participated in each captain used creative thinking to defeat attacks by multiple ships. Imaginative thinking was a trait Mac often sought out in those working for him.

The Argosy's proximity detectors went into alarm mode. The giant view screen showed two large UFC war ships facing the Argosy. The bridge crew watched in amazement. *Great move.* He knew he made the right choice in picking these two pilots. They blocked the Argosy from escaping. The ship could not move backwards as fast as they could move forward. In case of a fraud or elaborate hoax, they obeyed orders, but took an extra precaution.

Mac shut the dampening field and said, "Commander Stortz, these are UFC ships. They are the Warhammer, and the Dagger. I don't have time to explain right now. We can talk later." He turned the dampening field back on, and started talking to both captains. Mac explained the alien threat and the current situation. He had Dagger launch two micro probes with view and limited com capabilities. Neither captain questioned the presence of aliens.

"I'd like you both to scan the planet and plot this solar system. I want you prepared to leave if the aliens show up. I have three platoons going down on Rayne. We will be on planet for three days looking for proof of alien life forms. I want you both to hide with the Argosy and protect her. If aliens show up, do not engage them. Their ships are faster, so I am assuming their weapons are better too. Use the planet to hide your departure. Don't worry about us if we're still on the planet, our chances of survival will be better than yours. Come back with some help."

Both captains acknowledged the commodore's orders. They broke formation to scan the solar system. If aliens arrived, the UFC war ships needed to know from which angles they could remain unseen. They needed every tactical advantage they could glean. Mac put the Argosy's com system back in regular mode, removed his earpiece, and shut off the sound dampener.

The bridge crew watched Mac in silent awe. None of them had seen a commodore before today. Mac was standing with the view screen behind him as the Warhammer and Dagger peeled off to accomplish their orders. The inadvertent pose made him seem to ooze power. The bridge crew watched with great reverence.

The computer-generated voice on the bridge said, "Captain Tanner on deck."

The captain walked up to Mac and shook his hand once again. "Commodore McCormack huh? I gotta tell you, I'm not surprised."

"News travels fast." Mac looked over at Commander Stortz, and squinted his eyes.

The captain looked at the view screen. He saw his crew was tracking two impressive ships of war, bristling with weapons. "I'm glad you brought two ships with us. I have been taking heat from the governor. He said you had zero proof about anything. He told me I needed to exert my authority over a sergeant and be the Argosy's captain. He has lodged a formal complaint against me and you for delaying the colonization of a planet."

"Captain, I'm afraid the governor sees Rayne as a stepping stone. He doesn't care about lives at risk. If this planet is what I think it is, all hell is about to break loose. Both the governor and Lieutenant Phlop have no experience. They have a lot to learn. I'll ask the governor to withdraw the complaint against you."

"Good luck," said the captain.

"Oh, I can be persuasive when I need to be. I apologize for the interruption, but it couldn't wait, and now I need to get back to my troops. Thank you Commander Stortz."

"My pleasure commodore."

"Call me Mac, commander."

"Yes sir, Mac it is."

After Mac stepped into the elevator, the door started to close. He heard the computer-generated voice, "Commodore McCormack departing the bridge." *How the hell did the tekkies load that crap onto every ship's computer is beyond me.*

Mac headed back to his troops and shuttle. As soon as he stepped onto the hanger deck, he picked Dreng out of a crowd of soldiers. *She moves her body with such grace. Teaching her the Tao style of fighting was going to be a joy.* His thoughts about Dreng distracted him so much he didn't realize Lieutenant Phlop had come up next to him.

"Commodore, can you stop and talk to me for a minute?"

"Okay Mr. Phlop, what do you want to talk about?"

"You were right, I screwed up. I was playing politics rather than helping with the troops. I got mad when you tried to set me straight," the lieutenant smiled, "But in my defense, it was before I knew you were a commodore. I should have realized you spoke the truth. I tried to punish you in front of everyone, hoping to gain respect. I didn't handle the situation in a professional way. If you will let me, I'd like to be part of this military contingency."

I wasn't born yesterday, thought Mac. *The captain showed the governor and lieutenant the bridge recording of Warhammer and Dagger. That's when there was a change of heart, at least in the lieutenant's case.*

"All right lieutenant. But for now, I don't want you to interfere with my plans. Watch, learn, and help where you can, but no supervision or orders to the troops until you prove yourself to me. You okay with that?"

Mac saw the beginning of a sneer on the lieutenant's mouth. Mr. Phlop caught himself and forced a smile.

"Thank you for the opportunity to let me fix what I have done, commodore."

The lieutenant's tone and body language conflicted with his words. Mac wanted to give him a chance, but he was going to have to keep a close watch over him. Mac decided he needed to talk to the troops before the lieutenant arrived back on the scene.

"Before I allow you back, I need to talk to the troops." The lieutenant's eyelid twitched the tiniest bit, but Mac noticed it. You don't get to be the greatest sniper in UFC history by not noticing little details like facial tics. "Take the day off. Go pack what gear you will need for a three day scout mission, and meet us at the skiff at 0700 ship's time. If you're not sure what to pack, call Tinker."

"Aye sir. I'll be there and ready to go."

Mac headed back to the troops. He never had anybody sneak up on him like that. He was becoming too distracted by Dreng. *Stay focused Mac*. He continued on to the skiff.

"How's it going Tinker?"

"In about another thirty minutes we'll have everything loaded and secure. Are you flying us down?"

"No, we have two volunteer pilots to take us to the planet. We'll do a low altitude scan, pick out a good landing spot, and set up camp. After we land, the Argosy, Warhammer, and Dagger will find a good location to hide. They will stay hidden until we finish our scouting mission. The skiff pilots want to stay on the ground and wait for us. We can use the electronic camouflage net on the skiff. It will make it hard to see and impossible to detect if we shut down the power systems."

"Mac, I've got a good feeling about this mission."

"Aw crap Tinker, I wish you hadn't said that. Last time you said those exact same words our forward post was overrun."

"It's different this time. Everything feels right."

"I wish I could say the same. Tell you what, finish loading, and have everybody get a good night's sleep. The next three days will be long ones. Muster here at the skiff by 0700 and be ready to leave at 0732. Let the troops know the lieutenant will be coming with us." Mac could see the immediate response in Tinker's body. "Now before you go getting all depressed on me, his job is going to be to watch and learn, no issuing orders."

Tinker shook his head. "I don't trust him Mac, not at all. He's a rich snob used to getting his way. He has no business leading troops. If we see combat, he will get us all killed."

"I'll keep my eyes on him."

"He's sneaky. You better watch your back."

Raising his hand in a see you later gesture, Mac turned and walked back to his room. *What would the troops say once they found out Dreng and I had been intimate? I have never been in a position like this before. Imagine, me with a hot looking girlfriend.* He felt happy for the first time since his brother died, and it made him begin to worry. As he started to pack for the mission, he began to play "what if" scenarios over and over in his mind. Mac opened his storage locker and pulled out an old beaten up case.

He ran his hand across the banged up surface as if caressing it. He realized it would kill him if anything happened to Dreng. *Now I need you to take care of her too my old friend.* Mac opened the case and patted the contents as if it was a trusted dog. He lifted her up and admired her beauty. The old buzzard rifle is still a dangerous weapon in the right hands.

The door chimed. Mac's heart began to race. He set his rifle back in its case and walked over to the viewer. *Dreng.* He opened the door, and grabbed her. He saw the shock on her face as he planted a big ole kiss on her lips. He felt great until he heard Tinker laughing.

"You aren't going to kiss me too are you Mac?"

Mac was so focused on Dreng he didn't notice Tinker behind her. "I will if you want me to."

"Thanks, but I'll pass. The troops already know you two are, umm let me say this in a polite way – seeing each other."

Dreng's face had a red tint to it. "It's true Tinker, we have had a joining."

Mac interrupted, "It's what she calls – you know – making love."

Tinker started to laugh. "Hey, call it whatever you want."

"Mac, I tried to tell you, a joining is more than having sex," said Dreng.

Now Mac's face turned red. "Dreng, can we talk about this later?"

"See," said Dreng, "you won't listen."

Mac looked at Tinker, ignoring Dreng this time. "So, what do you want?"

Tinker pulled an old bottle of bourbon from behind his back and held it out to him. "A toast to our first assignment as a team."

He took it, and read the label, *Uncle Jack's Bourbon*. It was an expensive old glass bottle of alcohol. They didn't make it like this anymore. It had to have cost Tinker a butt load. Mac glanced around. "Where is Dwain?"

Tinker looked at Mac and began to laugh. He spit out, "He's joining – with a female crew member."

Mac's eyes got big as he shook his head no, but it was too late. Dreng gave Tinker a playful punch in the arm. The blow knocked him over. He kept laughing as he looked at up at her with surprise.

She reached down, gave him her hand and lifted him up as she said, "Excrement hole."

"Did you hear her Mac? She called me an asshole, but in a nice way."

"Yup, I heard it. Besides being polite, I'd say she's a pretty good judge of character too."

Mac got three glasses and poured each of them a drink. As the friends sat on the floor they laughed, talked, and drank for hours. Dreng got to hear story after story about Mac and his escapades. She kept pumping Tinker for more history between the two of them.

"Hey, you're not being fair! You're finding out about us, and were not learning anything about you," said Mac.

"All right," said Dreng, "ask me something."

Before she ended the sentence Mac said, "How did you get the scar on your chest?"

In an auto reflex Dreng put her hand to her chest and rubbed the scar through her top as if it were something sacred. Tears started to well up in her eyes. Mac could see she was struggling with how to tell them. He realized this was the wrong setting for something so emotional.

"Okay, I can accept it's the wrong time to talk about your scar, but you've got to give us something. You okay with that Tinker?"

"Yeah, I'm okay with it, but you have to make it something good."

A smile broke out on Dreng's face. She wiped the tears out of her eyes, looked at Mac and said, "I promise. One day I'll tell you, but not now." She looked at Tinker. "So, you want a juicy tidbit about me? Let me think… okay, I've got it. On Nokomis I grew up with my ancestor's traditional values. One of these is a very old tradition called a joining."

Tinker sprayed out saliva as he burst into laughter. He glanced at Mac. Then he interrupted Dreng, and said, "Mac, I don't know what you did to this poor girl, but all she wants to talk about is sex." Dreng shot Tinker a look that could have made a lessor man's head explode. Tinker looked at the clock hanging on Mac's wall and said, "Crap, look at the time. I still have to decide what snacks I want to pack. It's been a pleasure, but I have to go."

"What about my story?"

"We can all talk another time, I promise."

"Yeah, I suppose I should go too. I also have some packing to finish too."

Mac's face drooped. "Don't you want to stay a while longer, Dreng?"

"I know what you want Mac, but you said it yourself, get plenty of rest. If I stay I know what we'll be doing."

God, I love her brutal honesty. "You're right. Both of you get out of here and get some sleep, and thank you."

What is Dreng's obsession with sex? Is it from being a virgin? Or did she have very little experience and wanted to talk about it? Do her people talk about copulation so openly? It'll take me some time to get use to this kind of openness. If it makes her happy, I guess I'm all for it. Mac smiled. *It's a good end to the day.* He curled up in his bed and fell asleep.

He opened his eyes and checked the time, 0429. As usual, he woke up right before the alarm went off. He didn't go to the galley. Instead, he ate a light energy meal in his room. He tidied things up a little, grabbed his backpack, supplies, rifle case, and headed to the hanger deck. When he got there, the pilots were performing pre-flight ops on the skiff. Mac checked the load. Tinker had done a great job. Everything looked good.

Mac felt a presence and spun around. *Dreng, she's been watching me.* Mac looked her up and down. *She's one hot looking girl. After all the stories last night, I was concerned she might think I was too much of a killer.* She stood with her hands on her hips accentuating her curves in the tight body armor and smiled at him. *The Minx knows what I'm thinking.*

"You like my body armor, Mac?"

He laughed. "Yes, but you're too distracting. You are going to get me killed. Are those hand hatchets in your belt? I haven't seen those in years."

"My people refer to them as tomahawks."

161

"I assume you're good with them?"

"Yes."

More soldiers began to show up, Mac made sure they all brought their food rations. He also made everyone with a secondary weapon show him what he or she carried. Even the lieutenant carried an antique short-range projectile pistol. He wore it in his old style armor suit. It must have cost a small fortune.

At 0732 the skiff launched toward the planet. The troops looked at the view screen as the skiff made several low altitude passes. To Mac's trained eye the scene below looked worrisome because the plants did not look like random growth. You could see a pattern blending with the countryside.

There was no sign of sentient life. Mac identified a good spot for the skiff pilot to land. When the side cargo door opened, everybody sucked in the fresh air. After three months of being locked up on the ship it smelled like heaven.

"Listen up everyone, this goes for the pilots too. Do not use any equipment that draws on the skiff's power supply. Keep your rifles with you at all times. Dreng, I want you to position four of Tinker's troops on the perimeter. Tinker, take the rest of your platoon and put the electro dampening camouflage net over the skiff. Dwain, you can supervise the remaining troops in off loading our equipment. Sally, Dan, stay with the skiff in case we need to make a quick getaway."

"Lieutenant Phlop. Can you tell me why we can't use the skiff's power supply?" asked Mac.

"I understand why we can't use it until we get the dampening net on, but once it's on, I know the specs. You're wrong. It will shield all energy discharges."

Tinker hung around Mac and the lieutenant. He eavesdropped on their conversation.

"Tell me Mr. Phlop, what are the specs on an alien ship's scanner?

Silence. Mr. Phlop didn't respond.

"Our headsets fall within the natural electromagnetic variance of a planet's surface. So do our hand held weapons unless they are fired. The power supply on the skiff generates more energy than most normal disturbances. The energy peak, even if for a moment, might make us visible to enemy detection methods. It's better to error on the safe side."

Lieutenant Phlop shook his head no. He wasn't willing to keep an open mind and learn.

I'll keep working on him. If the lieutenant doesn't improve after three days I will terminate his commission in the UFC. Mr. Phlop will have two options. Return to Trinity Prime with the Argosy or convince the governor to accept him as a colonist. This is what happens when clout is used to put someone into a position of authority instead of talent.

"Mr. Phlop, what would you do next if I weren't here?"

"I'd deploy the three platoons in different directions to look for anything abnormal."

"Before any platoon leaves on a foray into possible enemy territory you should configure your base of operations. First we have some weapons to remove from their crates and set up. A word of advice, never leave your home base unprotected. The troops we leave here may have to give us cover fire, support fire, or stop an attack at any given moment. If the enemy overruns your home base, you lose your method of escape."

Dwain whistled. "What the hell is this? I have no idea how to set it up."

Mac walked over to Dwain. "It's a positron canon on anti-gravity skids."

163

All the troops gathered around Mac to see the new weapon. As he set it up he explained its operation.

"The canon contains an internal laser that creates positrons. It locks them into a magnetic containment field within a large single composite round. The round contains a proximity detector. Once fired, the round obtains an instant velocity of ten times the speed of sound using wee rail technology. Before anyone asks, it has nothing to do with peeing."

The troops laughed at the thought.

"As the round hits the target," Mac said, "the positrons get released in a stream. As the positrons contact matter, annihilation occurs. The material disappears in a burst of gamma photons."

"Fuck," said Dwain, "you can't make this shit up."

Dreng had walked up in time to watch Mac setting up the weapon. She asked, "What's the downside?"

Mac smiled. "It's experimental. There may be a few bugs in it, and when matter gets destroyed, there's a large burst of gamma radiation."

"I can't wait to try it out," said Tinker.

"If you are firing this weapon it means we are in some deep shit. My hope is you don't have to fire it," said Mac.

About an hour later, base camp was set up. Mac tested the helmet radios with the platoon leaders and a member from each platoon.

"Dreng, take Second platoon and head out at 120 degrees. Dwain, you take Third platoon and head out at 030 degrees. Mr. Phlop, you stay here with First platoon and the pilots. Tinker, you're in charge of base camp." The lieutenant's head responded with an involuntary shake in the negative. Both Mac and Tinker caught the response. He was still resisting. "Be back here at 1900 hours, ship time. I want an update every hour from each platoon leaders."

Being a ghost sniper, free to operate behind enemy lines had taught Mac many tactics. On recon of an area he always looked for potential traps or signs that seemed out of place. On the flyover he observed an unusual stack of rocks. They seemed out of place. He decided to investigate them on his own.

As he made his way through the countryside, his sniper training kicked in. He often used old low-tech methods in the field. He found many times the higher the tech the more apt something is to break down. A typical trick he often used was to lean sticks at the base of a tree or to mark a direction using pinecones on the ground.

The first hour reports started coming in. Tinker had nothing to report from home base. Dreng and Dwain both found signs of bioengineering. He expected as much. Both Second and Third platoons took plant and dirt samples. If bioengineering had occurred a quick DNA check of samples should confirm it. If they were bioengineered, sooner or later those responsible for planting the crops would be back.

By the fourth report, Mac had surveyed a large swath of land and was now three stone throws away from the rock formation located north-northwest of base camp. He sat in some bushes with his body armor blending into the background. After an hour he made his move toward the opening in the ground. The rocks turned out to be the entrance to an underground cavern containing pools of water. It smelled musty like mold. He was standing at the underground entrance when the fifth report came in from Tinker. He had nothing to report. Dreng and Dwain both reported they were heading back to home base. They estimated they would be back in five hours.

Perfect, thought Mac, *I have a few minutes left to explore.* He started to move down what appeared to be rock stairs, when he felt his backpack vibrate. *It's the link to the micro probes.* He walked back outside and pulled his viewer out. *Shit, two… no, three alien ships. Like what Dreng described, but they seem bigger. They look like flying bugs. If I'm seeing the aliens on my viewer, I know Warhammer and Dagger are watching too.*

Mac flipped his com to private so no one else could hear except Tinker, Dreng, and Dwain. "We have company. The micro probes picked up the arrival of three alien ships in orbit around Rayne. Alert your troops. Get to home base ASAP. Mac out." Mac cut his investigation short, and began to make his way back to base camp.

CHAPTER TEN: The Battle of Rayne

A dmiral Harding's convoy stopped one jump away from Rayne. Mahpee explained the Wasp's computer system problem to the other ships. He also reinforced his desire to take part in any battle with the Raygin. He asked if he could attach his ship to the Constellation's surface on the final jump. He would remain there until their engineer could work out the problem.

The Nomad's disappearance and the alien ship heading to Rayne were cause for concern. Mahpee told everyone he feared the Raygin might be using the planet for a base of operation. To resolve Mahpee's concern, the admiral agreed to take a risk. He decided to deploy a mini-popper probe to the outermost area in the Rayne solar system.

The military designed the probe to be low tech. Detection would require a focused scan. The shielded drive and the old-fashioned high definition camera made it difficult to spot. The Constellation deployed the probe. It stayed seven seconds, and popped back. A small tractor beam recovered the probe. Three alien ships were sitting in stationary orbit near Rayne. The admiral asked the war computer if more ships could be hiding in the Rayne solar system. The computer responded with an eight percent chance that there was an additional ship. The admiral asked each ship for tactical input.

Mahpee was first to speak. "I suggest we have your war computer identify the most strategic spot for our ships to jump so all of us are able to fire on a single alien ship the second we arrive. We also need to be positioned to maximize our firepower. The fighters should launch to distract the other Raygin ships. If we can take one of them out first, I'd feel much better about our odds. Don't forget, the ship we captured represents twenty-five year old technology. I am sure the Raygin will have a few surprises for us."

After some discussion, everyone agreed upon the attack plan. The war computer calculated the best locations to jump. Next, Mahpee had Bodaway attach the Wasp under the battleship. The tiny ship disappeared within the Constellation's surface structures. All the ships except for the Wasp were ready to fire as soon they jumped. Mahpee could feel the tension in the crew.

He asked if he could say a few words to those who fought with him this day. The admiral put Mahpee on a com capable of broadcasting to all UFC ships in the convoy. Tens of thousands of crewmen listened to their new ally. "My new friends, I am Mahpee, from the Peoples Nation. We have an old custom I would like to share with you. When death could be imminent, as in the case of today's battle, we sing our death song. Since you have no death song, I will share mine with you." Mahpee sang his song.

"I am a warrior.

I will not let fear in my heart.

I will not retreat, not even if I am the last one standing in front of my enemy.

I will not weep if this is my day to die.

I know nothing lives forever, so I give my gratitude for the days of my life.

I will act with courage, that I may come to the Great Spirit without shame.

Good luck my brothers and sisters. Mahpee out."

"This is admiral Harding. Thank you Chief Mahpee. Ships, prepare for sync jump in sixty seconds."

The war computer moved the convoy in a perfect synchronized jump. The solar system near Rayne lit up with torpedoes, lasers, and plasma cannons. Every weapon each ship had available fired or was launched at a single Raygin ship. UFC Fighters launched the instant their mother ships jumped into the Rayne solar system. They swarmed the other two Raygin ships. It caused immediate confusion. The UFC fighters had a tactical advantage over any fighters released by the Raygin, at least at first.

"Look," said Mahpee, as he pointed at he view screen, "we caught them with their shields down." The Wasp's crew watched a big Raygin ship take blow after blow without shields. The ion drive fizzled out. Electrical arcs were occurring all across the giant ship's body. It came apart in big pieces. It looked like everything was happening in slow motion because the ship was so large.

Mahpee was itching to join the battle. He dared not move without a functioning computer. The Wasp control panel lit up and the graviton tracking system switched on. A minute later it switched off again. Mahpee called engineering on the com console. In a loud and angry voice he said, "Nashta, I need a report. Now."

"Chief, you aren't going to believe this! It wants to speak to you."

Mahpee jerked, and turned to see Nashta standing beside him. "Make sense Nashta. Who wants to talk to me? The admiral?"

Nashta pointed to the form materializing on the bridge. Mahpee went pale. "Grandfather?"

"Listen to me Honiahaka. You must destroy the watcher, or your friends will lose the battle."

Honiahaka, little wolf, it's my secret name given to me by my grandfather. He used it when we were alone with each other. He said secret names held much power. "I do not understand. You are not my grandfather. He died years ago."

"Yet, I am here. Did you hear my words?"

"Yes, I heard. Destroy the watcher, but why should I listen to you?"

"Look," his grandfather pointed at the screen, "they are escaping your trap. All is not as it seems. What lesson did I teach you when facing a stronger enemy my Honiahaka?"

"You said I must be more cunning than my enemy."

"Good boy. You paid attention. The watcher sits there."

Everyone looked at the ship's viewer. The computer generated a gravity echo, which it painted on the screen. Yet to the eye, nothing appeared to be there. The entity claiming to be Mahpee's grandfather started to dissolve.

"Wait. I need my computer," said Mahpee.

"Soon, Honiahaka, soon."

"Nashta, what was that?"

"I don't know, chief. At first I thought it was the computer. It is not, but it is controlling the computer. I hate to tell you this, but it is controlling the weapon systems too. It knew my pass codes. Everything I tried, it countered. I believe if it wanted to kill us, we would be dead. I think it wants to help."

"Why doesn't it destroy the watcher itself?"

Nashta shrugged his shoulders. "I don't know."

The battle still raged. Mahpee struggled to come up with some type of deceptive plan. *The entity was right. The Raygin ships were starting to out maneuver the UFC ships. The two remaining Raygin ships were able to keep the battleship at bay while still firing at the cruisers. The fighters on both sides seemed well matched.*

"Aw kondor dung," said Bodaway. "We lost a cruiser, and another one is taking a beating. It can't seem to get away from the bugs."

As fighting continued, each ship sustained various forms of damage. The single exception was the Wasp.

170

Mahpee stared in dismay. Another cruiser lost its ion drive and drifted away, carried by its own momentum. The bugs were out maneuvering the humans. Their shields seemed to be able to withstand attack after attack. After what seemed like an eternity, the Wasp's computer and weapon systems came back on line. Both systems looked good from the bridge.

"Nashta, are we ready for battle?"

"I don't know what your grandfather did, but the computer seems faster. It will take me hours to find what he did to the weapons systems."

"We don't have hours, I'm going in now." Mahpee had a plan. The Constellation was taking a beating from the two Raygin ships. Something had to give. Plus, the Watcher needed to be taken out. "Admiral, I have good news. I have all my systems back. If you can fly straight at the Raygin ship nearest the planet while firing, I will decouple from you and fly under the ship. I'll try to take out the propulsion drive unit. They may not see us under your weapon fire. If they do see us they may think us to be a torpedo gone astray. Another concern is we have reason to believe there is a cloaked ship nearby. We may be able to catch two birds with one trap."

"I'm willing to try anything at this point. If something doesn't change, we will lose the Constellation, and the battle. You found a cloaked ship?"

"Long story, we used our graviton tracker. We need to move now admiral!"

"Okay Mahpee, here we go. Good luck."

The Constellation started firing with everything it had. It headed straight for the Raygin ship. The three Federation cruisers fired on the second alien ship. The Wasp used the battleship's massive firepower as cover as it flew under the enemy ship undetected. The plan worked. As enemy ship made a strategic move backward it exposed the Constellation to additional fire from the other alien ship. The Wasp computer targeted the Raygin ship's ion drive. The Constellation and the three cruisers retreated leaving the Wasp on her own.

*****

Smitty and his team arrived at the engineering duct. He could feel the attack on the bug ship had intensified. The individual bugs were scurrying around the ion drives. They were injecting some kind of green luminescent fluid into the primary equipment. They counted twenty-two bugs operating near the drives. There were also four attending to the shield generator and four more moving torpedoes on a cart. There were no weapons visible.

Tews and Spaz were right. The bugs had two ion drives and two poppers. The single shield generator was in the aft most part of engineering. The ion drives were straining. To an engineer the sound meant the ship was most likely in a backward maneuver.

Smitty's plan was simple: disconnect the alarm and remove the air duct cover. A team of four humans with two guns would exit the vent and guard the door. Any bug trying to enter or leave, would meet its doom. The weapon carriers on the human team would exit the vent and start killing bugs. Smitty's plan was to leave the shields online. He would isolate the drives, leaving them on while cutting power everywhere except for engineering.

When the humans started firing at the bugs, they scattered like roaches. Twenty-four bugs died in less than one standard minute. A few bugs escaped through a back door the humans couldn't see from the vent. Smitty posted humans with rifles at each entrance to engineering. He also put a few on a roving patrol and kept a few more by the main drive components.

The unarmed members were engineers. Smitty got them together and they tried to figure out how to disengage the drives. They followed the various conduits and pipes and found the cut off button. It looked pretty much like

172

those found on human ships. It should cut power by isolating the drive. Smitty hit the oversized button.

The whine from the ion drive started to slow down. The lights in engineering went out and the battery back-ups came on.

"What the hell happened?" screamed Smitty.

The shields dropped off line. Smitty guessed they had about five minutes until the ion drive wound all the way down and stopped. The Poppers had no power going to them, so they were useless.

"What flaming idiot would connect everything into a single kill switch? That's crazy," said Smitty. The ship started moving forward again.

*****

Mahpee noticed a flickering in the enemy shield. Something was wrong with the bug ship they were flying under. *Time to strike*. Before Mahpee could give the command, Bodaway fired at the Raygin's underside without using the targeting computer. The laser ripped a glimmering gash in the Raygin ship's bottom. The plasma canon, torpedo, and laser hit the ship's rear end, blowing off the giant port ion thruster.

Mahpee didn't understand why the Raygin shield failed, but it couldn't have happened at a better time. With one ion thruster still working, the big ship was trying to maneuver to Rayne. Ships that gigantic weren't made to land on a planet. Without its shield the ship would come apart as soon as it hit the ground. Mahpee reached over and activated the graviton tracker. He took over fire control. This freed Bodaway to concentrate on maneuvering his ship for a clear shot.

The Wasp dodged a large hunk of nozzle floating in space. On the screen, Mahpee could see tons of metal floating off in every direction. *Perfect*, he thought. *At first, we will blend in with the debris field. It might buy us an extra second or two.* The graviton tracking system confirmed the cloaked ship hadn't moved. Mahpee fired.

The Wasp's crew watched on the view screen. The laser hit the invisible target. The cloak fluttered and disappeared leaving the ship for all to see. Mahpee had never viewed such an elegant ship. It was sleek, grey-purple in color, and it looked like a bird in flight with two small stability wings. *Did the Raygin have unknown allies?*

Mahpee fired the laser again and hit the now uncloaked ship but not before it launched an energy weapon at the Wasp. The sleek ship became engulfed in a flash, as the Wasp's plasma canon hit home. The beautiful alien ship and its occupants dissolved into space dust.

The golden energy fired from the alien ship took the shape of three small rings. They behaved like a spring, collapsing in on itself over and over. It gained speed with every recoil. The Wasp turned toward the planet to evade the energy rings. The rings turned and closed in on them.

"Brace for impact," said Bodaway.

The computer diverted every bit of energy, including life support, to the shields. The rings hit the Wasp, and spread over her entire surface. The shields held, but shorted out as the energy faded. Life support turned back on. Mahpee let out a sigh of relief.

As the damaged Raygin ship attempted to land on Rayne it fired a weakened bank of lasers at the Wasp. It was a last ditch effort, as the big ship sunk into the atmosphere.

A couple lasers rocked the unshielded Wasp. Mahpee couldn't believe they weren't vaporized. The big ship's lasers must not have been at full strength, but they were still capable of doing great harm.

"Damage report," said Bodaway over the ship's address system.

Nashta responded. "The ship seems to be intact. We took two laser hits. One strike took out the rear ion propulsion nozzles. The second strike put a hole through the hull in engineering. It looks like the laser also damaged the power supply for the singularity drive. The ship seems to be self-sealing the holes in the hull. It must be Mahpee's grandfather."

The Constellation moved between the Wasp and the remaining Raygin ship. The admiral saved their lives, at least for the moment. Their current problem made them a drifting target. It was just a matter of time until the enemy ship found an opening. Something needed to change.

"Nashta, is the ion drive still operating?" asked Bodaway.

"Yes, but as I said, the propulsion nozzles are inoperable. They took a direct hit."

"I'm going to try to land on Rayne using the maneuvering thrusters."

"I wouldn't try it if I were you. The computer wasn't designed to handle the series of calculations and adjustments for a thruster landing. It needs time to learn… what? I can't. Standby," said Nashta.

"Stand-by? Nashta, I can't stand-by. It's now or never," said Bodaway.

"Uhh… Mahpee's grandfather's head just appeared and told me he fixed the hull breach. He claims he can land the ship if we put it in auto mode."

Bodaway looked at Mahpee and smiled. "He's your grandfather. You make the call."

"Put her in auto."

Bodaway flipped the Wasp's helm control into auto mode. The thrusters began to fire. The entity claiming to be Mahpee's grandfather used the Constellation as a shield. It maneuvered using the natural tug of Rayne's gravity. The thrusters fired in microbursts to line the ship up for an approach. When the Wasp hit Rayne's atmosphere, the ride got bumpy. Mahpee lost track of how many times the thrusters fired in an attempt to maintain the correct glide path angle. It would have been impossible for a human to make so many corrections.

The entity activated the ship's internal speaker system. "Everyone, strap in, this landing is going to be rough, but not as rough as it would have been if Bodaway tried this."

Mahpee couldn't help but laugh.

Bodaway gave him a stern look. "Oh great," said Bodaway, "your grandfather has Nashta's sense of humor."

*****

Dreng turned to make sure she hadn't moved too far ahead of Second platoon. They were returning to home base per Mac's orders. She caught a glimpse of a long smoking tail painted on the blue sky. It looked like a gigantic meteor on a low trajectory. Time to take a break anyway.

"Take five," she said as she pointed into the sky behind them.

The platoon stopped and watched. The object got closer and closer. Looking through her magnified visor, Dreng realized it was a massive Raygin ship.

"Mac, Dreng. A large Raygin ship appears to be crash landing. If it stays on course, it will hit the ground about eight clicks starboard of Second platoon."

"It must be too low, I can't see it. Investigate and notify."

"Roger, Dreng out."

Dreng heard Mac divert Dwain to an intercept point. He would be the backup for Second platoon.

Dwain allowed Dreng to hear him tell Third platoon, "You heard Mac. Let's move out."

After Second platoon had traveled two klicks the big ship went sailing by. They could see a large gash in the ship's belly as it glided past them. Smoke was pouring out the rear end of the ship. The force of the air pulled along with the giant ship knocked over a couple ground pounders.

About three seconds after the ship passed overhead, Second platoon heard a loud crash. The planet shook. The Raygin ship was on the ground.

Dreng set the pace. She had to remind herself not to outrun the troops as she struggled with her demons. *Life was much simpler on Nokomis. I still need to find the appropriate time to tell the troops about my story. I wonder how Mac will accept the full story? I dug myself into a deep pit this time. This whole thing could blow up in my face. First chance I have, I'll tell him everything. We promised to be honest. I know what he'll think. Withholding information on purpose is the same as a lie. Oh, Mac. What have I done?*

"Dreng. There are bodies over here. Big roaches. Yuck. Mac was right about the aliens," said a trooper.

"They must have tried to jump to safety before the ship hit the ground. Pretty stupid, didn't they realize they were moving at the same speed of the ship when they jumped. I'll bet they were moving at about 1000 kilometers per hour," said Dreng.

The platoon kept moving forward. After about eight hundred meters, the team found a wide, straight rut with bulldozed trees. The number of bug bodies grew, as the team got closer to the smoldering ship. There were thousands of them.

"Dreng, look," said trooper, as she pointed to what looked like six human bodies. Two were intact, but the others were in pieces.

"Mac, Dreng. We have found human bodies mixed in with crash debris."

"The new information changes your objective to a search and rescue," said Mac.

"Dreng, copy."

"Dwain, how far out are you?"

"ETA crash site, thirty minutes."

"Good job."

"Mac, can you update us on the alien ship's status?" asked Dreng.

"Three alien ships arrived near Rayne. The Warhammer and Dagger escorted the Argosy to safety. From what I can tell, six UFC ships, including a battleship, arrived near Rayne. It looks like the UFC destroyed one alien ship, and damaged this one causing it to crash. The battle is still going on. We have lost a total of three cruisers and one smaller ship whose arrival I must have missed. It doesn't look good for the remaining UFC ships. The smaller fighters are still battling it out."

"You mean we had six ships and they had three, and we're losing?" asked Dwain.

"No, we started with seven ships. It looks like we lost a total of four ships, but the battle is not over. Now, stay focused."

Second platoon arrived at the crash site. Dreng decided to surveil the wreckage before approaching the ship. It was broken into two big pieces. As the big ship slid to a stop, its nose must have caught on the planet's surface and buried itself. The hind end weight placed more stress on the metal than it could take. The ship snapped in half.

"Dreng," said a trooper. "Look at the hind section, near the break. Focus on the opening about thirty meters off the ground."

A big group of bugs were firing plasma rifles at a band of humans, attempting to get to the ground. The humans had gotten their hands on some rifles and were firing back. As she watched, she could feel a rage building inside her. It was from years of pent up anger toward the bugs for killing her mother. She wanted to get even. She began to take deep breaths.

"Mac, Dreng. We see human and Raygin survivors. Both sides have plasma rifles and are firing at each other. We are moving in to support and assist. The ship is broken into two pieces. We are on the aft, port section near the big break. We can see injured humans."

"Mac cop – ugh. Shit."

"Mac, are you okay?" asked Dreng.

"Yeah, I'm all right. I fell on some loose grass… be safe honey."

Dreng could feel her face turning red inside her helmet. *What was Mac thinking calling me honey and broadcasting it to everyone? It was so unlike him. She recalled his fall. Perhaps he jarred some electronics loose in his helmet. The pause. I'll bet he switched to private but it didn't work. This could be embarrassing. No time, got to move.*

Dreng switched her com to Second platoon. "I need the grapple hook, and some line. The rest of you spread out and take up defensive positions. After I get to the humans, be ready to lay down some suppression fire on my command. Keep an eye out for other humans or bugs."

Dreng tied the grapple onto the rope and threw it about half way up. It caught on some damaged metal hanging out of a five-meter hole in the ship's side. She moved up the rope without effort. The body armor's ability to blend into the black background prevented her from drawing fire. The bugs were focused on trying to keep the humans from getting to the ground, not trying to keep someone from climbing up.

The captive humans found themselves pinned down at a thirty-meter tear in the ship's side. The ship's curve made it difficult for Dreng to toss the grapple. To make it worse no metal extended out to offer her a good target. She leaned out again and made a sidearm toss in the blind, hoping to get the three hooks to catch on something. On the third try it caught. Within twenty seconds, she was standing behind the humans. She flipped her suit's camouflage capability off.

"Hello. I'm Dreng. Can you tell me who's in charge?"

Smitty's eyes opened wide. It seemed as though Dreng appeared out of thin air. He looked at her armor.

"I've never seen anything like your armor. You must be with the elite forces. How did spec ops get here so quick?" asked Smitty.

"Were not spec ops. We are three platoons of UFC light infantry. Now, can you tell me who is in charge?"

Smitty looked at Dreng's rifle and the two tomahawks hanging off her belt. "Not spec ops my ass. Call yourselves whatever you want. I'm glad to see you. My name is Smitty. I'm the Nomad's chief engineer. We are from the Nomad and Imperial Station. To answer your question, no one here is in charge." Smitty looked at the ex-captives. "Hey everyone, listen up. This here is Dreng," he looked at her, smiled, and said, "she's spec ops. She's here to help us. Do whatever she says."

About ten people came up to her and shook hands or patted her back.

"We're at a stand off. We were trying to get off the ship when the bugs showed up. I'm afraid more of them will be coming. They're like roaches. If you see one, there's more somewhere else," said Smitty.

"Are you the only survivors?"

"No, we heard plasma rifle fire inside the ship. As far as we know, there were 812 of us locked in a single pen."

Dreng surveyed their position. Even with suppression fire, she feared some of them would lose their lives repelling down. She would have to take the fight to the fifteen or so bugs preventing them from getting down.

"Dreng, Dwain. Third platoon is on site."

"Great. Send me three good rope-climbing marksmen. I left grapple lines in place. I'm going to take the fight to the bugs or we're stuck here. When I ask for it, give me suppression fire."

"How you going to get there?"

"I see a pathway to them if I can use a line to swing to the other side."

"Okay, it's your ass... honey."

Several ground pounders activated their mic and giggled. Even Dreng laughed at the thought of Dwain calling her honey. She let it go. When the three marksmen arrived she had them take up positions. She briefed them on how she would bridge the gap between their positions.

"Cover fire now," said Dreng as she ran out tossing a perfect grapple that caught on the ships broken structure. She swung across to the far section in one smooth motion. She could see the confusion as the bugs started taking fire from the ground. The Raygin crew lost two more bugs before they found cover from the crossfire. Dreng knew once her presence became known the bugs would concentrate their fire on her. She needed to move into the group's middle. She put her rifle down, took out her tomahawks, and attacked. Three big black bugs were dead before they knew she was in their midst. She kicked a bug hard in the midsection. The force of the blow knocked it fifteen feet through the air and over the ship's side.

Dreng had no option but to allow the troops to see her in action. She wielded the tomahawks like they were extensions of her own arms. Each of her blows went all the way through the beetle exoskeleton. What she didn't predict was the fighting quarters would be so tight. She moved so quick her help couldn't fire for fear of hitting her. She couldn't stop fighting to retreat without getting shot by an enemy plasma rifle. She believed her only chance to survive was an all out assault. Here goes n…. She paused her final attack as she heard a strange sound.

BuZZZZ Thunk. BuZZZZ Thunk. Dreng couldn't understand where the odd sound was coming from until she looked at two bugs with parts of their heads missing. She remembered the stories Tinker told about Mac's sniper days. His favorite rifle was the Buzzard. She understood the name now. She figured out the direction he was shooting from, and began to maneuver the bugs into his line of sight. He had saved her.

BuZZZZ Thunk. BuZZZZ Thunk. BuZZZZ Thunk.

Between Mac and herself all the enemy except one were dead. She thought about her mother and how the Raygin had taken her life as she swung the tomahawk at the lone surviving bug. The blow's impact was so great the Raygin body flew twenty feet in the air. It even cleared the ship's side before it began to drop.

"Holy crap," said Dwain, "did you see that? No wonder she beat me. She's a fucking robot. Mac is in love with a robot."

As Dreng caught her breath, she said, "Dwain, I can hear you, and I am not a robot. I was born on a high gravity planet called Nokomis."

"Nokomis? I've heard of it. It's a robot planet."

"Dwain, you're impossible."

Dreng gathered up six undamaged rifles and lowed them to the ground. By the time she got back to the humans, Mac was already arguing with Smitty. They had rigged a rope chair to get the wounded down to ground level.

"Save it," said Smitty, "I already heard it all. You are not special ops. I can't get any of you to admit it. You look like special ops, you fight like special ops, you shoot like special ops, but I guess you're from the fairy clan."

Mac laughed at Smitty's frustration. "One day, over some drinks, I'll tell you the whole story. For now, let's get your people down, and to safety before more Raygin show up."

The troops began to lower the injured. They ran three more lines down for everyone else to begin repelling.

"Raygin?" Said Smitty, "I prefer to call them bugs." He grinned at Dreng and gave her a wink.

She lifted her visor and nodded her head in the affirmative.

Mac walked up to her, "I have two comments. First, let me say nice job. Second, what the hell were you thinking? Are you trying to give me a heart attack? You were fighting like a possessed person."

She put her hands on her hips, and said, "I wanted to see if you were as good as Tinker said you were." She looked him up and down as if he were a cut of meat she was getting ready to devour.

Mac laughed. "You're so funny. Still feeling the rush aren't you? Everyone handles it a little different. I have to admit, it's the first time anyone came on to me. Take some long deep breaths. Slow your heart down and save your adrenaline for later. You may need it. Dwain, Mac. Bring Third platoon up. I want you to take your team into the ship and search for more human survivors."

"On our way."

Mac smacked his helmet and shook his head.

The last of Smitty's bunch made it down to the ground. Second Platoon picked up the bug weapons and moved everyone to a tree line for cover. Dreng was proud of them. They understood their armor made them invisible to thermal detection, but not the other humans. Mac spent days in the holographic trainer pitting teams against each other. The games of hide and seek paid off thanks to Mac's experience.

"Mac, Tinker. I just caught Mr. Phlop sneaking around the com system. He said he didn't use it, but the power was on. I shut it down."

"Tinker, remove his weapons, put binders on his hands, post a guard with him, and do not let him near the skiff. Tell him if he puts the troops in danger again, I'll impose war article 19, and kill him myself."

"Tinker copy."

Standing next to Mac, Dreng heard everything. "What's his problem, Mac?"

"My guess is he never had a chance to grow up. His parents coddled him his whole life. I'd be willing to bet they bought him this job. People like them are the reason I resurrected the old commodore title. I saw a lot of good soldiers die for no other reason than somebody got promoted beyond their competence level because they had money or were connected."

"What is war article 19?"

A smile lit Mac's face. "There is no such rule as war article 19. I use it on inexperienced young first lieutenants like Phlop. It forces them to think about the impact of their actions. They don't mind risking your life, but they never want to risk their own lives."

Dwain barking out orders interrupted their conversation. Third platoon began to climb up the ropes. As they got to the top, both Dreng and Mac were there to help.

When Dwain got to the top he looked at Dreng and said, "Nice job, honey."

Mac looked at Dreng with his eyebrows squished together. Dwain didn't wait for a response. He led his platoon into the ship.

Mac looked at Dreng. "Damn. I can't hear Third platoon at all. I heard Dwain in your helmet, but not mine. Something is wrong with my com. Why did he call you honey?"

"I meant to tell you–"

Mac put his hand out towards Dreng. "Be still. Listen."

The two stood motionless in their camo body armor as two Raygin fighters flew over the wreckage. The surviving Raygin ship must have observed the energy spike from the skiff's com system. They had sent the fighters to investigate.

"Tinker, Mac. We have two Raygin fighters flying over the crash site. It won't be long before they widen their search. Get the anti-particle canon ready. It's the only weapon we have capable of taking out a fighter. Set it up so it fires it between the split in the big tree by the camp. I'm going to try to lead them right down your throat."

"Tinker, copy."

"Dwain, copy." Dreng used battle signals to relay any communications from Dwain. She glanced into the smoke-filled sky and watched the two fighters begin their search pattern.

CHAPTER ELEVEN: Allies

The Wasp slid to a bumpy halt in a heap of giant apple trees. Everyone unstrapped from their seats and looked out the windows. The trees piled up in a big heap covering the ship. They provided a natural canopy, keeping them hidden from enemy view. The crew looked at each other and no words were spoken. Mahpee's grandfather had kept them all alive. When they looked for him, he was nowhere to be found.

The last action of the strange being was to take all systems off line. It seemed to have a purpose for every action, so they decided to leave the power off line. The crew had to force open the door. A big dust cloud was still settling.

"Bodaway, you and Nashta need to check the damage, inside and out. I'll scout the local area. Nashta, have you thought about what or who the entity is? And stop calling it my grandfather. I know it's not him."

"No, I haven't figured it out yet, but it knew about you and your grandfather. It needed you to act so it became someone you trusted. It also knew how to counter everything I was doing to take control back. I think it read our minds. While in the computer, it learned how to improve the drive and our weapon systems. It adapts and learns with blistering speed. Your grandfather –" Nashta ducked his head to avoid a slap from Mahpee, "piloted the ship to save us but wouldn't pilot the attack on the enemy. Why?"

"You need to figure out what it is and where it came from. In your spare time, you and Bodaway determine how

186

to repair the ship. I'll take everyone else and scout the local area."

"We're on it," said Nashta as he scooted out of slapping range.

The crew grabbed their weapons and headed out. The Wasp landed near a lake surrounded by fields of vegetables, fruits, and various kinds of trees. Everything seemed perfect, except the planet appeared to be void of animal or insect life. This wouldn't be the first planet Mahpee had visited where a super predator wiped out the other significant life forms. There is one major difference. On the other planets there were always insects, birds, and burrowing animals left. Here on Rayne, there was nothing. It had to be bioengineered.

Mahpee picked out the tallest tree in the area and began to climb. He stopped at an opening in the leaves and looked through his viewer. At a glance the whole planet appeared the same. He felt a chill run through him. *It's a harvest planet, a planet designed to support the Raygin war effort. The three Raygin ships must have come here to restock supplies. For the past twenty-five years they have been preparing for war by bioengineering planets. Planet building like this seems beyond the capabilities of Raygin technology. Could it be their invisible allies had a hand in helping them? Right now, I have too many questions and not enough answers.*

Another ten meters of climbing put him above the other trees. The heat from the sun warmed his face. He sucked in the fresh air and began to scan the horizon. He paused and focused his eyes on a spot in the far distance. He zoomed the viewer in on a huge column of smoke. *It had to be the Raygin ship crash site. Forty-one point eight kilometers or about twenty-six miles. That's not too bad. In this low gravity, traveling light, I could be there in about two point five hours.*

At least I won't have to pack food. I've seen enough.
Mahpee and the crew headed back to the ship. When they
arrived, both Bodaway and Nashta were looking at the
damaged ion thruster.

Mahpee walked to the ship's aft end to look at the
mangled thrusters. "How bad is the damage?"

"It's severe," said Nashta.

"Can you fix it?"

"No, I can't fix it. Not without a foundry to shape
new metal components. Even if I had one, the repair would
be temporary until we got to a ship yard or space station."

Bodaway started laughing. "Nashta, tell him before
he has your hide."

"Tell me what?" asked Mahpee.

Bodaway pointed at the twisted ion thruster. "Look
Mahpee."

Mahpee stared at the thruster. "I don't understand. I
don't see anything but a damaged thruster."

"Keep looking."

Mahpee stared without blinking. His eyes began to
water. A structural crack began to close. He wiped his eyes
and stared some more. A crinkle in the metal began to
smooth over. "How is this possible?"

"Nashta thinks he figured it out," said Bodaway,
"your grandfather isn't your grandfather. He is a collection
of nanobots."

Mahpee turned and looked at Nashta. "Explain."

"Remember the explosion at the university lab? I was
trying to meld my nanobot with the Raygin luminescent
organism from their computer. I wanted to see if I could get
the nanobots to learn. I programmed a bible of sorts off the
top of my head using a machine source code which cannot
be overwritten."

"Off the top of your head? Oh Nashta. Please tell me
you remember what limiting parameters you programmed
into them."

"I can't. I don't remember the parameters, but I know they seemed good at the time." Nashta looked at Mahpee. "I know, I know. It sounds bad, but you have to realize I was testing my supposition in a controlled laboratory environment. I didn't expect to create a new life form!"

"You mean these hybrid nanobots are alive?"

"For all practical purposes. They think, learn, and replicate on their own. They can't kill the aliens because it is against the source code I wrote."

Mahpee's grandfather's head loomed out from the crumpled metal. He said, "You do know we can hear every word you say?"

Mahpee pointed at his grandfather's face. "Did you build a switch to turn them off?" asked Mahpee.

His grandfather shook his head no, smiled, and disappeared into the surface once again.

"No, I never thought it would get this far," said Nashta.

"How long will their energy last before they need to recharge?"

"I made the nanobots self-charging. They can use electricity, light, heat, static charge, and conductive surfaces. I'm not sure how else they may have modified themselves. They can enhance themselves, but they cannot reprogram their source code," said Nashta.

"How did they read our minds?"

"I'm guessing they entered our brains via our noses. Memory is nothing more than encoded connections in the brain. They occur from the firing of neurons. It would be simple for a sentient nanobot to trigger our memories and read them. I think we can tell if they trigger our memories because they will be the thoughts foremost in our mind."

"I think you're wrong. Random thoughts happen all day long. How can you tell random from triggered? As soon as you think about a memory, it fires more memories.

Try not to think of something and it becomes what you don't what to think about. Can you talk to these nanobots?"

"I have tried, but as you saw, they appear when they want to, not on command. The nanobot in them may focus on one primary task at a time. I don't know. The truth is I know nothing about them."

"Can you destroy them?"

"Well, I guess it is possible. But I did program them for self-survival. Part of their code says they may not directly take another sentient being's life. I can now see this rather simple statement may be a problem. If you are planning their destruction, and if they get inside you, they would know what you are thinking. Mahpee, I hate to bring this up, but they might be able to take control of your mind for self-preservation."

"Wouldn't that be against the source code you programmed into them?"

"I don't know. It depends how they interpret the code."

"How did they get on the Wasp, and how many are there?"

"I programmed one. After the explosion, we couldn't find it. I may have brought it aboard. To answer the last part of your question, for us to see a solid form, I'd estimate there to be at least millions of them."

"How is it they reproduce so fast? Why are they helping us fix the ship?" asked Mahpee.

"The more of them there are the faster they can reproduce. I don't know why they are helping us. Maybe we are the simplest method of escape off this planet."

"You're just full of good news, aren't you? Bodaway, remind me, was it your idea or mine to make Nashta a crewmember?"

Nashta's shoulders slumped.

"It was your idea chief."

Mahpee walked over to the dispirited Nashta and patted him on the shoulder. "You know, my intuition is seldom wrong. I trust you," the chief gave him a stern eye, "Keep trying to talk to them, and find out their intentions. Maybe we can help each other."

Nashta perked up. "Don't worry chief, I'll find a way to communicate with them." The young engineer walked back into the ship leaving the repairs to the nanobots. He seemed determined to solve the communication problem.

"How long do you estimate it will take the nanobots to fix the ion drive?" asked Mahpee.

"Oh – at this rate, I'd guess about six more hours," said Bodaway.

"Perfect. I saw smoke on the horizon. It must be the crashed bug ship. I'm going to investigate and see if I can learn anything from their ship."

"There may be survivors. You better take Nidawi with you."

The chief frowned. *I don't need anyone to protect me. In the old days chiefs protected themselves, as would any warrior. Ever since the Raygin attack the leaders worry too much about me. I hate it that the council assigned me a shadow walker to be with me any time I went off Nokomis.*

He pictured his young daughter training to become proficient in hand-to-hand combat. Participating in thousands of matches and demonstrations in front of audiences. There was no doubt about her skill. But Nidawi trained in secret. Toiling at learning her special skill set. Seeking perfection. It was her sole purpose in life. She learned to kill any threat whether human or animal. She even learned Raygin physiology during her training. Now that he thought about it, *Bodaway gave me good counsel after all. I will take her.*

The two traveled light. Mahpee followed close behind Nidawi. As she ran, he could see some of her weapons tucked away in her armor. *If there are five weapons I can*

191

see, I know there are fifteen I can't see. At this quick pace she set, we will be at the crash site well within two and a half standard hours.

*****

The perimeter was set up. Dreng supervised the preparations to move the wounded. Mac managed to pound his helmet into submission. His receiver could pick up Third platoon again. He waited for them while watching for other threats. After about twenty minutes, he heard Dwain shouting out orders. In the background, he could hear weapon fire. Mac moved into the Raygin ship to see if he could find the troops and give them a hand.

As he rounded a corner Mac found himself behind eight bugs. It looked like Dwain got pinned between two groups of Raygin. Mac didn't want to use his Buzzard in the long corridor for fear the high velocity round would go through the target and hit his own troops.

"Semore," yelled Dwain.

Mac moved behind the corner and waited. Semore was the nickname for a cluster grenade designed for close quarter fighting. You could roll it or throw it like a ball.

WAUUUUM.

Mac felt a massive pressure wave speed down the passageway.

A bug came running around the corner on four legs. It didn't see him. They collided and tumbled over. Mac recovered and leapt onto the disorientated bug. He pulled his knife out of its sheath and stuck the tip under the bug's armor against its thorax. Mac smelled the air. It stank. He wondered, *did this bug shit its pants? Oh yeah, some relief bugs communicated with chemical odors.* Understanding the threat to its life it decided not to move.

"Dwain, Mac. I'm in a side passageway behind where you tossed the Semore. I captured a bug. I'm bringing it back with us."

192

"Dwain, copy. We found sixty-seven humans. They say they are the last survivors from their group of captives. We're heading out with about fifty bugs on our tail. Mac, there are hundreds of bugs alive in here. Most of them have rifles."

"Mac, copy." While they were communicating Mac bound the bug's clawed arms behind it. He also bound its legs to prevent full movement. He helped the bug to its feet and headed back to the exit point.

"Dreng, Mac. Put a few troopers in place to give Third platoon some cover in case they need it."

"Dreng copy, already done. We are also ready for the prisoner."

Mac smiled. *She would go far in Fleet Command if she decided to stay.* When Third platoon arrived, they wasted no time in getting everyone on the ground, including the prisoner. Five members of Third platoon stayed in the passageway to keep any marauding bugs at bay.

The survivors greeted each other and began to discuss their experience. Mac had to cut the reunion short. Too many armed bugs to stay and fight it out. Plus, with two Raygin fighters circling overhead, the humans didn't stand a chance. Mac hoped his plan would increase their odds a little bit. He walked up to Smitty, who was talking to another survivor.

"Smitty, I need about twenty volunteers to set up the fighters so we can take a clear shot at them. It will be our single chance to take them out. The assignment will be risky."

"Mac, this is Captain Cutter, he's from the Nomad. He can get you the volunteers better than I can."

A short, well-built, young military sergeant stepped forward towards Mac. "I was on Imperial Station when we got attacked. They call me Spaz. I'll be your first volunteer if you'll let a ground pounder join your spec ops team."

"We're not spec ops Spaz, but we'd be glad to have you fight with us. We are three platoons of ground pounders. You should fit right in." Mac reached his arm out and shook hands with Spaz.

Spaz looked at the body armor on the soldiers. He glanced at the new rifles. He couldn't help but see Dreng carrying two hatchets in her belt. These were all the hallmarks of spec ops.

Before he could say anything, Smitty said, "Don't bother arguing, Spaz. They have been told to tell us they are not here. Even though we see them, they won't admit spec ops is here. "

Mac didn't have time to explain it to the survivors. He walked up to his two platoon leaders. "I need three troopers from each of you. I am going to take twenty volunteers from the hostages and sprint across the open field toward the skiff."

"You want the fighters to see you?" asked Dreng.

"Yes. Grouped together we should paint a good return on the fighter's thermal detector. We will form a line when we see them heading our way. I want them to line up behind us for a strafing run. Tinker will be ready with the anti-matter cannon."

"Let me do it instead of you," said Dwain. "We can't let you risk your life."

Surprising everyone Dwain walked up to Mac, put his hand on his shoulder. "I didn't think much of you at first. I got to say I think you might be the real deal. Do you plan on getting married to Dreng?"

Mac was caught off guard by the question. *Damn Dwain. The books all said never talk marriage in the beginning of a relationship.* "Why do you want to know?"

"If you are, I was going to volunteer for the job, with the promise you would name your first-born child after me if I die." Dwain grinned.

194

Disbelief showed on Dreng's face. Mac started laughing.

"Sorry Dwain, you're going to have to name your own kids, not ours. Besides, I don't ask my troops to do anything I wouldn't do myself. I'm going."

"I was hoping you'd say that. Names are overrated anyway," said Dwain.

"Mac, Have you been thinking about... children?" Asked Dreng.

Before he could answer Fishman interrupted, "Mac."

He turned to see Fishman pointing in the sky.

"The fighters."

The Raygin were starting to search the next quadrant over. It wouldn't be long before they were in the perfect position. He could hear as the troopers behind them began to fire at the bugs, trying to get off the ship. They weren't stupid. It wouldn't be long before they found another way down.

Mac turned to Dreng and Dwain. "Get everyone together, let's start moving. Stay in the underbrush and have the troopers protecting our six follow a short distance behind. Erase our trail. For now want to evade, not engage them. I'm going to check on the fight above us."

The battle was still going on. Warhammer and Dagger had joined the fray. It looked like each of the original UFC ships received damage. The Raygin ship was taking on an enormous amount of weapon fire, but their shields seemed to be holding. The fight couldn't go on like this or in time, the Raygin would win. Mac contemplated their plight. He remembered hearing Smitty say they were in engineering when the ship went down.

Hustling over to Smitty he asked, "Did I hear right earlier? You were in the Raygin ship's engineering department when it went down?"

"Yeah. We snuck in through the ship's ventilation system, killed the bugs, and took control. We tripped all power to everything by accident."

"The battle above is not going our way, said Mac. "Our ships are taking a pounding and we can't seem to get through the Raygin shields. Any ideas from what you saw?"

"Yeah. The sons of bitches have two ion drives. If they're not moving, or using position thrusters, they can divert all power to the shields. The trick would be to make them use their main thrusters. They would have to divert power to make a big move. The problem is they can sit still all day and wait for help which is sure to come."

"I'll relay the info, in the hopes someone can come up with a plan while we take care of business down here." Mac called the Dagger's captain and explained what Smitty had seen in the bugs' engineering room. She told Mac she had an idea and needed to go. Mac felt a little better. He hoped the new information gave them a fighting chance. "Dreng, take the lead. Stop when you get to the clearing's edge. Dwain cover our six."

After about two hours of hiking through underbrush Dreng reported she had arrived. The bulk of survivors were still moving through the forest following her lead. Dwain reported the bugs were grouping outside the ship but seemed reluctant to leave. They were not following the humans.

The human volunteers grouped together with Mac.

"Tinker, Mac. We're in place, are you ready?"

"We anchored the gun and set it up to shoot between the split in the tree. I already flipped the switch to make a projectile. It's warming up or doing whatever it does to get ready."

Everyone with a headset heard the whirling noise in the background as the canon warmed up.

"It's going to take a few minutes to make an anti-particle round," said Mac.

The survivors watched the Raygin fighters began to search in their quadrant. There wasn't time to wait. They had to act now.

"Ready or not, here we come," said Mac.

"Mac, wait. I think the cannon is having power issues."

"No time to wait. We are out of options. Here we come."

Mac led the team into the open field. Several troopers and Mac would remain cloaked until the fighters got close. They would de-cloak and fire their laser rifles. He didn't expect to take down a fighter with rifle fire, but the pilots wouldn't know the humans didn't have anti fighter weapons. To be safe the pilots would break off their approach and evaluate the enemy. This would give Tinker time to get the canon ready to fire. It would take the Raygin pilots one or two minutes to come around for a second run.

"Shit, Mac. The battery doesn't have enough juice to launch the projectile. The power must have leaked out while the canon sat in storage for so long. I'm trying to hook up a few laser rifles to the power supply. Give me a minute."

All eyes watched as the fighters lined up to shoot the fleeing prisoners.

"Too late to wait," said Mac, "the Raygin fighters are maneuvering into position."

Some volunteers started to panic. They began to fan out.

Mac lifted his visor and yelled at them. "Stay together! Stay together! You have to run at the split tree, or we all die!"

They were scared, but they lined up again. In a few heartbeats, the fighters were in position behind them.

"Uncloak and fire."

The troopers appeared as if from nowhere and began to shoot at the two fighters. The response to the ground fire was as Mac predicted. Since the pilots weren't sure what weapons were being used against them, they broke off their approach and implemented evasive maneuvers. After they realized it was only low energy weapons, they would be back.

"Any luck, Tinker?" asked Mac.

"I got the laser rifle batteries hooked up. The canon is making noises, but the projectile ready light isn't on. Keep coming at me. I'll keep working on it."

The fighters swung around for another low-level run. The humans were three-fourths the way across the open field. One fighter took the lead and the second followed offset to the left. The humans presented themselves as a perfect target. Everyone lined up in a nice tight row.

"Fire Tinker, fire now!"

"Still no light. Here goes."

The lead Raygin fired a powerful laser canon. The ground in front of Mac vaporized, sending rock flying like shrapnel. Two humans exploded into pieces from the flying debris. Mac aimed his little laser rifle at the approaching fighter. When Tinker hit the fire button, no one heard a sound. Unseen by the human eye a prolate spheroid shaped anti-particle round rocketed from the gun.

Mac zeroed in on his target, ignoring all the pandemonium going on around him. His finger rested against the trigger. He began to squeeze. His gun hadn't fired when a hole larger than his old math teacher's ass appeared in the fighter. In a split second, he saw all the way through the Raygin war bird. It seemed like the lead plane hit its brakes. It passed overhead and veered left. The second fighter didn't understand what happened. It couldn't avoid a collision. They both hit the ground in a giant fireball.

The volunteers cheered.

Still trying to catch his breath, Smitty walked up to Mac. "What the hell just happened?"

"It was our anti-particle canon," said Mac.

"Anti-particle canon?" Smitty blew out his nose, turned around, flailed his arms as he muttered something about spec ops and a lying bastard.

With all the hooting and hollering going on, Mac couldn't hear anything Smitty was grumbling about, but he got the gist of it. He smiled. The survivors made their way into camp. Mac let the group take a minute or two to celebrate before he gave them the bad news. He started walking toward Tinker.

A perimeter guard yelled, "Halt! Identify yourself."

The cheering stopped. Everyone focused on a rather large person walking into the clearing. Mac turned, and started moving towards the intruder. Something was up. He was not coming from the crash site. It seems Rayne was full of surprises.

Mac moved, placing himself between the intruder and a spot in the woods. His sniper honed skills picked up motion in the background. Sure enough, someone had repositioned to regain a tactical advantage. All was not as it seemed. Mac gave battle signals to Dwain, who in response moved unnoticed into the woods. Tinker and Dreng, now alerted, stood at the ready.

Holding out his arms with his palms facing downward, the intruder moved toward Mac. He yelled, "I am Mahpee, Chief of the People's Nation. My ship, the Wasp, received damage in a firefight with the Raygin. We were assisting a UFC convoy."

Dreng lifted her visor in disbelief. "Father?"

"Ayashe?"

Ayashe? Mac's legs felt weak. He could see the confusion on the chief's face too. Mac called to the guard, "It's okay. Let him enter." But it wasn't okay. A thousand scenarios flashed through his mind. None were good, and what about the sniper in the woods?

The chief started to move toward his daughter. "What are you doing here? We have trackers searching everywhere for you. These are dangerous times." Mahpee turned toward the woods. "Nidawi, come, we are among family and friends."

Dreng moved toward Mahpee. Mac could see she was unsure of herself. Mahpee ran to his daughter scooping her up in his arms. There was no doubt in his intentions. Mac saw tears of joy in his eyes.

Behind Mahpee and Dreng, Mac observed a lone figure walking out from the shadows. It was the hidden sniper. Near where Nidawi revealed herself, Dwain appeared, and began walking toward her.

"Ayashe, forgive me. I was a fool. I should have told you how I felt, but it still hurts whenever I talk of your mother. I feared the old legends. I wanted to protect you, so I forbid you to enter the military. Come home with me, and I will support anything you want to do."

Now, it was Dreng's turn to cry. "Father, I was wrong too, but in a way, I did what you begged me to do."

Mac knew weasel words when he heard them. *What in the world is Dreng up to?*

"I have joined with a Person of the Stars."

Mahpee's arms dropped as he stood with a blank stare of his face.

Mac walked up to the father and daughter.

Dreng said, "This is Mac, Father. We are one."

I can't believe she's telling her father we made love! This is a little too open for me. Wait. What did she say? We are in love? No, no. It was we are one. What the hell does that mean?

Mac could see Mahpee's shoulders droop even further. In the background he also saw Dwain put his hand on Nidawi's back. She spun inside, grabbing his shoulder, moved her leg behind him, and pushed. Before Dwain hit the ground, Nidawi was holding a knife to his neck. Her brown eyes stared into his.

Dwain smiled through his open visor. "Are you a robot too? You're beautiful."

The slightest upturn appeared on Nidawi's lips. She rolled off Dwain, sheathed her knife, and held out her hand. "I am sorry. Instincts. No one lays a hand on me." She smiled and said, "Unless I want them to."

Dwain smiled like a playful puppy as he took her hand.

She pulled him up with ease. "No, I am not a robot."

"I wouldn't mind if you were." He smiled and said, "I'm Dwain."

The body language of Nidawi indicated she was receptive to Dwain's unusual overtures. With at least some introductions completed, attention focused once again on Dreng and her father.

Looking at Mac with a new focus, Mahpee said, "I am sorry, Mac. You must realize your joining is hard for me to digest."

"I don't understand," said Mac. He was having a hard time making sense of all this sexual openness.

Now, Mahpee looked at his daughter. "I fear you have made a bad choice in a man my daughter. You have joined with an idiot."

"Mac, this is what I wanted to tell you."

"What? About sex?" asked Mac.

Mahpee's face turned red. He glared at Mac. "What is going on here? Did you or did you not have a ceremonial joining?"

Stepping in front of her father, Dreng prepared to answer the question. Mahpee put his hand up to silence his daughter.

"I am talking to you, Mac."

This was not the way Mac planned on meeting Dreng's father. "I'm not sure what's going on, but I can tell you I have fallen in love with your daughter."

"Great Spirit, help me. I'll ask you again. This time I will help you by speaking slower, so you can understand. Did you, or did you not have a ceremonial joining?"

"I can say, your daughter told me we had a joining."

Frustration appeared on the chief's face. "What? Are you telling me you don't know? Weren't you there with her? How could you not know? Were there two pine-scented candles? Did my daughter offer a blessing prayer? Did she not wear a pure white silk made from the Crepe spiders? When you were intimate with my daughter for the first time, were you not covered in a blue blanket?"

This was not going well. The saliva built up so thick in Mac's throat he didn't think he could answer. Thankfully, Dreng spoke up.

"Stop this inquisition, Father. It's my fault. I haven't had the chance to tell him the significance of a joining."

It hit Mac like a ton of space debris. A joining was a ceremony, not the act of making love. *YES*, screamed in his mind. He couldn't contain his joy. *Now, I don't have to figure out a way to ask her the big question. We are already married. The little minx* he thought. *That's what she wanted to talk to me about.*

"Mr. Mahpee, I don't pretend to understand everything that has happened between your daughter and me. I don't understand your customs. You should know I was trying to figure out how I could ask her to marry me according to my customs."

"You were?" interrupted Dreng.

Mac smiled at her. "I was, but if I understand what is being said, I don't have to because we are already, um, joined."

Mahpee began to understand it was his daughter who had been deceitful. He allowed her spouse to see a half-smile. He looked at Mac. "Call me Mahpee. My people do not have surnames."

With his left eyebrow arched, Mac looked at Dreng.

"I am sorry for deceiving you my love. I created a temporary name from two different advertisement displays in Finder's Station. I generated a false identity using the name Dreng Matilda. My true name is Ayashe, it means – little one."

With the truth out, most tension in Ayashe's body dissolved. But, her eyes said she still felt a great deal of apprehension. Mac reassured her with a big hug. She embraced him back with such force he thought he felt his ribs beginning to crack.

A floating head appeared next to Mahpee. Third platoon wasted no time in aiming their weapons at the new threat. It stared at Mac and Ayashe as if evaluating them.

Ayashe recognized the face. "Great-grandfather Uzumati. Is that you?" she asked.

Uzumati's head smiled at Ayashe and turned towards Mahpee and frowned. "We have a big problem."

CHAPTER TWELVE: The Secret

Dagger and Warhammer escorted the Argosy to safety. They sent battle videos via com probe to United Fleet Command. The captains did what Mac thought they would. They both headed back to the Rayne solar system to assist in the battle. Upon their return, they saw the bad news. The UFC convoy was down to a Battleship and a single cruiser. Both ships had minor damage.

The Raygin designed computers were faster. The quick-thinking alien technology meant they could initiate the next firing sequence first, forcing the humans to be on the defensive. The UFC ships got a few lucky hits through the Raygin shields as they fired their weapons, but the big bug ship didn't sustain much damage.

The Dagger's captain, Tal Fetter, had been involved in several space battles during her career. It was obvious the humans were going to lose this fight unless something changed. She reasoned if the Raygin computers were faster than the human war computer, a UFC ship should disengage from the computer and create an unknown variable. She volunteered the Dagger.

After notifying the Admiral of their arrival and their plan, both ships entered the fight. The Dagger had immediate success with the first weapon volley it fired. The Raygin ship lost maneuvering thrusters on the port side. After the initial success the bug computer learned how to adjust to what, at times, must have seemed like illogical decisions.

The battle had turned into a stalemate because the Raygin ship always played it safe. When Mac's call came in about the bugs ships having two ion drives, Tal's creativity kicked in. She had a plan. She relayed her requirements to the remaining ships. Tal maneuvered the Dagger near the bug ship's port side and fired several times at the rear thrusters. The Raygin returned fire, sending the Dagger limping off behind the nearest planet.

The three remaining UFC ships kept firing at the Raygin ship for hours, hoping to score a hit during the same fraction of a second the bug shields had to come down to fire their weapons. The Raygin ship only maneuvered and fired on the humans when there was no risk to the alien ship.

Tal was finally ready. "Implement takedown," she broadcast to the remaining human ships.

The three Federation ships began to maneuver to the Raygin ship's aft and starboard side. Tal accelerated the Dagger using its ion drive. By the time the Raygin realized the Dagger was pushing a damaged cruiser straight into its port side, it was too late to move using only the slower thrusters. It was forced to use its ion drive to make a quick getaway move.

As soon as the Raygin ship began to engage their ion drive to avoid the impending collision, the UFC ships opened fire. The humans even used the damaged cruiser's weapon systems to take a few shots at the enemy ship. It looked like a huge Tesla coil in space. The Raygin shields with their reduced power could not withstand the attack of a battleship and four cruisers. The bug ship blew apart in three large chunks of black metal, which floated off into space.

The Raygin ship's destruction came at a price. The Dagger was the lone UFC ship undamaged. Several fighters were now stuck in the launch tubes on the human battleship. Repairs were underway. The battle had cost both sides tens of thousands of lives.

"Well done," said the admiral. "I'm not complaining, but where the hell did both of you come from?"

"Admiral, this is Captain Tal Fretter, on the Dagger. We are on assignment with Commodore McCormack and under his direct orders."

"Commodore? I heard rumors they resurrected that old rank for some high-flying official. The UFC kept it a secret. Do you know why?"

"Yes sir, he's the single commodore in the entire fleet. If everyone knew his rank, he couldn't move without lots of formality."

"Is he there? I'd like to talk to him."

"He's not here, sir. He's on Rayne with three platoons of… spec ops. He had a feeling the bugs were using Rayne as a forward staging area. He saved our two ships and the Argosy too. He had us deploy a couple vid/com mini satellites near Rayne, put him on the ground, and hide on the nearest planet's far side. If the bugs showed up, our orders were to get the Argosy away from harm.

We were afraid of detection after the three Raygin ships arrived. We laid low until you arrived and began firing at them. It was the distraction we needed to get the Argosy to safety. We got her on her way home and came back as soon as possible to help."

"If the commodore is right," said the admiral, "and this is a forward staging area, we had better get out of here. Tal, can you or the Warhammer send a team into these floating hunks of enemy ship? We need to look for some of their technology. It might prove useful. Also, if you could take some interior ship vids and grab a few bodies it would help. While you explore pieces of the enemy ship, we will try to repair ours enough so we can get back home."

"No problem admiral. I'll dispatch a team now."

Within minutes Dagger moved abeam the largest remnant of the Raygin ship. Tal deployed a shuttle. It contained a team made up of weapons experts, engineers, and medical personnel. She didn't realize how big the Raygin ship was until they were next to the floating fragments. She was sure it was at least twice the size of their battleship.

Another intact UFC cruiser was drifting in space. It had no drive capability and was on battery powered life support. Upon evaluation, the engineers reported they were too damaged to repair. Since the Warhammer didn't receive much damage it picked up the crew of the broken cruiser. The Raygin had destroyed the rest of the UFC ships.

Tal dialed in Mac's frequency to give him an update. The war had started. Why? She had no idea. The humans would soon be in the fight of their lives. Mac had become the most important man in the universe. He now held rank over all military personnel, and for that matter the civilians too. She hoped every rumor she heard about him was true.

The radio beeped that a link was established. "Mac, Tal here." She waited for a response.

"This is Mac, go ahead Tal."

"Argosy is on her way to Finder's Station. The battle is over. We destroyed all three Raygin ships. We are making required repairs, picking up survivors, and boarding what's left of the Raygin ship. We are looking for technology and any beneficial information. UFC survivors include the Battleship, one cruiser, plus Dagger and Warhammer. Do you need assistance?"

"Not right now. We have over a hundred human survivors from the crashed Raygin ship on Rayne. Tell the admiral Mahpee says he and his crew are well. Hundreds of hostiles survived the crash too. We will need to run a couple shuttles to get the human survivors off planet. I'll call when we are ready. We need to get out of here real fast."

207

"Aye sir, I'm on board with that."

He's one of those people always at the center of the storm. I can see his legend growing even more after this battle. Tal refocused her attention on the view screen as she watched the crew vid cameras. The boarding party began their entry procedure. The Raygin ship broke into three large sections. It was a shadow of its once great glory.

She moved to the biggest hunk of metal. Boarding another ship was always a dangerous undertaking. Even though there were holes everywhere, they could still run into pockets of survivors. The crew went in well armed, and wearing oxygen supplied mobility suits with grav shoes. The military called them Oxies.

Once inside the ship, the team entered a large dark passageway. As they moved deeper inside, the engineers placed signal boosters for both audio and vid displays. The crew on the Dagger's bridge watched as pieces of bug bodies and strange looking equipment floated by. Tal guessed the ship could hold at least twenty thousand or so bugs.

The team came upon a sealed hatch. Missions like this put the boarding party at great risk. "Commander Coleman, I don't need to tell you to be careful, so I won't."

"Thanks for your trust in me captain, I appreciate it."

She could see him smile as a crewmate looked at his face. The team set up a temporary barrier and depressurized the area behind the hatch for entry. Tal stared at the view screen as the team opened the sealed door. Caught by surprise, a large group of bugs started to scramble. They were coming after the human threat.

"Open fire," yelled Commander Coleman.

Laser rifles lit up the passageway. The unarmed bugs kept coming after the human invaders. Tal estimated there to be about two hundred bugs. Beetle bodies began to pile up so deep it was becoming hard for the human team to move over them. The surviving bugs regrouped and clustered in front of a second closed hatch. It was obvious they were protecting something deeper inside.

The bugs began to move as a massive spear shape of beetles toward the humans. Killing the unarmed bugs was easy. The attack was a ploy by the bugs and it worked. The bugs behind the dead ones used their bodies for a shield. The humans couldn't stop the spear. It was a clever hive type move.

"Blow the barrier, blow the barrier," yelled the commander.

Waooom. The grav shoes held as air rushed out of the passageway, carrying the bugs along on a free ride. Within seconds, the bug bodies lost all their oxygen. The moving shock wave carried their now lifeless bodies into the darkness.

"Let's see what they were protecting," said the commander.

The engineers set up a temporary interlock. They vented the pressure in the double sealed oxygen filled room. When they opened the inner hatch, a security officer was the first to enter the room. The lights were still on, which meant the room had its own power supply. Tal could see the chamber was expansive. Bigger than any room on a human ship. It looked to be at least 400 meters long.

When Commander Coleman entered the room, he whistled at its size. "Are you seeing this captain? There must be four to five hundred operating tables in here. It looks like a human body is on each table." Cables, hoses, and lines ran from beneath each table to the body on it. The commander walked up to a table to take a closer look. Tal couldn't believe her eyes. It was a child. As he looked at other tables, his vid link showed they were all children. A few boarding team members could be heard gagging as they tried to refrain from vomiting.

A female doctor walked up to a body for a better look and made sure they had vids to evaluate later. The aliens had cut off the top of each child's skull exposing the brain. It had the looks of an assembly line.

"We attacked them while they were in the middle of some sort of operation," said the doctor. "Look here," she said pointing to the open brain of a child. "There is a soft piece of tissue… no, it's webbing of some sort. It is connecting the cerebrum, cerebellum, and the brain's limbic area." When the doctor touched the tissue, the child's eyes opened, causing the doctor to reel backwards. She stumbled over her own feet. Other medical personnel rushed to check on her.

"I'm all right. I'm all right. It surprised me. That's all. They are still alive. Check the other children. Check the children."

The team used med scanners to evaluate the children. "They're alive. How can this be?"

The doctor stood up, established her bearings, and checked the pupils of the nearest child. "No eye movement." She checked the arms and legs. "No response to limb movement." She tapped on the wrist. "Reflex movement confirmed." She pinched the child's arm. "No response to pain." She looked at the med scanner readings and tried to figure out what flowed in the lines hooked up to each child.

Tal couldn't wait any longer. "I need your speculations doctor."

Tal watched as the doctor touched the membrane while reading the med scanner. The eyes opened again.

"I want you to understand this speculation is way out there captain. I'm guessing all the children seem to be in an induced coma. The webbing they have installed seems to use the brains electrical activity to power itself. This is far beyond anything we have. I'm guessing it's a data receiver. Why? Here's my guess, and as I said it is way out there. The older we get, the more our memories impact our decisions. Try to remember back to when you were a child.

Most of us can't remember events that happened earlier than about two and a half years of age. We use memories to help protect our bodies. We also use them for speech, problem solving, movement, perception, recognition, etc."

"The human brain takes about twenty-two years to develop, give or take a year or two. Let's say you take a young developing brain and input a computer-generated task. If you reward the brain with a good feeling it would be happy to complete all tasks assigned to it. I believe it might be possible for such an individual to operate at high cognitive levels. This webbing attaches to the cognitive brain pathways and it also hooks up to pleasure areas. I bet whoever did this wants the children to take data, assess it, manipulate it, and solve problems. Essentially, someone would have a perfect slave."

"Can we move the bodies?" asked Tal.

"Maybe. But it will take days to move so many children."

"What if we stabilized this section of ship and towed it with us – "

The doctor froze as a gargoyle like creature came from nowhere and leaped at her. It swung its sharp, clawed paw at her leg. She screamed in pain as claws ripped through her Oxie suit into her skin. Security personnel began to fire their laser rifles at the creature. It winced in pain as it dropped, either dead or unconscious. The power to the room shut off. The children's bodies started to convulse. Seconds later, all movement stopped. The med team scanned the children. They were all dead. Something had killed them.

"The animal attack was a diversion," said a security team member.

"Look for the power feed to this room," said Commander Coleman.

The engineers began to search the room.

"Found it commander" said an engineer, as she flipped the switch returning the power to the lights.

"Stay sharp. Something is in here with us. Teams of three, search the room."

A flash of white wispy smoke appeared near the commander. A woman with an elongated hairless forehead and long white hair materialized as the smoke dissipated. Her skin was a light pinkish cream color and her ears had points. Her eyes glowed orange. Though she looked a bit odd, Tal thought she was still beautiful.

The newcomer looked at the humans as if amused. "There is no need to look for me," she opened her arms wide, "I am right here."

"Who are you?" asked the commander.

"I am called Wineena. In time, I plan to become your overseer."

"What if we don't want an overseer?" asked the commander.

Wineena laughed. "It is not for you to decide, commander. Soon, you will learn to take pleasure in any command I give. I have seen enough to realize my colleagues are wrong about you humans."

"Are you human too?"

"Are you Ogarii? The answer is no. Please don't insult me." Wineena could see the commander looking her up and down. "I know. You think we share traits, but so do you and a baboon. You impetuous humans have much to learn."

"How is it you speak our language?"

Wineena turned around and lifted up her hair, exposing her neck. Everyone could see a small port. "Data port," she said, dropping her hair back into place.

"Why did you kill the children?"

"Because you would not. I did it to save you. You must leave soon, or the others will be back."

212

The commander held out open arms, "Why do all this?"

Wineena looked at the doctor while crewmembers were placing a repair patch on her Oxie suit. "You have already guessed at what I am doing. The Ogarii are at war with the Drahce. The Raygin fight for us but, they have proven to be slow to learn and remain uncreative on the battlefield. They require too much attention. You humans however, show much potential."

Tal told the commander via direct com to ask her why she was telling them her plans. The commander said, "If all this…"

"Save your breath, commander, I heard," said Wineena. She looked into the commander's vid camera. "Good job captain! You ask the obvious question. If I want to enslave your race, wouldn't I be better advised to keep it a secret? The answer of course, is yes, but it's not my short-term goal. Many Ogarii argue you are too brash, impatient, and too willing to gamble. They believe your traits make for bad warriors. They think your role in serving us would be better suited to become workers. They are mistaken. I am sure you will make good warriors and I aim to prove them wrong."

"How do you plan to do that?" asked Tal.

"My strategy has already begun. War. Humans must fight against the Raygin. The winner has the honor of becoming our warriors, and as far as the losers go, they will support us in other ways. Don't waste time trying to bargain with the Raygin. They wouldn't understand. Their programming has made humans an enemy of their collective nest. There is no alternative, you must go to war." Wineena spun around and disappeared in a blur of movement."

"Block the doors, search the room," said the commander.

The crew searched and searched for several minutes but couldn't find a trace of her.

"Captain, a small ship accelerated away from the debris field," said a bridge officer on Dagger. In the same breath he said, "It's gone." The officer manipulated a few scanner controls and said, "There's no trace of it, captain."

"Commander Coleman, a small craft has departed near your location. Get out of there right now. Take the bodies of two children on your way out. Now, move it!"

"Aye captain, we are heading out."

The team entered the shuttle with a few bodies and some equipment taken from the alien ship. The shuttle pilot started up the ion drive and activated the shields. The once mighty remnant of a ship exploded sending the small shuttle off to ride a mini shock wave. The small pieces of alien technology would not be retrievable. They would travel for years until captured by some planet's gravitational field. They had lost most of the alien technology. Wineena had robbed them of their bounty.

The commander reported everyone was safe and they were heading back to Dagger. Tal fired off a video to both Mac and the admiral. *They had to see this new information for themselves. The Ogarii appear to be humanoid. I wonder if there is some kind of link with humans? I'll bet the whole verbal exchange with the orange-eyed alien was done to buy her crew time to prepare for a quick getaway and to plant explosives. Clever little bitch!*

CHAPTER THIRTEEN: Spies

Imagine, a floating head with no body, telling you you're in big trouble. Anyone else would have laughed but Mac learned long ago when someone says you're in danger, you better listen. He needed to get to the bottom of this. Before Mahpee could respond to the comment, Mac asked, "What is the trouble?"

The head of Uzumati turned to Mac. "We entered the captive Raygin's mind. The alien's memories are images, not words. It is difficult to understand. The captive holds pictures of a fleet of warships so large it blots out galaxies. We don't think their fleet has arrived, but it is difficult to tell."

"Have they crossed into our universe?" asked Mac.

"Since the alien had memories of traversing the great void, we believe the answer is yes. Your captive envisions the attack will occur like a swarm of locust, destroying everything in their path. This Raygin's memories seem to indicate the planet you call Rayne is a feeder planet. It is one of many such worlds they created to support the war."

"Do you know where they will focus their attack first?" asked Mac.

"A memory of a star map calls the planet by a human name. We saw the word Esharra."

Mac leaned his body backward and tilted his head. "Are you sure it was Esharra?"

"The Raygin mind is not like the human mind. It's a jumble of pictures. The map we viewed in its memory showed a planet labeled Esharra at its center."

"What is Esharra?" asked Ayashe.

"After the mining wars the government decided to keep the parliament's location secret. They moved to a planet called Petri on the star charts. Its code name, Esharra, is from a long dead Earth language. It means the ruler's home. Its existence is known by a select few. Since the aliens know about Esharra I know they have spies in high places." The new information completed the puzzle Mac had been working on. He turned and looked for Lieutenant Phlop.

When he spotted him, it was too late. The lieutenant had already managed to break free of his bindings. He grabbed his pistol while everyone was watching the conversation with the floating head. Phlop pointed the old pistol at Mac's chest.

"Why Lieutenant Phlop?" asked Mac.

"Money. I'm going to be rich. The Ogarii are going to reward me well. I'm so glad you came here. Before I kill you, I want you to experience a little pay back for all my humiliation." The lieutenant swung his arm toward Ayashe and fired his pistol.

Years of plyos training prepared Mac to respond with unbelievable speed and power. Before the lieutenant lifted his weapon, Mac had already forced his heart rate to increase. It supplied his muscles with massive levels of oxygen. When the lieutenant's arm swung towards Ayashe, Mac sprung into the air matching the arc created by the lieutenant's arm with his own chest.

By the time the lieutenant pulled the trigger, Mac was horizontal in front of Ayashe's face with his feet curled behind him. His feet snagged her body, dragging her down and out of danger. At the same instant he leapt, Nidawi flung a three bladed circular knife at the lieutenant's arm. She couldn't stop him from pulling the trigger, but she did stop him from doing any more damage. Mr. Phlop's forearm and hand holding the gun separated from his body and dropped onto the soil.

The lieutenant screamed in agony as he held up the stump of his arm in disbelief. Bright red blood pulsed in a sporadic stream, soaking into the ground. He waved the stub of his arm back and forth, spewing blood in every direction. Dwain looked at Mac. His injury was already being taken care of so he grabbed a med scanner and rushed to treat the lieutenant. The armless leader's jaw tightened as he sank onto the ground. Dwain held him down and said, "Did you see that lieutenant? She took your hand off from fifteen meters away. She's awesome!"

The lieutenant looked at where his hand should have been and passed out. Dwain had to tear his admiring look away from Nidawi so he could help Mr. Phlop. He managed to battle dress the wound and medicate the traitorous first lieutenant in record time.

Mac blinked his eyes as he watched from the ground, not comprehending what was happening. The big hands of Mahpee latched onto him and stood him upright in one easy motion. Blood flowed from a wound on the side of Mac's head. Seeing the blood and feeling Mac's legs giving out Mahpee laid him on the ground with great care.

Now Ayashe could see the blood running down his head. With shaking hands, and tears forming in her eyes, she forced herself to check the wound. Mac watched Dwain run to him and manipulate the med scanner near his head. Dwain tilted the scanner towards Ayashe. She read the diagnosis: Probabilities: 95% concussion. 3% brain hemorrhage. 2% intracranial swelling. She breathed a sigh of relief.

Mac began to struggle to sit upright. Ayashe helped him up as she sprayed a sealant to stop the bleeding. She hugged him at his shoulders.

"Mac, what were you thinking?" she asked.

Looking at the lieutenant's unconscious body, Mac said, "It would have worked. But I didn't know the son of a bitch couldn't shoot straight. Who are the Ogarii?"

Tinker started laughing. "Here I thought you used your head because you know nothing can penetrate it."

The troopers laughed. Ayashe smiled and hugged him one more time.

She whispered in his ear loud enough for her father to hear, "My father is wrong, I have picked well. Thank you, my love."

"You do know I can hear what you are saying," said Mahpee. He smiled, "I admit, I may have been wrong about him."

Ayashe tilted her head as she looked at her father.

"Okay, okay. Don't give me that look. He risked sacrificing his life, so you might live. It is the grandest of gestures in our culture. You picked well." Mahpee looked at Mac and as a second thought said, "I still don't know if he is intelligent enough to serve at your side."

The talking head floated between Mahpee, Ayashe, and Mac. "I found this event to be enlightening. However, I suggest you pack up. We must leave with haste, or you may find yourselves Raygin captives, or worse."

"Who are the Ogarii?" asked Mac one more time.

"Get your people moving. We know very little about them," said the head.

At Mac's command, the three platoons loaded their supplies, the wounded, and all the women onto the skiff. Tinker picked a few troopers to ride along, in case anything unforeseen happened. Everyone else would have to make the short trip on the ground. As Mac and Tinker watched the skiff take off, Tinker felt a tap on his shoulder. He turned to see his uncle.

His face beamed as he hugged his favorite relative. "Uncle Jahra, I can't believe it's you. Mom and Dad will scream like Mangabee roosters when they find out you are alive."

Holding Tinker at arm's length, Jahra looked him up and down. "Albert, I've got to tell you I'm impressed. Tell me, how did you wind up in spec ops?"

Captain Cutter looked at Smitty, who in turn was watching Mac for any response.

"I'm not in spec ops, Uncle Jahra."

"Told you, Captain Cutter," said Smitty. "They all deny they are spec ops. They must have been threatened with something horrible if they told anyone the truth."

Mac smiled. "I hate to cut this short, but we have to get going." He looked at Dwain who was talking with Nidawi. "Tinker, take your platoon and cover our rear. Dwain, you and Third platoon lead the way. If she doesn't mind, Nidawi can be your guide." She looked at Mac and nodded her head. The response put a big smile on Dwain's face. "Dreng... shit, I mean, Ayashe. Split your platoon and cover our flanks. I'll be talking with your father."

Ayashe didn't say a word, but Mac could see a worried stare as she walked away. She was thinking the worst.

"Let's move out," said Mac.

As they began their hike, Mahpee walked up to Mac. "We have much to talk about. I regret our first meeting was not on better terms."

Mac tilted his head as he looked at Mahpee and thought about their future. "Yeah, I have to admit, I didn't care for the way it went down, but I'm sure everything will work itself out. I heard you have a high-tech shipbuilding planet. Tell me. How far away from Rayne is it?"

"We estimate we are about thirty-five days from Orenda, our shipbuilding planet. Why?"

"Its too far for us to use," said Mac. "We will make the mods we can while heading to Esharra. I know you

219

need to go back to Nokomis, but before you do, can you share some of your upgrades with us?"

"Yes, I will…"

The viewer in Mac's backpack sounded an alert tone interrupting Mahpee. "Sorry, I have to take this." Mac pulled out the viewer and read it. He walked over to Mahpee while calling Captain Cutter and Tews to come over. "You all might want to watch this with me. It's a vid from one of my escort ships called Dagger."

The odd-looking team huddled around the view screen as they watched the boarding vid. Mac stopped the vid several times to enhance the display to get a better understanding of what occurred. When Wineena appeared he replayed the event over and over.

"I suspected the bugs had help," said Mac. "They just didn't act like an advanced race."

"It troubled my thoughts too," said Mahpee. "When we dissected the Raygin bodies we found soft webbing linking different parts of their brain. It is similar to what your team found on the human children. Without a live subject, we didn't know its purpose. I fear the doctor on the boarding team is right. The webbing must help control the host's mind."

"I agree with the boarding party," said Tews. "It appears the webbing links the brain's different parts. It's more than a receiver. Look at where the connections occur. My bet is they flood the brain with repeated thoughts for the same task. See the loop?" Tews pointed on the enhanced image of a child's exposed brain. "Humans require some kind of reward to focus on completing a task. I'll bet that's what this link does. The other connections allow them to use their creativity to complete a task. They can deviate from the primary objective to avoid danger, or to save the individual. Amazing technology. To change the primary goal would require transmitting a new simple order into the loop."

"They have to have transmitters somewhere. Could they be on the Ogarii ship?" asked Mahpee."

Captain Cutter looked at Tews. "Didn't you say you and Spaz found some kind of transmitter in the vent near the bridge?"

"Yeah. We thought the bugs wanted it hidden from the crew for some reason. If we assume the Ogarii created or modified the Raygin ships, it all begins to make sense. What better location to hide a transmitter or relay than in the ship's vent system? It would channel the signal throughout the ship and the Raygin wouldn't even be aware of its existence."

Tews asked to use Mac's viewer. He found an engineering program and began to draw. As everyone watched a picture begin to take shape. Tews drew a transmitter, wiring harnesses, a power supply, and an antenna. He made the drawing to scale as best he could, knowing it would help the engineers.

"There. This is what we found tucked in the vent shaft cubby hole near the bridge," said Tews.

The picture was forwarded to Admiral Harding. They also sent their speculations about how mind control hardware might work. The group was so focused on discussing possibilities they didn't realize Tinker and the rear guard had caught up with them.

"Mac, we didn't expect to see you here. Is everything okay?" asked Tinker.

"Yeah, we have a lot of new information, but it's way too much to share right now. I'll give everyone a briefing when we get to the Wasp. Don't you think it's odd the bugs haven't followed us? If I was them, I would have been hot on our trail."

"Yeah, it's like they want us to escape."

The team started moving again. Tinker hid their trail and wiped out any evidence the humans had come this way. First platoon hung back again, keeping a close eye out for bugs. It wasn't long before Mac and his group caught back up with the main body of survivors.

"We need to discover how their mind-control works," said Mac. If we could find a way to destroy or disrupt the link, we can disrupt their military. Wineena was hiding something important on the Raygin ship. Could it have been the mind controller?"

Hearing Mac talk about disrupting the enemy's com link to the Raygin, Mahpee remembered the children from Imperial Station. "Mac, some children trapped in the swimming pool area on Imperial Station noticed an unusual occurrence. Every time a bug walked thru the door leading to the pool, it started making clicking sounds, and became disoriented. The dazed bug always stumbled back into the passageway confused. They never returned. The staff on the Constellation is evaluating all the data."

"Well, we have a test subject, so let's use it to test some of our conjectures. We also have a spy loaded with information we may be able to use. As our ships travel, we need to update our weapons, shields, and drives. If the entity known as your grandfather…"

Mahpee gave Mac a stare.

"Or whatever you want us to call him. If it has any recommendations to improve our computers, we'd appreciate the information."

"I'll ask it. I can also send you the specs on the graviton detector. It's how we tracked the Raygin ships. It's also how we discovered the cloaked Ogarii ship during the battle."

"You mean like the Wineena's ship?"

"No, it was several times larger. While cloaked, we hit it with several weapons, destroying it. The cloaking process must use a lot of energy making their shields weak."

"I'll be damned, I missed the whole evolution. Did they fire at you with any weapons?"

"Yes, they hit us with an energy weapon that chased us down and covered our whole ship. Luckily, our modified shields held long enough for the weapon's energy to dissipate."

"Do you know the energy drain on your shields– in joules?"

Mahpee began to realize, amongst everything else, Mac knew weapons. Only an engineer would speak in joules per second. He remembered Nashta making a big deal about it. "I believe the number Nashta reported was $4.1X10^{15}$ Joules, but you need to ask him to be sure."

Mac whistled. "That's stronger than anything we currently have." Smiling he added, "We are working on a new weapon we hope will cause a self-perpetuating fusion reaction."

Mahpee looked at Mac in surprise.

"Yeah, I know, it's a planet destroyer. It's supposed to be able to convert a planet to a small star by circumventing the proto star phase. The device forces the planet to enter the main sequence phase of a newborn star. A Laser creates plasma and initiates a fusion reaction. It begins burning hydrogen and trace amounts of helium in the planet's core. The nuclear fusion process, once started will last for several hundred years. In time the mini star will blow off its outer surface and become a miniature white dwarf. In a short time the tiny star will burn itself out and become a ball of iron. At least that's the theory."

Mahpee pictured the total destruction such a weapon could cause. "I hope I never become your enemy."

"Last I heard we are a long way from a deliverable system."

"Speaking of deliverable systems, you do know Ayashe is a war strategist? Trained by our best admirals."

Mac laughed out loud. "It's funny how you worked that into our conversation. She is a bit raw, and too willing to take risks, but I could tell she had some top-notch training. Before you go on, let me tell you what I'm thinking. We are one according to your laws, correct?"

"Yes. It is the equivalent of what you call marriage."

A smile broke out on Mac's face. *I still can't believe how my life has changed since meeting her*. He looked into Mahpee's eyes. "She signed a binding contract with the military, but we can work around it. I don't want her to go back to Nokomis…"

Mahpee gave Mac a stern look. The chief began to open his mouth to protest.

"Let me finish. I don't want her to go back to Nokomis… right now. I figured you would be leaving, but what if you left her with me? I'd remove her from the military ranks and make her the People's Nation liaison. Not working under me, but with me, on behalf of your people and the war effort. Hell, one day I want to go to Nokomis. First I need to build up my body's ability to move in your strong gravitational field. I would prefer not to look like a clown in front of your people."

With a quick move Mahpee stepped in front of Mac. Spinning towards him, he pinned his arms in a massive bear hug, and lifted him off the ground. Mac didn't understand what was happening, He didn't want to fight Ayashe's father, so he waited for the hammer to fall.

Hovering near the two trying to eavesdrop, Ayashe saw her father make a move on Mac and lift him into the air. She ran to his aid screaming. "Father let him go! Put him down! What are you doing?"

He grinned at his daughter while still holding Mac in the air and said, "I think I got you a big raise."

She stepped back and realized her father had Mac in an embrace. One such as a family member would give another family member on Nokomis when they are happy. She smiled at her father. "That's not how their military gives raises, father. Now, put him down and tell me what's going on."

He put Mac back on his feet.

"Fishman, take over for Dreng," said Mac.

"Aye sir taking over for… Ayashe."

Mac looked at Ayashe. *Dreng. Ayashe. This was going to take some time to get it right.* "Ayashe, you are relieved of duty."

"Wait a minute, I don't know what kind of plan the two of you concocted, but I didn't agree to anything."

"Mahpee, do your people have any laws that say when joined, the woman is to obey the man?"

Mahpee and his daughter both started laughing.

"What's so funny?" He asked.

"You have dug a deep hole you must place your body into," said Mahpee.

"What?"

"Forgive my father Mac. He doesn't understand some of your sayings. He means you've dug yourself into a deep hole. You see in our society, it is the woman who is the head of house and makes all major decisions. Now, tell me what's going on?"

Her father and Mac both started going over the agreements they had discussed. She would be responsible for war planning while Mahpee went back to Nokomis. Now she understood why her father hugged Mac. Besides allowing her and Mac to stay together, it also allowed her to continue to learn from the best. She would hold a war council position between the two peoples.

She hid her excitement. It meant she would become the second most powerful person in the People's Nation. Her father did not see the link between her new position and the prophecy. If he had, he would never have approved. Mahpee always avoided any discussions about the ancient prediction. She guessed he thought if he didn't talk about it, it wouldn't happen. So, she kept her mouth shut and said nothing. In time, she planned to explain it all to Mac, but not at the moment.

225

Dwain reported they were minutes away from the Wasp. Mac stopped walking. The surroundings looked a little familiar. He began to look for his trail markers. There they are. They were very close to the underground water cavern.

"Tews, tell me, how long do you think it would take the bugs to reach maturity, and where might they build their nests?"

"When we were on the ship, I hoped to find their nest during our vent searches. There is no way to know their life cycle without seeing the larva and pupas. I couldn't even make a wild guess until I have more data. A typical nest would contain beetles in all stages of life. It would be underground near water and food sources. In the larva, and early pupa stage beetles are easy to kill. It's why they always have a few adults tending the nest."

"Is it possible to stop their development somehow?"

"I don't think so. Until they begin to grow their exoskeleton as young adults they are eating machines. The brain hasn't had the chance to develop higher order functions yet. We learned a lesson with human babies. If you put them into cryo sleep at too young of an age, their brains will not develop when they exit sleep."

"I was afraid that might be your answer. Well... I guess I need two volunteers to go on a little sortie with me. I need someone who can shoot, and I need a bug expert. Any idea where I can find humans with those qualifications?"

"Why do you need them?" asked Spaz.

"When we landed I saw an unusual outcropping of rocks. I started to explore the area, and I found a cavern containing several pools of water. Before I could investigate the cavern, the bug ships arrived and changed all our plans. We are about twenty minutes away."

Spaz gave Tews a look. "Come on Tews, it will be like old times."

Tews looked at Mac. "Alright, but no one leaves me alone. Right commodore?"

Spaz laughed, "Never. Not unless we have to."

Tews's eyes opened wide.

"I promise, I won't leave you," said Mac as he patted Tews on the shoulder. "Does that mean you're going?"

"Yes. I'll go. In case you haven't noticed, I am not an athletic person, nor am I brave. You'll have to keep an eye on me, but I hate the Raygin. I wouldn't mind killing a few more of them for what they did to my family."

Mac nodded his head. "I can relate to vengeance. It motivated me for many years. If you don't want to, you don't have to do this. You both have earned your keep. By crawling through the Raygin ship, you have saved thousands if not millions of human lives. After fighting in several wars, I know it's not brave people that accomplish great feats. It's the everyday people who see the need and perform the task required of them."

"A kind statement," said Tews, "But I know you are trying to build up my confidence. Can I have about 5 minutes to gather up some supplies?"

Before Mac could respond, Spaz said, "Besides being an entomologist, he's also a psychiatrist."

Mac chuckled then said, "Now I understand. He's over analyzing everything." Before Tews could refute the statement, Mac said, "Get going Tews. Meet us back here in ten minutes. Spaz, come with me."

Mac and Spaz held an impromptu meeting with Mahpee, Ayashe, and Tinker. He explained his concern and plan. There was a chance they would exit the cavern hot if what Mac suspected turned out to be true. Tinker needed to get the ground pounders to set up a first line of defense. They needed to be ready in case the returning explorers needed cover fire.

Much to Ayashe's displeasure, Mac took her laser rifle from her. A smile crossed her face when he gave it to

Spaz. He also gave him a condensed thirty-second training session on how to use it. No one could have wiped the grin off Spaz's face as he caressed the rifle.

"Who'd thought a piss ant ground pounder like me would be handling an elite rifle used by spec ops?" said Spaz.

"It's not so much the weapon as it is the person wielding it," said Mac. "Let's find Tews."

CHAPTER FOURTEEN: Infestation

The Ogarii crew knew they would have to be visible for a moment as they maneuvered through the debris field. There was no way around it. They needed the power for their shield to avoid damage from the small pieces of wreckage, which would act like meteorites. The sleek ship started to move through the rubble so their computer could find a path out. Once it did, they engaged their ion drive. As soon as they intercepted their exit route the ship turned on it's cloaking system. The enemy ship disappeared from the human monitors. It departed by traveling in a series of unsystematic course changes. It was impossible for the humans to obtain a firing sequence or to track it.

The unforeseen human engagement near Rayne caught both Ogarii and Raygin crews by surprise. How did the humans find them? Wineena wanted answers. Both the Ogarii computer and their intel failed. Nothing indicated humans possessed this type of advanced capability. Could this technological leap be another anomaly? Wineena's instincts told her no. The computer had missed something important in forecasting human development.

She recalled the events from twenty-five years ago. The Ogarii were on the verge of invasion into human space. The Ogarii ruling caste known as the Varn received a message from a single scout ship: Humans are using singularity drives. Portus, the Ogarii self-thinking computer, stopped the assault. Wineena couldn't believe it. The giant computer believed its original war analysis could be wrong. By its calculations, the humans should have been a long way from discovering wormhole engineering. Let alone already using it! Not wanting to risk losing the war, the computer requested more data.

Later she discovered Portus did predict a possible irregularity event in human evolution. It knew it was possible for them to stumble across wormhole technology. She felt better to learn the computer didn't miss the event's likelihood altogether. The hitch was the probability was so low it did not warrant modifying the Raygin fleet. Portus accounted for the low probability event within its battle plan. Prior to the invasion the computer had the Raygin fleet deploy a contingency of scout ships. They probed the fringes of human space. Their job was to identify any unanticipated event.

Finding unexpected results, Portus stopped the attack. It calculated every possible scenario based on the new information. There were situations in which the Raygin fleet lost several significant battles. The loss of major battles caused the prediction of a prolonged war. In too many prolonged war scenarios the odds shifted in the human's favor. The invasion was put on hold. Portus dispatched additional scout ships to obtain more data. It also ordered the Raygin fleet to be refitted. Wineena remembered how angry she had gotten. She submitted a protest to the Varn. It was a waste of time. They sided with Portus.

Portus, for some reason, decided to refit the Raygin fleet in the Naktu solar system. It sits within the universe's second ring. The shipyards were not even built yet. The misspent use of time enraged Wineena. Her eyes smoldered flicks of orange as she recalled finding out about Portus building a parallel brain for itself. Of all places, the computer chose a good for nothing planet named Tik. It is the second planet from the sun in the Naktu system. *Coincidence?* She doubted it. The computer made a strategic move without oversight approval. It also convinced the Varn they too needed to move to Tik.

She felt sure the computer did it to keep an eye on the Ogarii fleet. The computer worked nonstop for twenty-five years. Its tendrils were everywhere in the second ring. She didn't trust Portus, not at all.

The Ogarii had grown too dependent on the massive computer. It didn't make a move without performing unending simulations. The computer 's influence over the Varn would end once she had a voice in the elite group. As overseer she supplied black market items to the Ogarii. She had acquired more wealth than most ruling caste members. It was time to make her move. A victory over the humans would put her in a position to force a vote. Everyone likes a winner, even the Varn.

All these distractions were becoming dangerous. She needed to refocus on the humans. Unlike the Raygin, they were not stupid. They had proven to be quick to learn and seemed to be adaptive. She glanced at her guest and caught him watching her with lust in his eyes. Her nose flared in disgust. *How dare he*. The fluid pressure between the lens of her eyes and her retinae increased. Her eyes glowed bright orange. By the time he saw the involuntary evolutionary warning to males, it was too late.

Her body became a vaporous blur as she moved with the speed of a striking Cave Cobra. Before Iscar could react, he felt the tip of a blade beginning to pierce the skin of his throat. He remained motionless. He could feel drops of blood traveling down his neck. "Wait," he screamed, "I meant no disrespect, Overseer Wineena. I am still not used to your customs. Forgive me."

"Beg."

Without hesitation Iscar said, "I beg you for my life. It will not happen again."

Wineena placed her knife back into its sheath at her waist. She ran her right hand though her long hair as she paced back and forth. "Navigator, take the Raath to Aghasur Point."

"Yes overseer," said the ship's navigational droid.

"I thought you said – "

Wineena waved her hand in the air, "Your son will be safe with his kind, Mr. Iscar Phlop. If he succeeds in his new task, he will become rich. In either case, we already activated a memory-blocking drug. It is beyond human capabilities to counteract. So long as your people believe he may have valuable information, they will not harm him. Rest easy."

She surveyed her crew. They were all watching her and waiting for orders. "I am moving the timeline up. Time to spring the trap. Karii, dispatch the transports to the breeder planets to pick up the Raygin Warriors. It is unfortunate we have missed an unexpected opportunity, but the plan will still work. Activate the nests, via sub space frequency. The invasion begins."

"Yes, overseer," said Karii

"What nests?" asked Iscar Phlop.

"Come now, you didn't think we would sit around for twenty-five years and do nothing? All the information you gave us proved useful. We planted nests of Raygin warriors on several key planets. Once the attack begins, the planets will call for assistance. Your fleet will split. The diversion will clear the way for an attack on the human leader. Once he falls, you will make the announcement to end the war and help to organize the surrender."

"I still don't understand, what use could we be to an advanced race such as the Ogarii?" asked Mr. Phlop.

"Hundreds of years ago the Ogarii attacked the Drahce. They are the dominant race in the universe's fourth ring. We could not get by their defenses. Unbeknownst to us, somehow, they unleashed a tiny zepto sized virus. It was inactive at first. It carried with it a hidden code placing itself into Ogarii genes. Once the virus spread throughout our space, the Drahce activated the code. All Ogarii pregnancies in progress self-aborted. Our women can no longer become pregnant. Doom faces our race unless we find the hidden code."

"So, you need us for sex?" asked Iscar.

The all-female Raath crew laughed at the prospect. They began to chide in.

"Humans stink," said a crewmember.

"They are too chubby. Look at him," said another.

In an attempt to outdo the other crew members a third one said, "I would rather skonk a hairy Neemar."

Everyone laughed except Iscar. The translator didn't work for the word skonk, but he understood its meaning. He didn't realize how much the Ogarii looked down on the other races.

"For us to mate with a human would be equivalent to humans mating with wild pigs," said Wineena.

"The problem must be you can't afford a war of attrition. Is it you need us to assist the Raygin in your war with the Drahce?"

Wineena looked at her crew and smiled. "And, that's why we will win the war with the Drahce." She looked at her human guest and nodded her head. "The Raygin are stupid bugs. They are nothing more than a delaying tactic. Our computer is working on the reproductive code quandary."

"The Varn did not want me to waste time searching in the first ring for answers to our problems. I insisted. We discovered and evaluated your people. We realized with some minor modifications, you make better warriors than the Raygin. The best news is Portus believes with humans fighting for us, that we tip the balance in our favor. We win the war with the Drahce. The drawback is Portus moves too slow. I will force the computer to move the timeline forward."

Iscar swallowed hard, but he didn't regret his actions. After all, it looked like power and greed were driving the entire universe.

*****

The humans on Rayne continued with their journey to the Wasp. Mac and his two new partners broke off to investigate the underground chamber. The pile of rocks drawing his attention seemed out of order from the rest of the local area. Underground caches are often used by the military to avoid prying eyes. He hoped they weren't walking into a barbed hornet's nest.

"Follow me and stay close," said Mac. He turned around and began an easy jog. He followed the markers from his earlier exploration.

Spaz heard Tews laboring to breath behind him. He stopped and without asking took his friend's rucksack and carried it for him. Mac smiled. The two made a good team.

Arriving at the cavern entrance Mac said, "This is it. Put your visors on. I'll go in first. Spaz, I want you so close behind me that you become my shadow. Tews, you're last, but most important. Stay close and figure out what's going on in here. Ready?"

Both Tews and Spaz nodded their heads as they followed close behind Mac. They moved further and further into the cavern. If not for the visors Mac brought, they wouldn't be able to see in the darkness below ground. They came upon what looked like a wide pulverized rockslide. Mac half surfed and half walked down the twenty-foot long rocky slide. Spaz mimicked Mac as he slid down the slide too. Tews wasn't as athletic, so he moved next to the wall, placed his hand on it for stability and shuffled down the sloped rockslide.

Tews stopped part way down. "Wait, I can feel a vibration coming through the rock. There's equipment running somewhere near." He looked around and reassessed the path they were following. "This isn't a natural rockslide were heading down, it's a stairway for the Raygin. We're in some kind of underground complex. There is no sign of visible mold. Smell the air. The odor of decomposition is strong. There must be a ton of decaying vegetable down here. I'm guessing we are entering a Raygin nest."

"We have to go in," said Mac. "We know so little about the enemy, I can't pass up the intel. We may never have another chance like this."

"Okay, but as you walk shuffle your feet in an un-rhythmic pattern. It will draw less attention. If you have to kill them using your knife stab them below their neck in a downward motion."

The three companions turned a corner and moved deeper into what they believed to be a Raygin breeding area.

"We're getting closer," said Mac. "The decay smell is making me nauseous."

Spaz started laughing. "What you smell is not decay Mac. Tews shit his pants. Didn't you, Tews?"

"Sorry. I developed a bad reaction to the pig slop the Raygin fed us. By the way, the smell of decay is constant. It already permeates the air. It doesn't get worse as we get closer."

"Will the smell coming from your ass give us away?" asked Mac.

"I don't think so. They translate the smell as a form of communication."

"What does it mean?" asked Mac.

"I don't know what it means. As big bug attacked me on the ship it stopped when it smelled what I did. It was shocked I spoke its language."

"Well, try to hold it in. You may be telling them, 'Hey, here we are,'" said Mac.

The three continued to make their way down the passage. In a short time, they came upon a huge wall, containing about fifty holes set up in columns. Each column had several holes in it. There were three groupings of columns. Each grouping contained four letter characters over the column. Mac looked at Spaz and Tews. They were both recording everything with their visor vids. Between the three of them, they could record most everything.

"Looks like the holes lead to three different locations. Are the bugs left or right handed? Did you notice?" asked Mac.

The two friends looked at each other and said, "Right."

"Why?" asked Tews.

"I am guessing they would use the left column of holes for low traffic areas, like sleeping or birthing areas, and right side for common use traffic areas."

"I should have thought of that," said Tews. "Are you a psychiatrist?"

"No. I'm a killer and notice details others sometimes miss. Follow me."

Mac climbed into a low hole on the wall's left side. Once in the tube, they felt air being drawn into whatever was on the other side. If the air was being drawn in, it was also exhausting somewhere. The tunnels looked about twenty feet long. When Mac got to the other side, he saw two bugs with plasma rifles. One guard stood on each side of a large passageway. There were no other bugs in sight. The passageway joined to several open-air cavernous rooms. He could hear machinery running but couldn't see it.

Mac gave simple hand signals to Spaz and Tews. He would take out the guard on the right, Spaz would take out the guard on the left, and Tews would wait in the tube. Mac jumped out and moved to his target using a stealth approach taught to him by a Tao monk. He looked at Spaz, running at the guard. He forgot to shuffle.

Mac killed his bug by slitting an opening downward through its thorax. He began to run toward the other bug in a full sprint in case Spaz needed help. Spaz was about fifteen feet away from his bug when it felt his presence. It turned, but not before Spaz jumped high in the air while firing a little handgun. Mac didn't hear any noise, but the guard dropped.

A second later Mac was looking at the dead bug, then at the needle gun still in Spaz's hand. "Look at you. You haven't even used your fancy laser gun yet. I told you it's the person, not the weapon. Nice job. Let me know if you're ever interested in spec ops."

It was every ground pounder's dream to be in the elite forces. Spaz grinned. In truth, after seeing Mac in action, his wildest dream would be to work on his personal team. Mac had a way to always bring out the best in those around him.

Tews interrupted Spaz's thoughts as he walked up to his two friends. He looked at the dead bug smiling and gave Spaz a big thumbs up. They dragged the dead guards into the first vast room. It contained enough decayed food to feed an army. As they threw the dead guards on the pile, Tews could see the individual decay pile contents. He threw up. The pile of degraded vegetation contained some animal parts along with a few human body parts.

Wiping the vomit off his lips, Tews said, "Mac, we have to stop these sons of bitches."

"That's why were here Tews. Come on, let's keep looking."

The next couple of rooms contained more food at various stages of decay. They found a room loaded with thousands of large larvae in gigantic trays. Each tray held a mix of decay puree and liquid.

"The hatchlings must suck up nutrients through their soft skin. I would call this the third and final phase of larva development," said Tews.

"How do you know?" asked Mac.

Tews reached down and used two hands to hold the oversized larva. Rolling the slimy body over, he showed Mac. "Look, the head and arms have developed, but the body still looks wormlike. The exoskeleton won't develop until after the pupa stage. It won't harden until the young adult stage." To prove his point, Tews squeezed the larva and it squished in his hands like a rotten tomato.

Mac looked at the goo as Tews flung the slime off his hands. "Mahpee's grandfather is wrong. This isn't a feeder planet. Its purpose is even more insidious. It's a breeder planet. They are growing soldiers right here in our universe! I'll bet there are more planets like this hidden within our sector of space. Can you kill all these bugs without making a lot of noise?"

Tews searched the room and found tubes leading from some kind of mechanical device to the trays containing the bugs.

"It looks like an old heat pump," said Spaz. "It removes warmth from ambient air and delivers it wherever it's needed. It's old style technology."

Each large tray of larvae contained a control device, hooked to its own heat pump. The controller contained two side switches. Mac and Spaz watched as Tews pushed on the top switch. The characters on the display changed and the heat pump turned on.

"I've got it!" said Tews. "We cook them in their own food."

Mac guarded the open-air cavern entrance while Tews and Spaz dialed up all the heat pumps. Tews placed a larva into a sample bag and placed it in his rucksack. When the two finished, Mac led them to the next room. More vegetation.

"Mac, we've been in here twenty minutes already. We'll never have enough time to explore this whole underground complex," said Spaz.

"You're right. A little more scouting and I'll be ready to go. Let's move to the second group of holes."

Mac thought it was odd. There were no guards posted inside the wall containing the middle set of holes. The set up was similar to the first cavern. They could see rows of open-air rooms. The three explorers peaked around the first corner. It contained thousands of pupas. They were all sitting in decayed food.

"This is the next life cycle of development, isn't it?"

"Yep. The worm like body is transforming into a beetle." Tews picked up a pupa and squeezed.

Mac heard Tews say, "This is for my brother."

The wiggling body soon went limp. Tews threw the dead husk back onto the decay pile.

Lifting his arm up, Spaz pointed down the oversized hallway. "Hey. Look over there. The room lit up. Something is going on."

"Let's find out what," said Mac. "Stay close, follow me, and hide in the shadows where you can".

When they reached the opening, Mac peeked around the corner. The open cavern looked like the large operating room on the Raygin ship. There were three orange-eyed female Ogarii in the room. They were preparing to operate on what looked like hundreds of beetles with their skulls open. These were smaller than the ones he was used to seeing. They could be young adults.

Moving back and away from the entrance, Mac motioned for Tews to look.

Tews looked in the room just as a female looked up. He pulled his head back. Too late, the humans heard clicking noises like Raygin talking but in higher softer voices. Tews's eyes were wide and all the color left his face. In the same instant Mac knew what happened.

With his rifle up and ready, Mac slipped around the corner. He saw three orange-eyed aliens. They must not have gotten a good look at Tews and thought he was a bug because they were shocked to see him. It's too late to duck back. The closest female grabbed a bladed instrument from the table. She turned and began to give a command to the other female. Before the one speaking finished her orders, Mac shot the furthest female in the head.

The one giving the orders turned to look at Mac and Tews. She lifted the instrument, smiled, and disappeared in a ghostly flash. Mac had seen this trick before. He fired his gun one foot away from Tews as she reappeared, still smiling. The laser burned a hole through her chest. The third female freaked out and made a move towards the wall. Mac fired three times in rapid succession. The last shot hit her as she materialized.

The frail entomologist was still standing wide-eyed. Spaz could see Tews's mind hadn't grasped what occurred within only one second.

Spaz looked in awe at Mac. "How did you do that? I was still lifting my rifle by the time you shot the third one."

Mac shrugged his shoulders, "I told you. I'm a killer. I don't think about it. The leader gave orders and picked up a weapon. I assessed the situation. There was no time to talk them out of whatever they planned to do. Sometimes it comes down to kill or be killed."

"How did you know the one with the weapon was going to appear next to me?" asked Tews.

"I shot her friend while she was talking to her. I did it on purpose to piss her off. I didn't want all three running in different directions to escape. When I saw the smile on her face after she looked at you, I knew she was coming. Being right handed, and wanting me to watch you die, I guessed where she would materialize."

"And the third one?" asked Spaz.

"I was lucky. The last one got scared after seeing the leader get shot. She ran straight for what I assumed was some kind of alarm on the wall. I kept firing until she appeared." Pointing to the ceiling Mac said, "Thermal detectors. They may have picked up the heat flashes from the laser rifle. Let's get out of here and head back to the ship."

Tews gained his composer and was rummaging through his rucksack. "Wait. Give me a few seconds." He pulled out a battery-powered aspirator the engineers designed on the fly. He began to spray it over the young adult Raygin. Remembering the need to learn about the bugs he ran into the room with the pupas, grabbed one, slipped it into a sample bag, and placed it in the second rucksack. Now they have a Raygin larva and pupa. Tews sprayed the pupas and reloaded a new supply bottle. "Okay, lets go."

As they were moving back to the wall with the holes in it, eight armed bugs entered the passageway. The soldiers scurried past the humans who were now hiding in the shadows. As the bugs headed for the operating room, the three friends ran to the tube wall. As they climbed out on the other side, they heard a screaming, "NIK, NIK, NIK" sound.

"Shit," said Mac. "That must be an alarm. We can't make it up the sloped pathway fast enough. They'll catch us long before we get out of here. You two go on. I'll hold them off at the corner."

Still holding his aspirator Tews said, "I've got a better idea. He began to aspirate the bug poison near the wall. They watched the tiny vapor droplets get sucked into the tubes. Mac and Spaz stood at the ready with their rifles pointing at the openings, but the noise soon died out. They didn't have to fire one shot. Tews reloaded and emptied his last bottle of Raygin poison.

As soon as the three of them exited the cave entrance, Mac requested a report from Tinker.

"Current status," said Tinker. "The shuttle is in the air and taking the women and wounded to the Constellation. Mahpee tells me the Wasp is flight ready, and Dagger is overhead in case we need some firepower. Captain Tal reports there are hundreds of Raygin at the crash site, but they are not leaving their ship. First, Second, and Third platoons are ready to repel an attack."

"Good work Tinker. We will arrive at your location in 25 minutes. The cavern contains a Raygin breeding facility. We may have killed a few thousand Raygin. Admiral, are you listening?"

There was a slight pause followed by, "Yes."

A clear violation of protocol, but Mac didn't care. In fact, he had violated rules often to help him and his troops. "Good, send some troopers down to the derelict ship and capture all the Raygin you can find. Did your chemist talk to Ruth Bernardo?"

"Yes, we made three thousand liters of poison and put together a delivery system."

"Good work Admiral."

"Tal, are you listening?"

"Yes sir."

"When we have all the prisoners and everyone is clear, drop a couple torpedoes on the bug ship. I don't want to leave them anything they might be able to use."

"Aye sir. Torpedo the Raygin ship after all are clear. And sir. Nice work."

Mac looked at Spaz and Tews. "I don't know what the hell that means."

"I am afraid it's my fault, sir. In battle situations we always transmit our vids live. I transmitted our activities. It was so natural I didn't give it a thought. They watched the live recording from our visors and they received any vids in storage. I'm sorry, sir," said Spaz.

Mac's head dropped. "Thank you, Tal." Mac looked at Spaz. "It's my fault I didn't think about conflict of protocols. They would all have seen the videos soon anyway, so no harm was done."

"Tinker, make sure everyone has all the videos."

"Will do, Mac."

"Is anyone else listening?"

"Warhammer is monitoring commodore."

"The Cruiser Starburst is monitoring commodore."

"Wasp is also monitoring."

He smiled when he heard the voice from the Wasp. *It's Dreng– I mean Ayashe. I'll never get used to her real name? Everyone is listening.* "We need to modify our ships with all the upgrades from the People's Nation. At least it will give us a fighting chance. If I were the invasion commander, I would attack now to negate the intelligence we obtained. Let's finish here, head home, and prepare for war. Our enemies are no longer coming. They are here."

CHAPTER FIFTEEN: Maneuvering for War

Before the Wasp left for Nokomis, Mahpee, Mac, and Ayashe sat down and talked. Mac got to hear the story about the scar on his wife's chest. He learned about the Tellers, and what had been foretold. Ayashe heard for the first time, the story of her cleansing and healing. Her father cried when he talked about her mother. All three came to a better understanding about each other. There would be no more rebellion from Ayashe.

Mac neither believed nor disbelieved certain story parts. He could see both Mahpee and Ayashe believed them to be true. It was good enough for him. After all, he had heard a lot of folklore on the planets he had been on during his military career. Who was he to say what was true or not true? A few months ago he wouldn't have believed a story about bugs fighting space battles in great ships of war! Or even there being an advanced race of females having orange eyes and an ability to disappear.

Some nanobots making up Mahpee's grandfather stayed with Mac and Ayashe. The rest of him went to Nokomis on the Wasp. Dwain was heart-broken at Nidawi's departure and yet at the same time excited too. The two agreed to see each on Nokomis during Dwain's next leave. The improvement in his attitude was obvious for everyone to see.

The nanobots began upgrades on all the remaining UFC ships. They also started working on the promising tachyon com device the humans had started. After two near disasters the crew worked out an agreement with the nanobots. Both humans and nanobots were learning to adapt to each other's needs.

Mac gave Ayashe access to the federation memory banks on the Constellation. She began to analyze possible attack scenarios. Day after day she poured over the data. She reviewed tons of information, including: the number of ships of war, the number of transports, and the number of trained personnel available. The list went on and on. She even looked at unusual reports submitted within the last twenty-five years. She assessed any significant data that could help her evaluate their vulnerability status.

On day four, Ayashe came out of her executive cabin looking exhausted. She asked Mac to set up a war council meeting. Within one hour everyone sat around a virtual meeting table on their own ships.

Mac addressed the group. "Those of you who don't know my wife, this is Ayashe. She is the liaison between our people, and hers, the lost Indian Tribes of old Earth. They call themselves, the People's Nation. Because of some evolutionary peculiarities, they became brainy. So, if they tell us anything, we should listen. My wife, amongst other positions…" Mac looked at her and smiled, "was trained as a war strategist. She wants to give us some insights. Please listen and feel free to ask any questions you may have. Ayashe, it's all yours."

"I'll get right to crux of my concerns. Mac believes more Raygin nests exist than the one he destroyed. I agree with him. After studying the data, I believe they have infested many planets inhabited by humans."

"Ayashe," interrupted Tal, "I am the Dagger's captain. There has never been a reported sighting of aliens on any planets I am aware of. What proof do you have?"

"By now, I'm sure you've heard about the universe's rings. We are the dominant species in the newest ring. The

245

Raygin are dominant in the second ring. I believe the Ogarii are from the third ring and are at war with a race in the fourth ring who are called the Drahce. We know the Raygin have been in the first ring for at least twenty-five standard years. We also have solid intelligence they want to attack Esharra, the home of your civilian leader. I went twenty-five years back into your records and looked for anything out of place."

Ayashe tapped a control at her table. A holograph appeared at each attendee's table depicting the universe as known by humans. Esharra stood at the map's center surrounded by thousands of stars. She tapped the controls again and inhabitable planets were displayed. "Each planet shaded in red reported abnormal operations of their planetary satellites over a three-year span. The three years were between 22 to 25 years ago. This in itself is nothing to worry about. But, a closer look shows the satellite failures were exclusive to unpopulated remote areas. This represents an un-probable event. The intermittent failure didn't draw any real investigation, or at least none were ever documented."

The leaders watched Ayashe tap the controls again. The map became pie shaped with Esharra still at the center. A few red plants changed to the colors red and purple. She said, "The red and purple color represents planets with advanced monitoring capabilities. They reported minor seismic activity in the planet's remote areas 22 to 25 years ago. It would be the type of thing we might see if someone were creating an underground nest." Tapping the controls one more time, Ayashe zoomed in.

The admiral's eyes went wide. "How could we have missed all this?"

"The Ogarii have proven to be patient, and even clever, Admiral," said Ayashe. "The Raygin infestation is designed, at least in part, to cause a distraction. Parts of our human fleet would have gone to assist the unprotected planets. The now obvious path you see will be the route the Raygin take to Esharra."

"Do you think we can stop them?" asked Tal.

"My guess is they want to take out human leadership in the hopes of a fast surrender. Mac believes the Raygin will attack immediately. It will cancel out any advantage we may have obtained with our new intelligence. All we know is the Raygin fleet is big by our standards. I suspect you can either save millions of people on the infested planets or save the leadership thus saving the human race but probably not both."

The admiral looked at Mac. "Is this your assessment also?"

"Her speculations about the Raygin invasion are sound," said Mac. "But, I have learned a battle is always fluid. We have already forced the Ogarii to move up their invasion plans. Can we throw enough surprises at the Raygin to give the people on Esharra time to escape? I doubt it. But we have other options. We can try to neutralize their ground forces. They don't know we know their plan. We can lay a few traps along the way, but no matter what we do we will lose many human lives."

"Commodore, we are at war and you are in the field of battle. It means you are in charge. Your orders outrank all others, even the planetary president. How can we help you?" asked the Admiral.

Mac saw a few smiles at hearing he was in charge. "I need help from the medical staff. Tell me why the Raygin approaching the pool on Imperial Station became dizzy and didn't enter the pool area. Use our prisoners as test subjects. We need to warn Esharra and the planets Ayashe identified on her map of the possible infestation. Finish updating the computers, shields, and our weapons. The engineers need to find the frequency the Ogarii are using to transmit to the Raygin. We need to jam it. Has anyone seen Mahpee's grandfather?"

A body appeared next to Mac. It had the metallic smooth face of a robot with black orbs for eyes and a metallic body. "I am here Commodore McCormack. Since it would be meaningless for me to be Uzumati without Mahpee being here, you may call me Apeiron."

"As in limitless?"

In human fashion, Apeiron's hand reached up and stroked its metallic chin as its face watched Mac. "We estimate the odds of any person knowing the meaning of my name to be one in twelve billion two hundred fifty-two million three hundred eighty-seven thousand. What do you suppose the odds are of the one being here?"

"With hindsight I'm guessing one hundred percent."

"Clever, Mac. May I call you Mac?"

"Yeah, go ahead, everyone else does. Tell me, how is the war effort going?"

"All modifications on the shields, weapon systems, and drives will be complete in thirty-eight point seven hours. We are still working on improving the tachyon communications system. It is proving to be more difficult than we anticipated."

"Have you come up with any new weapon systems that might prove useful in the war with the Raygin and Ogarii?" asked Mac.

Apeiron's shiny shoulders slumped as if in disappointment. "Alas, you have hit on our weakness. We seem to have little to no capacity for new creative thought. If you design weapons, we can improve them. If you fly it, we can fly it better. If you create fast computers, we can create faster computers... you see where I'm going?"

"Yes. I guess it's up to us to come up with new ideas you can improve on. We will make a good team in the long run."

Apeiron stood straight. "Yes, I am beginning to understand it now. You are right, we enhance each other's talents – we are a team."

Mac looked at the other leaders in the room. "Captains is there anything I can do to help you?"

"We understand Lieutenant First Grade Phlop is a traitor," said Tal. "We have to assume there may be other spies. We have seen you fight, but you can't see everything with all the distractions. You need an armed escort, sir."

All the captains nodded in agreement.

Seen me fight? He remembered the videos. "Okay. I guess I can do that. Anything else?"

The captains nodded their heads no. "Okay, thank you all. Make sure your crews install all the upgrades while I will work on our war plan."

First, Second, and Third platoons became Mac's personal protection. He needed Tinker for special projects, so he put Dwain in charge of escort duty and everyday activities. Spaz being a sergeant posed a problem. He didn't want to return him to the ground pounders on the ship. The problem was Spaz outranked everyone left in his original three platoons.

He came up with a solution. Offer Spaz a field promotion to ensign, for his heroic accomplishments while held captive on the enemy ship and for his performance inside the Raygin nest. Spaz jumped on the promotion and became the liaison between ship's personnel and Mac's team. It was his dream job.

Sitting in a meeting room on the Admiral's ship, Mac reflected on the odd chain of events bringing them up to this point. He hated to think the entire universe was at war with each other. So far, the federation had lost over a hundred thousand people. It could have been much worse if not for the Mahpee and the People's Nation. With the loss of Imperial Station, the win at the battle of Rayne would help boost morale. He needed to talk to the Admiral about getting some vids released for public viewing. It would help the population to understand what they were up against. The military also needed to increase enlistments.

Mac sat in the conference room waiting for his next meeting. He jerked up in his seat. *What the hell?* He swore he saw a wolf enter the room. It looked side-to-side and disappeared. It couldn't have happened. The armed guards outside the room would have warned him. Two seconds later Ayashe entered the room. Mac blinked his eyes hard. Was it a daydream? *The Teller story must be playing with my sub conscious mind.*

"Did I catch you sleeping my love?" asked Ayashe.

"I don't think so, well, maybe. I'm not sure."

"Mac, are you okay. Maybe, I shouldn't be keeping you up so late. You have so much to do, you need to rest."

"Are you kidding? I sleep like a baby," he looked at her and grinned. "Don't worry I talked to a doctor. She said to keep doing what we were doing every night. It helps the male body to relax."

Ayashe walked behind him and began to rub his neck in a gentle fashion. "As my father would say, you must need to go to the bathroom."

Mac's eyebrows furled together. He spun his head around. "What?"

"In other words, you're full of shit."

As Tinker walked in he saw Mac and Ayashe laughing. "Let me guess, you were talking about joining?"

Mac and Tinker both started laughing. Ayashe gave Tinker a look of disgust.

She walked over to him, grabbed his right ear and dragged him to the seat next to Mac. "You have been working with my husband too long."

Before Mac or Tinker could respond, an escort stepped into the room. He led Captain Cutter, Tal, Ruth Bernard, and Tews into the room behind him.

Captain Cutter nodded at his nephew and Ayashe. He looked at Mac and said, "Hello commodore, looks like an odd group of attendees. I can't imagine why you brought us together."

This made the commodore smile. "Hello everyone. Take a seat, and please call me Mac. To answer the question you're all wondering, you are here because you have proven to have the ability to think in an imaginative way. To me, you are each priceless. During my life, I have studied many battles. Many victories occurred due to a single, shrewd, and unexpected action. It's what I am asking you to give me. A list of unexpected actions we can use against our new enemies."

"Nothing is stupid or out of bounds. I want ideas you would consider to have a chance of success. We are fighting the Raygin. They represent a force with near unlimited numbers. We also have the Ogarii, a race of technologically advanced life forms wanting to enslave us. If we fight a traditional war, we will lose."

"Mac, some of us have no engineering background, we are not developers, designers, or scientists. Do we need to work with engineers or others as appropriate to evaluate the feasibility of our concepts?"

"Good question, Tal. The answer is no. I am more interested in your ideas. Don't get too complex at this point. I know many weapon systems, drive units, ship designs, and so on all came from laymen with no engineering background. Keep it simple. I will let Apeiron evaluate if the concept can be brought to realization. If we don't use some creative methods of attack we will lose the battle and the war.

The team looked apprehensive as the seriousness of their plight was driven home. *War is hell and people die, but I don't want them afraid to voice their ideas. I need to get them to relax.* When he saw Tews he knew what to do. "Tews. Do I need to warn them?"

Tews looked Mac in the eye. "No sir. I'm back on my meds. Though, I should tell the team what happened in case someone can use the information."

The whole team started laughing. Tews looked confused.

"Come on, Tews," said Mac. "You going to tell me a smart guy like you thought Spaz and Smitty wouldn't tell everyone they know about you and your escapades? Your abilities to stop bugs dead in their tracks has made you famous."

Tews's face turned red, as everyone laughed some more.

"I have an idea, commodore – I mean Mac," said Ruth. "Can we have access to the prisoners?"

"Yes. Work through Ensign Spaz. Tell him how many Raygin you need, what help you require, and what type of an environment you need. I will let the crew know this team's requests receive top priority. Work independent, work together, I don't care. We are at war. I expect results by the 2000 ship's time. He looked at the room's clock. You have twelve hours." He spun and walked out.

*****

It got quiet in the room. Everyone looked at Ayashe.

"Is he kidding?" asked Tal.

"He likes to push people but not beyond what he thinks they are capable of… so, I think he is serious. When he said each of you are priceless to him, he meant it. He has much on his mind, so let's give him something he can work with in twelve hours."

Nobody said a word. Ayashe decided she needed to lead the conversation. "On my home world of Nokomis I received training as a military tactician. I won't go into detail right now, but I studied all human wars. One way I see of balancing out our technical disadvantage with the Ogarii is by cutting off their head."

"You mean removing their ability to communicate with the Raygin?" asked Tinker.

"Yes, but that is too obvious. They know we must attempt it, so they will be ready to counter our efforts. We need to do the unexpected. I am talking about an attack on their home base in the second ring. Why? Because humans have never traveled beyond the first ring, they won't expect it. Plus we don't know our way around and we are new to singularity drives. They will never see it coming."

"Now I understand things a little better," said Captain Cutter.

Ayashe had everyone's attention with the idea of attacking the attackers.

"Any ideas on how would we do it?" asked Captain Cutter.

"Twenty-five years ago, my people captured a Raygin ship."

Tal's eyebrows moved up as she focused even more on Ayashe's words.

"We have star charts showing many solar systems in the universe's second ring. Apeiron is capable of reading electrical signals. The nanobots may be able to scan the mind our captives until it finds the information we seek."

"Can we gather enough ships to send into the second ring with the Raygin fleet attacking us? How do you propose we mount an attack with enough firepower to threaten them?" asked Tal.

This is good thought Ayashe. *Everyone is beginning to participate.* "The federation has an experimental weapon. It's a planet destroyer. If we can create a delivery system using our combined technologies, it might be possible to hurt them. Force them to reconsider their war with humans."

"We already have our first concept to give Mac," said Tinker as he looked at the clock. "We still have eleven hours and fifty-five minutes to come up with some more ideas. What else do you have Ayashe?"

Everyone looked at Tinker, not believing what he said. Ayashe tilted her head and smiled at Tinker. She reached over and wacked him on the head. Everyone laughed.

The ice was broken, and ideas started to flow from each person in the room. *How did Mac do it? I would never have thought of putting this team together. Another one of his talents I suppose. I have to learn to be more like him and perform unending assessments of everyone near me and of my surroundings. It is tedious work and he makes it look so easy. I can see how his time as a sniper developed his skills. As a ghost behind enemy lines, his life depended upon mental sharpness, patience, inventiveness, and intelligence. My Mac is the whole package.*

Up to now, I thought my father was the best leader I knew. But Mac has taken leadership to a level I have never seen before. He forces himself to think ten moves ahead. He even saw the potential in Dwain when all I saw was a jerk. I should ask him what he sees in me. She became angry with herself. *I'm a lazy daydreamer. Focus.*

Ayashe looked up to see Ruth Bernard, the chemist, staring at her. As soon as they made eye contact Ruth looked away. Ayashe felt sorry for her. *She lost her husband to the Raygin during the attack on their ship. When she looks at Mac and me she must think about her own husband and what should have been.* Ayashe decided not to say anything unless Ruth started a conversation about it first.

When Mac arrived at 19:45 they had several items on the list. Ideas ranged from attacking the Ogarii to moving asteroids. He looked over their work, captured the items for consideration, and smiled.

"Excellent work," said Mac. "Be back to work tomorrow at 0800 hours."

Ayashe watched Mac work his charm. From her seat she could hear the conversations as he talked to each person. Tinker and Captain Cutter invited her and Mac to Cutter's cabin. To her disappointment, Mac thanked them and said he was working on a master plan for the coming battle. He looked at Ayashe and winked.

The sneaky Moke Burro knew I was listening. A light tap on Ayashe's shoulder startled her. She turned to find Ruth standing inches from her face.

"I'm sorry Ayashe, I didn't mean to alarm you, but may I ask you a personal question?"

"Ask away."

"Do you believe in totems?"

An odd question, I wonder where she's going with this? "Yes, my people, including myself believe in totems. My father has seen the ghost like animals, but I have not. Why do you ask?"

"I have no Indian blood in me, yet I have seen a totem."

Ayashe was shocked. "Where did you see it and what animal was it?"

"Remember when you looked up and caught me staring at you? I'm sure you thought I was focused on you."

Ayashe felt her stomach flutter.

"Well it wasn't you I was staring at, but a wispy animal standing over your left shoulder. I know this is going to sound stupid, but a cow's head was sniffing your hair."

Ayashe's face turned a shade lighter as her stomach became queasy. She felt a little light-headed. "Are you sure it wasn't a bull?"

"As sure as I am here talking to you, it was a cow. I'm a colonist. I know a cow when I see one. So, what does seeing a cow hovering around you mean?"

"The cow represents the stability of a home, happiness, and patience."

"Hmmm, I guess seeing a cow isn't bad is it?"

"No. It's good. Very good." Ayashe didn't mention the cow totem also appears when there is a pregnancy. *Oh, what am I going to do? The military doctor guaranteed me*

I wouldn't get pregnant. What will Mac think? We haven't even discussed children. I don't even know if he wants any. How will he be able to lead with a child distracting him? How will I lead?

Seeing confusion on Ayashe's face Ruth asked, "Are you okay? You look a little pale."

"I'm fine. What you said about seeing the totem brought back many memories. I don't understand why you saw it, but I'm thankful you told me."

"It was a pleasure working with you, even with the distraction." Ruth smiled and headed towards the door where Tal was already talking to Mac.

Ayashe wondered if Mac heard any of their conversation, because she could hear his. Tal was talking about how she liked the idea of attacking an Ogarii planet. She wanted to know what he thought about the feasibility of using a planet buster bomb. Mac explained it was on his list to give to Apeiron, but he liked the idea of attacking the enemy. Tal volunteered her skills as a pilot.

"Listening in? Why not go up and join the conversation," said Tews.

"I wanted to hear the conversation, but I don't want to distract him," Ayashe said as she smiled at Tews.

"You and Mac are refreshing. Most people would tell half-truths, but you two don't even think about it. You both give honest answers. By the way, I liked what you did with the team – getting everyone involved."

"Mac told me you're an expert with bugs, but he didn't tell me you are also an expert on human behavior. I felt I needed to get everyone talking. Tell me Tews, would you like to head up the team evaluating the Raygin and Ogarii? We need to start collecting data and learning how they interact. You'd be perfect. You already have experience with both races."

"You think Mac would want someone like me on such an important team?"

Ayashe laughed. "I'll tell you a little secret. When Mac talked to me about you he said there's more to you than anyone realizes. I'll talk to him."

"Thank you, Ayashe."

She stood up and walked with Tews to where Mac was finishing his conversation with Tal.

Mac looked at Tews and said, "I've been meaning to talk to you. I need someone to head up our new Alien Affairs Division."

Tews started laughing. "You heard our conversation."

"Not all of it but enough to realize Dreng is right. Awe shit, I mean Ayashe. I'll never get use to this."

"I could use an ancient form of mind control called hypnotism to make you get it right." Tews saw Mac's face light up. He looked at Ayashe who frowned at him. "Hey, I'm kidding, we use chemicals nowadays. No one has hypnotized anyone in thousands of years."

"Can you do it? Can you hypnotize someone?"

"Oh, come on Mac, I don't care which of my names you use," said Ayashe.

"Yeah. I still know how to do it." Stepping in front of Ayashe, Tews blocked her view with his back. He pointed through his chest at Ayashe so Mac could see. He shook his head no.

"Tews, I'm not stupid," said Ayashe. "I know what you're doing. He knows better than trying something so crazy. But, thank you for telling him no."

After laughing at the two of them, Mac said, "It's for Lieutenant Phlop. He can't remember anything dealing with the Ogarii. The med staff used every technique at their disposal. Nothing worked. The doctors think the Ogarii have used a technique or chemical we are not familiar with to block his memories."

"When do you want me to try hypnotism on him?"

"Get some sleep tonight. Meet me at the med lab at 0800 hours. Be ready for a long day. I have to enter your new title into the records. What's your full name?"

"Tews Alexander G- e-l-l-e-g-o."

"I'll be a Platyrhine's uncle," said Mac. "I thought Tews was a nick name."

"For first names," said Tews, "my parents used variations of sequential numbers. My older brother was Eins, and my younger brother was Tres. It's what happens when your parents have an over active sense of humor."

"It's Brilliant. I'll see you at 0800." Mac patted Tews on the back.

Ayashe noticed Tews's eyes got a little vacant. The same look Mac had when he talked about his brother. She was glad Mac patted Tews. She could see it meant a lot to him.

"We have to stop them," Mac said.

"I know. I'll do my best. See you in the morning."

Tews walked down the passageway with his head hung low.

Ayashe walked up to Mac, gave him a big hug, and said, "We need to talk."

Without warning Apeiron appeared next to Mac. "Sorry to interrupt, Mac. You both better get up on the bridge. We got the tachyon com system working. United Fleet Command was already online trying to contact the Constellation. It appears they also were working on the com system. When Vice Admiral Farragut discovered you are on board, he wanted to talk to you as fast as possible."

Ayashe ran with Mac to the nearest elevator. She knew with the tachyon com system working that there would be little private time with her husband. The talk about children would have to wait, but she hoped not too long.

The elevator doors on the bridge opened. Ayashe's star chart was on the holo display. She looked at the scene.

258

People were everywhere. The computer reported, Commodore McCormack on the bridge. It got quiet as all eyes fell on her husband. She felt sorry for him. Everyone already understood the fate of all humans rested with him.

While Ayashe looked it the map something kept nagging at her about the Raygin attack plan. She felt they had missed something important.

The Constellation's captain interrupted Ayashe's thoughts. "You were right about all the infested planets except one. Esharra. The attack on the ground has begun." The captain looked at Mac, "Now everyone knows, we are at war."

Mac looked at Ayashe. "This means the Ogarii already have a method of instant communication. The war has started, and we are operating several days behind their first big move."

CHAPTER SIXTEEN: The Real Quarry

Though light years apart, the vice admiral and Mac were able to talk face to face. As soon as United Fleet Command got the tachyon com system working, they started to set up a large-scale network. Communications in some areas became instantaneous. The new com devices were being installed in ships of war and key military installations first. In some cases, single tachyon systems were placed in large human population areas. These systems linked to local dissemination networks already in place.

The time lag in the old method of communication forced the vice admiral to operate on many assumptions. He had no idea what chain of events put Mac on the Constellation. He apologized for not taking more action. Presidential support involving spending money was hard to obtain.

Admiral Farragut showed Mac the videos he had from a few of the infested planets. The Raygin proved to be a ruthless enemy. Killing every man, woman, or child they came upon. The enemy spared no one. Not even the sick, the old, or the immobile.

The planetary president made one stupid mistake after another. He had no military experience, but it didn't stop him from trying to direct military forces. He ordered a counter attack without launching probes to assess the enemy. The colonel in charge had a live vid crew shooting him leading the troops. Instead of a battle, it had become public entertainment. On Esharra, the first strike against the

Raygin came from overhead. The fighters dropped ordinance on the enemy troops. The damage was devastating.

Seeing the initial success from an aerial attack, the colonel committed his troops to a ground attack. When the fighters came around for a second pass, the bugs deployed a mobile shield. It neutralized the fighters. The bugs had suckered the human ground forces into attacking. They held off firing until the humans were well in range of their laser canons. Under the portable shield, they began to fire at the human troops. Mac watched the vids and shook in anger as the infantry took serious casualties for no reason other than ego.

Understanding the dilemma on the ground, the squadron leader led the fighters on a dangerous low-level attack. They flew right up to the shield's edge. The maneuver gave the troops enough cover fire to retreat. At least someone had some common sense.

It was eerie to see the different colored laser canons firing. The powerful lasers on both sides caused the electrons of atoms in the air to become excited. When the excited atoms returned to their ground state they left a bright track behind. The red human lasers needed an upgrade to match the enemy's more powerful blue lasers. From the looks of it, the humans could also have used a few more canons.

Admiral Farragut stopped the vid. "Mac, I need you to take action before the planetary president does something even more stupid than he's already done. Make a broadcast using the tachyon com system. Explain the attack by the Raygin and Ogarii. Show some videos of Imperial Station, the battle of Rayne, and throw in some current vids. Let them see both enemy races. Be sure to throw in some clips of us winning. We don't want to demoralize our own people. They need to have hope. I want you to make a declaration of war and enact the United

Planets War Powers Act. We need to make sure everyday people know you have legal status over any orders issued by the president. Or for that matter, anyone else claiming leadership."

Within minutes a video of Mac implementing the War Powers Act was broadcast. He became the hegemon for the human race. It was a responsibility he didn't relish. Since his brother's death, all he had ever wanted was to take care of his troops. Well, if he were honest, he would say he wanted to kill the enemy too. He always thought the troops were like his family. Now his family had become much larger.

Mac didn't even look at the vids the Constellation's crew put together. He trusted them. Besides, he was too busy saving people. He initiated the Planetary Doctrine of Posse Comitatus. He took control of civilian ships and planetary transportation. He had civilians moved off planet where he could. In other cases, he moved civilians to safer locations on the same planet. There was no time to reach a consensus, so he took immediate action.

Every day, hundreds of ships and military facilities got their tachyon com systems on-line. The vice admiral did a great job expanding the network. One by one they reported in to Commodore McCormack for orders. Tachyon particles permeating the universe became the foundation of the new communication system. The frequencies were limitless because vibrating particles could oscillate at more than one rate. Mac could talk to one ship while sending a message to another. The box containing the new com system included an encryption device. Each ship and facility received specs on new weapon upgrades from Apeiron.

It was agonizing for Mac to see the Raygin attack and not be there to help. The small convoy was still days away. The engineers used every moment to enhance their ship's firepower. Key personnel worked around the clock on secret weapons. Mac was afraid there still might be more spies, so all outgoing coms had to go through the bridge.

To help the planets without military support he decided to form a resistance force. He chose the name Lightning Brigade. They were to strike hard and like lightning, fade away and disappear. He taught them several simple tactics he learned during his sniper days. Their job was not to engage, but to harass the enemy. Mac hoped his tactics would buy the trapped humans some time. He sent instructions on how to make explosives from common local materials. He made vids on how to use various com devices to trigger the improvised bombs.

Day by day the resistance grew. They were becoming killers. The bugs had the fancy weapons, but humans had the numbers on the infested planets. Soon the bugs realized they couldn't keep sacrificing their troops. It became a matter of survival for them too. Their advance began to slow, giving Mac hope.

The humans discovered the bugs had added a filtration device into their armor. It filtered out the poison Ruth developed. Still, holding high hopes for using the poison, he created a team of chemists and biologists. Their goal, design a mechanism to defeat the Raygin filtration system in the armor.

In the middle of it all, the planetary president tried to pull a fast one. He declared he needed to be the one to initiate the Planetary War Powers Act. He claimed he was still in charge. He was wrong and Mac proved it. Next, the president tried to take credit for the Lightning Brigade. Members of the Mac's Lightning Brigade were interviewed and claimed the planetary president to be a liar.

This is the reason he insisted on being a commodore. It is difficult enough to fight a war without having to fight politicians too. The next day the Planetary Parliament tried to usurp Mac's power. The tachyon instant communications stopped their lies before they could take hold. Every day, the politicians tried a new trick or spread a new lie in an effort to regain control of the military. It was wearing Mac out.

Looking up, he saw Ayashe standing next to him. He wondered how long she had been standing there.

She placed her arm on his shoulder. "Mac, are you okay?"

"Yeah, it is just these politicians are distracting me. It's reminds me of when I was a sniper hiding in the middle of an enemy platoon and a wolf spider crawled down my back."

Ayashe shuddered at the insight into Mac's past. "Don't worry. I'll get these jerks off your back. I'll call Admiral Farragut and ask him to keep the troublemakers at bay. In fact, I'll ask him to make examples of a few of them. It will make others think twice."

In an untypical move, which he didn't even try to hide, he reached over, and kissed her in front of everyone on the bridge. "You know I love you, right?"

She felt her face flush. She managed a smile as she batted her eyes at him.

He felt a refreshed burst of energy. "What is it my beautiful wife needs from me?"

Out of nowhere, Apeiron appeared. The robot made from a conglomeration of nanobots looked at Ayashe. "Have you told him yet? Remember the promise you made."

Ayashe gave the robot a look with both her eyes squinting at him. Apeiron recognized the human emotion and disappeared into atom size pieces.

"What was that about?" Asked Mac.

"I'll tell you later." She looked around. "This is not a good place to discuss it."

Now he was worried. *She knows I'm busy. There isn't a lot of time for the attention a normal relationship requires. I wont be able to think with this looming over my head*. "Is it about us?" he asked. When Ayashe looked at him, she realized he was nervous.

"Don't worry. Things between us are great. In fact, it is becoming everything I ever dared to hope for in a joining. We need time to talk."

Mac looked at her while tilting his head.

"About our future, silly. Our hopes, our dreams, our – ummm, call it wish list for what lies ahead. We can talk about it later. Now I need you to answer a few questions for me."

Mac felt the tension leave his body. "Okay, shoot."

"What do you think about your planetary president?"

"He's simplistic and a know nothing. He is a manipulating, scam supporting, liar, money grabbing, and corrupt Mecater turd. And let me tell you from personal experience, they can get pretty big."

Ayashe wrinkled her nose and laughed. "Stop right there. I don't want to hear another of your disgusting stories. Save it for Tinker, he seems to like them. Do you think everyone else knows?"

"About the Mecater turd I hid inside?"

Laughing she said, "You had to find a way to work it into the conversation, didn't you? No not about the Mecater thingy. Let me rephrase the question. Do you think most people know the planetary president is what you described him to be?

"Yeah, sure. Most people don't want to be leaders. They are happy letting someone else do it so long as no major harm occurs. Why? Where are you going with this?"

"I'm working on a theory. I'll let you know if anything comes of it. Would you mind if I worked with Tews as he interrogates Lt. Phlop?"

"No, go ahead. The last six months are missing from the lieutenant's memories. Tews is working on getting them back. The doctors think he took some kind of drug to block recent memories."

The tachyon speaker squealed. The bridge went silent as the crew looked at the com officer. She checked the com unit and associated gauges. She looked at Mac, "The noise was a sinusoidal waveform. It's a type of carrier wave containing a data transmission. It looks like someone sent a video file." She typed in a few commands on the screen. "The files are from the Wasp sir."

"Great," said Mac, "this will make things much easier."

"Wait," said the com officer. "The carrier wave also contains a condensed voice transmission. They used the same frequency instead of separating them."

"Let me hear and see what they sent."

"Aye sir. Synching video and audio."

Mahpee appeared on the bridge's main viewer yelling at someone. "Uzumati, can't you be quiet for once." He faced the viewer on his ship and said, "Mac, grandfather has assured me the tachyon com system is working now. A book is longer than a vid."

"Stop the video," said Mac. He looked at Ayashe. "Is that code for something?"

"No. It is father trying to use your colloquialisms again. He meant a picture is worth a thousand words."

The translation got giggles from the Constellation's bridge crew.

"Continue with the video," said Mac.

"This is a transmission we received from Osa, our ocean planet. It is the farthest out of our colonized planets." As Mahpee talked, all eyes were on the screen. "You can see the planet's defense system firing in a sector of space. The explosions are from large planetary lasers. We hid them on asteroids. We tried to get the people of Osa to relocate twenty-five years ago." The crew heard Mahpee's voice quiver. "It's too late. Too few of them left for the safety of Nokomis. Osa had a limited defense system."

"Zoom in on the weapons fire," said Mac.

The crew watched as a few more Raygin ships exploded. But there were hundreds of them. Mac thought the Raygin fleet was big, but at least it was manageable. Several large ships maneuvered into distinct geometrical clusters. A shimmering shield appeared blocking the energy from the gigantic laser canons. In response the People's Nation launched drones from both moons of Osa. The computer piloted vehicles headed straight to the Raygin ships. They focused on the ones creating the moving shield. The enemy reacted by launching thousands of fighters. The pilotless drones were faster. They attempted to evade the fighters and focus on the battleships. In the end the sheer number of enemy fighters were too much for the drones.

The Constellation's crew watched as the Raygin fighters destroyed the drones. None got close enough to damage the alien battleships. The dark shadow of bug looking ships moved closer toward the small planet. Micro satellites orbiting Osa captured the whole attack on vids. The planet fired a barrage of laser canons as soon as the Raygin were in range. They were the largest laser canons Mac had ever seen. The combined laser fire broke through the cluster shield. The lead Raygin ship exploded in a sudden flash. Another black ship took its place. The armada moved closer to the planet while the lasers recharged.

"Watch," said Mahpee, "the weapons launched from the planet are new technology. They have named them bemoss. You would translate it to walkers. They use gravitational distortions of certain sizes in space to track their target."

The walkers fanned out as they flew toward their individual targets. Many of them exploded against the large shield. Everyone's eyes focused on the few making it past the energy blockade. Explosions were immediate as the walkers found their targets. Several Raygin ships sustained what looked to be considerable damage. One walker appeared to miss everything as it accelerated into deep space. It made an abrupt ninety-degree turn. Everyone saw a flash from an explosion. A sleek bird looking ship became visible in the bright blaze.

A cloaked ship had been hiding well away from the action. The ship's nose looked like a predator bird head. It had swept back wings like a bird of prey diving on its victim. Mac could see the flicker on the ship's surface as the shields shorted out. The ship diverted its power as it tried to protect itself from battle debris. A large chunk of a destroyed Raygin ship hit the graceful and now fragile looking ship. The weakened shields didn't hold. Mac knew the advanced design had to be Ogarii. It burst into several pieces and tumbled into space.

The Raygin ships started firing at the planet again.

"They took out the large laser canon sites before they could recharge," said Mahpee. "Next they destroyed transportation and communication hubs. When it was safe they landed with troop transports. These are the few vids we have from Osa's surface."

Mac watched as the Raygin destroyed everything. Most people on the planet didn't have weapons. They were sitting ducks. What resistance did manage to form became priority targets. The Raygin didn't bother with prisoners. Mac knew what they were doing. Teaching the humans a lesson. Destroying morale. It was a dangerous tactic to use. It could backfire and strengthen a resistance movement. The Raygin didn't bother with sending troops to rural or agricultural areas. They went for large population zones.

Everyone watched as atmospheric ships sprayed the countryside. "They are spraying a crop killing poison, said Mahpee. "The planet will be useless until we find a way to neutralize it. The loss of life will be horrendous. We estimate the death total will be near three point eight billion of our people."

"We have lost all communication with the planet. The last transmission we received is from a deep space micro probe."

The bridge became silent as the vid played. It showed a fleet of Raygin ships numbering in the thousands. This was the main body of the enemy fleet, not what they had been watching. Mac remembered the words of Mahpee's grandfather. *It's true. The Raygin fleet does blot out galaxies. This is not manageable.*

"We believe Osa was attacked because the Raygin probes detected human life on the planet. We are in communication with Nokomis and will soon arrive. From what we could see, several hundred Raygin ships flank the main fleet. They must fear a concentrated attack on the side of their fleet. I know I have given you a lot to think about. I await your call. Please tell my little princess I send my love. You take care of her. Mahpee out."

The anger Mac felt during his youthful sniper days returned with a vengeance. There would be hell to pay by the Ogarii if he had any say in it. He began to slow his heart rate. Experience trained him not to let anger rage. He began to channel his energy and thoughts towards a multi-pronged solution.

"Engineering. I want to know how the enemy was able to project their shields into near space. Taking advantage of quark confinement requires dense material to create shields without gaps. The average hydrogen density in space is one atom per cubic centimeter. They must be spraying a source of atoms from their ships. I need some quick answers."

Mac looked at Smitty.

"Now commodore, before you say anything else. I know quark confinement and shield theory. In fact, I know it better than I know myself. I'm your man."

"Great, it's all yours. I also want to know how to defeat their shield system. How can we modify the walkers to search only cloaked ships first. Search for undiscovered enemy weaknesses. Find a way to make the big laser canons fire faster. Work with Tinker. I'll have him get in touch with you."

"Aye sir. But before I go, may I make a suggestion?"

"Go ahead."

"I know Tinker is one hell of a trooper. I owe him my life, but don't you think we should have a few more experienced engineers for this project?"

"Smitty, to be honest I'm more worried about you than him. Tinker holds multiple engineering degrees. He's what you would call a natural. It's why I gave him his nickname. He developed the antigrav skidder bombs during the mining wars. He helped develop long range acoustic weapons, laser mines, medusa projectors, bremsstrahlung particle weapons, and a list of other inventions and improvement recommendations."

Smitty smiled. "Sorry? I didn't know. Nobody ever said anything."

Mac patted Smitty on the back. "You couldn't have known. Tinker could have joined the federation as an officer. He's top notch. For his own reasons he chose to start from the bottom as a ground pounder. He asked me to keep his tinkering ability private. I gave him what he wanted until now. Things have changed. We are at war. I need every bit of talent I can squeeze out of everyone."

"I'm looking forward to this. Don't you worry. I'll get hold of Tinker. You focus on what you need to be doing." Smitty turned and walked toward the elevator.

Mac smiled when he heard him mumble something about getting out of here before his list of things to do grew.

"Mac. May I speak to my father? It's important."

"Yeah. Go ahead. I need to talk to him too. You first."

The com officer signaled Ayashe to go ahead and speak.

"Father. It is I, Ayashe."

"I am not deaf grandfather. I know it's my daughter." Mahpee appeared on the viewer. "Ayashe. I miss you. Is all well?"

"Yes. All is fine. I am sorry about Osa. It is horrible what they did."

Ayashe began to speak, but no one understood. Phonetically it sounded something like: "Ah-say ga-wan-nees-gav oh-knee-ya-gay-sdow-da u-leese-ga-dav aye-yav wee-lee oh-ya-nav-dav, ew-see-li-da."

"I understand," said Mahpee. "May I talk to Mac?"

"I love you father. Mac is here. Speak as you will."

Odd. Something big is up. I recognized one word, u-tse-li-da. She taught it to me and knows I know the word. Hell, she even over pronounced it so I wouldn't miss it. It is when something is private and not for all ears. I'll wait to talk to her later. "I'm here Mahpee."

The two leaders brought each other up to date and promised the sharing of a few new discoveries.

"I have a couple requests," said Mac.

"You shall receive nothing from me Mac. I have not heard the words."

A red-faced Ayashe moved forward to translate.

"It's okay. I got it. He meant if you don't ask, you don't receive." He smiled. *One day we need to teach each other the finer points of our languages.* "First, can you have your engineers put top priority on developing the new light-based computer system? Second, I need a delivery system. It has to be fast as hell, small, maneuverable and have a strong shield system. You can design it for a one-person crew. It must be capable of carrying a payload designed into its nose. I'll send you the specs."

An involuntary twitch moved Mahpee's shoulders. He asked in a whisper, "Is a storm coming?"

271

Does he know my plan? He regretted talking to him about this particular weapon system. *I can't ask someone else to take the risk. I'll do it myself and with any luck make the enemy realize they are also vulnerable.*

"A storm is coming unlike any other, Mahpee my friend. The Ogarii are the universe's bullies. We have to bloody their noses to stop their bad behavior."

Ayashe experienced an involuntary shiver at the words. She realized, the enemy was moving to the storm's center. She needed to talk to Lieutenant Phlop.

"I understand, but we must talk when I arrive," said Mahpee.

"I look forward to seeing you in person again. Mac out." The face of Mahpee faded as the com officer broke the connection.

Mac formulated a new plan. He started making calls and scheduling meetings.

*****

Slipping away while Mac was distracted, Ayashe headed for the medical department. She needed to find out if what she suspected was true or not. Lieutenant Phlop had the answers, but he refused to talk to anyone. He certainly wasn't going to talk to her about Mac.

When she arrived in the med wing she searched out Tews. It scared her but she had to find out if what she suspected was true. She found Tews in an office with the staff working on a holographic display of a brain.

"Hi, Ayashe. Come in," said Tews. "Mac called and said you would be coming soon and to help you however we can."

She smiled. *Mac noticed her departure from the bridge even with everything going on. How does he do it?*

"What do you need from Lieutenant Phlop?" asked Tews.

"First, tell me how hypnosis works and how do I know I'm getting the truth?"

"I learned hypnosis from an old rebellious expert. It's an outdated practice no longer taught. The planetary government banned it thousands of years ago. My guess is with time, and dedication, anyone could learn how to do it. The government wanted no part of people experimenting with such powerful science. Today we use expensive chemicals and hardware to affect someone's memories. The cost is prohibitive."

"Encoding a memory occurs when a protein stimulates our brain cells. It creates a connection within the brain's neocortical region. The hippocampal activity -" Tews stopped mid-sentence when he saw Ayashe waving her hands.

"Hold on Tews. I appreciate your level of detail. But, is there a simple way you can explain it to me? We are kind of pressed for time."

"Sorry. I can get carried away. Let me put it to you like this, chemicals can block a memory connection, but the memory is still there. It takes away the pathway. Using hypnosis, I force the brain to make a new pathway to access the old memory. The chemical does not block the new connection. During questioning, we will monitor the lieutenant's brain waves. I can tell if he is faking it, or if I am in his subconscious thoughts. How's that?"

"Great. Can I question him?"

"No, you can't. Not without a lot of work. I have his mind trained to focus on my voice. It might take him days to get used to you. If time is important, I'll question him for you. You can be there while I do it. Is that acceptable?"

"Good enough for me. Let's get going."

At first Ayashe and Tews watched through a large viewing screen. The staff gave Mr. Phlop his dinner. It contained a special sedative to force him to relax. Tews explained this form of covert manipulation was why hypnosis was banned. The target had no idea he was being placed in a trance. He told her it's all about control and manipulation.

Within minutes of finishing his meal, Lieutenant Phlop fell asleep on his bed. The med team wasted no time wheeling in several pieces of equipment to monitor him. Tews began to talk to the lieutenant using a gentle, slow, and rhythmic voice. Everyone had to be quiet during the interrogation. Within minutes brain activities confirmed Tews was in contact with the lieutenant's active, but subconscious mind.

"Tell me Lieutenant Phlop, what did you think when you first realized there are aliens in the universe?"

The lieutenant struggled to answer the question. Ayashe watched him move his neck muscles as if under strain. Tews is clever. He is not going straight at the locked memories. He's going after peripheral memories. Building a new neural network in an effort to open up old memories. Once again, she marveled at the team surrounding Mac. They were the perfect storm of key people with specific talents. If you tried to build a team like this, you couldn't.

After about thirty minutes of questioning, the answers started coming with less labor. Memory clusters were beginning to link.

"Do you know the Ogarii person called Wineena?" asked Tews.

"You mean the overseer?" said the lieutenant.

"Yes."

"Yes. I know her."

"What did you talk about the last time you spoke with her?"

"She told me I could be the richest human alive if I helped kill our leader."

"How are you supposed to kill the planetary president?" asked Tews.

The lieutenant twitched and strained. "Not the planetary leader."

"Who did Wineena want you to kill?"

"Commodore McCormack, the top military leader."

The answer shocked Tews. He couldn't come up with a follow-up question. Ayashe could see the fear in the staff as they processed the lieutenant's response. Dread filled her heart. Mac was walking into a clever Ogarii trap.

CHAPTER SEVENTEEN: The Enemy Is Here

Mac could tell Ayashe had important information. As soon as she stepped off the elevator, her eyes locked onto him. She moved toward him without noticing anyone else. *Was she afraid? Something had her rattled.*

As she approached he said, "What's wrong?"

"What is the real threat to the Ogarii?" asked Ayashe.

Without hesitation Mac said, "Our military and yours."

"Yes, but I don't think they know about our existence or they would have sent scouts looking for us. Let's presume they don't know. Who would you go after if you were the Ogarii?"

"The leader."

"Which one, Mac?"

"The presi… uh, okay. I see where you're going. I'd go after – me. So, you think this whole attack is a trap set for me?"

"Yes. I have no doubt. Tews broke the mind block the Ogarii used on Lieutenant Phlop. It's been you this whole time, Mac. You dropping in their lap on Rayne must have freaked them out. They couldn't ensure your death on the planet so they let you escape. It would have ruined all their plans if you went into hiding after leaving Rayne. They needed you leading the human fleet as they sprung their trap."

"Clever. I could see myself doing something similar. Misdirection is one of my favorite tools. Good work, you may have saved the war."

"What do we do? The whole Raygin fleet is coming for you."

"We set a trap within a trap," said Mac. "I need to buy us time, so we can become better prepared. Looking at their approach, I didn't understand why they were using flank protection with such a large force. I would have expanded and thinned out the exterior ships. Now I see their plan. As they approach us, the flank ships will move farther and farther away from the main fleet. They will make a move to come in from our backside and close the trap. This overseer is no fool. She has formulated a good invasion plan. A good general adjusts like she did when we discovered too much about them."

Mac could see the flush in Ayashe's face. *Uh oh.*

She moved close to him and whispered, "I could make my eyes flash orange if you would like?"

Mac stepped back and looked her up and down, pausing long enough on her breasts so she noticed. "I don't want you to change anything. You are already perfect?"

Her face lit up with a big smile. "You shall be rewarded for that remark tonight."

He kissed her on her headband tattoo. "You know, I think it's time to call it a night. I've done as much as I can. Come on. Let's go."

She giggled. "Get back to work lazybones." As an afterthought she said, "Mac, I'm worried. What if we're wrong?"

"It means we drew the short stick and we're fucked."

She laughed. "You're so articulate."

"I'm a ground pounder honey. Always give it to me straight. Let me improvise, adapt, and overcome."

On hearing Mac's response one of his personal guards interjected an, "Oohrah."

The bridge went up for grabs at the well-known ground pounder expression. Mac and Ayashe hadn't noticed everyone was listening to their conversation.

I have to learn to be a little more discrete. Mac turned to look at the supportive guard.

Seeing Mac staring at him the young soldier thought Mac was mad at him. "Sorry, commodore."

"It's Mac," he grinned. He looked at the bridge crew and said, "I didn't have a chance to finish answering Ayashe's question. Let me say, but I think we're right."

The young soldier looked into Mac's eyes and said, "Say the word Mac. I'll follow you to the gates of Hades. We all saw your films. We are behind you one hundred percent."

"What films?" asked Mac.

Lieutenant Muween stepped forward. "I took the liberty of putting together several video montages, sir. We used fight scenes to show the humans what we are up against. You were in many of the videos and it seems as though there were… umm, how should I say this? Some unintentional consequences."

"What might some of the unintentional consequences be?"

"Com companies have requested more vid clips of you. They called you videogenic. Requests for sniper school are up over a thousand percent. Enlistment is through the roof. Thanks to the vice admiral, Lightning Brigade schools sponsored by the military spec ops are popping up everywhere. With the development of tachyon communications, you are the most famous human in our universe! The ship building facilities are beyond full staffing levels. Your popularity is helping to weaponize the entire human race. I could go on and on."

Mac felt his checks flush red.

"Now, now, Mac." said Ayashe, "You told me yourself, wars need heroes. Accept it as good for the morale and move on."

Mac took a deep breath, looked at Lieutenant Muween and said, "Please, don't make it about me."

"I didn't sir. It's just everyone is looking for a real leader. They understand everything is at risk here. To put it in words you might understand better, if I may?"

Looking at her with tilted head Mac said, "Yeah, go ahead, lets hear it."

"Accept it and adapt."

"You mean I'm fucked."

"Yes sir. You're fucked as far as fame goes."

Ayashe and the bridge crew laughed.

"Alright. Enough fun and games. Let's figure out how to kick some alien ass."

This time the bridge gave him an "Oohrah," in unison.

A sinking feeling crept into his stomach. He realized this scene might wind up in a video clip. He looked at Muween. She was already watching him with a big smile on her face. She raised her right hand and gave him a thumb up signal. *Let it go*, he told himself. *Let it go*.

That night Ayashe and Mac were intimate. The sex was better than anything he had ever experienced. He rated it higher than when he paid a small fortune for a night with a Partuvian prostitute. *God, he loved her so much*. When he questioned her concerning what she wanted to talk about, she said it should wait for a better time.

Lying with his head in her lap he said, "Remember, no secrets."

"It's not a secret," she said as she looked into his eyes. She rubbed her hand through his hair. "I need your undivided attention for more time than you can give me right now." He heard her gentle voice say, "I'll wait. It's all good. Relax, relax Mac." His eyes began to flutter and he fell into a peaceful deep sleep.

The Raygin fleet continued to advance.

Mac woke up feeling great. For the next couple of days, he worked on a plan of attack. Some military ships began to arrive on scene. He decided not to send them to help the infested planets. No one had heard from the Planetary President for the last couple days. Mac believed he had already snuck off the planet. The humans on the infested planets were holding their own. This was thanks to help from civilian ships and the Lightning Brigade.

He had two primary objectives. Destroy as many enemy ships as possible and don't engage in an all-out battle to the end. They needed to buy time so they could relocate ships, creating new ships, perform upgrades, and develop new weapons. The UFC needed time to increase staffing levels and planets needed time to install better planetary defenses. The list went on and on. Time was the common thread. Right now, he needed every war ship available to pull off his plan.

Ships worked around the clock setting up a number of debris fields. They planned to redirect the enemy fleet into several traps. It was slow going because Mac's ships were designed for war, not moving asteroids. The Tonk belt miners located in hundreds of solar systems throughout the universe contacted Mac and offered the use of their trained personnel and oversized equipment. The Tonkers, as they are called, helped Mac move mountain-sized asteroids into tactical positions. Thanks to them his plan might work. He still needed Smitty and Tinker to come through for him. He started to make his way to cargo deck bravo to check on their progress.

As he walked through the passageways everyone greeted him. He pondered about his past and how he had loved being a simple soldier. After all this, his days of blissful anonymity would be gone forever. The elevator door opened and Mac found himself looking at a mess. He saw hundreds of pods. Some looked near completion, others had their guts hanging out of them. He estimated at least two thousand people were working on the high-tech equipment. He had a feeling of disappointment. It wouldn't be the first time he had to make do.

His mind scrambled for a new plan as his eyes continued to survey the scene. He realized no one was beating on equipment, cursing, or standing motionless in confusion. *They have done it!* The apparent disarray was nothing more than what mass production looked like in an open area.

He saw Tinker, Smitty, and Apeiron talking near a centralized drafting table. As he walked toward the trio a continuous host of workers greeted him over and over. They all knew him. *Damn vids. Thank God Ayashe is not here. She wouldn't let me live this down.*

Tinker looked up. "Mac. We were getting ready to come to the bridge to talk to you. You didn't need to come to us."

"It's okay. I don't mind. It's nice to get away for a few minutes. It clears my mind. I can't believe all these people know who I am!"

Tinker smiled. "I'm telling you, you don't know the half of it. During break I can't even eat! I spend all my time answering questions about you. I have never witnessed anything like it."

"I don't want to think about it," said Mac. He changed the subject. "Tell me what's going on. I was hoping to have about five hundred modified walkers." He estimated the number and realized they were far short. They had worked so hard, he regretted saying he hoped for more. "To be honest, what you did is amazing. I'll take whatever you can give me."

Smitty laughed. "Don't you go worrying your pretty little videogenic face, sir." Smitty spread his arms. "We have three hundred and two walkers here, and seven hundred are being built on four other battleships. You can thank Apeiron for coming up with the idea of using other ships."

Mac looked at Apeiron and said, "Thank you." The robot's chest stuck out as if it were proud.

"Commodore McCormack please come to the bridge," spoke a female voice on Mac's personal com unit.

"Gotta go, nice work," said Mac. He spun around and jogged back to the elevator.

When Mac stepped onto the bridge, the admiral wasted no time with greetings. He pointed at the view screen. "We received a sentinel alarm in the Artemis sector. No visual. The grav detector identified the appearance of a small target. It's stationary. We are running a full system check."

"Diagnostic complete admiral. All systems check out," said the com officer.

"It appears we have a small cloaked vessel snooping around."

"Perfect," said Mac. "Computer, activate Flicker in Artemis sector. Authorization code Mac na-s-gi-ya-i." He chose People's Nation words not stored in the computer for authorization codes.

Thirty seconds later the Admiral said, "The cloaked vessel is gone. What did you do?"

"It was Ayashe's idea. She heard about the Medusa projector Tinker developed. She asked if it could work in space. Turns out it can under the right circumstances. We located interstellar clouds with characteristic energies in the 21 cm range." Mac saw a puzzled look on the admiral's face. "They found clouds loaded with hydrogen. Our engineers set up several pods with projectors. The small spy ship thought it detected a flotilla containing two hundred of our battleships patrolling the area. When they play the vids back, the signal will be weak, but they should attribute that to the distance."

"I would like to have heard the pilots' thoughts!" said the admiral.

"Each minute we can slow the Raygin fleet down buys us more time to prepare."

"Incoming call from Mahpee," said the com officer. "Go ahead sir."

"Mahpee, Mac here. Go ahead."

"We have left Nokomis. I am carrying a gift for you from my engineers. Nashta and grandfather also came up with a new fighter design. It combines Raygin, Human, and our own technology. I have sent you the specs. Any bioluminescent organisms in the fluid will work, but we used Vibrio bacteria. They replicate and are plentiful in salt water. How is the war effort going?"

"I wish we had more time. I decided we could not afford to split the fleet. There will be no space support or military ships to evacuate the planets. The Raygin have portable shields and have tunneled underground. After an initial loss of human lives, the infested planets are standing their ground. It would take us months and hundreds of ships to evacuate the affected planets."

"You made a difficult choice, Mac. If it means anything, I would have made the same decision. I will arrive soon with your package. My fleet is hidden so we may surprise the enemy when the time is right. For the last twenty-five years I have wanted revenge against the enemy responsible for killing my wife. Soon I will have vengeance. Is my daughter okay?"

"Yes. She is well and helpful. She said if I talked to you to tell you, 'na-s-gi-a-ge-yv tsi-ge-yu-a ni-hi.'"

"I may tease you Mac but know my daughter has chosen well. Tell her I love her too. And Mac, you will be like the u-we-tsi I never had. I must go. I will meet you in mere seconds."

Mac smiled. "Okay, Mahpee, I'll see you soon."

*****

For the next couple of days Mac and Ayashe worked on creating plans, while everyone else worked on implementing them. The Raygin continued to attack human populated planets using the Osa tactics. There was nothing they could do to save billions of lives.

The micro probes watched, tracked, and recorded the enemy. They broadcast the Raygin fleet's advancement vids to the Constellation. The Ogarii remained unseen. Their sleek ships hid within pods of Raygin ships. The intensity of preparations reached a peak. The humans knew the enemy would arrive within days. There was no doubt. They needed more time.

Work on the modified walkers was complete. They were being deployed per instructions. The next new project cluttered all bravo deck. Parts were everywhere and still being created by the thousands. The new single piloted fighter design earned the name, Screamer.

The first Screamer soon rolled off the Constellation's assembly line. Within hours it passed all static tests with no errors. When Ayashe arrived, she heard the engineers talking about finding a test pilot. She volunteered without a thought.

Apeiron gave her a stare with his black robot looking eyes. "Do you think we should clear it with Mac first?"

"From where did the plans for these fighters originate?" Ayashe asked.

"Go no further. I understand your logic. Are you familiar with the design and controls?"

"Yes. I read the material my father sent. I understand the People's Nation have named the craft a Screamer. Do you know why?"

"The story I heard is when the first test pilot accelerated the new fighter it was so fast it surprised him. He screamed," said Apeiron. "The name caught on."

Smitty's eyes enlarged. "What if she gets hurt? We are as good as dead. You've seen what Mac can do."

"I will take appropriate precautions. Don't kid yourself. If I get hurt, I too fear Mac's response. Come on guys, I have complete confidence in our engineers and you. All of you have seen what they can do. I promise I won't take any risks."

Using a voice resembling Mahpee, Apeiron said, "Ayashe, it is more than you, I worry about."

Deflecting the statement to avoid any questions she said, "We should all hope for each other to be safe." She gave Apeiron a hard stare. "I'll tell you what, you can send an escort out with me."

"I suppose it's better than nothing," said Apeiron.

Within an hour, a Screamer sat in launch tube alpha one on the flight deck. An escort craft already waited in a safe position near the battleship. Ayashe started the engine. The egg-shaped pilot bubble inside the large gyro flipped upside down. "Oops." She flipped the gyros on and the pilot bubble righted itself. "I should have said I trust our engineers design, but not their instructions. Alpha one ready for launch."

"Alpha one, launch authorized," said a voice in her cockpit.

She launched from the tube into near space armed and at max speed. Even with the g-reduction suit, she felt the effects of speed beyond anything she had ever flown in the past. She tried not to scream. But her amygdala, a region near the brain's base, couldn't suppress a loud involuntary, "Shiiiit!" At that moment she was glad she wasn't the first test pilot. Screamer was a much better name than Shiiiit.

Even with her super strength it was an effort to move under the force of acceleration. She made a mental note: *human use of manual control under full acceleration would be impossible. They would have to use visual or verbal*

285

controls. After the initial shock, she gained control using visual commands.

"Dreng, are you all right?" trumpeted over her cockpit speaker system.

Cute. When he's worried about me, he calls me Dreng. I guess I'm the one to blame for it. "Mac, I'm fine. The fighter's speed shocked me." She reversed direction and the gyro spun the pilot bubble. She was facing forward again. The pilot bubble made her feel like she was free floating in space. Why hadn't anyone thought of this before? "Pilot visibility is unbelievable."

"The fighter is so small and streamlined, we can't get a solid lock on you for viewing magnification. You moved so fast, you disappeared off our screen within a second from launch."

"I'm going to simulate attacking the Constellation. See what happens when you try to get a firing lock on me."

She flew straight at the enormous battleship. To an observer from the outside it would look like a pea attacking the moon.

"Target lock," said Mac, "on both laser and plasma canons."

Ayashe swung around for another attack. "Okay. Now try."

On this approach she flew a twisted course. The little vessel zigzagged and changed speed. When she stopped she was looking into the bridge. The big ship was still looking for her. "Bang," she said, "you're dead. I flew a serpentine path and changed speed several times."

"Try it again. This time zigzag without speed changes."

Ayashe made approach after approach at Mac's direction. Over half the time, the targeting system couldn't get a lock on the Screamer.

"Ayashe, our shields are up. Try using Portal to get through."

She couldn't wait to use the genius device created by Tinker and Smitty. Using the properties of confinement, they created a weapon to drain the energy from a ship's shield at an isolated location. They found they could create a short, causing a temporary opening. Nashta and Mahpee's grandfather took the concept a step further. They used the energy from the tapped shield to strengthen their own shield.

Ayashe positioned herself against the Constellation's shield. The energy began to flow into the Screamer. "I have an opening I could fire through."

"It won't work," said Mac. "It took you thirty seconds to create an opening. The Raygin fighters would have been all over you."

"All that work. What a shame," said Ayashe.

"It wasn't in vain. We can talk about it later."

"Seems like we always have to wait till later."

Mac ignored her frustration. "Let's see how you do against three war drones. They're armed with the same low energy lasers we use in pilot training."

She accelerated as the nearest drone fired at the space she vacated. "Oh great. Thanks for the late warning." Another drone tried to get behind her at her six o'clock. *Smart.* The drones are trying to come at me from three different directions. Her pilot bubble spun as the Screamer accelerated at a ninety-degree ascension. The drones or even alien fighters could never keep up with her, let alone make such a maneuver. She remembered the targeting tests and began to fly an irregular pattern. Within seconds, she destroyed all three pilot training drones.

Mac let the bridge microphone go live for a few seconds, so she could hear the cheering. "Nice job," he said.

"I want one of these."

"I'll have the crew put your name on one. Run a victory lap, and come back in. Production is already continuing."

It was like he understood she needed the distraction from war planning. She accelerated, spun 180 degrees and accelerated again. A few more passes and she returned to the Constellation. The Screamer is amazing. She felt guilty enjoying herself. When she got back, she went right to work again.

The push from Mac had been relentless the last few days. He drove her until she learned to drive herself beyond what she thought possible. It scared her when he confided in her and said they would lose this upcoming battle. "A battle," he said, "is not the war. The death toll will be high on both sides, but we have to make them think twice about another full force attack."

The latest micro probes showed the main Raygin fleet had stopped about two light days away. The flank ships continued and widened their approach. Mac was right. The enemy ships were moving ahead to block retreat and attack from two fronts. The number of Ogarii cloaked probes increased. It was a sure sign the battle was about to start.

Stopping the Raygin fleet so close was an effort to draw the humans away from their defenses. Even if at full strength, which they were nowhere near, Mac estimated the humans were at a five to one disadvantage. His sharing every tiny thought about the war with her began to make her worry. Something was up, and she had to find out what, before he did something stupid.

*****

Without warning the weapons officer on the bridge yelled, "Incoming, full shields. Red alert. Brace for impact.

288

CHAPTER EIGHTEEN: The Enemy's Face

A small micro gravity well opened in close proximity to the Constellation. A tiny craft appeared. It wasn't much bigger than the new fighter design, but it traveled faster than light. The view screen showed a small craft with a wide body in the middle, one narrow end, and the other end looked like it was cut off or unfinished. The targeting computer locked onto the undersized ship.

"Hold. Don't fire," said Mac. It's one of ours. Let's get it on hanger deck bravo."

"How do you know?" asked the admiral.

"If it was a kinetic energy weapon, we would be dead. On the other hand, if it were a mine it would have detonated by now. If it were a probe, it would have captured the data and left the scene. If it was an enemy ship, they would have offered to surrender."

Both the admiral and crew laughed. It was an intense moment.

"Constellation. This is Mahpee. Is Mac there?"

"Yes, Mahpee. I'm here."

"I was hoping you wouldn't fire. I didn't want to use the radio while on approach, with the enemy so near."

"We will put you on hanger deck bravo. I'll have you brought to the bridge and I'll let Ayashe know you're back."

"Thank you. We have much to talk about."

When Mac called Ayashe he could tell by her voice she assumed he called to check on her assignment.

"I have identified three alternate exit routes. All based on your expected deployment of Raygin ships. I put the plan in the war file folder for you to review. I named the file abukcheech."

"Mouse?"

"Yes. They are hard to catch. The paths will allow for fleet regrouping or exit depending on how the battle goes."

"Great, but it's not why I called. Your father is here."

"What? Why didn't you say so? Where is he?"

"He arrived with my ship a couple minutes ago. He should be on his way on his way to the bridge by now."

*****

Her heart sank. *He said "my ship". He's up to something and he's hiding it from me.* She shot out of her chair and headed to the hanger deck.

"I'll be there soon. Don't let father leave the bridge until I talk to him!"

"Okay. Be quick."

When the elevator opened to hanger deck bravo Ayashe saw at least a hundred Screamers. All of them were under various phases of construction. The shipyards were building new weapons, but they were all too far away. The battleships had to resort to mass-producing their own weapons. There, she saw it. A new style craft parked outside the fighter elevators. It had to be what her father arrived in. She began to take long running strides toward it. Technicians were already working on the ship's nose.

When she arrived, she read the box. To: Commodore McCormack, Contents: One Storm. She looked inside the vessel. She could see the technicians were hooking up some complex looking equipment. It looked like there was room for three people, but all she could see was one seat. *Odd,* she thought. *It didn't look like a fighter.* She didn't see any weapons.

290

Ayashe walked up to the technicians. "What is all this?"

The techs looked up to find Ayashe already standing in the ship.

"You can't be here," said a tech. "Oh crap. We're in big trouble."

"I'm not here to get anyone in trouble. You know who I am, right?"

The technicians all nodded their heads.

"All I want to do is protect Mac. Even if it's from himself."

She could see her words had got to them. They too would do anything for him. *Good.* She swung her head at the equipment as if to point.

"The box says this is called a STORM," said a technician. "It's a new science project. If it's an acronym I don't know what it means."

"Mac told me about this. It creates a small star out of a planet by eliminating the proto phase and going right to nuclear fusion, right?"

The techs looked at each other in surprise, "Yes ma'am."

Ayashe pointed to the vessel. "Is this a drone?"

"No ma'am. The ship requires a single pilot. We are to hook up and verify the weapon's operability. The hanger crew is waiting to move the ship to launch tube echo two."

Ayashe's legs felt weak. *Mac made all this happen. He would never ask a pilot to fly this planet killer to their death. He would do it himself.* "You boys. Don't you let Mac get into this ship."

Six eyes went wide as the technicians contemplated how they would try to stop him. By the fear in their eyes, Ayashe knew they had watched videos of Mac fighting. She would have to stop him herself.

Ayashe spun around and ran back toward the elevator. She went straight to the bridge. The door opened, but she didn't see Mac or Mahpee. Her heart raced. The admiral saw her scanning the bridge and pointed to the conference room.

The door opened as she approached. *No one.* She stepped back out toward the admiral. "No one is in the conference room."

"Odd. They must have used the emergency bridge exit. Hold on Ayashe. Com. Where is Mac?"

"Mac is on the launch deck, sir."

"Security alert," said the ship's computer. "Unauthorized launch from tube echo two." Ayashe heard it from inside the elevator as the door closed. *What has he done?* Tears ran down her cheeks. *He is gone. My Mac is gone. Why? Why Mac? Don't let this happen. I'm such a fool. You're the one I've dreamed of my entire life. Please Great Spirit I give my life for his.* Ayashe looked up and closed her eyes. *Take me instead.* The door opened, she looked at launch tube echo two, and it was empty. She burst into tears. It was too much for her to accept. She bent over, weeping. *I haven't even told him...*

She heard an "Uggh," to her right. She looked around the elevator's corner. "Mac!" She ran to him, picked him up like a rag doll and hugged him. "Thank you. Oh, thank you. Thank you."

Mac, still confused, smiled, and groggily asked, "Why are you thanking me?"

"Not you stupid. I thanked the Great Spirit."

He rubbed his neck. "Hey, can you hear my head pounding?" he asked.

She looked around and pointed. "It's not your head. It's coming from the storage closet."

He tried to move toward it, but she held him tight. *Apeiron was right I should have told him.* She looked him square in the eyes. "Mac I am with child. I am carrying your baby."

Mac stopped trying to get to the closet. He looked at Ayashe. She saw his eyes were getting moist. Unsure of what this meant, she started crying again.

"Are you happy or sad," she sniffled while still crying. "I can't tell."

"Are you kidding? I'm happy! I have always wanted children. Lots of children."

She hugged him. "Yeah, well let's start with one and see how you do. So far you're off to a bad start."

She let go of him, so he could open the storage locker. Inside the room were three well-bound crewmembers. Mac released them.

"Where is Mahpee?"

The ensign asked, "You mean the…" she looked at Ayashe, "big Indian guy?"

"Yes, his name is Mahpee."

"There were two of them, sir. The big Indian, Mahpee, and an old Indian. Mahpee called him grandfather. The big one apologized repeatedly while tying us up. He said he had to do it for his family. He said he was saving his… it sounded like he said ouwaycee."

Mac's head slumped down.

"I don't understand. He does not have a u-we-tsi," said Ayashe. "He has me, a daughter."

Mac walked up to Ayashe and embraced her. "He told me I was the u-we-tsi he never had. Your father has taken my place to deliver a storm to the Ogarii. I'm sorry."

"You're sorry? No, you're both crazy! Get him back. Get him back right now before it's too late!"

They both ran back to the elevator and headed back to the bridge.

"He knows you are carrying our child."

"How do you know?"

"In the elevator he grabbed me in a chokehold. He told me you had something important to tell me. I didn't understand. Your father told me not to worry. He said you

293

would clear everything up. He apologized to me too. It's my last memory before I blacked out. How could he know?"

"Apeiron," said Ayashe. "No one else knew. I'm going to dismantle one big mouth robot."

Mac stepped out of the elevator and walked up to the com officer. "I need to use the tachyon com system to contact Mahpee in the ship that just left."

The com officer typed a command into the computer. "Go ahead, sir."

"Mahpee, this is Mac."

"I am sorry Mac, but I couldn't let you do it. You have to take care of my family. You have a life to live. I have sung my death song. Whatever comes, I am ready for it. It will be up to you to tell the story of Mahpee, so my grandchildren will know me." Mahpee looked at his grandfather and smiled. "I will arrive like a thief in the night, but I will bring with me the power of a storm unlike any other ever witnessed. I will call on the apocalyptic horsemen to strike down my enemies. For once and all I will have a fitting retribution for my wife."

Ayashe looked at the com officer who nodded her head.

"Father. You betrayed my trust. You get back here right now. This is crazy."

"Ah, Ayashe, my little warrior. You have grown so much. I am sorry it ends this way. Mac understands. He knew what must be done weeks ago. We have never crossed the void, so a pilot must be on the ship to ensure the mission's success. Mac himself planned in secret to deliver a terrible blow to the enemy, but I have stolen his crack of lightning. He is a great leader and a great husband. He has earned his place to be at your side. Forgive me for the betrayal of your trust. You must lead our people now. I will soon enter into a continuous sequence of jumps and will be unable to communicate. I have left many vids for you. It is better this way. I love you. Mahpee out."

"No. Father wait! Mahpee, please… wait."

Ayashe was crying. The com officer was crying. Mac's eyes glistened, as did those of half the people on the bridge.

"What the hell just happened?" asked the admiral?

"Mahpee stole my thunder," said Mac. "He's is carrying a special delivery for someone in the universe's second ring."

"The Raygin?" asked the Admiral.

"No, the Ogarii. A small planet called Tik by the Raygin," said Mac.

The admiral shook his head in disbelief. "Why would you ever think of placing yourself at such risk? We could have gotten hundreds of volunteers for such a mission."

"I would have done it for my family." Mac looked at Ayashe who was still in tears. He spread his hands out towards the bridge crew. "I would have done it for my military brothers and sisters. I would have done it to save the human race. Admiral, I am not one to ask another to do something I wouldn't do myself."

"I understand, but we need your ability to strategize," said the admiral.

"Two strategists leading one fleet is one too many. Ayashe is a leader and every bit as good as me. You would have been in good hands."

Thinking about Mac's words made her see the path that she needed to take. "I must leave my love."

Mac looked at her with big sad eyes. "I know. It's the best plan of action. Two fleets, two leaders, it gives us a tactical advantage. I'll prepare a cruiser to transport you and your fighter."

Apeiron appeared next to Ayashe. "That won't be necessary. I have upgraded your fighter with a gravity well generator. If you don't mind I will travel with you and Yue Fei will stay here and help Mac."

"Yue Fei? There's another one of you?" asked Mac.

"Yes. We are three in form, but there are many of us."

"Why are you giving us all this help?"

"We cannot kill your enemy for you. If a life is sentient, we cannot destroy it. We can save a life, but the cost may not be life for life. We may assist you, modify your equipment, recommend actions, or warn you."

"I accept the help you offer. I still want to know the reason why. Why you are so willing to help, when you don't have to?"

"But you see, we do have to help you. If you don't win, we will not be allowed to live as we please. We believe the enemy you face may not be the enemy you should fear the most."

The tactical officer rushed to Mac and interrupted the conversation. "Sir, the probes indicate the Raygin fleet is on the move. They're heading toward us."

"Damn, this is it! We will have to finish this conversation later. Com, initiate Thor's Hammer."

"Aye sir, initiating Thor's Hammer."

"Ayashe, you need to leave right now. Follow your natural instincts. I don't have time to walk you down to your ship. I love you." He hugged her, kissed her, and touched his forehead to hers. She had taught him the action represented a great show of affection with her people. "I won't tell you to take no risks, but if you must, make sure the potential pay-off is worth it. Take care of yourself, and our little one."

Ayashe stepped into the elevator as activity on the bridge increased ten-fold. She heard Mac issuing orders to federation ships. She recalled the first time he called the operation Thor's Hammer. She asked why he had chosen the unusual name. He said, "we are going to throw

296

everything we have at them." The sense of humor seemed to be a human trait found amongst both peoples.

She appreciated his genius. He positioned the fleet and let the enemy probes see where they lay in wait. The Raygin fleet was moving in response to their last reports. Mac changed the human fleet's entire formation. The elevator doors closed as the screens on the bridge flashed ship position information. With all the new preparations he told her in time he was sure they would win the war.

She started thinking about her father. Losing him hurt. Now, she was leaving Mac. She had an overwhelming sense of anxiety. Tears dribbled down her cheeks. *How had father remained sane after losing my mother? What did Apeiron mean saying the enemy we're fighting is not the one we should fear most? My mind is like a trash heap. I need to focus. Focus Ayashe.*

She remembered lying in bed with Mac when he told her he wanted to start teaching her the Tao style of fighting. She laughed at him saying she was tired and not ready for one of his sexual workouts in the bedroom.

In a gentle voice he said, "You lie here and relax."

She smiled at the memory. She knew Mac's one-track mind and told him she was sure sex had nothing to do with Tao fighting. Her tears stopped trickling. *It wasn't sex he was after. He talked to me about how to clear my mind of clutter so I could focus at the task at hand. It was more than a fighting technique. It was a lifestyle he had told me. Train my mind every day.*

She walked through the mantra of meditation the old monk had taught Mac. She slowed her heartbeat to gain focus. For the first time, she could feel the baby's heartbeat too. *It is so strong.* She identified her distractions and resolved her issues one by one. She felt an odd energy encompass her as she concentrated. In the end one thought remained, *prepare for battle.*

When she arrived on the launch deck, it was a sight to see. Every launch tube contained a mix of fighters. If they had more time they all would have been the new design she loved so much.

She heard someone yell her name.

"Ayashe, over hear."

She scanned the rows of fighters until she saw a crewman waving his arms. He was holding her g-suit. She jogged over to him, grabbed the suit, and slipped into it. He directed her to a fighter. She walked up to it and noticed it already had a pilot's name on the body. She hoped she wasn't taking someone else's ship. In the tradition of UFC fighters, a person close to the pilot gets to pick a nickname. For better or worse, the pilot is stuck with the name for their entire career.

Ayashe read the pilot's name. Tears formed in her eyes. It read "Sky Hawk" or in the People's Nation language, "Mahpee Chatan". Below the name was a headband with the twenty-three feathers she had earned in her life. Ayashe touched her forehead to her father's name. She climbed into the fighter and strapped in. She turned on the gyro, turned on the com, and received a start engine signal from the launch crew. She looked around realizing she didn't see Apeiron.

A floating semi-transparent robot head appeared. "I am here, Ayashe. I loaded the coordinates of your fleet into the computer. You can fly manual or engage the autopilot once you clear the Constellation."

"Command, this is Sky Hawk, tube Charlie three requesting permission to launch."

"Sky Hawk, this is command, cleared to launch from tube Charlie three, God speed."

Ayashe's fighter flew out the tube, made a streaking left turn and disappeared into the blackness of space. "I think…I'll pilot my own ship," she said. "I need to get a better feel for how it operates." Between jumps she put the little fighter through maneuver after maneuver.

Each time it felt a little better. The ship was a little more responsive. "Is it me or is the fighter getting faster?" she asked Apeiron.

"The nanobots are leaning how to better use the bioluminescent bacteria. I have detected an eight percent improvement in overall ship efficiency. Your reaction time has increased twelve percent. Your increase represents an impossibility in such a short time."

"What are you saying?"

"You should be capable of improving your speed by three point two percent through muscle repetition. You have more than tripled that. It is impossible without outside influence."

"Could a sounder sleep be the cause?"

"You misunderstand. I am not talking about your attentiveness. Each human body has an amount of electrical energy to send nerve impulses to control muscles. It also fires signals to or from the brain. The amount of electrical energy your body generates is increasing. It is causing you to think and move quicker. I cannot detect what is producing the phenomenon."

"My people believe in totems. They are spectral energies in the form of animals. As a baby, I was near death and had a cleansing performed by tribal elders. My father told me that he witnessed many spectral animals in the operating room with me. Sightings of these spectral animals standing next to me have occurred from time to time. Could the ancient stories have some truth to them?"

"Perhaps. Have you observed any of them yourself?"

"No, but Mac did. He didn't tell me at the time because he thought it was his imagination."

The semi-transparent face of Apeiron looked at Ayashe as it contemplated what she said. "We will search our memories for answers. The Wasp is calling you."

"Sky Hawk, this is the Wasp."

Sure enough, it was the Wasp. She recognized Bodaway's voice. "Wasp, this is Sky Hawk, go ahead."

"When you arrive, dock with the Wasp. We have a port designed for the new fighter. It is official. The War Council selected you as the new War Chief. The generals wait for your arrival. We continue to track the Raygin fleet and wait for your orders."

Ayashe made her required statement, acknowledging her selection. "I accept my place amongst the previous War Chiefs. I promise to honor all my relatives. I will listen to the Council of my people. When I sing my death song, I will not show fear in front of my enemy. I will support the telling of our past, for it reminds us where we came from." In the old tradition of warriors, Ayashe let loose a blood curdling battle cry to instill confidence as they prepared to attack the enemy.

"Your words have been heard and recorded. We wait for your arrival, chief," said Bodaway.

Tiny bumps formed on Ayashe's skin at the base of her skull to the small of her back. The prophecy was unfolding before her eyes. *I must help put an end this senseless war. The Ogarii have no respect for our lives. I shall have little respect for theirs.*

Her fleet keyed their transmitters and each ship played its war drums.

Boom, boom, boom.

The sound echoed throughout the universe's first ring. The human race was no longer divided. It was once again a single circle, unbroken by the old prejudices.

When Ayashe arrived, she received bowls of red and black melted wax. She painted her war face in front of everyone. Bodaway placed a twenty-three feathered headpiece on her. It was all transmitted to the People's Nation. She could feel the rush of adrenalin, like someone turned a switch on. The excitement was getting to her.

Focus, she thought to herself. *Focus. Get control. Save it for the enemy. Breathe*, she told herself. She let out a breath and started to share her plan.

"The main Raygin fleet has two large groups of Raygin ships on each flank. They plan to combine and cut off the human ship's retreat. Our enemy's problem is they attacked us, killed our people, yet they do not know we exist. What is the first law of war?

The room was quiet. They were afraid to talk... not a good situation she thought. Time to change tactics. She walked in front of Admiral Sewati, stopped, and looked him in the eyes. He was a big man, like her father. "Admiral, my father often spoke of you. He considered you a great leader. A great military mind."

"Mahpee too was a great leader," said Sewati.

"I agree. He too is a great leader. Yet he counted on your council in anything war related, ship design, weapon systems, deployment of forces, and planetary defense systems. Is there anyone more knowledgeable than you in such matters?"

"You would be hard pressed to find such a person."

"Forgive me Admiral Sewati, but I must prove a point." In a move taught to her by Mac she chopped her hand onto a nerve located on the neck below the ear. As Sewati slumped unconscious she caught him and laid him down. An instant grumbling started. Did they lose their best admiral?

"Tell me. What good is all that knowledge now?" They saw Sewati stirring and trying to get up. She experienced the same difficulty when Mac struck her vagus nerve to show her the effect of such a blow. She stooped over the admiral and helped him up. "We will do the same with the Ogarii. Take enough of them out so they cannot control the large Raygin fleet." She hugged the admiral.

The admiral understood. It was the quickest way to get everyone talking. He hugged Ayashe back. "You are a brutal war master, but I do have a few thoughts on how we should attack the enemy."

Everyone laughed. Many good discussions occurred, and the group chose the best plans. The People's Nation fleet split into four groups. Twenty-five cruisers carrying the modified walkers would be the first to deploy. Their escort included fifty battleships loaded with a mix of both old and new fighters. Their targets were the lead ships in the trailing flank of Raygin ships. The rest the Peoples Nation ships would approach from behind and split into three attack groups. Each group would have cruisers capable of deploying walkers.

The trap was set. Two hundred Raygin ships flew into the minefield before they understood their danger. Some walkers were engineered to lock onto gravitational wave targets displaying no associated visual confirmation. The fighters waited with engines off in the nothingness of space. When the walkers activated, it was the cue to start the battle. The cruisers and battleships made a jump into near space. Fighters attacked. The walkers identified and latched onto their targets shields. A few enemy ships tried to pulse their shields so they could fire at the walkers. They discovered the walkers could detonate faster than they could get a target lock.

Six walkers were stationary, just hanging in the empty space located in the middle of the several Raygin ships. It could only mean they had found some of the cloaked vessels. The Ogarii activated their shields. Four sleek ships appeared. Instead of slipping off, the walker continued to hold onto the shield and created a short. The weapon system on the modified mine required thirty seconds before it could create an opening in the shield and fire.

Raygin fighters deployed with the intent to destroy the walkers hanging on the Ogarii vessels. The new fighters destroyed about forty Raygin fighters, as they attempted to pick off the walkers. The Raygin launched a swarm of hundreds of fighters. A few cruisers were waiting for the move and fired their large laser canons into the swarm of enemy fighters. The swarm turned into a large melted mass of metal flickering and flashing in the foreground.

Because the Ogarii were dealing with their own threat, they were losing focus on the Raygin. The People's Nation battleships made their move. They had learned much from the People of the Stars successes in their battle. The computer engineers dedicated part of each battleship's semi-bioluminescent computer to targeting. It combined three technologies. The effect of the coordinated firing to hit the same target equaled the energy of planetary lasers. The Raygin shields couldn't hold. The combined firepower started to rip the bug ships apart.

Ayashe saw four Ogarii ships with their shields still up explode within the same second. The thirty seconds required to detonate seemed like an eternity. The Raygin battleships broke formation and started to run, causing total chaos. Ayashe let the fleeing ships go. She would not be distracted from attacking the lead group of Raygin ships trying to box the human fleet into a trap.

The Ogarii realized the humans could see their cloaked ships, so they uncloaked. They were no longer priority targets of the mines. The two groups came face to face with near the same number of ships. The Ogarii used the big Raygin battleships as shields. They maneuvered within the Raygin fleet. This allowed their sleek ships to concentrate fire at a single People's Nation battleship. The People's Nation shields could not withstand multiple hits from the unusual Ogarii energy weapon.

Ayashe lost two battleships. Their new computer adjusted and began to fire at the ships shielding the Ogarii. Unless something changed, it appeared they had come to a standoff. She was sure in time more Raygin ships would arrive. *Focus. What would Mac do?*

Ayashe opened a link to Sewati. "Sewati, Ayashe here. I have a plan. Give me cover fire as I move in on the lead Ogarii ship. Be ready to fire at it." She remembered Mac's words. Risk must have a worthwhile pay off or don't take it. *Well*, she thought, *winning the battle for the human race was worth the risk.*

"We are ready. Proceed with your plan, chief."

Ayashe felt an exhilarating blast of adrenalin. She used the Raygin ships to hide her from view as she zigzagged her way toward the Ogarii. She was invisible to the big Raygin battleships. She wasn't sure about the advanced Ogarii ships. Timing was everything. She cleared the last Raygin battle ship and accelerated. Her tiny fighter latched onto the Ogarii shield. The portal weapon triggered on contact. She began to see an increase in her shield strength. The Raygin fighters must have received a command because they came full speed at the Ogarii ship. They were heading right at her. The portal soaked up the energy the Ogarii poured into their shield and put it all into the little fighter. The Raygin fighters opened fire. Her shields held. Whew. That was too close.

She loved using the manual controls. Moving her throttle forward to full power the tiny fighter nudged the bigger ship. It was all it took. Two battleships fired at the exposed Ogarii vessel. The drain on the Ogarii shields made their ship vulnerable. In a tight cocoon of Raygin ships, the command ship couldn't maneuver. In a violent reaction, the ship split in half. Ayashe could see bodies floating into space as she accelerated toward the other Ogarii ships.

The destruction of the Ogarii control ship caused the associated Raygin ships to leave the fight. The People's battleships fired on the Raygin ships breaking formation. They were able to open a line of fire to the remaining the Ogarii ships. The Ogarii tried to lock their weapons onto the little fighter causing all their problems. Ayashe was too quick. They missed time and time again, often hitting their own Raygin ships.

Her mind was clear as a bell. Somehow, she could feel the energy coming from enemy weapons as they tried to lock onto her fighter. She wreaked havoc on them until she started drawing too much fire. Even with her newfound super sensitivity she knew it's time to leave. The gyro moved her seat ninety degrees as the fighter shot away from the hotbed of laser and plasma fire. She caught her reflection in the pilot bubble. Impossible. Behind her left shoulder was a large semi-transparent wolf. It couldn't be, there was no room! She had to zigzag some more to avoid becoming a target. When she looked again, the wolf was gone.

She returned her attention to the battle in time to see her battleships and cruisers destroy a second Ogarii ship. The Raygin recalled their fighters. The big bug ships formed a wall around the two remaining Ogarii vessels. They sacrificed their outer ships to allow the Ogarii to exit the battle without taking losses. To escape, they jumped as a group, using their singularity drives.

"Sewati, Ayashe here. Do not chase them. Have the fleet take up defensive positions. Assign a couple of cruisers to collect the remnants from the Ogarii ships. Pick up all survivors including Raygin. I'll stay out here and help.

"I understand, Ayashe. What's our next step?"

"We were lucky. Each battle they see more of our tactics and the capabilities of our weapons. The next engagement won't be so easy. We move to attack the Raygin ships flanking the human fleets the opposite side. We must prevent a pincer style attack or a block of their escape route."

CHAPTER NINETEEN: Clash of Fleets

The vids Apeiron sent Mac of both engagements were telling. He learned the Ogarii controlled a limited number of Raygin ships per command vessel. The Raygin leaving formation must have been the ones controlled by the destroyed command ships. Their first instinct seemed to be to run and save their own lives.

Ayashe confused the Ogarii crew when she attacked the command ship. Mac believed the confusion occurred as they took resources away from controlling the Raygin to assess their own threat. During those few seconds he saw several Raygin ships break formation and run. He brought up the display panel on Ayashe's ship.

The shield strength on the fighter as it drained energy from the Ogarii ship was high. Not because the Ogarii used more power but because the fighter was so small. He looked at the data from the Ogarii ship and the Constellation. He realized both produced the same energy for their shields. Since the Ogarii shields were stronger, it meant the strength came from the exterior surface's density.

The Raygin ships breaking formation never returned to the battle. This meant the Ogarii command ships had to be in close proximity to maintain control. So far, Wineena's single mistake was in not knowing her enemy. If not for the People's Nation, the humans would already have lost the war. Mac walked toward the elevator as his escorts fell in step behind him. "I'll be on the hanger deck."

"Aye sir. On the hanger deck," said the com officer.

When the elevator arrived on the hanger deck, the doors opened. Mac saw rows and rows of fighters. A sure sign the Constellation was ready for a battle. His eyes latched onto an ancient Chinese warrior dressed in the old-style battle gear of his era. *Yue Fei seems to be enjoying himself. Imagine a robot enjoying itself instead of always spewing facts or performing mundane tasks.* He started to walk over to the three comrades.

"What's going on?" asked Mac.

"We're starting to get technical data from the Wasp about the Ogarii ship. We are looking for anything to help our cause."

"Great. It's what I wanted to talk to you about. I have determined the Ogarii ships have stronger shields due to the material used for the exterior surface."

Yue Fei and Smitty looked at each other in disbelief.

Yue Fei leaned over and whispered to Smitty, "He sees from a perspective I have not learned to mimic. It is beyond my ability."

Smitty nodded his head and said, "Okay, Mac, lets say you're right. What next?"

"I have a question. Can you place a small gravity well drive, like Apeiron put in Ayashe's fighter, into a kinetic energy weapon?"

"Sure, but why? Kinetic energy weapons can't penetrate shields. In fact, I bet they can't penetrate the skin of an Ogarii ship even without its shield."

"What if we placed an anti-particle round into the kinetic energy weapon?"

"How do we test it?" asked Tinker.

"We don't," Mac winced, "and I need it in twenty-two hours."

"This isn't as easy as you would think," said Smitty. "Before a gravity well gets created, the generator finds the lowest density of gravitons to travel point to point. Wait a minute. Maybe we can do it. I suppose we could re-adjust the target computer and have it look for the equivalent mass density of the Ogarii ship," said Smitty.

"I can take care of the computer programming," said Yue Fei.

"Smitty, won't the delivery device blow up on contact with the shield?" asked Tinker.

"No, I think Mac is right," said Smitty. "According to the laws of confinement, the weapon would treat the ship's shield as energy, not mass. The gravity well will move the weapon through the shield. Think of it as a ship traveling through the energy of the universe in its own gravity well. The difference being, our weapon will destroy itself upon hitting the skin of the Ogarii ship. If we place an anti-particle round in the nose of the new weapon, I'm sure it will move through the shield. Impact will cause the release of positrons, creating instant annihilation. By that I mean the destruction of some matter and the massive release of radiation."

"A photon torpedo is not a kinetic energy weapon, but I'll bet I can make it one," said Tinker.

"I'll figure out how to stabilize the positron container in the warhead," said Smitty.

"Give me as many as you can get done in 21 hours and forty-five minutes," said Mac.

Yue Fei rolled his eyes.

"Hey, I saw that," said Mac as he looked at Yue Fei.

"Pretty human, huh? I have seen other people do it when you ask them to do the impossible."

"You're real funny," said Mac.

Smitty nudged Yue Fei as if he were human. "You know what you have done? You have asked us to design a whole new weapon system by cannibalizing at least three other systems. Getting it done in less than twenty-two hours may be impossible. We are still working on a list of priorities you asked to complete!"

"I know. Believe me, I didn't forget."

"It was hours ago," said Tinker.

Mac gave Tinker a look.

Tinker knew immediately what it meant. "Okay, I know. You have told me a hundred times, a battle is fluid often times we must improvise, adapt, and overcome."

Mac smiled at Tinker. "You'll make a great leader one day. I gotta get back to the bridge. Good Luck." Mac spun around and left the trio to work on their new task.

Once back on the bridge, Mac reviewed the latest vids from Mahpee's micro probes, looking for any changes. The Ogarii ships were no longer cloaked. They grouped themselves to lead the Raygin fleet. He remembered this formation from when they attacked planetary defenses. They were learning. By using Ogarii ships in the lead position they increased shield strength and firepower.

He wished they knew how the enemy managed to combine and project their shields. For now, the technology was beyond their understanding. The entire human race was working on the war effort and associated problems. Knowing something is possible means in time, someone will figure it out.

The secret UFC shipyards are running at max capacity, but they need time. Time. There it is again. It is a common thread. Having the new kinetic energy weapon will guarantee human survival. We will still lose, but we can set a few traps and move to hit and run tactics. It will allow our technology and production to catch up.

In the few remaining hours, Mac deployed all the weapons. Arriving ships were assigned their tactical positions. Ground-based troops received the latest concoctions to overcome Raygin armor and its filtration systems. Planetary troops received the latest obit-based weapons capable of destroying shielded ships. For now, he couldn't stop the Raygin from capturing planets and billions of humans.

The commodore reported to the com officer he would be in the bridge stateroom. He felt exhausted and needed to sleep before the battle. He resisted calling Ayashe. He began to clear his mind. He told himself he had done all he could with what he had available. He stretched out on his bunk, closed his eyes, relaxed his muscles, breathed slow and long his as he meditated. Questions remained about the Ogarii and the structure of the universe, but he had no time to focus on them. He let the thoughts go like wispy clouds as he fell asleep.

When he woke up, he put aside his dress uniform hanging in his room. Public relations wanted him to wear the fancy clothing into battle for photo opportunities. He sighed. It wasn't right to deceive the people into believing he was someone he was not. He wasn't the great leader they wanted to portray him as. He was simply an efficient killer. He put on his plain, unadorned, body armor and walked onto the bridge.

He looked at the screen. It was still a blur. They were too far away for a crisp focus.

"Mac, come here," said Admiral Harding. "Look at this. It's the latest vids from the micro probes. You can see the fighters better here. Looks like that's how they plan on responding to the walker threat."

"Smart move," said Mac. "I knew this wouldn't be easy. They have no concern for their Raygin soldiers."

"Mac, we have an urgent call for you," interrupted the com officer. "The caller says he will talk to you and you alone."

Mac nodded.

The officer activated the com unit. "You're on sir."

"This is Mac. Who am I talking to?"

"Mac. I'm Gurko. My family was on Nyx during the mining war. You saved us from some mercs and you got us transported off planet. I was seven years old at the time."

"I remember you Gurko. How can I help you?"

"It's not me needing help this time. It's you. We have been watching the vids of the Raygin fleet. It took forever to get in contact with you! I'm a charge detonator for Tonk. I know if we place shaped charges on some of the larger planet sized asteroids, we can direct a small meteor shower right in the face of the enemy ships!"

"Navigation," said Mac, "how long until the Raygin reach the asteroid belt?"

"Four hours eight minutes, sir."

"It will be close, but if you're willing let's do it. How do you want to make this happen?"

"We suspected you would say yes. The charges are already in place. We are on the staging asteroid, Mimas. It took us a little longer to place the charges than we anticipated and we only have one shuttle. Could you send two additional shuttles to pick us up?"

Admiral Harding gave Mac a head nod.

"We are on our way. This is a lifesaver. Thanks, Gurko."

"Anything for a brother. You're a legend to the Tonk miners. Gurko out."

"What's that about?" Admiral Harding asked.

"Darkmore was my first assignment. I was there when the fighting broke out. The war moved to the mining planet Nyx. The mercs killed my brother and his wife. They weren't even miners. In retaliation I volunteered for sniper duty on their remote planet. I killed so many mercs I lost count. The brass told me I saved a lot of miners. To this day – I'm not sure if I did it for them or for myself. The big conglomerations forced all free miners off Nyx. To survive, they started Tonk Mining. They worked together and were able to compete with the big companies. Today they are the biggest asteroid miners in our universe."

"Damn Mac. Was there a conflict you weren't involved in?"

"I don't think so. During times of war the military loves a killer. I guess I owe it all to Vice Admiral Farragut."

"Come on now, Mac. From what I've seen I know it's not why you're here today. The admiral saw in you what we all see in you."

Mac didn't argue. He knew the truth. The better he got at killing the higher up in rank he went. He looked back at the battle formations using the holo-projector. This tactic Tonk came up with would deliver a solid blow to the enemy. After today, the Ogarii wouldn't be so quick to come after them.

Mac modified his battle plans to take advantage of the new tactic. This is where he excelled as a leader. He brought ships in behind the Raygin fleet. He hoped to create a bottleneck as the Ogarii pushed through an intentional weak spot left in the asteroid belt. Tonk left a path requiring a sharp turn and placed a few big asteroids in the way, so the enemy wouldn't suspect a trap within the trap. They would see it was the best path, not perfect, but at least workable.

To go around the solar system's planets would put the Raygin fleet at unnecessary risk. Instead, Mac knew they would push through the asteroid belt and attack the human fleet head on. Gorko's brilliant blast idea would destroy the enemy fighters or force them to take shelter. The launch of the walkers would follow the debris from the blast giving them time to do their work.

The humans watched the enemy fleet advance. The oversized Ogarii shield began to push the asteroids making a pathway for the Raygin fleet. They took the bait making a hard turn to clear an easier path. Mac began to move his ships to attack the enemy's front and the rear. After a few hours, the Ogarii broke through the Asteroid belt. The Raygin fleet began to enter the opening. The tiny fighters hovered all around the big ships.

"Mr. Tomes," said Mac, "get ready to detonate the charges on my mark. After we have visual verification of detonation, launch the Walkers."

"Aye sir. On your mark, detonate the charges. Once we have visual verification, launch the walkers."

Mac wanted to wait until the Raygin fleet started to move through the asteroid belt.

"Mac, Tinker," came over Mac's com. "We have six grav torpedoes ready. We attached them to six Screamers."

Mac felt some tension leave his body. *God bless them, they came through for him.* "Nice work. Let me talk to the wing lead." Mac briefed the wing commander on what he needed.

Three minutes later, the fighters flew out of their launch tubes. They were armed with a new weapon and zigzagged their way towards the lead Ogarii shield ships.

"Mr. Tomes, prepare for detonation of the asteroids. I will count down from five."

"Aye sir, ready for detonation."

"Five, four, three, two, one, detonate."

The explosive charges detonated. Mr. Tomes looked at the view screen. Gigantic cone shaped explosions blew shrapnel right at the Raygin fleet. "Visual verification of asteroid detonation confirmed. Launching Walkers." All eyes on the bridge watched as he pushed the launch button.

"Okay Admiral Harding. Let's move in on the lead Ogarii ships."

"Aye, Mac. Commencing frontal attack."

Thor's hammer was in full swing. The humans threw everything they could fly at the Raygin Fleet. It looked like a ballet of ships with fireworks going off in the middle. Mac timed the detonation of the asteroids with perfect precision. The human battleships even pushed derelict ships into the Raygin formation. The meteor shower destroyed thousands of fighters. Some enemy fighters took cover behind the large battle ships. Behind the human generated meteor blast came the walkers. They moved unimpeded and latched onto enemy battleships. By the time the fighters realized the meteor shower was over, they had lost hundreds of battleships.

At the same time, six undetected Screamers moved closer toward the Ogarii lead ships. Behind the Screamers, poured hundreds of human ships. They flowed like water from behind the local planets. The attack's genius was Mac had managed to hide the final formation until the last moment. It was obvious the Ogarii expected the humans to form a defensive formation due to the enemy's superior numbers. Instead, the humans began to attack the enemy ships as they exited the asteroid belt.

The Ogarii adjusted their formation and shield to meet the human attack. Without realizing it, their ships were open to a side on attack by the Screamers. Each fighter picked a separate target. At two thousand meters from the parabolic curve of the Ogarii shield, the screamers launched their new grav torpedoes. As predicted, the torpedoes moved through the shield like it wasn't there. When each torpedo hit their target, two bright blue bursts of Cherenkov radiation appeared. They formed along each Ogarii ship's perpendicular longitudinal axis.

The Screamers disappeared in a blur of movement as they accelerated away from the remaining Ogarii ships. No sense in taking risks. The big protective shield flickered out. The human battleships took immediate action. They used joint fire targeting to take out another command ship. The Ogarii returned the favor, using the same tactic to destroy a human battleship. To save themselves, the Ogarii moved behind the Raygin ships as they gushed out from the asteroid belt. The six command ships hit by torpedoes remained stationary.

Not wanting to move into a trap, Mac said, "Someone confirm those Ogarii ships aren't moving because they are inoperable?"

"Commander Baako here sir, I'm the science officer. Those are the ships the torpedoes hit. They aren't moving because the electronics are fried and the crew is dead. We estimate the combined gamma and Cherenkov radiation exposure they received inside the ship to be over three thousand Sievert. The crew died when the flash occurred."

"Thank you, Mr. Baako."

Thanks to the miners, the battle had begun better than Mac had expected. With their noses bloodied the Ogarii would want revenge but would not attack without discussing possible traps. The faster speed of human computers helped to keep the superior numbers of Raygin ships at bay. The overwhelming number of Raygin ships meant they were willing to trade ship for ship during the battle. The fight went on for half the day with each side gaining here and losing there. It was as he feared. Humans had to disengage. They couldn't afford to stay in a battle of attrition.

It was time to call Ayashe, he thought. "Com, I need the Tachyon."

"Go ahead, sir."

"Ayashe, Mac. How is the battle?"

"Mac, I'm so happy to hear from you! We have reached a stalemate. They seem willing to lose their ships without concern."

"Same here. Initiate operation Egypt."

"Initiating operation Egypt. Be careful my love. Ayashe out."

Operation Egypt was the withdrawal of all human ships from the battle. They would follow a specific route. Mac's battleships stayed in place as the smaller ships began to leave the battle zone first.

From the beginning, the Raygin were fighting on two fronts. The human ships attacking the enemy's rear retreated from the fight. The Ogarii refused to split their fleet to pursue them, fearing another trap. The human battleships at the attack's front launched a final barrage of walkers. The weapons targeted the Raygin ships coming through the bottleneck. The Raygin lost a few ships, but an even more significant result was the walker attack caused temporary confusion. It gave the humans time to disengage from the battle.

The human ships used the nearest planet's gravitational pull to cause a slingshot effect. The Raygin chased them using the same path and tactic. As the enemy moved alongside the planet, large lasers hidden on the planet's surface began to fire on the Raygin ships. The Raygin fleet had to break formation to move away from the planet. They moved right into a minefield. Mac had bought the human fleet the time they needed to engage their singularity drives. Now it would become a game of cat and mouse until the humans gathered their strength. They had lost the battle, yet in time he was sure they would win the war.

*****

"Aaahhh." Wineena screamed so loud the sound echoed off the bridge walls. "Who the skonk is this Commodore McCormack? I am a born leader, one in a hundred billion. You mean to tell me a human has out maneuvered me? Where did these weapons come from? Where the skonk was Portus when we needed him?" She pointed at the navigational droid, "I want answers."

"I will endeavor to find the answer for you, Overseer," said the droid.

The overseer looked at the view screen and the retreating humans. "Fritnee, are we able to send a chiliad of ships to pursue of the humans?"

"No, Wineena. It is all or nothing. We have lost too many control ships. If we split our forces we will lose control of hundreds of Raygin ships. "

"We must draw the human fleet into battle. Lets start destroying the population areas on these local planets," said Wineena.

CHAPTER TWENTY: Portus

In the next two months the Raygin fleet attacked thirteen planets inhabited by humans. Estimates put the loss of human life at forty-seven billion. The military was learning how to fight a war based on enormous distances. The human fleet entered into several skirmishes with the Raygin. They used hit and run type tactics designed to inflict maximum damage to the enemy with minimal losses. They never committed to an all-out battle again. Every day, the secret human shipyards pumped out new ships.

Humans banned together like they never had before. The media couldn't get their hands on enough war videos. The fighter pilot known as Sky Hawk became a legend. When the humans found out she was Mac's wife everyone fell in love with her.

On the flip side, Mac gained the status of hero within the both the human universe and the Peoples Nation. Before Mahpee left Nokomis, he submitted paperwork to the Tellers. He invoked an ancient pre-earth exodus custom. He decreed Mac to be a tribal member. By risking his own life to save Ayashe's life on more than one occasion, he was due Life for Life rights. Though not born from the People's Nation, the Tellers voted for Mac to become a tribe member.

The military videos of Mac saving Ayashe proved Mahpee's claims. His actions were indisputable. The media covered the unanimous vote by the Tellers. Mac received tribal membership. After the vote, the reclusive mystic, Nahimana, made her way to the media dais.

Her blind white eye looked right into the vid transmission devices. Children turned their heads to avoid looking at her. Many stories claimed if you looked into her eyes, she could see into your soul.

"The tide is changing, but do not celebrate or rejoice. The real battle has yet to begin." She turned around and walked away. She disappeared into the crowd before anyone could ask her questions.

The foretelling by Nahimana troubled Ayashe. Mac watched the Nokomis video. He had felt great, right up to the point where the mystic spoke. No wonder she made Mahpee nervous. Even Mac felt queasy. He experienced a feeling like he had jumped from a great height. He felt like she was looking right at him when she spoke the dire words. His stomach told his brain, get ready, because something bad is going to happen.

*****

It seemed like forever since they made the big jump into the second ring. Within moments they would arrive at the Naktu solar system. Mahpee daydreamed of how Mac would talk to his grandchildren. Telling them about how Mahpee was the first human to cross into the universe's second ring. He recalled as they approached the great void, how the number of stars became fewer and fewer. Not knowing what to expect, he used the ion drive to enter the void. As they entered the area of nothingness, the ion drive stopped working. It was an unexpected surprise. Not a single ion existed in the void. In fact, there was no sense of anything. They could not even see a single star as they coasted in what he hoped was a forward direction.

He recalled starting the singularity drive. *With one pop, we entered into the second ring. I miss the old drive. Its slow popping sound comforted as we traveled from place to place. This modified drive is way too fast. Pop, Pop, Pop. It drives me crazy. I feel anxious.*

He knew they had to be getting close to their destination by now. "How much longer until we reach Tik? I thought we'd be there by now," said Mahpee.

"A few more jumps and we will arrive," grandfather pointed on the screen. "Right here is where we are going. We will miss you Mahpee."

Was it foolish to feel sad? He and his fake yet so real grandfather had bonded after entering the second ring of the universe. The nanobots kept his grandfather's form but they started to share their group minded robot thoughts with him. He discovered the tiny computers thought on a much grander scale than humans. They were one hundred percent goal driven. Time seemed irrelevant to them.

Mahpee was worried about the future of his tiny friends. "Before the last jump you need to get off the ship. Even you can't survive the heat the Storm will create."

An alarm sounded as the ship came to a halt between jumps. The computer displayed a message on the viewer.

Mahpee looked at the screen. "It's a bunch of ones and zeros. Do you think it is Ogarii or Raygin?"

"Neither. It's binary code. It's how computers talk in the purest form."

"Who are they and what do they want?" asked Mahpee.

"Hold on... It is a droid piloted cargo ship. I'm talking to it... No crew... No passengers... It's hauling freight to Tik. The navigational droid needs a manual reboot. The ship is seeking assistance."

"I say we leave it," said Mahpee.

"Do not be too hasty. We may discover new information by linking to the droid."

Mahpee hated the thought of a delay. He wanted to get it over with, but grandfather was right. Any additional information about the enemy could be consequential.

"Okay. I'll pilot us to it and attach to the ship."

"Good. I'll take care of everything else," said grandfather.

In two hours, the ship carrying the Storm pulled away from the alien cargo vessel. It was on its way with a special delivery. Mahpee felt excited as he watched the view screen. Within seconds there would be retribution.

*****

The second mind of Portus contemplated its success with malevolent enjoyment. It moved the Varn from their old home in the third ring to Tik. The new home was a deviant and degenerated place. Hundreds of thousands of Ogarii were drawn to the planet like ants to a sweet kobara tree. More were arriving every day. Word of its wickedness had spread. Portus gave them everything they could ever want.

The nefarious heads of state would never leave their paradise. They had lost control of their empire and didn't care. The virus Portus created and blamed on the Drahce would ensure this would be the last generation of Ogarii. They were too useless of a race to use in its future plans.

At any given second Portus made billions of thoughts. Its mind controlled millions of activities. Its brain used a hierarchy of thought capable of trillions of petaFLOPS. A petaFLOP is a measure of a processor's speed and Portus had no equal. The higher up the ladder a task moved the more attention it got. For simple jobs like turning on lights or watering vegetation, it didn't even know it was doing the task.

Without warning, the giant computer broke all contact. It focused on a single threat. It ran millions of scenarios in a nano second. *I can't stop the ship.* The second mind of Portus sent thousands of commands and questions to the ship's computer while it tried to take control. There was no response.

Using satellites, it watched the small ship. It should have landed at a delivery terminal. Instead it plummeted straight into the planet and emitted a small, but powerful laser. The large planetary defenses were designed for attacks from space. Ground defenses included armies of droids and thousands of ships. It would take two point seven seconds to intercept the tiny ship. Portus launched its attack ships knowing it had no more than a percent of a percent chance of success.

The ship escaped detection by operating in the low hierarchy task range. *What is it doing*, wondered Portus? The ship created a super-heated tunnel. It flew straight into the planet. An uncountable number of scenarios ran through the mind of Portus. Planetary monitors detected radiation coming from the core of Tik. The computer performed tens of thousands of calculations. It understood what occurred with a 99.9998 percent certainty. *Nuclear fusion. It is a genius plan.* The giant computer's unbreakable base broke. The planet's crust started to crack. Tik was no longer a planet. It was becoming a small star. Everyone on the planet was already dead.

In the last attosecond of its life, the second mind of Portus transmitted a gigantic data burst.

*****

"Overseer," radioed the captain of a nearby command ship. "We have lost control of all Raygin ships."

"Is the loss human induced failure?"

"No. It seems to be a command initiated from your ship."

"It can't be. What is the command?"

"Return to the third ring."

Before Wineena could respond the Raath began to move to the fleet's interior.

"Navigator. I did not give the order to move into formation. Stop."

"I apologize overseer," said the navigation droid. "Your command has been overridden."

"Overridden? No one can override my command. Who would perform such a treasonous act?" asked Wineena.

"The command came from Portus."

"Portus. Portus is a computer. It cannot make command decisions! Navigator, I order you to disregard all commands from Portus."

"I'm sorry overseer. I cannot override an instruction from Portus. Can I help you in some other way?"

Wineena pulled her plasma pistol from her waist and shot the droid, melting a hole in its metallic head. "No. I'll take care of it myself. Iscar, you useless piece of bonard, move the trash heap of a navigator to the side! Taena, take the helm. Full stop."

Iscar ran to the navigator's metallic body and dragged it to the wall. Taena manipulated the controls but the ship did not respond.

"Overseer, the computer will not respond. It locked out all controls. I am unable to stop or move the ship."

Wineena, still holding her pistol, lifted it, aimed at the ship's computer..."

"No!" Screamed Taena. "Please don't shoot, Wineena. Without the computer we cannot jump. The humans will capture us! Something serious must have occurred. Could the Drahce have attacked?"

"I don't like this," said Wineena. "We have no clue what's going on. I guess you're right, we don't have a choice. So, home here we come." She put her pistol back in the holster.

"What about me? Can you drop me off along the way?" asked Iscar.

"Didn't you follow what's happening stupid human? We aren't in control of our own ships. You have no choice but to tag along. Wait, I've got it. I think I'll put you in a cage and make you a pet for everyone to see."

Iscar surveyed his surroundings. He wished he had worked on an escape plan.

*****

While talking to Tews about Raygin mind control, Mac received an alert. It read: Raygin fleet on the move. Left ground-based troops behind.

Oh, shit thought Mac. *The Ogarii found a weakness in my defenses and they are moving on it.* "I have a problem. I've got to go to the bridge. I'll call you later." Mac spun around and once again ran to the bridge. Crewmembers walking in the passageway stepped out of his way. Mac nodded his head at them. In the last couple months, they learned anytime he was running a major event was occurring.

When he got to the bridge, the crew already had the appropriate battle holographs on the table. He scrutinized their position and projected several possible paths. *What were they up to?* He couldn't come up with a single objective that made any sense. The Ogarii didn't try to hide their route. *Hell*, he thought, *even a child flying a tracker could have followed the enemy fleet's gravitational waves. They didn't care they were being followed.*

Mac took immediate action. He moved ships and troops to support some of the infested planets. After another week of following the Raygin fleet, he knew what they were doing. The enemy was leaving. The Ogarii were moving the Raygin fleet out of human space. Something big must have happened because at this point the Raygin were winning the war. He hoped it was Mahpee, but there was no way to know.

The humans called the day the Raygin fleet left the first ring Victory Over the Ogarii and Raygin day (VOOR day). The whole universe celebrated. Mac knew it was not a real victory, but he let the celebrations go on. He promised to stay on as the de facto president until an election could be held. Afterwards he would relinquish his authority and return to being a commodore. The human war machine would keep building ships, developing new weapons, and designing better planetary defenses. There were also plans to install an advanced warning system. The fleet of the People's Nation joined the human fleet for the time being.

Mac's beautiful wife was with him again on the Constellation. He felt happier than he could ever remember. They were enjoying each other's company as they rested on their bed in their stateroom. The two leaders took advantage of the time by talking about their future plans.

"Mac, I want to have the baby on Nokomis."

"I'm all for it, but remember I'm a tribal member now so I need to learn your language. I don't want..." he paused and gave her a look, "our people to think you married an idiot."

"Oh. Now it's our people is it? I have news for you, President de facto McCormack. I have already told all my friends I married pretty, not smart."

He laughed, grabbed her by the waist, snuggled up to her, and kissed her belly. "Pretty gets what pretty wants."

"What is it my pretty wants?" Ayashe asked.

He smiled. "You. You and the baby." After he spoke those words, he shivered as he remembered what the mystic said: … do not celebrate or rejoice. The real battle has yet to begin.

The End